Fic
25/04/14
1/05/14
15-05-14
15-02-16

JUNE FRANCIS's maiden name was Nelson, and athough she can't lay claim to the famous Lord Admiral, she can boast of at least six mariners in her ancestry who came from far and wide. June's mother worked in service and her tales of the old days have inspired several of June's novels.

ACC. No: 03131201

The Pawnbroker's Niece

JUNE FRANCIS

Allison & Busby Limited
12 Fitzroy Mews
London W1T 6DW
www.allisonandbusby.com

First published in Great Britain by Allison & Busby in 2002.
This paperback edition published by Allison & Busby in 2012.

Copyright © 2002 by June FRANCIS

The moral right of the author is hereby asserted in accordance with
the Copyright, Designs and Patents Act 1988.

All characters and events in this publication,
other than those clearly in the public domain,
are fictitious and any resemblance to actual persons,
living or dead, is purely coincidental.

All rights reserved. No part of this publication may be reproduced,
stored in a retrieval system, or transmitted, in any form or by
any means without the prior written permission of the publisher,
nor be otherwise circulated in any form of binding or cover
other than that in which it is published and without a similar
condition being imposed on the subsequent buyer.

A CIP catalogue record for this book is available from
the British Library.

10 9 8 7 6 5 4 3 2 1

ISBN 978-0-7490-1300-4

Typeset in 10/14.2 pt Sabon
by Allison & Busby Ltd.

The paper used for this Allison & Busby publication
has been produced from trees that have been legally sourced
from well-managed and credibly certified forests.

Printed and bound by
CPI Group (UK) Ltd, Croydon, CR0 4YY

My thanks go to Bob Evans, whose
Mersey Mariners was invaluable to me
in writing this book. As was
The Autobiography of A Liverpool Slummy
by Pat O'Mara.

CHAPTER ONE

Rita lifted a fist and rapped on the door alongside the pawnbroker's shop. The sound was barely louder than a mouse scrabbling behind a skirting board. She half-hoped the Miss Sinclair named on the note wouldn't hear. Then she would be able to scurry back home and say she'd done what Mam told her and that there had been no answer. The trouble was her mother might not believe her. She often called her a little liar in a tone of voice that sometimes scared the hell out of Rita. It was no wonder she did tell fibs because on more than one occasion she had received a clout over the ear when telling the truth. She just couldn't win.

Rita was about to bang on the door again when

a noise behind her caused her to whirl round and stare up at the black-clad figure looming over her. Glinting dark eyes, a slender nose and pale skin stretched over angular cheekbones caused the girl's legs to turn to jelly.

'What is it, girl? Have you come to steal my money? I know what devils you kids are!' The woman lifted her umbrella. Rita ducked and would have made a run for it but was seized by the arm. 'No, you don't! Explain yourself or I'll take you to the bobby and you'll be locked up and the key thrown away.'

'But I haven't dun anythin', missus! I came with a message for Miss Sinclair from me mam.' Rita reached for the scrap of paper which to her annoyance her mother had pinned to her thin coat as if she was a little kid in danger of losing it. She tried to undo the bent rusty pin with one hand but couldn't.

The woman slapped her hand away. 'Stop that! I'm not going to be able to see in this light. Let me get the door open and you can come inside and explain yourself.'

Go through that door with this woman! Rita thought in alarm. Not on your nelly! What wouldn't she do to her once she got her inside? She might bake her in the oven like the wicked witch in *Hansel and Gretel*. Nah! She was letting her imagination run away with her but, even so, she didn't know this Miss

Sinclair so why should she trust her? 'Couldn't I just give yer the note and go? Me mam'll be wanting me for supper.' That was a lie because a man had been waiting outside their room and the last thing Eve Taylor would want was her daughter home early.

'No!' Miss Sinclair pushed the girl and she tripped over the threshold. By the time Rita picked herself up the door had closed. 'Move!' Knuckles dug into her backbone and propelled her along the lobby and into a rear room that was in darkness but for the embers glowing in the grate. 'Don't move!' The woman pulled a chair from the table and climbed onto it.

Move! Don't move! You should make up your mind, missus, thought Rita.

A match flared and there was a pop as the gas mantle flamed, chains were adjusted and the shadows in the corners of the room fled.

Miss Sinclair removed the pins from her hat and placed it on the table. She had nut-brown hair and looked no less frightening by gaslight to the fourteen-year-old girl. Clad in an old-fashioned long black skirt that rustled and a black velveteen jacket that hung on her gaunt figure, she reminded Rita of a picture in a fairy-tale book. She beckoned her forward with a black-gloved hand.

Reluctantly Rita left the relative security of the wall next to the door and stepped onto a rug, which felt soft and warm beneath the soles of her shoes with holes in. She fumbled for the note again and cursed her mother for treating her like a parcel needing a label.

Miss Sinclair clucked with her tongue and teeth and removed her gloves before pulling Rita closer. Her chin was forced up and long fingers unfastened the pin. She was told to sit.

Rita sat on a chair next to the green chenille cloth-covered table. On it was a glass jar half-filled with chocolates. Her lips parted and she drooled. It seemed ages since Christmas and the bar of chocolate her mother had given her. She imagined its creamy taste on her tongue. She rested her elbows on the tablecloth. Some chocolates were wrapped in gold foil, others shiny purple, but most were unwrapped. If there had not been a lid on the jar she could have easily slid her fingers across and taken one. She could have crammed it into her mouth before the woman could prevent her. The treat was worth a smack.

She glanced at the woman and, as if sensing Rita's gaze on her Miss Sinclair looked at her through wire-rimmed spectacles. 'Eve must be raving mad to think I'd take you in. She says I owe her but the way I see it she owes me. As for trying to recall me to a sense of duty where you're concerned, she's had it!' She removed the spectacles that had magnified her eyes to an alarming size. 'You can take me to her before she clears off. I've got a bone to pick with her.'

Rita stood. 'What d'yer mean, *clears off*?'

'It's plain enough, girl. She's dumping you.'

'I don't believe yer! Mam wouldn't leave me. ''Sides, she's got a man with her. A big black fella off the monkey boats that anchor in the Coburg Dock.'

Miss Sinclair did not appear surprised to hear this. As she pinned her hat on she said, 'Not daft, is she? Those tribal-scarred fellows from the West Coast of Africa make good husbands. They draw a steady wage and are away at sea for a good nine months when trade's good. Although with the Slump . . . still that's no reason to dump you. Unless . . . I suppose it's possible she hasn't owned up to you.' Her sharp eyes rested on Rita's thin pallid face with its patches of scurvy and remarkable liquid brown eyes. 'I don't suppose you remember your father?'

'He was a lord,' said Rita stoutly. 'He had a palace in Timbuktu just like the King's.'

Miss Sinclair's lips twisted in what was a travesty of a smile. 'Eve could always make up a good story.' Taking Rita's arm she hustled her out.

She struggled. 'Yer hurtin' me!'

'Am I now? Well, you'll know what pain is if you try and get away. Eve's kept her whereabouts secret for years, and, as I say, I've a bone to pick with her.'

'But, missus, I won't run away. Honest!' Rita crossed her fingers behind her back. The pressure on her arm did not slacken and she realised Miss Sinclair did not trust her.

She feared the woman was telling the truth about

11

her mother, as she was quickly led through narrow cobbled streets until they reached a tall house not far from Cornwallis Street baths. It was situated in an area named after famous sailors: Grenville, Hardy and Nelson. It had been built during the last century to house merchants within walking distance of the waterfront so that in no time at all they could inspect their cargoes when they docked.

The front door was open and an elderly man with corkscrew hair and dusky skin sat upon the step, a clay pipe jutting from between teeth rotting from eating too many raw molasses. He whittled at a piece of wood with a penknife.

'Let me by!' Rita dragged her hand free from Miss Sinclair's and tried to force her way past him, only to have the back of her collar seized. She gagged as a button dug into her throat.

The pressure eased as Miss Sinclair placed a knee in her back. 'Is Eve inside?'

'She's gone, missus.' The man screwed up his eyes. 'Told me to tell any who came looking she was leaving Liverpool tonight.'

'Yer a dirty liar! Me mam wouldn't leave me!' Rita clawed at the woman's hand and tried to get at the man.

Miss Sinclair twisted her round and the girl's plaits swung and hit Rita in the face as she shook her. 'I'll have none of that!' The woman was furious. 'Why didn't you stop her, old man?'

12

'Stop that one?' he said in a deep voice, and he licked the blood pouring from a finger. 'See what the kid's gone and done?'

Miss Sinclair barely glanced at the wound. 'Do you know where Eve's gone?'

'You think she'd tell me?' He got to his feet and turned to go inside.

'You might have heard her talking!' She took out a coin. 'Thruppence if you tell me what you know.'

He stretched out a hand but she closed her fingers over the coin. 'Information first.'

Rita scrabbled at his sleeve. 'Hurry up and tell us!'

'Cardiff! He's got a sister and Eve and her fella are gonna help run her boarding house.'

'Address?' said Miss Sinclair.

He shook his grizzled head and reached for the coin.

The woman's grip slackened and Rita pulled herself free and shot off like a rocket. She did not stop running until she passed St Vincent de Paul's church and was halfway along Park Lane. She slipped like an eel between those paying a visit to various pawnshops for their husbands' Sunday suits. Hope glowed in her eyes. She would find her mam and go with her to that place ol' Lucas had mentioned. She refused to believe Eve would deliberately leave her behind. They'd been through all sorts together. Which way would she have gone – by sea? Plenty of ships in the Mersey although some were doing nothin'. Crews laid off because trade had dropped due to the Slump. How to find the right ship? Her footsteps faltered. Then she told herself she must try. Cardiff, Cardiff, Cardiff!

She turned left into Cornhill Street, heading for Wapping and the docks. A whiff of salt-laden air caused her nostrils to flare as she raced past the Baltic Fleet pub. She crossed the dock road passing beneath the overhead railway and came to high stone walls blackened with the soot of several decades enclosing the docks and warehouses.

A stitch caused her to slow down and she pressed her hand against her side. Her breathing steadied as she walked the length of the wall, remembering that on the other side lay Wapping, then Salthouse, the massive Albert Dock and Canning. Beyond these was the Princes Landing Stage where the ferries and liners came in. What cargo ships went to Cardiff? Would they be bringing coal on sooty coasters? She was unsure. Her heart sank. Without the right dock and the name of the ship she had no chance of finding her mother. What about sailing time, too? She had heard many a Jack tar enter their room, half-drunk on her mother's arm, talking of tides and sandbanks and far-distant lands.

Rita's attention was suddenly drawn to the huge bulk of the Customs House across the road, with old salts sprawling on its steps. Taking a deep breath she went over.

A number of men were clearly drunk. One was fast asleep, each snore lifting his straggling moustache before it flopped down again. His clothing was torn and smelly. A middle-aged man of shabby appearance was playing the mouth organ. She decided he must be reasonably sober to hold a tune.

'Excuse me, mister! Could you tell me when high tide is and where I'll find a ship to Cardiff?'

The man shook his mouth organ, sending gobbits of spit flying. 'What's that yer say, queen?'

'Cardiff! Is there a ship going tonight?'

'Caadeef! Not te night! Sure, yer'll find the Welsh coming in to Canning and Salthouse docks but not te night. Yer best gettin' home to yer mam. It's not safe for a young 'un being here at this time of night.'

'But me mam—'

He launched into 'What Shall We Do with the Drunken Sailor?'

Dragging her feet, hands looped behind her back and her head bent, she walked away. Perhaps her mam and her fella were going by train! She lifted her head and hurried round the corner of the Customs House and into Canning Place; looming across the way was the Sailors' Home. She had heard kids talking about their sailor fathers calling there before a voyage. Her spirits rose as she stared at the blackened walls of this refuge for mariners. It had rounded windows and towers soaring into the starlit sky.

Rita moved towards it, but cautiously, not wanting to draw attention to herself. A drunk was bellowing 'Blow the Man Down', arm in arm with a woman. In the shadows was another raddle-faced streetwalker lighting a cigarette, so the girl sidled over to her and said, 'Dolly! Have you seen me mam?'

The woman's painted face registered alarm. 'What the bloody hell are you doing here, kid? Now yous hop it!' She shooed her away. 'Yer don't want a fluke catching yer round here. Yer young and clean and there's many who go for your sort. Scram before yer end up like me.'

'But me mam's gone off with a black fella!' Rita tugged on Dolly's arm. 'Did she say anything to you about him?'

'No, she bloody didn't!' The prostitute sounded fed up and appeared about to say something else when a couple of men emerged from the Sailors' Home. They parted and one made his way in their direction. Dolly muttered, 'He mightn't have much after the do-gooders have had him but what he's got left is gonna be mine.' She stubbed out her fag and, pushing Rita away, stepped out of the shadows, clad in a shortened yellow satin frock that had once graced the stage, making a beeline for him.

Rita followed, only to be threatened by an arm the size of a ham. 'What did I bloody tell yer? I'll squash yer into the ground if yer don't beat it!'

Rita had seen Dolly claw a woman's eye out and trembled at the memory of blood and gore. She turned and fled up the nearest opening. It did not take her long to know she had made a mistake. The street might appear deserted but somewhere a ukulele was being strummed and a man was singing. She quickened her pace, her heart hammering in her breast.

A voice called down from the window. 'Where are you going, flower?'

Then, like a medieval strolling minstrel, a young man appeared singing in a foreign language. She tried to dodge him but he sidestepped and blocked her way. 'Now where are you rushing off to, petal?' The flat café-au-lait features of the fluke relaxed into a smile. 'You looking for someone?'

Rita stared at him with all the fear of a mouse caught by one of the many cats living in dockland.

'There's no need to be scared of me. You come inside my house and get warm. Have a drink and some food and rest. It's late. Will someone be missing you?'

Rita dodged to the side of the street but he moved with her and held out a hand. 'Come with Uncle Johnny! I'll look after you. Get you a nice room and decent clothes.' He placed his ukulele on the ground.

Her eyes darted left and right, looking for a way of escape. He made a grab for her, caught her and held her against him. She screamed and he laughed. She screamed again.

'That's enough, Johnny.' The voice took them by surprise. 'Let her go or I'll have you in court before you can say *Davy Jones' locker*.'

Johnny released Rita. 'I wouldn't have hurt her, Padre.'

'You'd have set her off on a path that leads to Hell,' said the dark-haired man with silver wings of hair at his temples, dressed in black. 'Come, girl!' He held out a hand.

Rita hesitated and Johnny smirked. 'She hasn't a pick on her but if that's your taste, Padre, I hope you enjoy her,' said Johnny.

'Shut your filthy mouth!' rasped the older man.

Rita stared at the padre, doubly unsure about accepting his help as she remembered Eve warning her about pimps, police and priests – one lot were after your body, another were out to squash your spirit and the latter wanted to imprison your soul – not to mention the perverts.

The girl made a run for it, fell and lost a shoe, got to her feet and ran on, not daring to go back for it. She was out of breath by the time she came to Paradise Street and found an empty doorway. She retreated into the shadows, shaken still by her encounter with the two men. Gradually her breathing steadied and she had the courage to peer out of her doorway.

Many a sailor looking for a terrestrial Paradise had ended up in the gutter, feeling like nothing on earth, stripped of the new suit bought with some of his pay-off money and every other penny gone.

The shops were closing but there were still people about as pubs began to empty out. She hunched her knees and rested her chin on them, gazing in the direction of Cleveland Square and the heart of Chinatown. A building festooned with paper lanterns caught her eye.

Many times in her life Rita had coped by escaping into her imagination. She remembered spinning a globe in school in search of Timbuktu, wondering if it was in China and the place where her father had once had his palace. Not that she looked Chinese at all but something about that race interested her. She knew Chinese men had signed on British ships during the Great War, claiming to be from the British colony of Hong Kong and so in possession of British citizenship. After the war, some had settled in Liverpool where there was already a thriving Chinese community founded in Victorian times. Some married white women but on the whole they kept themselves pretty much to themselves as did most Jews, Africans, Swedes, Spanish and Greek in the Granby ward of the city.

Rita had never dared enter Chinatown. There had been talk of a trade in young girls smuggled to China on tea clippers. She had mentioned it to her mother. Eve had laughed. 'No need for you to worry, kid. You'd need to be a blonde like me. Still, keep away from there. You just never know – someone might fancy you one day.'

A tear rolled down Rita's cheek. Why couldn't she have been blonde and had style like her mother instead of skinny with hair the colour of a new penny? It was not that she really wanted to be attractive to men and smuggled abroad – not on your nelly! She could have got a job in one of those classy clothes shops such as Cripps or Bacon's in Bold Street.

Where were Eve and her fella now? Rita felt too tired and scared to wander the docks looking for them anymore. She tucked her bare foot beneath the skirt of her coat and dozed off.

The squawking of a cat woke her. Immediately she was aware of the hardness of the step beneath her and opened her eyes. The sky was silvery grey and the stars had paled. She shivered. The streets were Sunday quiet but across the way she could see a couple of Chinese men putting out the lanterns. One was carrying a sack.

She stood and stretched. Her mouth was dry and her stomach craved food but her first thought was of Eve and her fella and that Miss Sinclair. Why had her mam sent her to that woman? How come they knew each other? Rita had noticed the three golden balls hanging over Miss Sinclair's shop and knew some pawnbrokers lent money. Could Eve owe her money and that's what this was all about? Maybe Lucas knew more about Eve's whereabouts than he was cracking on. She'd go back home and find out.

Perhaps she would even take a shortcut through Chinatown – should be safe enough at this time of day.

She limped across the square, inspecting the ground for any rusty nails or stones, wary of ending up with a septic foot. *Chink chonk Chinaman bought a penny doll,* echoed in her head, remembering kids chanting the words to half-caste Chinese children.

Immediately she entered Pitt Street she was aware of an unfamiliar sweet odour and wondered where it was coming from and what caused it. She passed confectioners and grocers, an eating house with lanterns and poultry hanging from hooks. Other windows displayed ornamental models of willowy men and women dressed in Chinese costume and little fat bald men with bare tummies, their belly buttons painted gold.

She jumped out of her skin as a door opened with a crash and a man came flying out. He landed on the pavement. A Chinese man stood in the doorway, arms akimbo. 'You don't come here again. You trouble!' He went back inside and shot the bolts.

Rita would have made a run for it if the dark-haired young man wearing a reefer jacket and peaked seaman's cap had not looked so ill. His face was pale and clammy as he staggered to his feet and leant against the wall.

'Yer look terrible,' she said.

'I feel terrible.' He closed his eyes.

'What have yer been up to in there? What's the funny smell?'

'Get lost, kid. Get home to your mam.' He moved away from the wall but swayed so much she darted forward to prevent him from falling.

'Yer drunk!'

'No, I'm not. Besides, what's it to you?' He pushed her away. 'I'm skint, so yer wasting yer time. Got to get to the Home.'

'I'm not what yer think I am,' she said, flushing. 'I'm looking for me mam. Where's your home?'

He shook his head as if to clear it and leant on her. 'Give us a minute.' Closing his eyes he took several breaths before saying, 'Sailors' Home.'

Rita nodded sagely. 'It's not that far away. I'll be a crutch for yer for a tanner to buy a bun and a mug of cocoa.'

'Are you deaf, kid? I told you—'

'So you're still here, Billy! Pops said you would be,' interrupted an irate voice. 'I hope you haven't spent all your bloody pay-off money!'

Rita gazed at the newcomer who was blonde and good-looking with the bluest eyes she had ever seen. He wore a tweed cap with the peak turned sideways and a shabby jacket. He smelt of horses. 'He was thrown out of there,' she said, pointing to the closed door.

'You didn't have to tell him that,' said Billy, frowning. 'He thinks he has to know the ins and

22

outs of everything. Wheedled the fact I was here out of me dad, I bet!'

'I was thinking of Mother and Alice. We'll lose the bloody yard if you don't help us.'

Billy clenched his jaw. 'Your mother called me a bloody thief. I'm no thief and you know it! And I've stopped bloody caring about the yard. I've offered help and had it turned down. You want it – you find a way of getting rid of the debt. Why the hell d'you think I ended up here but to try and stop Dad gambling?'

'Well, you didn't succeed, did you!'

'He would have lost more if we hadn't had a row and stormed off. Anyway, I've got to get going. I've a ship to catch. Come on, kid!' Billy urged Rita forward.

'You're not going with that little tart, are yer? She had money out of you?'

'No, I haven't,' said Rita crossly. 'And I'm no tart.' She felt bowed under by the weight of Billy's arm. 'I'm looking for me mam and I just happened to be passing when he appeared.'

Tawny eyebrows elevated like humped caterpillars. 'This is bloody stupid! Get out of the way, girl! I'll take over.' He attempted to detach Billy's arm from about her shoulders but Billy resisted.

'I don't want your help, Jimmy. Get off home.'

'Don't be bloody stupid. Alice is going to love

23

this when I tell her! You know she worries about you. Don't you care?'

Billy blinked and rubbed his eyes. 'She's the best thing that came out of the marriage between your mother and my father but you won't get me back to the yard. I'm leaving on the morning tide.' He squeezed Rita's shoulder. 'Come on, kid. I'll see you get something to eat.'

Those words were enough for her to stick with Billy despite Jimmy's good looks drawing her gaze to him. She allowed herself to be hustled along but Billy moved so fast she tripped over one of his feet and it was only Jimmy's outstretched hand that prevented her from dragging Billy to the ground.

'Beat it,' said Jimmy, pushing her away and turning to his stepbrother. 'I get it. You've left most of your money at the Home. I'll come with you and see it gets to where it's most useful.'

Billy laughed. 'You never give up, do yer? But you're too late. I took a leaf out of Dad's book and tried to treble my stake. I've still got a few bob to my name but in future I'm not going to worry about saving the bloody yard or my father. I'll spend my money the way I want.' He reached for Rita and pulled her against him as Jimmy stepped back. 'Come on, kid. I don't want to lose my berth.'

'I've stubbed me toe! It's bleedin'.' She did not expect any sympathy but it would have been nice to get some.

'I'll get one of the women to stick something on it,' said Billy.

Jimmy swore and stormed off.

She went with Billy, hoping he would keep his promise of seeing she got some food. By now she was consumed with curiosity. All her life she had wanted to be part of a proper family with a mother and a father, brothers and sisters. She knew that families fell out sometimes but the ones she knew stuck together despite the rows and helped each other out. No doubt the man beside her would change his mind about his family next time his ship docked.

They came to the Sailors' Home and went inside. Despite the early hour all was hustle and bustle. Rita's eyes widened as Billy detached himself from her. She followed him, her gaze taking in the soaring columns and the galleries of cast iron decorated with nautical themes. She was to learn the foundation stone had been laid almost seventy years ago when four thousand ships a year had docked in the Mersey and there had been a desperate need for safe accommodation for the seafarer, too often a victim of the wicked rapacity of crimps, pimps and prostitutes. The building was modelled on a ship's quarters and had rooms like cabins arranged around an internal court.

'You in trouble again, Billy?' said a deep voice that Rita recognised.

She shrank behind Billy but she had been

25

spotted and he pulled her in front of him, resting his hands on her bony shoulders. 'I need to get back to my ship and could do with a gallon of coffee first but I promised this kid something to eat, Padre.'

'I don't want to go with him,' said Rita in a trembling voice. 'I've heard things about him.'

The padre shook his head. 'Foolish child! You shouldn't believe anything a pimp says.' He turned and shouted a name.

Almost immediately a small rotund man dressed in black and wearing a dog collar appeared. 'Yes, Padre! What can I do for you?'

'Take the young lady to the kitchen and see one of the volunteers gives her something to eat.'

Billy smiled at Rita. 'You'll be OK now, kid. Thanks for your help.'

Before she could say *tarrah* or ask where the yard was he and his stepbrother had mentioned, he had turned from her and she was whisked away by the clergyman.

In the kitchen several women were preparing breakfast. One of them looked disapprovingly at her. 'Who's this you've got? She's only got one shoe and looks like a slummy.'

At the sound of her voice several heads turned and to Rita's dismay she recognised one of them as her former teacher, Miss Turner. 'Rita Taylor! What are you doing here? No fibs, mind! You tell me the truth or you'll be in trouble.' Her dark eyes were like gimlets and her voice real schoolmarmish.

'I always tell the truth, Miss Turner!' Rita crossed her fingers behind her back.

'Don't give me that, girl! I wasn't born yesterday,' said the teacher.

'Now isn't this nice that you know each other,' said the parson, eyes gleaming behind the thick lenses of his spectacles. 'Father Jerome said you were to feed her.' He left them staring at each other in an unfriendly fashion.

'Where is your mother?' said Miss Turner, spreading margarine on toast and placing it on a plate. She indicated Rita sit down at the corner of a table.

Rita ignored the question, her gaze on a steaming urn. 'Any tea goin'?'

The teacher frowned. 'Finish your words, Rita. Go-*ing*! All those years teaching you wasted – and answer my question.'

Rita bit into the toast. She munched, savouring every mouthful. No way was she going to tell Miss Turner her mother had left with a black fella and gone to Wales.

A thick white mug was placed in front of her. 'With a man, is she?' The teacher's voice was not unkind. 'Don't you worry, dear. I'm not judging you by her slatternly ways. I'll see you home.'

The colour rose in Rita's thin face. 'Yer don't

have to worry about me,' she muttered. 'Mam's moved. I can find me own way there.' She lifted the mug and a tear ran down her cheek and dripped into the steaming tea.

'"My", not "me", Rita,' corrected Miss Turner. 'And I don't care what you say, I'm coming with you. I know my duty.'

Rita decided to take the teacher all over the show until she was sick and tired of walking. But things did not work out the way Rita planned. The teacher cottoned on to what she was up to and frogmarched her to her old home. She hammered on the door and eventually someone came.

'What the bloody hell d'yer think yer playing at knocking me up at this time of morning?' said a woman with pipe cleaners in her hair. 'Oh, I'm sorry, miss,' she added hastily, seeming to recognise the teacher at a second glance. 'What are you doing here with Rita? Evie's gone and the kid's supposed to be staying at her aunt's place.'

Rita was stunned. 'I haven't got an aunt. She's lying.'

'Don't you call me a liar! I'll get Lucas! He can tell yer where she lives.' She vanished up the lobby and they heard her yelling, 'Luu-ca-as! Get yer arse down here. Yer wanted.'

Several minutes passed before he appeared. 'What do you want with me? Don't you know this is a day of rest?' He stared at Rita. 'You shouldn't have run off like that, girlie. That Miss Sinclair was real annoyed.'

Miss Turner frowned. 'You have this aunt's address?'

'Sure do.' He dug into the back pocket of his trousers and produced a scrap of paper. 'Here yerrah!' He slapped it on Miss Turner's palm, and stepping back closed the door firmly.

Rita did not want it to be true but was remembering how Miss Sinclair had called her mother 'Eve' and said she had a bone to pick with her.

'Well, Rita?' said the teacher sternly.

'If I had an aunt, Mam would have told me,' she said desperately.

'Where is your mother? No lies now.'

Rita was silent.

Miss Turner gazed at the address on the slip of paper. 'Right! Let's go! I'm going to get to the bottom of this.'

CHAPTER TWO

Margaret Sinclair lifted a cardboard box from the shelf and placed it on the pink cotton eiderdown. Removing the lid, she gazed at the wax doll. Made in Germany, it was one of a pair, a gift from her brother Donald when life had been full and happy. 'The stylish Sinclair sisters' they had been called just before the Great War, part of a group whose parents met in each others' houses for musical evenings. The last one had been in 1910 and had been a happy occasion. They were not to know that within the year Donald would be dead, his ship having foundered in the North Sea. Their mother had gone mad with grief and refused to get rid of anything of his – and even today his bedroom remained as it was before he died. This doll had been taken from her and placed in his room, sacred because Donald had bought it.

Her mother had been furious when Margaret's interest in clothes had resulted in her undressing the doll to see how its garments were stitched together. She had been working at Bacon's in Bold Street, a real classy shop, at the time. Despite her eighteen years her mother had shoved her in the cellar and refused to let her out. She had been scared stiff not so much of the dark but of this example that her mother was becoming more and more unhinged. She had not been in the cellar long before her father freed her after a screaming match between his wife and younger daughter. Within six months Eve had got herself pregnant by a married man and run off.

The door knocker sounded but Margaret decided to ignore it, fingering the doll's satin skirt, feeling afresh the loss of her family and those far-off happy days.

The knocker sounded again. 'Don't they know it's the Sabbath?' she murmured. Still, it would be foolish to turn down the chance of making money and what was the Sabbath to her these days? After her mother's suicide her father had lost his faith, and her own had been sorely tested after God had taken her fiancé, Alan, as well.

She replaced the doll in the box and put it back on the shelf and went downstairs. Drawing back the bolts, she whipped the door open and was about to say it would cost them extra on a Sunday when she recognised her niece – but not the woman dressed in a navy coat and a dated cloche hat in a lighter shade of blue.

'Miss Sinclair?'

'Yes?'

'Is Rita here your niece?'

'Of course she is! Her mother is my sister.' She held out a hand imperiously, 'Come in, Rita! I hope you won't be so silly as to run off again.'

What was it about these spinsters of a certain age that they had to always be bossing a girl about? Rita did not want to admit it but she was scared of Miss Sinclair and determined not to show it. 'If yer me aunt, how is it I've never heard of yer before? I think yer not telling the truth.'

'Don't be rude, Rita,' said Miss Turner. 'I won't hand you over until Miss Sinclair proves what she says is true.'

Margaret said coldly, 'My father ran this business nigh on forty years. He died last month and I've taken over. Anyone in this neighbourhood could verify who I am. More to the point, who are you?'

'She used to be me teacher,' said Rita. 'So don't think yer can put one over on her. She's a brainbox!'

'Rita, be quiet!' Miss Turner sighed heavily.

'I have my sister's note so you can see that,' said Margaret. 'Come in.'

She led the way along the lobby and into the

kitchen. She waved Miss Turner to a chair in front of the fire, and said, 'I don't know why you are interested in my niece when she's left school. In the note Eve sent she says Rita will be fifteen this year, although she looks much younger. Apparently her father was a sailor and died during the war.'

'No! Me dad could be living in Timbuktu!' cried Rita. 'It's hot there and people wear silk robes and carry funny little sunshades. One day he'll come back for me and buy me ice cream and chocolate.'

'Stop! Such imaginings only lead to trouble. Sit and be quiet!'

Rita did not want to do either of those things, she just wanted to beat it, yet her knees felt weak and her stomach was quivering. She sat by the table determined not to give in to her fear of her aunt. She felt lonely and rejected because of her mother's desertion, but tried to buck herself up by telling herself Eve had just gone on ahead to Cardiff to see what the place was like and would send for her. She glanced at the jar of chocolates on the table and imagined the creamy taste of them on her tongue, listening to the women's conversation with half an ear.

Margaret had produced Eve's note and Miss Turner had read and returned it to her. 'I'm sorry if I offended you by asking for proof. I've been concerned about Rita since she finished school. So many girls in her situation end up going down the wrong road. I'm sure I don't have to cross the Ts and dot the Is for you to understand my meaning.'

'I understand perfectly. I wouldn't have chosen to have my niece live with me, and no doubt I'll have my work cut out licking her into shape, but I was never one to sit down and die.'

'I wish you the best of luck. Will she work in the shop? She's had less schooling than she was entitled to. Your sister kept her away times without number until we were sick of sending the man from the school board around. Rita's not stupid. In fact she's sharp in her own way. Even so . . .'

'I'll have to give her a few lessons then, won't I? She'll need to work out percentages amongst other things.' Margaret stood and moved towards the door. 'Now if you don't mind I have a lot to do. She'll need a bath, clean clothes and something to eat, no doubt.' Suddenly she noticed her niece was no longer sitting at the table but had vanished.

Miss Turner was unable to prevent a tiny smile. 'You are going to have your work cut out. God help you and I hope you both gain from having found each other.'

Not the right phrase to use, thought Margaret, because she and her niece had not gone looking for the other. As soon as she closed the door behind her she checked the bolts were still drawn top and bottom on the scullery door and then she went into the storeroom behind the shop where she kept unclaimed knick-knacks, pictures, small pieces of furniture and racks of clothes, the latter depleted today. On Monday they would fill up again with Sunday-best clothes.

'Come out from where you're hiding and I will not hurt you. If you don't, you'll be sorry for wasting my time like this,' called Margaret.

Silence.

She walked about the room moving this and that but there was no sign of her niece. Unlocking the door that led to the shop, Margaret stared at the pitted mahogany counter where her father had performed so many transactions of a profitable nature. She placed her hands on it, levered herself up and looked over the other side, but there was no Rita crouching on the floor.

Margaret hurried upstairs but there was no sign of her niece there. She returned to the kitchen and looked under the table, and then walked into the scullery, frowning as she gazed about her. Then she felt a draught fan her skirt and her gaze went to the cellar door. She called down the steps. 'Are you down there?' Her voice bounced back off grimy cobwebby walls and then she heard the slightest of movements. Was it a mouse, the cat or her niece?

There was nowhere else she could be, so she had to be down the cellar.

'Rita! Will you come out of there?'

Again came the slightest whisper of movement

but not a word spoken. 'You're being silly!' Still there was no response. 'Well, if that's how you want it, then you can stay down there,' she said losing patience and letting the latch fall into place. Sooner or later the girl would see sense and ask to be let out. She, herself, had not forgotten how the darkness had felt like a living presence threatening to smother the life out of her. It had been filled with imagined demons and ghoulies she remembered from the descriptive ghost stories Alan's twin, Will, had told her when they had played games with the lights out. What had happened to him after she refused his proposal of marriage, the one after Bella's death?

Margaret put on the kettle and then returned to listen at the cellar door. All was quiet. What was Rita doing down there, that's if she was there? 'If you want to come out you only have to say sorry.' Again there was no answer. This is ridiculous. Ignore her!

Margaret took the teapot into the kitchen and sat down. She poured herself a cup and then reached for the jar of chocolates. It was not there! A chocolate a day was all she ever allowed herself. She had been reared in ways of thrift, and treats had seldom come her way. Even now, when she had inherited her father's business and had a nice little nest egg, it was difficult to break the habits of a lifetime. She had worked hard for those chocolates. In fact, since her father's death she had been overworked. One of the reasons she had changed her mind about her niece staying with her was that she needed help in the shop and the girl was family.

Margaret became aware of knocking coming from the scullery and was up like a shot and into the scullery. 'Did you steal my chocolates? I warn you that act will not go unpunished.' She waited for the girl to admit the theft but there was only silence once more. Margaret could feel herself losing control of her temper. If she let the girl out now she would not be able to contain herself and would land her a clout. She would leave her there for a while longer; to try and keep her mind off her she would do some work.

She went into the shop and took a ledger from beneath the counter. The figures blurred before her eyes and, with a muttered curse, she went for her spectacles. The banging had begun again. Margaret went to the door and demanded an apology. All she got for her pains was silence. She thought of the darkness in the cellar and could not understand the girl's stubbornness. She would have been terrified, but then Margaret remembered leaving the door open between the two rooms of the cellar. In the far room was a grating high on the wall that let on to the pavement. She fetched the ledger from the shop and sat at the table in the kitchen and tried to pretend her niece was not there.

When the singing started, Margaret could scarcely believe her ears. She shot up and went and opened the cellar door. 'Come out of there,' she said in an angry voice.

Something came flying out of the depths narrowly missing her head. It smashed on the red-tiled floor. Before she could recover her equilibrium her niece was up the stairs and forcing her way past her. She made a grab for Rita but missed. She whirled round and saw her niece picking her way through broken crystal. The sight caused Margaret to see red. 'You little bitch!' She sprang at the girl, whose face bore evidence of the chocolate she had devoured. This time Margaret managed to grab one of her pigtails.

Rita screamed and put up her hands to ease the pressure on the roots of her hair. 'Let me go, yer ol' hag!'

Margaret's breath hissed through her teeth. 'Shut up, you stupid girl! Do you want to go back in the cellar again?'

'I don't care. I just close my eyes and pretend I'm in a palace. If you hadn't been so cruel as to shut me in I would have eaten only half of the chocolates, but I got hungry and then thirsty and so I ate them all just to show you yer can't have yer own way all the time. Yer know where people like you go? To hell!'

'I can't believe your cheek! Can't you see the danger you're in?' Margaret almost choked on the words and her free hand was twitching. 'There's no one here to save you. That jar you broke was pure crystal. I've a cane in the shop that my father used on naughty boys who came into the shop and shouted rude words.' She felt a shiver go through the girl and added in a quiet voice, 'Understand?'

Rita nodded and said huskily, 'I'm sorry about your jar but I was cross with you.'

Margaret gasped. 'You cross with me! How do you think I felt when I found my chocolates missing? You can sweep up the mess while I decide what I'm going to do with you.' She went for the hand brush and dustpan.

As she watched the girl clear up the broken crystal she wondered how her sister could have let her get into such an undernourished and filthy state. 'You'll have a bath. I can't let you between the sheets in the state you're in.'

'Yer wha'? A bath! I don't like water.' Her dismay shone in her eyes.

Beautiful eyes, thought Margaret. Far better than a doll's glass ones. 'You will do as you are told,' she said distinctly.

'I don't get yer. Yer didn't want me last night so why d'yer want me now?' Rita's eyes widened in alarm. 'I know! Yer going to do something nasty to me 'cos of the chocolates.'

'I'm going to improve the way you talk, for starters,' said Margaret. 'My mother wouldn't put up with such sloppy speech from us so why should I from you? As for you having a bath, you're not getting out of that. You could have fleas so I'm not

39

taking any chances. We'll try drowning the . . . the horrors.' She would have liked to call them little buggers but her upbringing stopped her this time.

'Drownin'!' Rita's voice was horror-struck. 'Yer not getting me in no bath. I'm off!'

Margaret reached the door before her and put her back to it. Rita flung herself at her, pummelling her stomach with bony fists. She remembered one of Eve's men dunking her in a tub. The water had come right over her head and she had thought her last day had come.

Aunt and niece struggled against each other but the woman's superior strength told and her strong fingers imprisoned the girl's wrists. She managed to lift her and swing her over the sofa and then dropped her. Margaret wiped her hands on her skirt as if to rid herself of all contact with her niece.

Rita huddled in a corner of the sofa, wanting to weep, but she was determined her aunt would not see her cry. She buried her head between her knees and forced back the tears.

Margaret went into the storeroom and her hands trembled as she took several items from a cardboard box. Then she brought in the galvanised zinc bath from the yard. Fortunately there was a boiler behind the fireplace which provided her with hot water. She placed a bucket in the sink and began to fill it. She washed the scratches inflicted by her niece, then from a cupboard she took a purple bottle and painted them with gentian violets. She replaced the bottle and took carbolic soap, a loofah and flannel from the same cupboard, as well as two towels.

It was after the umpteenth trip with buckets she noticed Rita had vanished again. She had that desire to hit out once more and yelled, 'You smell, girl. By hook or by crook you're having a bath!' She went in search of her.

She found her in the shop gazing at a wall of shelving where unclaimed goods lay gathering dust. 'You shouldn't be in here,' said Margaret sharply.

Rita looked up at her from eyes swimming in tears. 'What harm am I doin'? I don't want to stay here but right now I don't seem to have a choice.'

'Of course you have a choice,' said Margaret. 'You can live on the streets, there's the workhouse or you stay here and work for me. The latter means, though, that you have to be clean. Now back to the kitchen.'

Slowly Rita followed her but she hesitated just inside the kitchen and stared at the water in the bath. 'Couldn't I just wash?'

'No! Fleas spread diseases. Now take off your clothes!'

Rita shook her head and placed her hands beneath her armpits. Margaret's lips tightened and before the girl could prevent her, she managed to lift her fully clothed and dunk her in the water. Rita let out such a scream it echoed in Margaret's head. The girl clung to the bodice of her aunt's frock as her skinny legs thrashed the water, and then she brought them up and wrapped them around her waist.

Margaret could have screamed. 'Will you stop being so silly and act your age!' she cried, exasperated.

'You're going to drown me!'

'Don't tempt me!' Margaret struggled to get her niece's legs from about her waist but as quickly as she got one into the water, Rita drew it up again. In the end, Margaret kicked off her slippers and stepped into the bath water in her stockinged feet. 'I will not let you drown. I don't know where you've got this fear from but take off your frock and underclothes now and wash yourself standing up in the water if you must.'

'OK! But turn your back! I don't want you looking at me in the nuddy.' Slowly Rita lowered her feet into the water and released her hold on her aunt.

Margaret turned her back, wondering if she had gone quite mad stepping into the water the way she had and letting her niece have her way. Rita stripped but for her knickers and picking up the soap and loofah gingerly began to wash herself. 'I don't have to wash me hair, do I?'

'Of course you do! Undo your plaits and I'll wash it for you.'

'No thanks! I can manage meself,' she muttered.

'It'll need rinsing.'

Margaret heard her niece take a deep breath. 'OK! But not until I say I'm ready . . . and I want the two towels handy. I don't want you looking at me.'

'This is silly,' said Margaret turning round.

Immediately Rita placed the loofah in such a way as to cover her private parts. Margaret tried to conceal her dismay at the amount of red marks, which she presumed were bug bites, all over her niece's body. She had little in the way of breasts and Margaret could have counted her ribs if she had wanted. She went and filled a pan with warm water from the tap.

After rinsing her niece's hair Margaret picked up the smaller of the towels and averted her eyes as the girl dropped the loofah and wrapped the larger towel about her slender body. She waited until she climbed out of the bath before fastening the smaller towel about her hair, turban fashion.

She handed Rita a nightdress. 'Put that on,' she said brusquely, turning her back so she would not have to look upon her niece's naked defenceless body, and left the kitchen to change out of her damp clothes.

When she returned it was to find Rita kneeling on the fireside rug with her wet hair dangling in front of her face as she tried to dry it in the fire's heat. In her mind's eye Margaret could imagine fleas dropping onto her rug. 'We're going to have to cut your hair,' she said abruptly. 'I should have done it before you washed it. Tomorrow you can go to the chemist and buy a fine toothcomb and a bottle of nit lotion, as well as some special soap.'

'Your hair's long. Why should I have mine cut?' said her niece, slanting her a glance from those lovely brown eyes.

Margaret did not answer. She had thought of having her hair shorn six months ago and her father had almost had an apoplexy when she mentioned doing so, even though cropped hair had been fashionable for years.

'Up, Rita!' She beckoned her niece with a finger.

The girl stayed where she was, her eyes wary. 'I don't want my hair cut.'

'OK. But right now I need to look at your hair, so don't try my patience to the limit.'

Rita got to her feet. Margaret picked up a comb and gingerly began to part the girl's hair as she looked for the telltale tiny white specks that were nits' eggs. They were there all right and Margaret shivered. Fleas spread disease. She went over to the large dark-oak sideboard and took a pair of scissors out of a drawer. 'You're going to have to have it cut. If you don't you'll have another lot of fleas in the morning crawling all over your head.'

Rita was mortified and as the cold steel touched her head she cried out, 'How do I know you're not gonna slit me throat?'

'You're letting your imagination run away with

44

you again,' said Margaret, exasperated once more. Yet she could not help wondering where her niece got such ideas. Had she ever been threatened in such a way? Or had she been taken to the cinema and seen one of these American gangster films?

'I'm gonna look terrible,' moaned Rita. 'Mam said the fellas like it better long.' She attempted to pull her head out of Margaret's grasp and received a light slap.

'Do you want me to cut your neck? Eve has deserted you and if you are to live with me you must learn to do what I say.' Snip, snip went the scissors. Snip, snip, snip.

'Why d'yer want me here?' asked Rita. 'Yer don't like me and by the sound of it yer didn't like me mam either.'

'Your mother . . . if I could find her I'd . . .' Margaret stopped. What was the use of thinking of what she'd like to do and say to Eve if she had her in front of her? 'There!'

Margaret stepped back to view the results of her handiwork. The ends were not quite even but they would do. She reached for the towel and rubbed dry the dark-red cap of hair. She had decided not to allow Rita to share her bed, but perhaps she had best sleep in her room. She might be frightened in a strange bedroom on her own. Tomorrow she would see what her niece thought of Donald's bedroom or the small back room, which her father had moved

45

into after her mother's death. Tonight she could sleep on a mattress on the floor beside her bed.

Margaret told Rita to dry her hair properly and went into the scullery and made a jug of cocoa. She watched her niece drink it down with such an expression of bliss on her face that she had to smile. Then they went upstairs and, taking the mattress from the bed in the small back room and clean bedding from a cupboard, she showed Rita where to sleep.

Straight away, the girl curled herself up on the mattress and dragged the bedcovers over her head. She fell asleep immediately much to Margaret's surprise. She, on the other hand, did not sleep very well at all. Her mind was too busy reliving that day and wondering what the future would hold now she had taken in her niece and whether either of them would ever hear from Eve again.

Eventually Margaret did fall asleep but she woke with the dawn to immediately recall the happenings of yesterday. She turned and looked over the side of the bed at Rita, who lay on her back, her rust-coloured lashes fanned out on her thin pale cheeks. The sleep of the innocent, was her first thought until she recalled what she knew about the girl. She was a thief and a liar and she must not forget that her upbringing had been very different to her own.

Downstairs Margaret drew back the curtains and looked out on the backyard. The rays of the rising sun caught the broken glass embedded in cement on top of the dividing wall between her property and the next. For a few seconds the glass reflected dazzling light. She thought of diamonds and engagement rings and all those single women who had lost fiancés. She thought of Rita and hoped this day would not disappoint, and that the weather and her mood could be sunny all day.

She went into the yard and deposited Rita's frock, knickers and odd shoe in the dustbin. Back in the scullery she lit the gas under the kettle and put on the oats she had left in water to soak overnight. Then she heard footsteps on the stairs and, turning, braced herself as the door opened.

CHAPTER THREE

'Where's me frock?' asked Rita, her rusty hair an unruly cap on her small head and her thin bare legs like sticks beneath the hem of the nightgown.

'Where it belongs – in the dustbin,' said Margaret.

The girl scowled. 'You had no right to do that. I'm not staying, yer know. I'm going to find me mam. I've always looked out for her.'

'Have you indeed?' Margaret would have laughed if the girl had not looked so pathetic – the very idea of her being able to look after anyone was ridiculous.

'Yeah! Me!' lied Rita, strutting into the scullery like a cock bantam. 'She's choosy, is Mam! Some fellas she just couldn't be doing with but she wouldn't have no pimp looking out for her skimming off some of her earnings.' She gave her aunt a calculating look from beneath her sweeping eyelashes to see what she made of that. 'I don't suppose you've got a fella? Naw! Not with the way you dress. Yer've got to dolly yerself up to attract the men.'

Margaret's lips tightened. 'I think I've heard enough about men for the moment. If you want to eat, wash your hands in the sink here.'

Rita held up her hands and looked at them. 'They're not dirty.'

'Don't argue with me! If you don't wash your hands and face you don't eat. If you're going to look for Eve you've got a long journey ahead of you so you'd better get something in your stomach.'

The girl's mouth fell open. A satisfied smile gleamed in Margaret's dark eyes as she brushed past her niece. Rita rallied quickly and followed her into the kitchen. 'You mean yer don't want me to stay, you want to be rid of me after all?'

'I'm not forcing you to stay. Why should I?' said Margaret, setting two places at the table. 'You could prove more trouble than you're worth. How you're going to get to Cardiff interests me, though. Got money hidden away somewhere, have you?'

Rita glowered at her. 'Yer must know I haven't. All I got is what I arrived in.'

'Then you'll be walking to Cardiff in your bare feet if that's the only way you can get there.' Margaret

49

glanced at those appendages. 'I threw your shoe in the bin, as well as your frock. What happened to the other one, Cinderella?'

'Very funny! I was running away from someone, if yer must know.'

'You mean me?'

'No! If yer must know it was a couple of blokes. One was after me body, the other wanted to save me soul. Still, yer had no right to throw me shoe away. I could have gone back and found the other.' Rita's bottom lip jutted out as she folded her arms across her thin chest. 'Yer going to have to get me a new pair.'

Margaret gasped. 'You've got a nerve! Have you forgotten already about the cane I keep by for impudent boys? Don't think just because you're a girl I won't use it on you.'

'But I'm your niece!' Rita delivered the words as if they were a password that would open doors. 'You have a responsibility towards me!' There was a look of triumph on her face.

'Exactly! If you weren't so against your soul being saved then you'd know that in the Bible it mentions not to spare the rod and spoil the child.'

'What's that supposed to mean?'

Margaret made an exasperated noise, raised her eyes to the ceiling and hurried into the scullery to check the porridge hadn't caught.

Rita followed. 'I'm not thick, yer know!'

'So your teacher told me.' Margaret stirred the

porridge with a wooden spoon. 'Although she also told me that Eve kept you away from school more times than was good for you.'

'That's because she always felt terrible the morning after and wanted me by her. Besides the place was always in a mess and I couldn't abide that.'

'You surprise me. It's a wonder she didn't take you with her then, if you were so useful to her.'

Rita's small face looked stricken. Immediately Margaret regretted those words and tried to make up for it by saying, 'She probably had no say in it. The bloke she went off with most likely laid down the law and said he wasn't taking you with them.'

The girl's expression lightened a little but she made no comment about that, only saying, 'Life was getting pretty tough for us. Mam's still a looker but she's not as young as she was and yer'd be surprised how many women are going on the game to feed their kids. She's always had a yen to be respectable so maybe this bloke promised to marry her.'

'Maybe! We can only hope,' said Margaret, marvelling at her niece's philosophical statement, while trying to conceal her shocked reaction to its content. She knew only too well of the deprivation that so many families suffered and could only hope that Mr Ramsay MacDonald's Labour government could do more for the poor women of this country, who had lost so much and been given so little in return after the Great War.

51

Thinking of all the men who had been killed she thought of Alan, although she had not lost him in that conflict. He had gone out as a missionary to China before the war and vanished. She had waited for his letter telling her to follow him out but it had never arrived. She could only believe that he had been killed in one of the uprisings out there.

She caught herself up on the memory, chiding herself for dwelling too much on the past since her father had died. She filled two bowls with steaming porridge and carried them into the kitchen.

Rita was still drying her hands when she followed her in. Margaret pointed to one of the dining chairs and the girl sat down. She watched her aunt sprinkle salt on her porridge. 'Where's the sugar? Mam always had sugar when we had porridge.'

Margaret felt a flicker of irritation. 'Eve isn't here. I eat it with salt. You're going to have to learn my ways if you stay.'

Rita put down the spoon and placed her elbow on the table, resting her chin in her hand. She sniffed before saying in a trembling voice, 'You don't know what it's like being me and having your mam leave you with someone you don't know.'

'Don't I?' said Margaret, not looking at her. 'My mother left me in spirit if not in body and put a stranger in her place. You probably don't understand what I mean by that but I can tell you it's just as difficult to face up to as having your mother leave you and go off with a man. Now try your porridge with salt. It's the way my parents always had it and I learnt to enjoy it that way.'

Reluctantly but prepared to have a go Rita sprinkled salt on her breakfast. Then she picked up her spoon and began to eat as if every mouthful was an effort. She gagged once and Margaret shot a glance across the table and watched her force down the food. 'Do you know your tables?' she asked abruptly.

Rita put down her spoon and said sullenly, 'What d'yer want to know for? Yer thinkin' of having me stay here after all and have me working for yer?'

'That depends on whether you're going to behave yourself. If you want to go to Cardiff and try to find your mother you're going to have to earn money, even if you decide to walk all the way. I reckon it's going to be nigh impossible you finding a job elsewhere the way unemployment is. I'm presuming you don't already have a job or want to earn money by . . . by selling your b-body to men the way Eve . . .' Margaret's voice trailed off.

Rita blanched. 'I tried to find work but . . . Anyway, Mam didn't always make money that way,' she said fiercely. 'It's only since things got really tough that she began hanging out where she knew there'd be sailors. She did a bit of singing and dancing before that, playing the squeeze box.' Margaret remembered her sister playing that well. Her niece continued, 'But she had to pawn that in the end to pay the rent on the new place we'd flitted to. Now that was a real dump and not worth sacrificing the ol' squeeze box for. I was real sad to see it go because it was one way we made a bob or two and, besides, the music used to cheer me up.'

'Your mother should have got in touch with me sooner, then.'

'Maybe she had her pride. If yer were my sister I wouldn't have wanted yer knowing how low I'd sunk.'

'Perhaps.' Margaret reached for the teapot but drew back her hand at the sound of the door knocker.

They both half-rose in their seats. 'You can stay where you are!' ordered Margaret, waving her down. 'You're not dressed! And it's probably only Mrs McGinty who does for me.'

She swept out of the kitchen, thinking it could just as easily signal a troublesome customer. One she'd lent money to who was supposed to pay back a small sum weekly including interest. Some got into difficulties and after a sleepless night worrying about how they were going to ever be free of the debt, could get really truculent in their demands for her to lower her interest rates; rates which were set legally by the government. It was something they wouldn't have dared do to her father.

To her surprise it was Rita's former teacher. Although she was not alone, because just behind her was Mrs McGinty. The cleaner excused herself, easing her way past Miss Turner who said, 'Good morning!'

'Good morning to you,' said Margaret, a slight pucker between her brows. 'What can I do for you?'

'I'm just checking whether you found Rita or not? I was worried about the girl. As we both agreed, the last thing we want is her to take to the streets.'

'I couldn't agree more but there's no need for you to worry. She's here and having her breakfast.'

'Thank the Lord for that,' said Miss Turner, smiling. 'When I was in bed last night I couldn't stop thinking about you. It's not easy to take in a girl like her.'

'No. But I'm sure we'll sort ourselves out,' said Margaret, her voice distant.

Miss Turner flushed. 'Well, if you need any help I don't live far. I could put in a couple of hours of private tuition with Rita if you wished. Since Mother died I have time on my hands. We also have a Bible study at the church for girls of Rita's age, if you were interested.'

'Thanks for the offer. I'll let you know.' Margaret bid her good day and closed the door, hoping the woman was not going to be a nuisance. It was obvious Miss Turner was lonely and in need of extra income, as well as being a do-gooder, but at the moment Margaret felt she had enough on her plate, coping with the shop and her niece.

Back in the kitchen Margaret found Mrs McGinty staring at Rita, who was down on her knees in front of the fireplace cleaning out last night's ashes. The char shot a look at her employer and folded her arms across her scrawny bosom, which was covered by a sacking apron. 'Who's this? What's she doing here taking over my job?'

Before Margaret could answer Rita glanced up from beneath her eyelashes at the char. 'I'm Miss Sinclair's niece and I'm makin' meself useful. She's not going to be needing yer anymore.'

Mrs McGinty's mouth fell open. 'Is this true? What am I going to do? I need this money with my Alf's back being bad again. He hasn't been able to do any roofing work lately; only had a few hours of cocky watchman's work.'

'Of course she's not taking over your job,' said Margaret soothingly. 'Get up, Rita! You'll get filthy! When I said I'd put you to work you know I had no intention of having you scrub floors or clean out the grate. Into the scullery and out of that nightgown and wash your hands and face. Then upstairs and wait in the bedroom for me.'

'OK! I was only trying to help. It's what I used to do for me mam.' Rita shrugged her bony shoulders and, brushing ash from her palms, walked out of the room, her head held high.

'Well, I never,' said Mrs McGinty, looking flabbergasted. 'Where did she come from?'

Margaret did not answer, having no intention of letting the woman know the ins and outs of her business. What she knew already would soon be all over the neighbourhood. She left the char to take over from where her niece had left off and hurried out of the room and into the storeroom.

Rita watched Margaret pull at the seams of the plain blue frock as if to reassure herself that it was not going to come apart, before placing the garment on the top of a small pile of clothing. She made a satisfied noise in her throat. 'These should fit you.'

Rita could not make her aunt out. Right now she was a very different person to the one who had threatened her with an umbrella that first evening they had met. She should be used to changes of mood. Her mother was the same. One day she would be as bright and cheerful as a sunny day and then the next it was as if a cloud had descended and she wouldn't get out of bed. Still, they'd been together through thick and thin and Rita could not dismiss easily those memories. There'd been times when Rita had never been able to get warm and as for food . . . gosh, her stomach had never been full. She remembered begging for a stale loaf on a Saturday night from the bakery and stealing fruit from handcarts. She had been caught once but got off with a severe reprimand from the bobby on the beat. He had frightened the life out of her and she'd told her mother never again. The worst day of her life, though, had been when she'd arrived home from school and found her mother in bed with the rent collector. They hadn't stayed in those rooms, though – Eve had disliked him as much as Rita and they'd flitted. That had been when they had lived the other side of Liverpool, not far from Great Homer Street. It had been the start of Eve carrying on with the men. Some had been good to them both and some had been bad.

'Will you stop daydreaming!' Margaret nudged Rita's foot with the toe of her shoe.

'I'm not daydreaming! I'm thinking of Mam.'

Margaret's expression became austere. 'That's a waste of time. Get dressed and be downstairs in five minutes!'

Rita nodded and picked up a pair of camiknickers and sniffed them cautiously. They smelt of camphor but she wasn't going to complain. One thing was for sure: she was going to be warmer this chilly March day than she had been for a long time. She put them on and reached for the hand-knitted black stockings, which itched slightly but were as warm as toast, reaching just above her knees to be held up by proper fancy garters, not just elastic bands. Next came a vest, which was a bit long but at least it would keep her bum warm. After the vest came a liberty bodice. My Aunt Fanny! she thought, this is the gear! I'm feeling snug already. She began to hum

'What Shall We Do with the Drunken Sailor' as she put on the blue frock, and deftly did up the dozen or so tiny pearl buttons which fastened up the front. After that there was a navy-blue wool cardigan.

She went over to the dressing table where she remembered catching a glimpse of herself earlier. She hadn't liked her reflection, mourning the loss of her hair, but now as she turned her head this way and that she thought she didn't look half as bad as when wearing the nightgown. Pity she didn't have Mam's blonde hair and blue eyes, but there – she was as God had made her. If only Eve could see her now. Suddenly Rita was angry. Whatever her mother's motive had been for sending her to her aunt, she should not have done it in the way she did. It wasn't what mothers should do! It was wicked sending her to the aunt she didn't know existed and then leaving her without a goodbye or an explanation. But her rage did not last long and she began making excuses for Eve.

Maybe a proper goodbye would have been too upsetting for them both! It was possible that her mother would write asking how she was getting on and, when she wrote back and told her how unhappy she was, then Eve would send her a postal order for the fare with orders to come to Cardiff right away. She mightn't know where her mother was but Eve certainly knew where she was. Presuming Rita stayed on with her aunt.

She heard her name being called but made no move to hurry. Instead she took Margaret's silver-backed brush from the glass tray which contained a comb, a pair of small scissors and hair grips, and brushed her shorn hair, smiling at her reflection before replacing the brush and tripping downstairs to remind Margaret that she had no shoes.

Rita remembered how she had lost them and thought briefly of the two men she had met. What had been their names? Billy and Jimmy, that was them. She hoped the sailor had caught his ship and that the younger handsome one saved the yard he had been going on about. If only she could meet him again – now she was looking so fine.

Shoes were found for Rita among the unredeemed goods in the storeroom. They were a little too big but with newspaper stuffed in the toes they were comfortable enough.

Margaret handed her a note and two half-crowns. 'I want you to go to Lomax's the chemist in Berry Street. I expect you to be no longer than half an hour. So don't go wasting time looking in shop windows.'

'What about me coat? Did you throw that in the bin as well?' Rita looked up at her aunt who was taller than Eve by at least three inches and lacked her glamour. It was difficult to believe that they were sisters.

'No! That'll do you for now. You need a hat, though.'

A small green felt cloche was found in the storeroom. Rita had never owned a hat and she spent several minutes looking in the mirror, tilting the hat this way and that until she was satisfied. Then she skipped out into the street, aware of an overwhelming sense of freedom. For the moment the pain of her mother's desertion and the strangeness and apprehension she felt being around her aunt were put aside.

Rita made for Berry Street, thinking how well her aunt had her taped. The girl had never had money to spend on herself in her life so the next best thing was to window-shop. Cripps in Bold Street was already displaying tailored suits for the race-going middle classes. In a few weeks, Liverpool would be horseracing mad because of the Grand National at Aintree. Visitors from all over the country and even abroad would crowd the streets.

Another lovely shop was De Jong's, specialising in lingerie made of lace, satin and silk. Then there was Pacquin's, who catered for a Jewish clientele. Further down right in the city centre there were Lewis's, Bunney's and Frisby, Dyke & Co's stores, crammed with all sorts of things, dresses and furnishings and pretty knick-knacks; things she could only dream about. Right now, though, Rita was prepared to settle for the smaller shops in Berry Street.

But the first thing she did, as soon as the three

golden balls hanging above her aunt's shop were out of sight, was to open the note. She grimaced as she read *One fine toothcomb, one bottle of nit lotion and a block of Derbac soap. Please write the cost of these items down for me and enclose the note with said items. Miss Margaret Sinclair.*

'Damn!' murmured Rita. 'She doesn't trust me! But surely she'd realise I'd read the note . . . or was it that she thinks I can't read well enough?'

She pocketed the note, feeling annoyed as she walked in the direction of Berry Street. As she turned the corner where Lunt's the bakery was situated opposite St Luke's church, she noticed a youth in a shabby torn jacket and trousers kneeling on the pavement next to a grating outside a shop. He held a cane with a large bent spoon tied to it, which he lowered through the grating. Guessing what he was up to, she crossed the road and stood next to him.

'Any luck?'

He did not answer immediately, concentrating as he scooped around in the rubbish below. Then, holding his breath, he cautiously withdrew the bent spoon through the grating. Swiftly he pocketed the silver thruppenny bit in the bowl of the spoon before dropping it through the grating again. Only then did he look up at her from grey eyes that appeared too large for his thin face. There was a purplish bruise on his jaw and his bare wrists were bony. 'You done this, have yer?' he said.

She nodded. 'When I could get a place where there were no lads hanging around, but I wasn't very good at it.'

'Yer have to keep trying.' He looked through the grating and she watched as he jiggled the cane again but this time he had only caught a farthing.

'Can't yer get work?' asked Rita.

'A bit here and there, fetching and carrying for people. Yer know the kind of thing, but on Saturdays I work at Fitzgerald's the chandler's.'

'Better than nothing.'

He snorted. 'Yeah, yeah! Thanks for your interest but I'm losing me concentration. Could you go away now, luv?'

'Me name's Rita.'

'Sam!' Without looking he held up his free hand.

She shook it. 'Good luck, Sam! See yer around!'

He nodded.

Rita walked along the pavement until she came to Hilton's confectionery shop and there she paused to gaze longingly at the jars of sweets in the window. After that, it was on past the Temperance Hotel, the post office and Grosvenor's Motors. Next to which was the chandler's shop mentioned by Sam. On past a hairdressing salon and more sweet shops until she came to Lomax's. She hesitated outside and a sigh escaped her. Why hadn't Eve got rid of the nits properly? On Christmas Eve she had hunted them out, catching and cracking them between her fingernails, but you didn't get shot of fleas properly like that. Their eggs had to be exterminated completely and the only way to do that was with nit lotion and a fine toothcomb, as well she knew – but the shame of having to go in the chemist for those things! They would look at the note and look at her shorn head and know that she had fleas. They'd think she was dirty.

Rita steeled herself and pushed open the door, wishing that she could spend the money on face powder or perfume because the smell of them would have made her feel better than any old Derbac soap and nit lotion would. Still, it had to be done, and she handed over the note and the money and within five minutes was back outside the shop with her purchases, and the change burning a hole in her pocket. As she walked slowly between housewives with toddlers hanging onto their skirts, and men old before their time shuffling along the uneven paving stones, she fingered the coins. She thought of her mother and the indignity of having nit lotion combed through her hair by the aunt who was a stranger to her and she felt really fed up.

She stopped outside Hilton's confectionery shop again and gazed in the window at the glass jars filled with a variety of sweets: pear drops and Pontefract cakes, chocolate dragées and fruit pastilles, sugared almonds and toffee whirls, and lots more. Her greedy eyes lingered on each jar, imagining the taste of their contents. She debated what punishment her aunt might dole out if she gave in to temptation and spent tuppence on sweets or chocolate – and decided to chance it. So she might get a whack with that cane her aunt had mentioned, but it wouldn't be the first time she had been whacked. So with a determined step she went inside and bought a bar of chocolate.

She could only think of how good it tasted as she allowed the first creamy square to melt on her tongue, but by the time she had eaten four squares she could not get Margaret's furious face out of her mind and those words: 'You stole my chocolates!'

Sam was still hovering over the grating and so she placed the remains of the chocolate a few inches from his hand resting on the pavement. He glanced up with a startled expression. 'I'm muggin' yer!' she said jauntily and hurried across the road, not wanting him to thank her for something she had stolen.

Back at the pawnshop she noticed activity inside the shop. Its entrance was situated discreetly up a side street so, bracing herself, she opened the door and eased herself through into the dark and musty interior. It was only when she saw how crowded it was that she remembered it was Monday and people were 'popping' their Sunday best.

She skirted the queue and managed to reach the counter, which was piled high with clothing at one end. Her aunt spotted her immediately. She was working the pen machine, a useful little gadget, which linked three pens together. By writing with one the other two were put into operation so that a pawn ticket and two copies could be written at the same time.

'I would have been here sooner only—' Rita was stopped in mid flow.

'Never mind that now! Take these suits and hang them on the racks in the back.' Margaret's tone was brusque.

Rita burrowed her hands beneath the pile on the counter and managed to lift them. As she balanced the suits against her body a strong smell of tobacco made her sneeze, not once but three times. She was glad to drop the clothing on top of a chest of drawers in the storeroom. Taking a hanger from the first rack, she hung up the first suit.

By the time Rita had finished, her arms were aching and she had counted thirty-five suits as well as several women's coats, skirts and dresses. She felt quite buoyant, thinking about the money that would be her aunt's at the end of the week when most of the wives and children would reappear and redeem the family's Sunday best. These people weren't the poorest of the poor. They might be struggling to make ends meet but someone in the family must be in work to be able to get the clothes out of hock to attend church.

At one o'clock prompt Margaret turned the sign

on the shop door to CLOSED and shot the bolts top and bottom. 'Time for lunch,' she said.

'Who's cooking it?' asked Rita, easing her shoulders as she stood behind the counter, watching her aunt.

'Why, are you volunteering?'

Rita shrugged. 'I can fry egg and bacon and make porridge and a pan of scouse but that's pretty much my limit.'

'Just as well, then, that Mrs McGinty is a capable plain cook who sees to lunch.' Margaret locked the till. 'Inside, then, and let's have a cuppa and the stew she's left us. Wash your hands first.'

Again, Rita thought, but decided that she might just as well seeing as there was hot water, a decent block of soap and a dry towel available. Besides, she'd handled all those suits and felt grimy.

As they entered the kitchen a strong smell of Mansion furniture polish mingled with the appetising one of rabbit stew. Rita closed her eyes in ecstasy as her tummy rumbled and then opened them again remembering that she had spent tuppence of her aunt's money on chocolate. Hell! She just hoped that she could get the stew down her before her aunt asked for her change.

Hands washed and sitting at the table, spoon in her hand, Rita waited nervously as Margaret came into the kitchen with two bowls of stew on a tray. Big chucks of meat, thought Rita, almost drooling as she dipped her spoon into the bowl. As she lowered her head to take a first luscious bite, her aunt said, 'Your hair! You did get the things on the note I gave you?'

'Y-y-yes!' Rita did not look at her.

'Where are they?'

'In my coat pocket.'

'With the change?'

Rita nodded.

'Then go and fetch them.'

'Can't I get them after I've finished me dinner? I'm starving!'

'Lunch, Rita.' Margaret picked up her own spoon. 'Yes, of course. What was I thinking of? The food'll get cold. Eat up!'

Rita gulped with relief and gobbled down the food in case her aunt suddenly changed her mind.

Margaret's blue eyes rested on the girl with a frown. 'It isn't good for the digestion to eat that quickly but it's obvious to me you need building up. You're far too small for your age. You don't seem to have developed in the places you should.'

Rita thought if her aunt thought that then it was worth asking if there were second helpings.

'Yes,' said Margaret with a faint smile. 'But don't gulp your food. It's not nice to watch.'

Rita hurried into the scullery with her bowl before her aunt could change her mind. This time she ate more leisurely but she was beginning to tense with the anticipation of what was to come.

When her aunt asked her, 'How many pennies are there in a shilling?' Rita jumped out of her skin and for a moment she could not think. Margaret frowned. 'Come, Rita! You must know.'

Suddenly it came to her and was such a relief. 'Twelve, of course.'

'Then recite your twelve times table to me.'

Blow! Rita's smile faded. It would have to be the hardest one. Nervously she nibbled a finger. 'One twelve is twelve,' she muttered.

'Take your finger out of your mouth!'

Rita kept her eyes on the tablecloth as she recited, 'Two twelves are twenty-four. Three twelves are thirty-six. Four twelves are forty-eight. Five twelves are sixty. Six twelves are . . .' she cogitated, adding twelve onto sixty and said in a relieved voice, 'seventy-two. Seven twelves are . . . eighty-six.'

'No! Eighty-four and you are much too slow.' Margaret's frown had deepened. 'You should have them off pat. Eight twelves?'

Rita's mind went blank again and her heart pounded. There was a long silence.

'Think, girl, think! Seven twelves are eighty-four. Eight twelves are . . . ninet-ty . . . ?'

Rita moistened her lips, hating her aunt for doing this to her. 'Ninety-six?'

'Nine twelves are?' There was another silence. 'Come on! It's like getting blood out of a stone. Nine twelves are?' Margaret banged the table with her fist.

'I don't know!' cried Rita, her thin cheeks aflame as she sprang to her feet. 'I don't know! I always have trouble when it gets to a hundred and something.'

'Then how can you possibly handle money?' said Margaret, exasperated. 'You can't be of any real help to me if you aren't good at arithmetic.'

Rita's heart sank. She had to be of help to her aunt if she was to stay off the streets, as well as save money to go to Cardiff and look for her mother. 'I'm sorry! But I can learn.'

Margaret rested her elbows on the table and placed her chin on her hand and scrutinised Rita carefully. 'I hope so. Now go and get those things I sent you for and the note and change.'

Rita felt her knees start to quiver and was that nervous she almost stumbled on the carpet but managed to get out of the room to the lobby where she had hung her coat on a hook. She took the money and the note from her pocket and picked up the bulging paper bag with the weapons to wage war on fleas and returned to her aunt.

Margaret looked at the note and compared the sum total of the purchases with the coins on the table. 'There's a discrepancy here.'

'Is there? I wouldn't know. I'm useless at arithmetic, as you've said,' said Rita, trying to bluff it out.

Her aunt stared at her and then suddenly sniffed the note. For a moment she held that pose before placing the paper on the table. 'Chocolate!' Rita could not help but start. 'Own up! You spent some of my money on chocolate!' Margaret's expression was grim. 'If there's one thing I can't stand that's a liar! There's a very good reason why 'Thou shalt not bear false witness!' is one of the Ten Commandments. Not telling the truth leads people into terrible trouble.'

'I'm sorry!' Rita's expression was conciliatory. Her shoulders were hunched and she clenched and unclenched her hands.

'I should hope you are, but that doesn't mean you're going to escape punishment. To stop you going wrong you have to learn that bad behaviour doesn't pay. In fact it's painful.' She got up and left the room.

Rita wondered if she should make a run for it but where would she go – and she needed money? She just had to take her punishment like a man. Margaret was back with a cane. 'Hold out your hand!'

For all her fine thoughts, Rita hesitated to do as she was told. What happened next she should have expected. There was a swishing noise as the cane came down and caught her on the leg. The black knitted stocking deflected the blow somewhat but she still felt the sting of the cane and attempted to dart out of the way of the next swipe. She was too slow and the cane came down twice on her other leg. 'You must not lie and you must not steal. I

71

cannot have you staying here if I can't trust you,' said Margaret firmly.

'I'm sorry! I said I'm sorry! I won't do it again!' cried Rita, holding out her hands in supplication. 'I don't need to be hit again to know what I did was wrong.'

'I'm glad to hear it. There'll be no more chances for you to mend your ways. You must turn over a new leaf from this moment on.' Margaret threw the cane into a corner. 'Now show me you can be of some use. A fresh pot of tea to make amends.'

Rita shot out of the kitchen and put on the kettle. When she took in the teapot her aunt said, 'You're going to have to practise your tables, right? I've an abacus that my brother brought home years ago when I was a little girl. You can use that.'

Rita did not argue.

Yet when she saw the abacus she felt a rush of shame, remembering having used one in her early days at school.

'You'll practise counting in twelves.' Margaret moved the beads on the wires. 'Afterwards you should have some idea how many twelve times twelve is. Then I want you—'

'It's a gross,' murmured Rita.

'So you remember some things. Good,' said Margaret, and smiled. Then she left her alone and went to open the shop.

That evening Margaret took Rita upstairs after

closing up for the day. 'This can be your bedroom if you wish.' She flung open the door of Donald's room and hurried across the floor to open the curtains. Dust billowed from the material catching her throat and making her cough.

'Whose was it?' said Rita, taking a hesitant step forward.

Margaret did not answer but took a box of matches from the pocket of her waistcoat and lit the two gas lamps on the wall above the bed. It took her several attempts before the mantles caught and two pools of light reflected off the blue painted walls and lit up the room. She glanced down at the bed, remembering being unable to wake up her mother who she had found lying here. It had been a terrible shock. She blew out the match and turned and faced her niece, thinking how Eve had escaped such moments. 'This is my brother's room.'

'Brother?' It was one surprise on top of another, thought Rita. 'Where is he?'

'Dead! I should have said it *was* his. He was killed at sea.' There was a tremor in her voice. 'It turned my mother's mind and that's why nothing has changed in here in all that time.'

'How sad!' said Rita in heartfelt tones. A ship in full sail in a bottle caught her eye. 'Did he do that?' she asked, going over to the chest of drawers on which it stood.

'No. It was brought into the shop and immediately

73

Mother laid claim to it for him.' Margaret followed her over and picked up the bottle. 'He was only a boy when he made up his mind to go to sea,' she said with assumed briskness. 'At the time there were two other boys in the family so he wasn't discouraged, but they both died before I was born. Donald was thirteen years older than I and never married.'

Rita's gaze swept the room. There was a huge very masculine-looking wardrobe of dark wood and next to it in a corner were a cricket bat and several small balls, as well as a leather football. Against another wall stood a crowded bookcase. She went over to it and peered at some of the titles. *Two Years Before the Mast, Robinson Crusoe, Ivan the Terrible and his Reign of Terror.* She stopped reading and looked at her aunt, who was unlocking one of the wardrobe doors. 'Nothing there I'd like to read,' she said.

'No. I suppose I'll have to empty this out, and the chest of drawers.'

'You mean all his clothes are still here?' Rita could not conceal her amazement.

'Yes,' said Margaret ruefully. 'I told you Mother wouldn't have anything changed, although there's not that many clothes. He spent most of his time in uniform. Sometimes I can still see him here.' Thinking of her brother reminded her of the Brodie twins again, but William in particular this time. He and Donald had both done their naval training on the old *Indefatigable* which had been fitted out with sails as well as steam and been anchored out in the Mersey. Although William had been nine years younger than Donald, they had got on well. Will, unlike her brother, had not joined the Royal Navy but had become a merchant seaman, taking ship to the Far East more often than not. She felt a flutter beneath her ribs remembering his reaction to her refusal to his proposal, and her fingers tightened on the edge of the wardrobe door.

Rita startled her when she spoke. 'It's spooky in here! Isn't there another room I could have?'

Margaret realised her niece's words echoed her own feelings. She closed the wardrobe door and turned off the gaslights, hurrying Rita out. She took her to the back bedroom, simply furnished with a single iron bedstead, wardrobe and chest of drawers. Her father's life had been the shop after his son and wife died and he had left no impression behind in here at all. 'Will this do?'

Rita nodded. She had never slept alone in her life but she supposed she would get used to it and, although this room was much smaller and not as brightly decorated as the other, there were no ghosts.

CHAPTER FOUR

'How now, brown cow!' recited Rita beneath her breath as she walked along Berry Street to the chandler's shop. The December sun glinted off her shiny hair, lice-free these days. She had put on weight and had curves where it was good for fifteen-year-olds to have them and had even started her periods. She had been living with her aunt for nine months and although she still felt as if part of her was missing at times, due to her mother's absence – she had not written or sent a postal order, which hurt and annoyed Rita immensely – she had adjusted to her circumstances.

Having her tables drummed into her and remembering that there were two hundred and forty pence in a pound, that one per cent was one part of a hundred whole ones, had not been too difficult once she set her mind to it. As Miss Turner said – to whom Margaret sent Rita for an hour's elocution lesson on a Saturday morning – it was all down to practice, practice, practice.

Rita hated being taught to talk proper – or properly, as Miss Turner would have it. She didn't want to be changed into somebody else who didn't sound a bit like her and set her apart from the only young people she knew.

'Henry Hall hops on his heels!' she recited in breathy tones, sounding every H as she stopped outside Fitzgerald's chandler's shop. Galvanised buckets hung like garlands in the doorway. She said the rhyme missing off all the h's and got a grin from Sam, who was placing an enamel bowl inside another which was inside another and so on piled up on the floor.

'What's that yer saying, Rita?' he asked.

'It's a rhyme supposed to help me talk *propar*. My aunt's idea! I call it daft because the only people I talk to are those who come into the shop, and most of them are ordinary folk just like me,' she said with a chuckle.

'She probably has her reasons. I've only been in her shop a couple of times and she doesn't strike me as daft.'

'Well, if she has she's keeping them to herself.'

'So what is it yer after?' asked Sam, rubbing hands reddened with the cold.

She was just about to tell him when there was the

clatter of hooves and a horse and cart pulled up at the kerb a few feet away. A young man with tawny hair, wearing his cap sideways, sprang down. 'Is your boss there?' he called out.

'Yeah! I'll get him for yer!' Sam turned to go inside the shop but there was no need. Mr Fitzgerald was already there and was frowning. 'You're late! You should have been here yesterday, Jimmy.'

'It wasn't my fault the horse threw a shoe.' The young man's annoyance showed on his face. 'I'm here in plenty of time for wash day and that's the main thing, isn't it?' He went to the rear of the cart and let down the back and called to Sam to give him a hand.

The youth hurried forward and was soon staggering past Rita hugging a large cardboard box that had GREEN WASHING SOAP printed on the side. Watching him, Rita thought, he does try but he's still the skinny runt I met in the spring, whose father is a drunken bully, because Sam had a bruise on his cheekbone and a hint of a black eye. She knew that he was the youngest in his family and that three of his brothers had been killed in the Great War. Since then the rest of his brothers and sisters had left home except for his eldest sister – she had taken the place of his mother, who had died when he was born. He was seventeen but sometimes the expression in his eyes belied his age.

Her attention shifted to the young carter, who was carrying two boxes of soap with seemingly little effort. He spared Rita only the briefest of glances but it was enough for her to recognise him because she had never seen anyone with such deep blue eyes before. It was obvious he did not remember her and she was glad of that; she would rather he forgot altogether her appearance in Chinatown. He was altogether a very fanciable bloke. Despite it being winter he wore no jacket – only a waistcoat over his shirt, the sleeves of which were rolled up to reveal muscle.

He finished his business with Mr Fitzgerald and, brushing past her and Sam, he climbed up behind his horse, flicked the reins across its glossy back, clucked with his tongue and the cart rumbled off. As it did so Rita noticed a name written on the side: Wm Brodie Ltd. Haulage Company. She might have been tempted to follow it and see where he worked, but from the load in the back of the cart he obviously had other deliveries to make. Besides, she had another errand to run for her aunt. She could catch him another time if he was a regular delivery bloke here.

'Sorry about that. What is it yer wanted, Rita?'

She turned to Sam. 'A pound of salt, please.'

This commodity was piled up like blocks of frozen snow for an Eskimo's igloo. As Sam cut it with a knife, she breathed in the scents of paraffin, the liquid soap called aunt sally, mothballs, wax polish, soda and washing blue. All were delicious smells. Sam weighed the salt and then wrapped it up in newspaper and handed it to her. She paid her penny and went on her way in the direction of Rathbone Street and the home of the McGintys.

Mrs McGinty had not turned up that morning so Rita had been dispatched to call at the house and see what had happened to her. As she walked her head was in the clouds, thinking of Jimmy, imagining him beside her, holding her hand and saying that it didn't matter at all that her hair was short and the colour of rust instead of ripening wheat. He loved her and would take care of her forever. She had never been kissed and tried imagining what it would be like to feel his lips pressed against hers. She closed her eyes a moment and walked smack into a lamp post. She rubbed her nose, which really hurt, and told herself to be sensible and curtailed her daydreaming.

The brown paint was peeling from the McGintys' front door. There was no knocker – only a letter box, which she rattled.

A young man opened the door. He had a face like a ferret and looked her up and down in a way that she did not care for one little bit. 'Who are you?'

She presumed he was one of the McGinty sons. 'Rita Taylor, and your mother works for my aunt.' She enunciated every vowel carefully as taught by Miss Turner.

His eyes became even more slit-like and he sneered. 'Oh, so yous is the one who thinks she's Lady Muck.'

Rita was so annoyed by his rudeness that she

80

forgot to behave like a lady. 'Watch yer mouth, mister, or yer mam won't be having a job to go to when I tell me aunt about this. Why didn't she turn up this morning?'

Before he could answer a man's voice shouted from inside the house. 'Who is it, Bert?'

He bellowed back, 'Ol' Sin's niece! She wants to know why Ma didn't turn in, Pa!'

'Bring her in! Let's have a decko at her!'

'Dad said yer to come in,' said Bert, an unfriendly expression in his eyes. He flung the door wide and stepped to one side.

'I'm not deaf,' said Rita. Her curiosity had been roused by her aunt's description of the char's husband, whom she considered to be a lazy good-for-nothing, whose wife waited on him hand and foot because he was supposed to be a martyr to a bad back and also only had one eye. She said that she might have believed in the bad back if she had not seen him coming out of the pub, his back as straight as a ramrod and crouched on the ground, playing pitch and toss with a whole gang of men that summer. Now Rita was to see him for herself.

He lay on a sagging sofa, his head resting on a neatly darned cushion. His greasy greying hair was much too long and hung about his ears. He wore a black patch over his left eye and surveyed her unblinkingly from his undamaged one like she was a specimen on a slab. He had not shaved for a few days by the look of it and there were food stains down the front of his pullover. A bottle of beer stood on the floor near to hand.

'So yous are the niece!' His voice took her by surprise. It was thin and reedy. 'Yer can tell yer aunt the missus'll be in this afternoon. She's gone an' cut her finger to the bone and's gone round to her sister's to see what she can do about it.'

Rita winced at the thought. 'Poor Mrs McGinty! I am sorry.'

'Aye! I bet yer are. Yous wouldn't be wanting to slave away like my Gert does for buttons getting yer clothes dirty. We know why you're there and what yer after!' His expression was ugly.

Rita bristled. 'Do yer now! Yer must tell me! I can tell you something, though. I work just as hard as your wife does and for a lot less. I'd watch what I was saying if I was you, Mr McGinty.' She turned and walked out.

Rita entered the pawnshop on the bounce. 'That man! He's horrible!' She placed the parcel of salt on the counter.

'What man?' said Margaret, without looking up from the handwritten list she was perusing.

'Mr McGinty! He really got up my nose,' said the girl, placing her elbow on the counter and resting her chin in her hand. She scowled at her aunt. 'I don't want you sending me there again.'

Margaret lifted her head and there was a tiny

crease above her nose. 'You're giving the orders round here now, are you?'

Rita flushed. 'You know I'm not. It's just that I didn't like the way he looked and spoke to me so I walked out.'

'Not before finding out what was wrong with Mrs McGinty, I hope,' said Margaret with a long-suffering sigh. 'You really do need to learn to control your emotions. Mrs McGinty's jealous of you. Daft as it seems, she got it into her head that after my father died I would ask her and her husband to come and live with me.'

'Gerraway with yer!' said Rita, her eyes widening. 'Now I've seen him I wouldn't trust him as far as I could throw him. He looks like a pirate with that black patch.'

'Don't let people's looks affect the way you judge them, Rita. I know it's not easy but there's many a man lost an eye in the war.'

'Is that where he lost his?' said the girl, thinking reluctantly that perhaps she should feel sorry for him. Although she had thought he looked too old to have fought in the war.

Margaret shook her head. 'He was in prison during the war. It was in a fight. His eye was gorged out.'

'Ugh!' Rita shuddered. 'Should I feel sorry for him?'

'No! He hit the other man over the head with a flat iron and he ended up like a vegetable. I think Mr

83

McGinty got fifteen years for that,' she murmured. 'Mrs McGinty assures me that he used to be really wild but that he's calmed down a lot since. Did his back in breaking stones in prison, apparently, and that's stopped his gallop. Her words.'

'Blinking heck!' said Rita. 'Yer just never know with people, do yer?'

'"You", Rita, not "yer",' corrected Margaret. 'And yes, you're right. We never do know with people. Now, what's wrong with Mrs McGinty?'

Rita told her and Margaret frowned. 'Let's hope that sister of hers knows what she's about. If it's as bad as he said, Mrs McGinty could end up with septicaemia and that wouldn't be nice at all. She's going to have to keep the finger covered and out of water. You might need to give her a helping hand.'

'OK!' said Rita, hoping she sounded willing. At least now she knew why Mrs McGinty was forever muttering about intruders and saucy misses who were out for all they could get when she was in earshot.

As it was, when Mrs McGinty turned up with the thumb of her left hand tied up with a piece of bloodstained rag she made it known in no uncertain terms that she would rather struggle on her own than accept Rita's help, which suited the girl fine. Although, for the first time ever the girl did feel sorry for her, not only because she was obviously in pain but also for having a husband like Mr McGinty.

That night Rita dreamt of pirates coming up the

Mersey in a sailing ship and running off with all her aunt's money. One had a black patch over his eye but fortunately he was seen off by a swashbuckling youth wearing a scarlet kerchief over his golden hair, who clasped Rita in his arms, but as his head came down close to hers and he was about to kiss her, he vanished.

The following morning she relived her dream, bringing it to a satisfactory conclusion – but then she began to imagine cruising down the river with him. Twice Margaret scolded her for writing the wrong figures in the ledger and was so exasperated that she ordered her to fetch the ladder on wheels that reached the top shelves. 'Most of those on the top shelf have been there for more than a year and a day, so fetch them down and we'll put the best in the window. Christmas is coming and hopefully we'll make quite a few sales.'

Rita was to be kept on her toes that week because Mrs McGinty's finger was so painful she couldn't work properly. Margaret insisted on removing the bloodstained rag with some kind of herbs and grease on it. What she saw resulted in her demanding that the cleaning woman accompany her to her own doctor in Rodney Street. Mrs McGinty returned as white as a sheet but with the finger neatly bandaged and, although it was still painful and she could not work as normal, she was obviously grateful to Margaret for having had the finger seen to by a doctor.

'I could have died if it had been left any longer,' she said to Rita and a couple of customers, regaling them with a description of how the doctor had cleaned out the pus.

The week before Christmas was far busier than Rita had expected with such poverty around but people were pledging all sorts of things: sheets, towels, false teeth – anything to buy food for the table on Christmas Day, even if it was only a pan of scouse or a rabbit.

There were those who had money to spend and bought gifts from the display in the window and the glass cabinets inside. Rita had got to know some of the girls of her own age who were in work and came into the shop looking for little gifts and they would chatter about boys, clothes and films. She enjoyed these times but never really felt one of them.

Sam also called into the shop when Margaret was not around. Rita had seen him a few days ago drawing chalk pictures on the pavement in the city centre. She was surprised how good he was and dropped a penny in his cap. Now she made him a cup of tea and a jam butty. Mrs McGinty glanced in on them and when she saw who Rita was entertaining she nodded at the youth and said, 'Hello, Sam!' Then she returned to her work.

'You know Mrs McGinty, then,' said Rita.

He nodded. 'Her husband is one of Dad's drinking cronies.' His eyes darkened to the colour of slate. 'I wouldn't trust him as far as I could throw him.'

'Aunt Margaret said he's an ex-jailbird and knocked some bloke silly.'

'Dad still talks about that. It was a matter of thieves falling out.' Sam held the steaming cup between his hands, warming them. 'He's supposed to be keeping his nose clean these days but I reckon he's up to no good.'

'What d'you mean?' She was all ears and, resting her elbows on the counter, brought her head closer to his.

'A couple of real tough-looking men called round at the McGintys' house the other day with a handcart,' he murmured. 'They went up the back entry and came back with it loaded up and covered by a sheet of tarpaulin.'

'You think it was stolen property?' she whispered.

'Wouldn't be surprised. I bet old Gert doesn't know anything about it. She believes everything he tells her, even that he was wrongly imprisoned.'

'I can believe it,' said Rita, her expression thoughtful. 'She's a hard worker but she thinks the sun shines out of him.'

'Gullible,' said Sam and, draining his cup, thanked Rita for the tea and jam butty. Taking from his pocket a bar of chocolate, he wished her a Happy Christmas. She was touched but before she could thank him he was out of the shop. By the time she reached the door and looked up the street he had vanished.

It was just before midnight on Christmas Eve that

the shop finally closed. Margaret was in a buoyant mood so the girl guessed they had done well enough to satisfy even her expectations.

'Put the kettle on, Rita, and make some toast! The fire's just right.'

It was true the fire had a glowing heart and once settled with tea and hot buttered toast and their feet on the fender, Margaret surprised Rita by saying, 'Do I look old and ugly?'

There was only one answer, thought the girl.

'You can be honest,' said Margaret with a rueful gleam in her eyes.

Rita wondered what this was all about but did not like to ask. 'You could make more of yourself. Mam always said there was room for improvement even after she'd dollied herself up.'

Margaret bit into her slice of toast and brushed crumbs from lips that curved sweetly when she took the trouble to smile. The trouble was, thought Rita, she didn't smile often enough.

'There was a card from Eve but I ripped it up,' said her aunt.

'You did what?' The girl sprang to her feet, her elfin face incredulous. 'Mam sent me a Christmas card and you ripped it up?'

Margaret waved her down. 'It wasn't addressed to you. It was for me!' She added in exasperated tones, 'That sister of mine's got a nerve! It's something she's never lost.'

Close to tears, Rita paced the floor, hugging herself. 'How can she write to you and not to me?' she said fiercely.

'She sent you kisses.'

Rita turned on Margaret and her brown eyes were filled with pain. 'A fat lot of use that is! Better not to have written at all than send me paper kisses!'

'Far better,' she said with a sigh. 'I wasn't going to tell you about the letter, expecting you to react like this, but then I thought you had a right to know that you're going to have a little brother or sister.'

Rita reached out a hand to the back of a chair to steady herself. 'I don't believe it. She's always avoided having a baby before!'

'She's married now. Anyway, she wanted me to send you to Cardiff to help her when the baby comes, but you can imagine how I felt about that.' Margaret stood up and put an arm around her niece. 'I'll not have her using you as a skivvy. Now sit down and eat your toast – and tell me what I can do to improve my looks,' she added with a faint smile.

Rita did not feel like eating or giving advice. She was sick with anger and disappointment and dropping her toast on her aunt's plate she muttered, 'Cut your hair and get it Marcel waved. Shorten your skirts or even better *buy* some new clothes.'

'That means spending more money than I really want to.'

'You've got money, so why not spend it on

yourself?' said Rita irritably. 'You'd think you were on the breadline the way you go on.'

'Don't be cheeky!' Margaret flushed. 'I'm saving up for my dream house.'

Rita could not help but stare at her. 'Your dream house? What's wrong with here? You're right on top of the shop, saves time and money.'

'I want shut of the shop one day.'

Rita could not believe it. 'Why? It's a right little gold mine.'

'It's hard work and there's times when I can't sleep for worrying someone might get in and knock me over the head and take everything Father and I worked for. No, I'd like to be a moneylender pure and simple. I wouldn't need the shop then,' she said, pacing the floor. 'All these things people bring need so much space.'

'Well, it's up to you,' said Rita with a shrug. 'But getting back to you improving your looks, it's your choice to whether you want to spend money on yourself or not. Have you a man in mind to live in this dream house with you?'

A sharp laugh escaped Margaret. 'There's only two men I've ever thought anything of and wanted to marry and they went out of my life years ago. I can see why you're thinking the way you are but a woman doesn't always dress to please a man.'

'Mam did,' said Rita in bitter tones. 'She said she had to and that's why I only ever had rags on my back. Anyway if you want to look good then you'll have to fork out some money. You can get ideas about fashion from the women's magazines.'

Margaret said scathingly, 'They're full of nonsense written by middle-class women for women who've got nothing better to do than waste their time drinking tea and reading in the afternoon.'

'Working-class women read magazines, too,' protested Rita. 'Mainly stories, though! There's the *Red Star* and *Secrets*, although they don't print many pictures. You can have a flick through them at the newsagents or you could always buy an *Echo* – that has a fashion page once a week.'

'I'll think about it,' said Margaret. 'Now, you eat your toast.' She returned it to the girl's plate. 'I don't want you getting scrawny again.'

Rita wondered if there would be any more shocks that Christmas. She was going to have a brother or sister but when would she get the chance to see the baby? There was part of her that wanted to rush off to Cardiff because hadn't she always wanted to belong to a proper family, but she was angry with her mother for not writing to her. What else had she put in that letter to her aunt? No money to pay for her fare, Rita would have bet on that. Probably she expected Margaret to pay for it. Rita made up her mind to put her mother out of her mind for ever, although that was easier said than done.

Christmas Day passed without any excitement at

all. To Rita's amazement and delight Margaret gave her a pound note and a large box of chocolates. This was wealth indeed because Rita's wages were only a few shillings a week since, as Margaret always reminded her, she paid for her keep and provided her with clothes, and recently she had even bought her a new pair of boots.

In return the girl presented Margaret with three handkerchiefs on which she had embroidered an 'M' in the corner, as well as a small box of chocolates and a glass jar with a lid on it. 'I know it's not crystal but I thought it would do to keep your chocolates in,' she said with a twinkle.

Margaret thanked her. 'You've come a long way since the day you scoffed nearly a whole jar. I'd never have believed you could change so much, but then you've been keen to learn and that goes a long way.' The compliment pleased the girl and she determined to ask for a rise in the new year.

Rita had believed that business would fall off after Christmas but she was wrong. There was a steady stream of customers 'popping' whatever they could to keep body and soul together in the winter months to come. She waited to see if her aunt would do anything to improve her appearance but she waited in vain.

CHAPTER FIVE

It was early spring 1931 and Rita was up the ladder dusting the top shelves in the shop when the door opened and a young woman entered. She had fine-spun blonde hair that curved in points on rosy cheeks. Her face was fine-boned and she was very pretty. Dressed in some style in a plum-coloured coat with a fur collar and a cloche hat, almost the same shade of purplish red, she wore strapped black Cuban-heeled shoes on her long feet.

Rita bet a pound to a farthing that her eyes were blue and felt a pang of envy as she paused in her task to watch the girl place a brown paper parcel tied up with string on the counter. 'I want to pawn this,' she said in a voice that was barely audible.

Margaret stared at her for a moment before reaching for her spectacles. 'I haven't seen you in here before.'

'No. But the name over the door is Scottish so I thought I'd give you a try.'

'You don't sound Scots,' said Margaret, picking at the knot in the string.

'No. My step-grandfather was Scots and I liked him very much.'

'He's no longer with us, I take it,' said Margaret, placing the string in a tin. She removed the brown paper and tissue paper to reveal a vase decorated with hand-painted oriental figures. She let out a breath.

'That's nice,' said Rita from her perch up the ladder.

The young woman glanced up and smiled. 'My stepbrother brought me it from China. I don't really want to part with it but needs must when the devil drives.'

'As bad as that, is it?' said Margaret, turning the vase over carefully between her hands. 'I'll give you two pounds for it.'

The girl gasped. 'Jimmy thought it was worth at least five pounds. It's real porcelain!'

Margaret raised her eyebrows. 'And how do you know that?'

'Because Billy said so and it was he who gave it to me so he should know.'

Margaret tapped her fingers against her chin. 'I'll give you two pounds ten shillings and I'm robbing myself. What with the Depression, it's a tough business I'm in now.'

The young woman gnawed on her bottom lip and drummed her fingers on the counter. 'Couldn't you make it three pounds ten shillings? Jimmy said we need—'

'I don't care what this Jimmy says,' said Margaret firmly, shaking her head. 'Two pounds ten shillings is all I'll give you, unless . . . I'll tell you what I'll do – I'll give you three pounds two shillings if you sell it to me and that's definitely my last offer.'

'Sell it!' The girl groaned and there was a long silence. Then she sighed and nodded. 'I didn't really want to get rid of it but I'll take what you offer. We need to buy feed and bedding for the horses, you see. Things are pretty dreadful at the moment and we could lose the yard.'

'If that's said to make me up my offer you're wasting your time. There's plenty of people round here who have trouble enough buying food to put in their children's mouths, never mind animals,' said Margaret, her expression severe. 'Now, Rita, get down from there and write out a receipt while I put this vase somewhere safe.'

Rita descended the ladder and reached for her aunt's fountain pen on the ledge beneath the counter. She drew the receipt book closer to her. 'Name?'

'Alice Martin.'

Rita lifted her head and stared at her. Alice was an uncommon name. Yet she had heard it a while ago. Where? She wrote the name down. 'Where do you live?'

'Brodie's haulage yard.'

Rita felt a stir of excitement. 'Where's that?'

'D'you really need to know?' Rita nodded. Alice sighed. 'It's up off Leece Street but you won't be having to look me up, will you?' she said anxiously. 'The vase is mine.'

Rita did not answer but was thinking the yard was within easy walking distance of Berry Street. She handed the receipt to Alice. Having seen Jimmy on several occasions round and about she had not yet plucked up the courage to speak to him, but something inside her now wanted to remedy that. She could not wait for lunch closing time so she could go up to the yard and see what else she could find out about him. What was this girl to him, for instance?

Rita watched as horse and cart and Jimmy disappeared into the yard. She could scarcely believe her good fortune and wondered if she dared follow him inside. It was cold standing out here waiting on the corner. Despite it being early April the wind whipped round it like a knife and the sky was full of scurrying clouds. She tucked her hands into the sleeves of her coat, mandarin-fashion, and crossed the road. The gates were wide open and she walked straight in without being stopped.

The cobbled yard was void of people but the horse that Jimmy had driven in was still hitched between the shafts of a cart and was munching from a nosebag. She could hear voices that seemed to be coming from the stables straight ahead of her.

As quietly as she could, Rita walked across the cobbles. On her left was a house and to her right were more stables and a smaller brick building. Smoke was coming from the chimneys of both brick buildings. There was a stench of horse manure, which she realised came from a heap of soiled straw bedding near the stables. She could hear the voices clearly now.

'You shouldn't have accepted her offer!' She recognised Jimmy's voice and felt a thrill dance down her spine.

'I had no choice!' Alice's light tones held a pleading note. 'Believe me, Jimmy, I did my best. I doubt we'd have got any more from Solly. Anyway, I'm wishing I hadn't sold it now. It meant something to me, and Billy'll be upset if he finds out I've got rid of it.'

'How's he going to find out? He's back at sea, and even if he wasn't, he said he's never going to set foot in this place again since Mother accused him of theft yet again.'

'It's not fair! I don't believe he is a thief,' said

Alice stoutly. 'There's no need for him to steal. He has money in his pocket – unlike you and I.'

'You try and get Mother and his father to believe it. Anyway, it's neither here nor there. Whatever we say isn't going to change what the parents think. As long as you and I stay friends with him that'll keep you and him happy, won't it?'

There was a long silence and then Alice said, 'I suppose so. I mean, I'd rather he stayed here when he was home but I just hate it when people I love are at each other's throats. So what are we going to do with the money? Is there enough to pay the feed bill? Will you give it to Pops to pay?'

'Not bloody likely, if you'll excuse my language! He might gamble it away.'

'He wouldn't! He might like a flutter – and he's saved us that way before – but he's not stupid. And what about the moneylender? He has to pay some of the interest off, at least.'

'The moneylender can wait. He's bluffing about sending the bailiffs in.'

'How d'you know?' said Alice, a catch in her throat. 'I'm terrified he might mean it this time.'

'It's a bluff! He's not going to kill the goose that lays the golden eggs. The horses have to be fed, so don't say a word about this money to Pops and I promise you if that vase means so much to you I'll find some way of getting it back. Anyway, I've a load to get to Crown Street. See you later.'

Rita fled, knowing she should not have been eavesdropping on a conversation which was obviously terribly private. Even so, she had found it fascinating and there was no doubt in her mind that the family was in deep trouble.

When she arrived back at the shop she was annoyed to find that she had to pass some youths messing about outside. A couple wolf-whistled as she passed. She told them to go and chase themselves and hurried inside where, to her annoyance, she saw Mr McGinty hovering over one of the locked display cases that contained jewellery and knick-knacks. A cigarette dangled from the corner of his mouth, dropping ash onto the glass. A vision of him dressed as a pirate popped into her head. What was he up to? She stared at him suspiciously as she made her way to the counter.

'So you're back,' said Margaret, without glancing up. 'Get the yard brush and get rid of those boys outside. They're causing a disturbance.'

'I'll do it for yous, Miss Sinclair. Yer can't expect lads to take notice of a young slip of a girl like yer niece,' said Mr McGinty in his reedy voice. 'I saw her flirting with them on her way in.'

'I was not flirting with them,' said the girl indignantly, grabbing the brush as Mr McGinty made a beeline for the lads.

He raised an arm in a threatening manner. 'Hoy, yous lot! Shift yerselves!'

The boys jeered at him and proceeded to run rings round him, entering the shop in the process. Rita went for one of them with the yard brush but the lad grabbed the pole and almost wrenched her arm out of its socket. 'You swine!' she cried, enraged.

Margaret made an exasperated noise and reached for the cane. 'Get out of my shop!' There was a swishing sound and the cane thwacked the youth across the shoulders. Hastily he released his hold on the brush pole. Again the cane came down and he yelped as it stung his ear. He shot out of the shop.

Rita turned on Mr McGinty who was standing with his back to the display case. 'A fat lot of use you were,' she said.

He darted her a poisonous look but smiled ingratiatingly at Margaret. 'Sorry I couldn't catch them for yous, Miss Sinclair, but this eye of mine makes me blind on one side.'

'Yes, Mr McGinty, I can accept that, but what are you doing here?' said Margaret, her hand shaking as she replaced the cane.

'I came to see if the missus was here.'

Margaret looked at him as if he had run mad. 'Mornings, that's all she does here. I suggest you look elsewhere and stop taking up room in my shop.'

'Right yer are, Miss Sinclair.' He lifted his cap and scratched his head, then replaced his headgear. 'I was wondering if yous had any odd jobs yer needed doin'?'

'If I had, then I'd let Mrs McGinty know. Now if you don't mind . . . Out! I've work to do,' she said firmly.

'Good day to yous, then,' he said with a sniff, and slouched out of the shop.

'I hate it when that happens,' said Margaret, resting her back against the counter. She scrutinised Rita's face. 'And where did you disappear to, miss?'

'I needed fresh air.' She replaced the sweeping brush in its corner. 'I wonder what Mr McGinty was really doing in here. He and those lads . . .'

Margaret nodded. 'That kind of horseplay wouldn't have happened when my father was alive.'

'You could do with a man about the place.'

'It's finding one I can trust. Right now we'll just have to make sure that kind of thing doesn't happen again. I'm certain nothing was stolen this time because we moved fast, but we must be on our guard constantly against such tricks. So many people are having a hard time of it they could be tempted to do things they wouldn't normally even dream of.'

Rita agreed.

That night she dreamt again of pirates coming up the river but this time there was no golden-haired youth to rescue her. Black Patch the pirate had a large cutlass and was about to cut her head off when she woke in a sweat, her heart pounding. It was such a relief to know that it had all been a dream.

A week passed before Rita saw Jimmy again. It

was raining and he was coming out of a building not far from the Fascists Club on Berry Street. His hands were in his pockets and the way he held his shoulders showed that he was either feeling down in the dumps or the cold. He appeared deep in thought. She backtracked to the building he had come from and read the brass plate on the wall. It belonged to a financial broker. She did not delay but rushed after Jimmy and tailed him all the way to the yard.

He was about to go inside when he stopped and turned round. She had no time to retreat. He had spotted her so she walked up to him. He was scowling. 'You've been following me. Why?'

For a moment she could not think what to say, then, 'Is there any harm in my following you?'

He looked startled. 'So you don't deny it?'

'No. I was curious.'

He stared at her. 'I've seen you before.'

She smiled. 'You're quick. I've spotted you around delivering. I've seen you at Fitzgerald's several times.'

Light seemed to dawn on him. 'You're the girl I've seen talking to Sam. You his sister or something?'

Rita shook her head. 'We met even before that.' She had not meant to say that but something was driving her on. 'You don't remember, do you?'

'Should I?' He continued to stare at her from those deep blue eyes.

'No. I suppose not.' She paused and changed the

subject. 'I've met Alice. She's pretty, isn't she? And very like you.'

'She's my sister, that's why. Where did you meet her? In church?'

'No! She came into my aunt's pawnshop.'

'Your aunt?'

'Yes. Miss Margaret Sinclair. I'd like to help you if I could. Your family's in debt, aren't they? You've been threatened with the bailiffs.'

'How the hell do you know that?' he said wrathfully. 'Do you belong to that bloodsucking, heartless lot in Berry Street?'

'Of course not,' she said, hastily taking a step back. 'My aunt's no bloodsucker.'

'Sez you!' He turned his back on her and went inside the yard.

Rita followed. 'Look, I'm sorry. I didn't explain myself properly.' Her elfin features were repentant.

He ignored her, striding across the yard to the house where Alice stood in the doorway. His sister seized his arm. 'You've been ages. Mother and I were getting worried.'

'What d'you think could have happened to me?' he said with a laugh, shaking his head and sprinkling her with raindrops. 'That he'd have me beaten up or put in prison?'

'No, but—'

'There's no need to worry.' He put his arm round her.

103

'You mean . . . he listened to you and not Pops?' Alice smiled in relief.

'Of course he did.' His voice was warm and tender. 'You've said it yourself, haven't you? I've got a way with me. Now let's get inside. I need to talk to you.'

The door closed behind them.

Rita stared after them and was tempted to bang on the door and plead to be let in. There had been a tone in his voice when he spoke to his sister that made Rita yearn to bask in the heat of his affection. He had lied, of course. The family was in a lot of trouble. Suddenly a shiver went right through her and she hurried home.

'And where've you been?' Margaret gazed at Rita standing in a puddle of water that had dripped from her clothing.

'It-it's not half r-raining out there,' she said, teeth chattering.

Margaret came from behind the counter, turned the sign to CLOSED and took off the snick on the lock before hustling Rita through into the kitchen. She left her shivering in front of the fire while she fetched a couple of towels.

'Get your hair dried and out of those wet clothes!' She thrust the towels at Rita and went upstairs, reappearing a few minutes later with a blanket. 'Wrap that round you while I make a hot drink. You do realise you could go down with pneumonia and cause me a lot of trouble?' She vanished into the scullery.

'I'm sorry!' Rita's voice was husky as she took the two aspirins handed to her. She gulped them down with the hot sweet tea. 'I was following a bloke. He's in trouble and I wanted to see if we could help him.'

'We?' Margaret sat down, a forbidding expression on her face. 'I hope you're not starting to fancy the opposite sex.'

'What's wrong with that?' said Rita with a touch of defiance.

'Your mother,' said Margaret.

Rita rolled her eyes. 'I'm not like Mam. This fella doesn't even like me. He's the Jimmy that girl Alice mentioned. The one who brought the Chinese vase in! The family's in debt and they've been threatened with the bailiffs.'

'Why are you telling me this?' Margaret's attitude was still stiff.

Rita struggled on. 'As I said, I thought we – you might be able to help them. Maybe buy off their debt so they'd have more time to find the money to pay it off.'

Only for a moment was Margaret speechless. Then, 'Have you gone mad? Why should I do that? I don't even know this girl or her family! I'm not in the business of doing favours.'

'You're in the business of making money!' Rita flung the words at her.

'Aye, but I'd have trouble getting money out of this family if their moneylender's talking of sending in the bailiffs.'

Rita could not dispute that and, for a moment, she could not come up with an answer to it. Then, 'I'm sure they'll be able to find the money eventually. They're probably going through a bad patch like lots of people at the moment,' she persisted. 'It can be done, can't it? You can take over a debt from another moneylender? You won't miss the money. You're rich! You could easily afford to help them out. You've carpet on the floor, a roof over your head, three meals a day and you don't have to cook on the fire. You've several outfits in your wardrobe and you don't have fleas or bed bugs. As well as that you have Mrs McGinty to do the housework. That's rich!'

Margaret made an exasperated noise in her throat. 'You know nothing about it! There's only me to look after me into my old age. Riches to me is not having to work for a living, and having a proper house and someone to see to my every need. The other day I saw the house of my dreams, but can I afford to take over the lease? I'm not sure.'

Rita was distracted from her purpose. 'What's it like, this dream house?'

'Large! And it has windows from floor to ceiling. It's in Abercromby Square and overlooks a garden in the centre.'

106

'I've seen them houses from outside. They look huge! I bet they're nice inside.'

'The one I like is more than nice but it'll cost money to buy the lease and decorate and furnish it to my satisfaction. I'd still have to earn a living but I want to be a moneylender, pure and simple, like I said to you at Christmas. None of this having to be open all hours with the need for storage space and the worry of the shop being broken into. It would be a respectable business, of course! Not a bit like those fish-and-money women Father used to tell me about. They operated in the mean streets of the Irish Catholic area. Tough as old boots; they'd give those that didn't pay up a beating. As well as that, the debtors had to take part of the amount lent in rotten fish.'

'Yeuk!' exclaimed Rita.

Margaret was silent, thinking of how her father had taught her a lot about making money. 'Charge tuppence in the shilling,' he had advised her. She had worked out that was a sixth or approximately sixteen-and-a-half per cent. At the moment she charged fifteen per cent to encourage his old clients to continue to do business with her, but if she did what she wanted, then she would up her rates once she was really established.

Rita leant forward and touched her aunt's knee. 'House or no house you could help them. I'm sure they'd find some way of paying you back.'

Margaret blinked at her. 'Haven't you listened to a word I've said? I need all the money I can lay my hands on. I don't have a husband to provide for me. Anyway, what's the name of this family?'

'The name of the yard is Brodie's. The owner is Jimmy's and Alice's stepfather.' Rita drained her cup and stretched out her legs, placing her cold feet on the warm brass fender.

Margaret stiffened. It couldn't be! Even so, curiosity compelled her to ask what kind of business this Brodie was in.

'Carting. They have a yard just off Leece Street.'

Competitive, thought Margaret instantly. There must be hundreds if not a couple of thousand carters in Liverpool transporting goods from docks to yard and businesses to shops. 'Now if you'd said motors I might have thought of putting some of my money behind them. But no, I can't see my way to helping them.'

'But they need your help,' insisted Rita. 'Miss Turner says that we're put on this earth to love God and love our neighbour and that means everyone.'

'Huh!' Margaret's eyes glinted and her mouth set in a straight line. 'Don't you be quoting Scripture at me, girl! I know my Bible and I also know that nobody's ever helped me.'

'That's because you're so good at helping yourself.'

'Don't try and soft-soap me.'

Rita kept her eyes on her face, smiled and kept on looking and smiling at her.

Margaret banged her fist on the arm of her chair. 'Don't look like that! You'll have to give me a better reason than Miss Turner's Bible-bashing to convince me. Tell me more about this family!'

Rita grimaced. 'I don't know that much about them. There's Jimmy and Alice who are brother and sister and they have a stepbrother, Billy. The one who gave the vase to Alice! He's a sailor. I think it was his father who married their mother. He doesn't get on with the mother. She called him a thief apparently but Alice thinks that that's a lie.'

'The father?' Margaret was watching her intently.

'I honestly don't know much about him . . . except he seems to be against his son. I think his name's William.'

'How do you know that?'

Rita thought her aunt was looking a little pale. 'Because I saw W. M. Brodie painted on the side of the cart . . . and that's all I know . . . except their moneylender has his offices in Berry Street if you need to go along there.'

Margaret was silent. In truth she was feeling dizzy and a little sick. Surely there could not be two William Brodies with a son called Billy living this end of Liverpool. She took several deep breaths before getting to her feet and, taking the girl's empty teacup from her, she forced her legs to propel her out of the room.

For the rest of the day Margaret was good for nothing. Rita had to ask her things twice or even three times before getting an answer to customers' enquiries. Margaret could not get the Brodie twins out of her mind. The one lively and full of fun, reckless and with the habit of making any girl he talked to feel like she was the only one who meant anything to him in the whole wide world. He liked people – and that was the trouble. It had driven her mad to see him talking to the shy girls in the group, bringing them out of themselves. Maybe if her sister hadn't been the glamorous one she might not have been so jealous but Margaret had been unable to help it, and Bella had been the last straw.

No wonder she had turned from Will to his twin Alan – sensible, self-controlled, idealistic, religious almost to saintliness, with a passion to take the gospel to China.

She rubbed her forehead where it ached. Could this W. M. Brodie really be Will? He had been a sailor, so what was he doing in the carting business? She had to find out. If she helped him she would have power over him. What was she to do? What her father would have recommended, she supposed. Sleep on it.

But when Margaret went up to bed, sleep was a long time coming. She rose and, moving the rug from beside her bed, she took up the loose floorboards and dragged out the tin box in which her father had

110

kept all his money even before Wall Street crashed. She had seen no reason to break with tradition. She unlocked the box with the key she kept on a chain about her neck, and began to count the money.

Rita could not sleep either and so heard the noise of the box being dragged across the floor. Then she heard a clinking noise. Curiosity aroused, she slipped out of bed and, not pausing to find her slippers, tiptoed out of the room. She inched her way along the landing to her aunt's bedroom where light showed beneath the door, and bending, peered through the keyhole. It took a few seconds for her eyes to adjust to the light and a couple more for her to realise the importance of what she was seeing as Margaret placed the last of the money bags inside a tin box and locked it. Then, frustratingly, she and the tin box moved out of Rita's range of vision. The light was extinguished and then the bed creaked.

Rita could not help but be excited as well as thoughtful as she crept back to her own room. No wonder her aunt was worried about being broken into. Without that money there'd be no dream house and no capital for her business. She snuggled beneath the bedclothes. If only she had a little of that money it could save Jimmy's family from the bailiffs. She tried to sleep, but the thought of all that cash in the house was making her nervous and her imagination went into overdrive.

The minutes ticked by. She heard the long case clock downstairs strike midnight and then the half-hour. Every little sound caused her to start up, such as the rainwater dripping from the leaking gutter. Then she really did hear a noise that frightened her. A door squeaking on its hinges. She did not move for several minutes, straining her ears, but all she could hear was the rapid beating of her heart. Unable to bear the suspense any longer she got out of bed again.

The linoleum felt even colder to the touch than earlier. She reached for the slippers Margaret had bought for her birthday and crept out of the room and downstairs. She paused in the kitchen to pick up the poker and then went through into the storeroom. The door to the shop was open. She heard a match being struck and immediately froze as she caught a glimpse of the bottom half of a face. Then the match went out and all was in darkness. She couldn't prevent an intake of breath and gripped the poker tightly, sensing someone was near. Slowly she turned, raising her weapon, but it was too late. Something hit her on the head and she sank to the floor.

CHAPTER SIX

'Aunt Margaret! Aunt Margaret!' There was a sense of urgency in the voice. 'Wake up! Wake up!' The doorknob rattled.

Margaret came up from fathoms of sleep as the voice continued to disturb. She struggled out of bed, eyes still closed, and stumbled across the floor. 'What is it, Rita?'

'Open the door!'

Margaret forced her eyes open and fumbled for the key which was on a nail on the wall next to the door. She had never left it in the lock since reading in a crime novel how a thief had got into a bedroom by sliding a sheet of newspaper under the door and pushing the key from the other side with a length of wire. She opened the door and saw the shadowy outline of her niece slumped against the banister. 'What's happened?'

'There's been a break-in. I disturbed whoever it was but they hit me on the head,' gasped Rita.

Margaret felt for the girl's shoulder. 'Are you all right? Did you see who it was?'

'Just a bit of a face . . . a chin, a nose.' She caught her lower lip between her teeth. 'I felt sure if I'd seen only a bit more of his face I'd have recognised him.'

'Did he get anything?'

'I don't know! I didn't stop to look.' Gingerly she felt the spot where the blow had landed and her fingers were wet. 'I'm bleedin'!'

'Assault and battery!' Margaret's voice quivered on the words.

She snatched up the dressing gown flung over the foot of the bed and knotted the belt tightly about her slender waist. She lit a match and ignited the candle she used to light her way to bed. Then she inspected the cut on Rita's head. 'It's a good job you've got a thick head of hair. You should have come for me if you heard something instead of going downstairs on your own.'

'I didn't want to disturb you. I thought I might be imagining things. Anyway, I did pick up the poker and took it with me but I didn't get a chance to use it.'

Margaret muttered, 'I don't know what the world's coming to. You'll need something on that. Come downstairs and I'll see to it . . . have to go anyway and see if anything's missing.'

Rita nodded her throbbing head, then winced. She followed Margaret downstairs, feeling slightly dizzy. She wondered about the burglar's identity. Youngish! Could he have been one of the youths who had run rings round Mr McGinty? She was convinced that had been a put-up job to enable one of them to filch something from the shop.

Holding the candle aloft Margaret surveyed the interior of the shop, noticing that the bolts top and bottom of the door were drawn back. 'He probably got out that way,' said Rita. 'But how did he get in?'

Margaret made no answer, having noticed that the lock on the tall display cabinet which had contained jewellery, watches, a couple of enamel pillboxes and quality vases had been smashed. She knew exactly what had been in there and saw that a couple of rings, a child's silver christening bracelet, the Chinese vase, which she had purchased only the other day, and a silver watch and fob chain had been taken. She felt extremely angry. How had he got in?

She went into the back premises followed by Rita. Margaret gazed about the kitchen by the light of the flickering candle but could see no sign of it having been disturbed. Even so, she crossed to the window and drew back one of the curtains to find as she expected that the snick was in place. She hurried into the scullery and found the door and window securely locked. The cat, obviously not accustomed to such activity at this hour, mewed and stropped her leg but she ignored it. A terrible suspicion was dawning on her.

'Are you sure you actually saw someone?' she said.

'I didn't dream it,' said Rita.

'Then it's a mystery to me how he got in unless he can walk through walls, and I don't think burglars can, do you?' She turned away from the door to stare at her niece, holding the candle aloft so she could see Rita's face.

'D'you really expect me to answer that?' said Rita, annoyed. 'It's a stupid question! You know they can't, so it can only be that you're accusing me of-of being in cahoots with the thief. Have you forgotten I was hit over the head?'

'That could have been done to make you look innocent.'

Rita gasped. 'I don't bloody believe this!'

'Don't you swear at me, girl!'

'You're giving me cause to swear! Accusing me of being a bloody burglar! I'm nothing of the sort and I don't know how you could think that of me.'

'You've stolen before and Mrs McGinty told me you were entertaining that Sam, who works at Fitzgerald's, in the shop here, giving him tea and jam bread.'

'So what's wrong with that? Aren't I allowed to have friends?'

'He's a young man who's hard up.'

Rita bristled. 'He's no thief! And there's no way

116

that he would hit me over the head. She's probably protecting that husband of hers and . . . and perhaps one of her sons. Mr McGinty's been in prison, remember?'

The reminder brought her up short for a moment and then she remembered what her niece had said about seeing part of the burglar's face. 'Do you think it was the son?'

'I can't say!' Rita's voice was stiff with disappointment and hurt. 'I wish I could.'

'Then you're best keeping your thoughts about them to yourself. Don't get me wrong, Rita, I don't want to believe the worst of you. I've been pleased with the way you've worked and fitted in, but what am I to think? Can you explain to me how he got in?'

Rita was not the least bit mollified by her aunt's words and said tartly, 'I'd have to be in cahoots with him to know that, wouldn't I? Although maybe you left a window open upstairs! Maybe the burglar didn't go out the door here but even now is up there. Maybe in your room – because you didn't lock it behind you – looking for something else to steal.'

The girl got a swifter reaction than she expected. Without a word Margaret hurried out of the scullery which was immediately plunged into darkness. Rita swore and waited a few moments until her eyes became accustomed to the dark, then she made her way out of the room, considering herself lucky not to fall over the cat.

When she arrived upstairs it was to discover her aunt's bedroom door firmly locked against her. That did it! Rita lost her temper completely and kicked the door. 'I'm not a thief and I know you've got money in there so there's no point in trying to hide it from me.'

Margaret ignored her, too busy making sure her nest egg was safe. It was a relief to discover its hiding place undisturbed. She came out of her bedroom and locked it behind her. 'I'm going to make a cup of tea.' She headed for the stairs.

'I want an apology,' said Rita, racing after her. 'I'm really upset that you could even think for a moment I'd steal from you. I'll prove I'm innocent if it's the last thing I do!' She flounced back upstairs, having no idea exactly how she was to prove herself innocent, but one thing was for sure: she wouldn't speak to her aunt until she did.

The following morning Rita realised that not talking to Margaret was going to be extremely difficult, although neither she nor her aunt had much to say over the breakfast table. On the woman's side it was mainly because she was thinking of what to say to the local bobby. She knew exactly what time he passed her shop and planned on reporting the burglary to him.

As soon as Margaret told the constable that a thief had got into her shop, despite every door and window being locked, she could see that he did not believe she had locked up properly. He insisted on going over the whole building with her – even into the attic.

'Aha!' he said, spotting the skylight in the roof open several inches. He inspected the surrounding paintwork and even Margaret could see that it had been scuffed. 'This is where he got in. I can see it as plain as the nose on my face,' said the policeman with a triumphant gleam in his eyes.

Margaret's gaze went from the window to the floor. 'I find it incredible that someone should climb all the way up here, risking their life without even knowing whether they could get in or not, and all for a-a few . . .'

'There's lots round here who haven't got much of a life so would think it's worth the risk.' He stroked his moustache and shook his head. 'And some of these burglars are very sure-footed. Otherwise they wouldn't be called cat burglars.' He beamed at her.

'Yes, I see that,' said Margaret in a dry voice.

'There's been an outbreak of rooftop thievery lately. Lead being stripped from churches, etcetera . . . They could have spotted your roof from the top of the nearest church.'

'Have you any suspects?'

'None that we can pin anything on right now but the super thinks it's a gang who are operating right across Liverpool as far as Bootle.'

Margaret's mouth tightened. 'Well, I wish they'd picked on someone else. I expect in future for you to keep a better eye on my property.'

'Always check your place, Miss Sinclair. Can't be in

119

three or four places at once, though, I'm sorry to say.' He took out a notebook and pencil. 'Now if you'd like to give me a description of what's missing. Let's hope we can get your property back. I don't like to say this but there's some in your line of work that aren't fussy about where what they buy comes from. Anyway, I'll have the fingerprint expert come round and see if he can get any prints. Not that I've much hope. Most of the villains know to wear gloves these days from watching the films and reading penny dreadfuls.'

Margaret saw him out with little hope of her property being recovered. She told Rita what he had said about the skylight and then added in a stiff voice, 'I should never have suspected you. Just because it appeared impossible for anyone to get in without someone being on the inside. I'm sorry for upsetting you. How's your head this morning?'

'I'll survive.' Rita turned over a page of the magazine she had on the counter. 'And OK, I accept you are sorry, but maybe you should get someone else to help you here and I'll go and live with Mam.'

The silence that greeted these words was so long that Rita gave in to temptation and glanced up at Margaret. What she saw in her aunt's face made her feel uncomfortable.

'We all make mistakes, Rita.' Margaret toyed with her fingers. 'That could be one of yours. So why don't we put this behind us and go on from here? We'd both like the burglar caught. He just might come into the shop and you'll recognise something about him.'

Rita doubted it but let go of her hurt pride. 'There's so little for me to go on, but I suppose you could have something.'

'So you'll stay here a bit longer?'

Rita hesitated, then nodded.

Margaret took a deep breath. 'Good! Perhaps I should think of taking out some insurance. Father never believed in it but the way things are going these days . . .' She did not finish but instead said, 'The lock on the cabinet is going to need replacing so I'll get along to the locksmith in Renshaw Street. You'll be all right here on your own?'

Rita realised that by going to the locksmith herself instead of sending her, Margaret was saying that she trusted her. It was just a pity that she'd doubted her in the first place but perhaps the blame for that lay as much with her as her aunt. If she had never stolen the chocolates and spent some of her change that time, Margaret wouldn't have any examples of bad behaviour to throw in her face.

Rita was still thinking about this and the burglary when Sam entered the shop. She presumed he was there because word had got around already about the burglary. Then she noticed he was carrying a musical instrument case.

'What have you got there?' She leant across the counter towards him.

'It was me sister's.' His voice was subdued. 'I need at least a couple of quid for it . . . more if you can. I've no idea what it's worth.'

She sensed there was something wrong but did not like to pry so unfastened the snips of the case and opened it. Her eyes widened when she saw the accordion. 'Does your sister really have to get rid of this?'

Sam seemed to have trouble speaking and only after clearing his throat noisily did he say, 'She's dead. Otherwise I wouldn't be here with it but I had to come before *he* gets his hands on it. She told me to take it just before she died and to get out and go down to Mam's sister's place in Shrewsbury.'

'I am sorry, Sam!' She reached out and squeezed his hand. 'I know how fond you were of her.'

'Yeah, well, these things happen.' He glanced at her; his eyes were bright with unshed tears.

She felt like crying herself and had to look away but she hung on to his hand. 'Do you really have to leave Liverpool?'

'Yeah. I'm a coward, yer see. With our Flossie gone there's no one but me to stop him doing his worse and I'm not much of a fighter. She and you made me life worth living, but if I stick around he'll find me and I've had enough. Our Flossie said that me aunt's husband might be able to get me a job. He works with motor cars, has a garage. So I've got to go down there and see if I can make something of meself.'

Rita looked down at the frayed cuffs of his jacket. She did not need to ask him to step away from the counter to know that his trousers were too short in the leg. She withdrew her hand and placed it on the accordion. 'I'll tell you what, Sam, I've no idea how much this is worth but I'll give you four pounds for it.'

'Thanks!'

'And I'll give you a second-hand suit from out back. The bloke it belonged to died, so he won't be wanting it.'

His grey eyes brightened. 'Yer good to me, Reet. I know I look a scruff.'

'It's nothing,' she said gruffly, determined not to worry about what her aunt might say when she discovered what she'd done. 'The suit might be a bit on the big side but maybe you'll put weight on once your aunt feeds you up.'

He smiled slightly. 'I can live in hope.'

'Right! That's sorted out.' Rita did not look at him because she was a bit choked. She wrote out the pawn tickets and gave him one. 'Just in case you're ever able to redeem it.' She also gave him four pounds in various coinage and notes. 'Now come into the back and I'll get them clothes.'

He followed her into the storeroom, looked at the pinstriped suit, felt the fabric. 'Good stuff. Could I put it on now?'

'Of course you can! That's the idea, Sam. I want

123

you looking smart when you go off on your big adventure.' She went back into the shop while he changed, thinking that she was going to miss him. He had been part of her life since she had come to live with her aunt.

'Yer can look now,' he said.

She turned and thought, not for the first time, what a difference clothes made to how you saw a person. She smiled. 'How d'you feel, Sam?'

'I feel different,' he said, pulling back his shoulders and stepping down into the shop.

Rita knew exactly what he meant. She had never forgotten the sensation of being decked out in a decent set of clothes by her aunt. 'You look like someone going somewhere.'

'I am, aren't I?' he said with a grin, dragging on his tatty cap.

Rita shook her head. 'Hang on there!' She darted into the storeroom and dived into a large cardboard box that contained odd items of clothing. She produced a trilby and gave it to him.

He smoothed back his dark hair and put it on and then went to have a look at himself in the mirror. 'I look the real thing,' he said, turning up the brim of the trilby slightly and then tilting it to a rakish angle. 'I just wish our Flossie could . . .' His chest heaved and he turned away.

Rita slipped her arm through his and hugged it. 'She'd be pleased for you, Sam. You go out there and do what you've said. Make something of yourself. I just wish I could be there to see it.'

'Me too.' He took a deep breath. 'Thanks for being like a mate to me. Yer a real gud skin and I wish there was something I could do for you.'

She could not speak but squeezed his arm and held it against her. When she found her voice she said, 'You write. I'd like to know how you're getting on. I'll expect to hear great things.'

She saw him out and for a moment they stood there looking at each other. Impulsively she kissed his cheek. 'Promise you'll write?'

He rested a couple of fingers on the place her lips had touched. 'Promise.' He turned and walked away.

Rita watched until he was out of sight and then went inside the shop.

To her surprise Margaret said very little about the price she had paid for the accordion. 'I played it when I was young, but the music stopped here when my brother died.' She said no more.

The burglary was a four-day wonder. People came into the shop, including Mr McGinty, just to look at the display cabinet and ask how they got in. It seemed completely daft to Rita. 'They'd get more excitement at the cinema,' she said to her aunt, busily polishing the brass items that were for sale.

'But this is real life, Rita,' said Margaret. 'You haven't told anyone where he got in, have you?'

'I do have some sense,' said her niece. 'I just wish we'd hear something about the stolen goods.'

But weeks passed and they did not hear anything.

In all the excitement, Rita's plea to help the Brodie family had been pushed to the back of Margaret's mind but she was to be reminded of it one sunny day in May when a seaman came into the shop. Rita had been sent to Lunt's for a couple of sausage rolls for their lunch. Mrs McGinty had gone to a funeral, so Margaret was on her own. She had to grip the counter tightly to steady herself, because looking at the sailor was like seeing the Brodie twins all over again. He wore a navy-blue reefer jacket and peaked cap, just like William the last time she had seen him.

He removed his cap and smiled, placing a small brown paper package on the counter. 'I want to sell this.'

'Your name wouldn't be Billy Brodie?'

Instantly his eyes were wary. 'You know me?'

'I can't say "know". You were only a child last time I saw you. But I knew your parents. Although I haven't seen your father since just after Bella, your mother, died.'

'I don't remember you.'

'Why should you? I saw little of your parents after they married.' She reached for the scissors beneath the counter and snipped the string, opening the wrapping to reveal a small length of ivory intricately carved with flowers and birds. She was

126

enchanted, and fingered it gently. 'Now this is lovely. How much do you want for it?'

He placed his cap on the counter. 'Ten pounds!'

Her eyes dilated. 'You're expecting a lot. I had a young woman in here not so long ago with a Chinese vase to sell. She mentioned having a stepbrother called Billy who went to sea whose ideas on prices were rather inflated. It wouldn't be you, would it?'

'I wouldn't have thought so. Although . . . what was her name?'

'I can't remember. My niece wrote it down.'

'I see.' He frowned.

Margaret said, 'If she didn't send you, then why come to me?'

'You were recommended. I was speaking to the padre at the Sailors' Home about selling this,' he touched the ivory with workmanlike fingers, 'and Miss Turner, who's a volunteer there, suggested I do business with you.'

Margaret was surprised but pleased. 'That was good of her.' There were several questions she wanted to ask him but before she could do so he spoke again.

'Can we get back to business? Are you interested in buying or not?'

She nodded. 'I'll give you six pounds.'

'Not enough!' His voice was firm. 'Nine.'

'Seven.'

'Make it seven pounds ten shillings.'

Margaret's expression was steely. 'You drive a hard bargain.'

He grinned. 'Do I have a sale?'

'Yes. Although I'm not in the habit of paying over the odds for what, after all, is just a rather nice piece of ivory.'

'It's a Chinese artefact and you know it.' He rested an arm along the counter and fixed her with his blue eyes in a way reminiscent of both his father and uncle. 'There's more where that came from. Refugees are flooding into Hong Kong because of the civil war. It's going to get worse now the Japs have got a foothold, too, and are after more land. Those getting out of the country are in need of cash and desperate to sell their family treasures. I know it's lousy for them but it's a bit of good luck for hard-up sailors like me. Lucky for you as well, if you know a buyer for such things. You could make a nice little profit.'

She did not betray by the flicker of a smile that knowing such a person was a strong possibility. 'You're forgetting these are difficult times, Mr Brodie. Trade worldwide has slumped badly since '29.'

'Tell me something I don't know, Miss Sinclair,' he said. 'Will I come and see you next time I dock?'

'I don't see why not.' Her voice was light.

She reached for the receipt book. 'But tell me how your father's getting on. Last time I saw him he was still a seaman. Now I hear he's in the carting business. How did that come about?' She glanced over her spectacles and saw he was tight-lipped. 'Come on, don't be shy, Mr Brodie. I won't go repeating what you tell me but I have heard the yard was in trouble. Maybe I can help.'

'You mean . . . ?' He hesitated.

'It is in financial trouble?'

He nodded. 'The business belonged to my great uncle, whose only son was killed in the war. Pops inherited it, so he gave up the sea.' He lowered his eyes and drew an invisible pattern on the counter with a finger. 'It was something my stepmother had been on at him to do ever since she married him, from what I gathered.' He lifted his head and met Margaret's gaze. 'She didn't like being left to look after me all on her own after my grandparents died. I was a bit of a lad, you see?'

'Yes, I do see.' She could not prevent a smile. There was something attractive about him. 'I can't imagine it being easy for either of you. A husband and father away at sea more than he was home.'

'If Mam hadn't died things would have been different.'

'Yes, that must have been a great upset for you.'

He nodded.

She said no more but wrote out a receipt. She was just about to go into the back and get some banknotes when the shop door opened and Rita entered. 'Here's my niece,' said Margaret. 'Your parents knew her mother, as well. You have something in common. She lost her father at an early age and you lost a mother.' She went into the back, wondering why she had to bring Eve into it.

Rita was wearing a long green jacket over a pale green and oatmeal frock; she was pleased with her appearance, knowing green was her colour. She removed her hat and smiled at Billy. 'We've met before.'

He returned her smile. 'Where? Surely I'd have remembered someone as pretty as you?'

Colour rose in her cheeks. 'Flatterer. But I didn't always look like this. What are you doing here?'

'I've sold this to your aunt.' He touched the ivory with the tip of his forefinger.

Rita spared it a glance as she lifted the flap in the counter and passed through. 'That's nice.' She placed the bag of sausage rolls on the ledge beneath the counter before resting her elbows on the mahogany and staring at him.

He looked puzzled. 'Are there wanted posters out for me? Your aunt recognised me, too. Although that's not so surprising because apparently she knew my father and I'm like him.'

'I was a scrawny little slummy when we met for the first time.' Her brown eyes twinkled and she held out a hand. 'Rita Taylor. You were getting thrown out of a gambling club in Chinatown. I was the girl that helped you stay on your feet.'

He looked surprised but took the hand she offered. 'Thanks for that! I haven't forgotten you. I'll admit I wouldn't have recognised you. Did you ever find your mother?'

Rita was impressed. 'Fancy you remembering that.'

'How could I forget? You made it memorable. Between us we really got Jimmy's goat. He still hasn't forgiven me for gambling my own money away.'

'That's because he wants to save the yard.'

'You remember him going on about that?'

'No, I've seen him since.'

Billy's mouth formed a silent 'O' but he didn't pursue the subject. Instead he said, 'So how is it you ended up here?'

She smiled and withdrew her hand. 'It's a long story. I never did find Mam but I know she's in Cardiff and has married and had a baby, despite her being the world's worst letter writer.'

'That's parents for you,' he drawled. 'My dad never writes but then I never write to him. Not since he took my stepmother's word as gospel instead of my side.'

Rita sighed. 'I never knew my father. You're lucky having a family.'

'Ha!' He pulled a face and rested his elbows on the counter so that they brushed hers. 'You need to get to know my family better and you'll realise just how wrong you are.'

'I've met Jimmy and Alice; they seem OK.'

A small cloud seemed to descend on him. 'You've met Alice?'

'She came in here. She sold a Chinese vase to my . . .' Rita bit her lip. 'I shouldn't have told you but she was upset about selling it.'

'Can you show me it?'

She said with a moue of regret. 'Sorry. We had a break-in a few weeks ago and it was stolen along with some jewellery and stuff. My aunt was really angry.'

'What was I angry about?' said Margaret.

Rita whirled round, feeling guilty at being caught gossiping. 'I was telling Billy about the burglary.'

Margaret stepped down from the storeroom and placed several banknotes on the counter. 'Well, now you've done that you can go and warm up the sausage rolls.'

Reluctantly Rita said *tarrah* to Billy.

'I'll probably see you again sometime,' he called, an appreciative gleam in his eyes.

Margaret pushed the money across the counter. 'Give your father my regards.'

'Why don't you give them yourself?' said Billy, picking up the money. 'I'm sure my stepmother would love to have you drop in sometime.' He winked and walked out.

Impudent, she thought, but definitely has some of his father's charm. A charm she was surely immune to after all this time, knowing she was going to have to find out if that was true or not.

CHAPTER SEVEN

Margaret gazed at her reflection and thought she should have taken Rita's advice when she asked for it months ago. Although asking her niece what to do to improve herself instead of relying on her own judgement showed an amazing lack of self-confidence.

What had William's son thought when he'd looked at her across the counter? Well past her best? She fingered a handful of hair, glossy as the skin of a horse chestnut and drew it across her face beneath her nose. 'Aha, me beauty! Your money or your virtue?' she growled.

You're going off your head, said an inner voice.

Maybe! She went cross-eyed trying to see the strand of hair close up and spotted a couple of grey hairs. Determined not to let them get her down she told herself that it was never too late to improve oneself. A cut, a perm, a new outfit and she would feel ready to face William Brodie.

Having made up her mind, Margaret lost no time in having her hair done. She did not find it a pleasant experience sitting for hours with tubes sticking out of her head – and as for the smell of the lotion! But when the hairdresser had finished with her she was astonished by the transformation. There was a bounce in her step as she made her way home.

Rita seemed to need to look at her twice before recognising her. 'Blinkin' heck! You're a new woman! What an improvement!'

'I'll take that as a compliment.' Margaret smiled and went into the back premises where Mrs McGinty was cooking lunch. 'So what d'you think?'

The char's mouth dropped open. 'Yer going to have to buy a new hat.'

'Never mind a hat! Do I look younger?' Margaret looked at herself in the mirror above the sideboard.

'Ten years, at least,' said Mrs McGinty, knowing which side her bread was buttered on. 'You got yerself a man?'

Margaret rested her hand on her springy curls. 'I just thought it was time I took myself in hand. If I'd done it while Father was alive it would have been too much of a struggle, but with him dead well over a year now, I can please myself.'

'And why not?' said Mrs McGinty with an unexpected burst of fervour. 'He wasn't the easiest of men to live with.'

Margaret could agree with that but it seemed rich coming from the wife of Alf McGinty.

Two days later, Margaret left Rita in charge of the shop again and went to Bacon's in Bold Street, where she had once worked as a finisher, and watched a parade of that summer's fashions. She was persuaded into parting with more money than she had intended on a calf-length artificial silk frock in peach and cream. It had a scooped neck and long sleeves with a double layer of frills at the cuff, and there was even a matching coat. When she saw herself in the outfit she felt wonderful.

I have gone crazy, she thought on her way home, the bag with the shop's distinctive label swinging from her fingers. This outfit is more suitable for a dance or a wedding than for a business visit. So the next day she went to Lewis's and purchased an 'off the peg' navy-blue frock with the tiniest of white spots: to go with it she bought a white straw hat with a navy ribbon round its brim, a pair of two-tone strapped shoes, navy gloves and bag.

The next early closing day she waited until Rita had gone off to the matinee at the Trocadero with one of the shop assistants from Berry Street before changing into the navy-blue frock. To all outer appearances Margaret looked smart and confident but inside her stomach it was as if a hundred moths were doing the Charleston.

When she reached Brodie's yard, she was surprised to find the gates closed. She tried the Judas door and was relieved when it opened. Her heels made a ringing sound on the cobbles as she walked across the yard. She noticed several slates missing from the roof of the house and three carts had their shafts resting on the sunlit cobbles. It was the silence she found disturbing. Was she too late? Had all the horses been sold off to pay William's debts? She headed for the stables, peered inside and was relieved to see several horses in the stalls. She re-emerged, puzzled.

'Can I help you?'

Margaret started and turned to gaze at the man standing a few feet away. She would have recognised him anywhere, despite the creases at the corner of his eyes and the lines running between nose and mouth. She felt a catch in her throat, thinking that he would never see forty again. There were threads of silver in his dark curly hair but he still had good shoulders and stood erect in the black shabby suit.

'That roof needs a few slates fixing, Will.' Her voice sounded breathless in her ears.

He lost colour and did not answer immediately. Then he appeared to collect himself and covered the space between them in two strides. 'Maggie?'

'I wasn't sure you'd recognise me. It's been a long time.'

'Yes!' He gazed at her with an intensity that made her blush. 'What are you doing here?'

'Curiosity! I've only recently heard that you'd remarried and given up the sea.'

'Who told you?'

'Does it matter? You swore undying love to me.' She had not meant to say that and knew she shouldn't have by the change in his expression.

'You turned me down! I had the boy needing a mother. If you're having second thoughts now about marrying me in place of Alan, then you're fifteen years too late.' His tone was harsh.

For a wild panicky moment she wanted to flee the yard, mortified at having plunged them immediately into an argument. Perhaps that desire had been simmering in her subconscious all this time, waiting for the right moment to erupt, needing to sort out the unfinished business that was between them. But did she have that right? He had taken a second wife. She drew on that inner strength which she had needed to call upon so many times in the last twenty years. 'I'm not here to go through all that again. I've tried to put the past behind me.'

'But haven't quite managed it, obviously!' He smiled.

So might his twin have smiled if he had still been alive! She felt sadness along with that fluttering excitement she had experienced on her way here and placed her arms across her chest in a subconscious defensive action. 'True.'

'So what can I do for you?' He patted his pockets and brought out a tobacco pouch. 'I presume you didn't come just to tell me that you'd heard I'd married again and accuse me of being a liar.'

'Is that what I said?' As soon as the words were out she had wanted to retract them. 'Sorry. The truth is I heard you had money problems.'

His hand stilled a moment and then he resumed shredding Old Twist. 'And who told you that?'

Margaret did not reply but looked about her. 'It's so quiet. You've horses in the stables and carts not getting used.'

'The men are out at a funeral. I've just got back. They'll be here soon. One of my drivers was killed down at the docks. A chain snapped and a bale of cotton fell on him.' He rammed the tobacco into the bowl of the tortoiseshell pipe with long fingers, then struck a match on the sole of his shoe. 'Doesn't rain but it pours. Isn't that what our mothers used to say when one thing went wrong after another?' He raised an eyebrow as he lit the tobacco, flicked out the match and drew on his pipe. 'I lost a horse the other day, broke a leg and had to be shot. Jimmy, my stepson, said it was more of a loss than the man who died because men can easily be replaced, the way unemployment is these days. Unfortunately I can't afford to replace him. Not for the first time my moneylender is threatening to send in the bailiffs.'

'I'm sorry! How's your wife coping with it all?'

Margaret felt a need to bring her into the conversation to see how he reacted. She would like to meet her.

'I keep as much as I can from her about the business.' He encompassed the yard with a sweep of his pipe. 'She doesn't enjoy good health.'

'I'm sorry to hear it. Is that why you gave up the sea?'

Margaret wanted to hear his reasons from him.

'Good God, no! Billy was the problem. He went a bit wild after losing his mother and then I married Maud, who had two kids of her own. My parents died and he just did not get on with my wife. Not that I blame him entirely for that but she has a daughter, Alice, and she didn't want them getting close. As well as that, she considered him a bad influence on Jimmy.'

'The poor lad! No wonder he went a bit wild.'

'You feel sorry for him?' A tiny smile flared in his eyes. 'Ohhh, Maggie! If only you'd married me, how different all our lives would have been.'

'You know why I turned you down! And as it is you've proved me right. We weren't meant for each other. You found someone else.'

William's smile faded and he drew on his pipe before saying, 'You know where I met Maud? At Aintree during National week! Her father owned a couple of horses and she told me to back them. I won a packet! She'd just been widowed and was doing everything she could not to face up to life without her husband. Her father had money and was prepared to indulge her. When I was on leave, my mother looked after Billy and we hit the high spots. Not the right way to handle loss, perhaps. But we were two needy people.'

She felt pain, imagining the kind of life he had lived while she had struggled to forget him and his brother, telling herself that she had done the right thing in refusing his proposal. She had been convinced he could have got Alan out of China but hadn't done so because he was jealous of him and wanted him to die. 'Are you still gambling?'

He frowned. 'I don't think that's any of your business. Have you come here to gloat?'

'No! I came to see if I could help you. What tune is the business in debt to?'

He laughed mirthlessly. 'Who told you about it? And what is it to you?'

'My niece, Rita. Your stepdaughter came into the shop with something to sell. So come on, Will, humour me!'

'Why should I?'

'It might be to your advantage.'

He stared at her for what seemed a long time and then, 'What the hell!' He named a sum that made her reel.

Instantly Margaret knew that if she took on his debt she could say goodbye to that dream house of hers. If his business went to the dogs, most likely she'd lose most of her money, but what would happen to him if she did not bail him out?

'A crazy amount, isn't it? Terrifying how it's doubled, trebled, quadrupled from the original amount I borrowed.'

She knew exactly what he meant. 'What'll you do if you were to lose the yard?'

'If I only had myself to think about I'd go back to sea. As it is . . .' His teeth clenched on the stem of his pipe.

'You'd rather not think about it.'

'Yes. But it's all I *can* think about. I'm in a downward spiral and it's a bloody struggle trying to get out of it.'

'What happened to your wife's father? You said he had money.'

William grimaced. 'What d'you think, Maggie? Thousands have gone bankrupt in the last couple of years. He was no exception. On top of everything else, Maud's had to cope with her father shooting himself.'

'Oh, my God!' A shiver convulsed Margaret. 'She has my sympathy.'

'Thank you!' His voice had softened. 'Now, if there's anything else I can do for you, Maggie, say it now or go. The men'll be back in a minute and—'

'I could save you from the bailiffs.'

'What!'

'My father died a year or so ago and left me everything.'

'Lucky you!' He paused. 'What about Eve?'

Margaret's smile vanished. 'Do you always have

141

to worry about other women? Eve went off and left me to deal with the mess Mother was in after Donald's death – and I worked damned hard for Father. Anyway, she isn't your concern. Now do you want me to take over your debt or not?'

He did not answer immediately but looked towards the gates as men began to trickle through the Judas door. Then he faced her. 'Can I trust you to treat me fairly?'

She almost choked on her indignation. 'You've got a nerve to ask me that. When did you ever treat me fairly? Don't answer that! I know the answer myself. I work within the law. I won't cheat you.'

'Then it's a deal.' He held out a hand and she hesitated only a second before taking it. 'So when will you give me the money?' he asked.

She could not help but throw back her head and laugh. He smiled. 'What's so funny?'

'D'you think I'm daft? Give me the name of your moneylender and I'll take over the debt from him.'

Only for an instant did he show annoyance and then his expression changed to reluctant admiration. 'Your father's trained you well. If anyone can turn this business round it's probably you. My heart's never really been in it.'

'Cut the soft soap,' said Margaret, flushing with pleasure nevertheless. 'You've still got to work damn hard. You'll pay me just as you would the moneylender you have now but my rates will be slightly lower, I should imagine, and I'll give you more time to pay. One bit of advice – stop gambling. You must have let hundreds slip through your fingers.'

'Do you take me for a fool?'

'Do you take me? I remember Alan writing to me after finding you in that gambling den in Shanghai.'

William's eyes glinted. 'Did you ever wonder what he was doing there?'

'You're insinuating he was a gambler, too? How low can you get?'

'Pretty low,' he said quietly. 'But remember, nobody was as close to him as me. Although you might think you knew him, I knew him better.'

'Oh, go to hell!' she said, and almost changed her mind about helping him. 'You make me mad!'

His lips twitched. 'Then neither of us has altered that much.'

'You certainly haven't.' She got control of herself. 'Now, give me the name of your moneylender and your credit agreement and I'd like to see the books.'

'Come over to the house and I'll let you have them.' He led the way.

Margaret hoped to meet his wife but William took her into a small room that obviously served as an office. Despite the paperwork that littered the desk, he seemed to know where to find the agreement because he produced it in no time and handed it to her. 'I'll be glad to have him off my back. Would you like me to come with you when you visit him?'

Margaret shook her head. As long as she turned up with the money – with a bit extra for interest after checking the wording on the agreement with a fine toothcomb – she felt certain she would have no trouble. 'I'll send my niece round with the new agreement for you to sign in a few days.'

He looked surprised. 'I didn't know Eve had a daughter?'

'Rita lives with me.'

'She works for you?'

'That's right.'

'And you keep in touch with Eve? I got the impression—'

'That Eve and I have nothing to do with each other?' Her laugh had an edge to it. 'You're right! She sent the girl to me eighteen months ago and ran off with a man – and you feel sorry for Eve?' She walked out of the room, hoping she had given him plenty to think about.

Over the next few days Margaret wasted no time getting William's financial affairs sorted out. She would like to see him again, but had mentioned sending her niece because she thought it better for them both if she appeared businesslike, rather than too friendly. She must not forget he had a wife.

'What's this?' Rita turned the envelope over between her hands and noted the address.

'It's a credit agreement between Mr Brodie and me.' Margaret glanced up from the book open on her knee. 'I want you to take it to the yard and make sure he signs the original and the copy.'

A smile lit the girl's face. 'You've decided to help them. I'm really glad.'

Margaret raised her eyebrows. 'It's a business agreement, Rita. Nothing to get excited about. I just hope I've made the right decision. If I haven't, then you'll be out on your ear for bringing their troubles to my door in the first place. Now go!'

Rita went. She was happy and swung her arms, humming a tune from the Ivor Novello film she had seen the other day. She came to numbers chalked on the pavement and did a hop, skip and a jump, taking in most of the squares. She remembered Sam chalking on the pavement for money and wondered how he was getting on at his aunt's. She had yet to hear from him and hoped he would keep his promise and write.

She reached Brodie's yard and walked between the open gates. Carefully avoiding a heap of steaming manure she approached an old man clad in a tatty jacket and trousers shiny with wear. He was in the act of climbing onto a wagon behind the scrawniest horse she had ever seen.

'Where can I find Mr Brodie?' she asked.

He jerked his head in the direction of the house and mumbled words she didn't quite catch. He flicked the reins and told the horse to walk on. She approached the house and was about to knock when the door opened and Billy came out, almost knocking her over in his rush. He saved her from falling by seizing her shoulders and bringing her against his chest. Her nose caught one of the buttons on his reefer jacket. 'Ouch! That hurt!'

'Sorry! I wasn't expecting anyone to be there!'

'Apology accepted.' She smiled up into his angry face. He released her and pushed his cap to the back of his head; a clump of black curls sprang out onto his forehead. She thought how unfair it was that between them he and Jimmy had hair and eyes that any girl would envy.

The anger died in his face. 'You're Rita from the pawnshop. What are you doing here?'

'I've come to see your father.'

'About what?' His tone was clipped.

She hesitated. 'I'm not really supposed to talk about business to anybody but the client.'

'Client? That sounds official.'

'It is.'

He changed the subject abruptly. 'Has your aunt had any luck getting her stolen property back?'

The question surprised her. 'Not so far. But I have my suspicions about who's behind the dirty deed. He hit me over the head, you know!'

Billy's expression froze. 'He hit you! I didn't know that.'

'Yeah!' She grimaced. 'Not too hard but hard enough to stun me and make his escape.'

'The bloody swine!' He put an arm about her

shoulders. 'I'm sorry to hear that. I didn't know you came that close to seeing who it was.'

She quite liked the feel of his arm around her. 'Not close enough. Although, as I said, I have my suspicions who's behind the theft.'

'And who would that be?'

'Mr McGinty. Well, he couldn't have done the actual deed but I think he's the brains behind it. Although . . .' She wrinkled her nose. 'Has he got that many brains?'

'Who's Mr McGinty?'

'Our char's husband.'

Billy looked thoughtful. 'I can see how that would make him a number one suspect. I suppose she could have let him in?'

'No! She doesn't live on the premises. Besides, the burglar got through the skylight. I tell you – he won't get through there again if he was to try. Aunt Margaret had the locksmith out.'

'Very wise,' said Billy.

Rita thought he was about to say something else when a voice behind her said, 'I thought I told you to go, Billy! I'll not have you stirring up trouble here again.'

Rita whirled round and saw a man so like Billy that he could only be his father. His face was set in uncompromising lines.

'Don't worry; I'm going!' Billy's voice quivered with anger. 'There'll come a time, Pops, when you'll want my help. I tell yer – you'll have to beg for it!' He brushed past Rita and strode towards the gates.

She stared after him in dismay.

'What can I do for you, young lady?'

Reluctantly she turned and marvelled afresh at that amazing likeness to Billy.

'It's rude to stare,' said William.

Rita drew herself up to her full height of five foot two inches. From her bag she produced a large brown envelope 'My aunt, Miss Margaret Sinclair, sent me. I have an agreement here for you to sign regarding the debt she has taken over on your behalf. I'm to wait while you read and sign both papers.' Rita's tone was brisk. 'You will keep one of the copies for your own records.'

'You must be Eve's girl.' He made no move to take the envelope but folded his arms across his chest and smiled.

It was a smile of such charm that she was bowled over. 'Of course, you knew Mam!'

'Yes. We spent a fair amount of time in each other's company. She was a laugh. D'you hear from her?'

Rita hesitated, wondering how much Margaret had told this man about them.

'Ha! I see. You don't.'

She recognised sympathy when she saw it. 'She's written a couple of times but not to me. Mind you, if she hadn't left, then I wouldn't be here because I wouldn't have met Billy and Jimmy.'

This was news to William. 'Where was this? I seem to remember your aunt mentioning you meeting my stepdaughter but not the lads.'

'That's right. She came into the pawnshop and—'

'And when was that?'

'Months ago. She . . .' Suddenly Rita was remembering the conversation she had heard between Alice and Jimmy in this yard.

'She what?'

Rita gripped her lower lip between her teeth and gazed at him helplessly. 'Ask her!'

He smiled. 'Don't look so worried. I'll get to the bottom of it myself.'

Relieved, Rita held out the agreement to him.

He took a fountain pen from his breast pocket, glanced through the typescript and signed both sheets.

She was horrified. 'You should never sign anything without reading it first.'

'I think I can trust Maggie not to diddle me,' he said smoothly, placing the papers back in the envelope and handing it to her.

She frowned. 'It doesn't show good business sense not to read an agreement – and you should have kept one of the sheets.'

She removed a paper from the envelope and handed it to him.

A clatter of hooves caused them to look round.

Jimmy brought the horse to a standstill and sprang

from the cart. 'You've got to do something about Billy, Pops. He nearly caused an accident, standing in the middle of the road forcing me to stop. I nearly ran him down! And what does he do but bloody drags me down from the cart and punches me. Look!' He thrust his jaw almost under William's nose.

Rita could see the swelling on one side. 'Why should he do that?'

Jimmy's head slewed in her direction and consternation showed in his eyes. 'What are you doing here?'

'She's here on business. Get inside and have Alice put some witch hazel on it.'

'B-but what business?' demanded Jimmy.

'Later!' William faced Rita. 'Thanks for bringing that, and give my regards to your aunt.'

Rita had no choice but to leave. She paused at the gates and looked back, wondering why Billy had punched Jimmy. He and his stepfather had vanished, but on the doorstep stood a woman in a dressing gown. Her greying hair was dishevelled, her face haggard and unfriendly. She clenched her fist and brandished it in the girl's direction before going back into the house and slamming the door.

Margaret handed the suit over the counter to the young girl, thanked her and said, 'See you Monday.'

Rita held the door open and closed it after her.

'Well, did he sign?' said Margaret.

'Yes, but he didn't read them properly.' Rita frowned as she placed the envelope containing the credit agreement on the counter.

Margaret smiled as she picked up the envelope. 'Trusts me, does he?'

'So he says.'

'Good. Then everything will be fine as long as he keeps up the repayments. If he doesn't then things'll get awkward.'

Rita could imagine. 'I saw his wife. At least I *think* it was her.'

'And?' Margaret stared over her spectacles.

'In a dressing gown at this time of day.' Rita rested her arms on the counter.

'What did she look like?'

'A mess.'

'Poor her! Poor Will! I get a feeling that's not a happy household,' said Margaret, going into the storeroom and placing the credit agreement in the filing cabinet.

Rita thought that herself – and it wasn't only because Mr Brodie was up to his eyes in debt. Why had Billy punched Jimmy? And why were he and his father at loggerheads? And what was wrong with Mrs Brodie? Would Alice tell Mr Brodie that she'd pawned the vase Billy had given her? She wished she could have eavesdropped on the conversations going on at the yard, but that night she was to have other things to worry about.

CHAPTER EIGHT

Rita was having a bad dream. She was being buried alive, could hear the sound of the spade against the coffin! She screamed but no sound came out and so she hammered with her fists against the lid, but this time she could hear a distinct thud, thud. She woke, lying on her stomach with her hands against the bedhead. Oh, the relief! Her thudding heart slowed its beat and, realising her pillow had slipped off the bed, she picked it up and placed it behind her head. Not daring to close her eyes yet in case the nightmare came swooping in again on bats' wings, she remained sitting up until the memory of the dream faded and she felt brave enough to climb out of bed. Desperate for a drink, she went downstairs.

By the time she reached the scullery her eyes were accustomed to the dark and she could make out cupboards, cooker and sink. The moggy approached, purring. 'Not mousing?' she whispered, glad of its company.

She put on the kettle, talking to the cat in whispers as she put a match to the mantle; only then did she notice the door to the cellar was open. She clicked down the latch and poured milk into a saucer for the cat, and took a bourbon from the biscuit tin.

She felt much better after the tea and was washing her cup and saucer when she heard the stairs creak. Her heart seemed to bounce into her throat but then she pulled herself together. It would be her aunt. She put the crockery away, expecting Margaret to join her, but when she didn't Rita experienced that peculiar sensation of the hairs rising on the back of her neck. Could a burglar have got in again? She tiptoed through the kitchen and into the lobby, pausing there to listen. At first she did not hear anything and then there was the sound of movement in the storeroom.

She inched her way in that direction and it was as if the last break-in was being repeated as she crept through the open door. A rasp of a match and light flared but this time the face she saw was long, unshaven and its owner wore a black eye-patch. She almost dropped on the spot. So Mr McGinty had been behind the last theft! The match went out.

Rita should have learnt her lesson from the last time and froze, but she had been holding her breath without realising and it came out in a whoosh. She heard him curse, and she decided to run upstairs and get her aunt. But she only managed to get through the door when she was grabbed from behind. She screamed and then a hand covered her mouth. She kicked out but only succeeded in stubbing her big toe, which hurt like hell. The next moment she was falling backwards and landed on top of Mr McGinty. She struggled to get up while he was cursing and swearing – such words that she had not heard since a fight between Dolly and another prostitute when she was a kid. Then she was seized by the arm, dragged upright and thrust aside. Startled, she stared at the dark shape bending over the man on the floor. Then came the crunch of bone on bone as Mr McGinty attempted to get to his feet, only to be sent crashing to the floor.

The black figure straightened and she could see the faint gleam of his eyes. 'Who are you?' she whispered.

He grabbed her arm and hustled her out of the storeroom and closed the door on her. She heard something being shifted about and when she tried to open the door, it wouldn't budge. She put her ear to the panel and heard a faint screeching.

'Rita, is that you?' She spun round.

Immediately she shaded her eyes from the light of

the torch. 'Aunt Margaret, Mr McGinty's in there.'

'How d'you know?'

'I saw him! He grabbed me, but you're not going to believe this – another fella all dressed in black dragged him off me, KO'd him, then pushed me out here. I don't know how he got in, but he's looking for something.'

'Then out of the way and let me get in! I've got the poker with me.' Margaret handed the torch to Rita and brandished the poker in the air like a sword as she turned the doorknob and pushed. The door barely moved.

'He's put something against it but perhaps if we both push we'll be able to shift it,' whispered Rita.

They threw themselves at the door and, after several attempts, managed to move whatever was behind it, enough for them to squeeze through the gap.

Margaret played the torch about the room and caught Mr McGinty in its beam. He was on the floor, groaning and trying to get up. Without saying a word they hurried over and sat on him. He swore and attempted to throw them off and would have succeeded if Margaret had not hit him on the head with the poker.

She and Rita stood up; the girl hurried into the shop and saw the door wide open. She stepped outside and looked up and down the street but it was deserted.

Margaret came and stood beside her. 'Got away, did he?'

Rita nodded.

They went back inside and closed the door. 'You get dressed, Rita, and see if you can find the constable. If not you'll have to go up to the bridewell.'

'You'll be OK on your own with him?'

'If he makes a move I'll bop him over the head again. In the meantime, I'll find something to tie him up with.'

Rita was dressed and out in five minutes. As she went in search of the bobby she wondered whether to mention the man in black. After all, he had done to Mr McGinty what she would have liked to do herself since setting eyes on him.

Margaret used the washing line to tie up her char's husband, grateful for the lessons in knots her brother had taught Eve and herself. It only seemed like yesterday, and she thought he would have been proud of her. After she trussed Mr McGinty up as fine as a piece of brisket she went and dressed. When she came downstairs again he was stirring and struggling against his bonds.

'I wouldn't bother if I was you,' she said, pulling up a chair.

'Oh, me bleedin' head,' he groaned. 'What did yer have to go and hit me for? I meant yer no harm.'

'Pull the other one! What were you doing here but to steal from me?'

156

'I haven't taken nothing,' he said sullenly. 'Yer can search me if yer like.'

'No thanks!' She shuddered at the thought of going through his pockets. 'I'll leave that to the police.' As if on cue, there was a knocking on the shop door and she hurried to answer it.

The first thing the two policemen did was to compliment her on her knots. Then they searched Mr McGinty, despite his protesting his innocence.

'Then what's this?' said one, pulling out a small cotton bag drawn tightly at the neck with string. He loosened it and shook the contents out on the counter.

Rita and Margaret stared at the rings and silver watch. They glanced at each other but neither said a word.

Rita sat on her bed with her knees hunched and her chin in her hands, trying to remember every detail of those moments when the intruder in black had hustled her out of the room. There was something niggling at the back of her mind. What was that smell which had clung to him? Some kind of polish, but not the stuff used on furniture. A little click had gone on in her brain. Could the intruder be the same as the one from the last break-in? If only she could remember where she had come across that smell.

Margaret entered the room and sat on the bed. 'Perhaps you can tell me how my stolen property from months ago turned up in Mr McGinty's pocket?' she said pleasantly. 'Its description seems to have slipped the police's mind but you recognised it, didn't you?'

'Yes! And I'm convinced the intruder put it there.'

'Which means that he must have taken it.'

Rita nodded. She felt unhappy about that. 'So what are we going to do?'

'Why didn't you mention him to the police?'

'I didn't like to. Have you told them?'

Margaret pleated the bedcover between her fingers, her expression absorbed, head bent, with her hair curling like a huge halo giving her a definite aura. 'I told them that I never saw him, but Mr McGinty told them that there was definitely another man in the storeroom, and that he's innocent. They don't believe him. He's admitted he came after my money but couldn't get in my room. As you know, I always lock it and since the last break-in I place a chair beneath the doorknob.

'So what . . . ?'

'They have enough on him to put him away for years. They went back to his house and searched the place. They've been wanting an excuse for ages, apparently.'

Rita sat up straight. 'They found something?'

'Lead under a tarpaulin in the yard.'

The girl laughed. 'Got him! So Sam was right.'

'What's he to do with this?'

158

Rita told her what Sam had said months ago about some real tough blokes going round the back of the McGintys' house and coming back with a loaded cart covered in tarpaulin. 'I bet Mrs McGinty's up the wall with all this. I bet she's told them he's been framed.'

Margaret smiled. 'You're wrong. Apparently she went for him because he went back on a promise to her . . . said he'd never get involved with the bad 'uns again. She's washed her hands of him.'

'Marvellous!' Rita wanted to dance round the room. 'So it doesn't matter whether we mention the black intruder or not?'

Margaret shook her head. 'Want to know how he got in?'

'Yes, please.' She stared at her, bright-eyed.

'Sawed through the chain on the grating and dropped into the cellar. He was able to open the latch from the other side with a gadget they found in his pocket.'

'You think our black intruder got in the same way?'

Margaret shrugged. 'Possibly! Although why he took such a chance to return my property to me is a mystery. Maybe his conscience got to him.' She rose from the bed. 'Anyway, I'm glad he knocked Mr McGinty down for us, and when Mrs M gets over the shock I'm sure it'll be the making of her.'

'Will she still be coming here?'

Margaret paused in the doorway. 'What'll she

live on if I sack her? She's a hard worker and with him gone I'm sure she won't be so bolshie.'

Rita agreed. 'I'd still like to know who the mystery man is.'

Margaret said grimly, 'Me too. Don't forget he hit you over the head last time. One thing's for sure: he won't get in again. I'm having thicker chains and a good strong lock put on the grid and bolts top and bottom on the cellar door. If he wants to visit in the middle of the night a third time he'll need to come down the chimney!'

Strangely enough, Rita was thinking about what her aunt had said a few weeks later when she saw Jimmy down by the docks caught up in a traffic jam. The fumes and noise of vehicles, the tooting of horns and shouts of carters were enough to give anyone a headache, and she had a blinder. Mr McGinty's trial was coming up and she was to be called as a witness. She dodged through the traffic and came alongside the cart, looking up at Jimmy. His swollen jaw was back to normal and he was as handsome as ever but looking really cheesed off.

'Hello!'

He glanced down and flashed her a disarming smile. 'Hello! I hope you're going to forgive me for being so rude last time we met. I meant to visit the shop and say thanks. I'm sure it's down to you that your aunt got us out of trouble.'

'You're forgiven,' she said cheerfully. 'Things better up at the yard now?'

'Yeah! Pops bought a new horse.'

'That's great!' she shouted above the noise of the traffic. 'Didn't think of getting a lorry, though?'

Jimmy scowled. 'Don't like bloody lorries! The smell and – look at this jam.'

She was of a mind that lorries took up the same space as a horse and cart, and that the smell of manure was just as bad as petrol fumes, but she kept her thoughts to herself, and said in way of comfort, 'It'll all be sorted out once the tunnel's finished. There won't be those queuing up for the luggage boat.'

'They reckon it won't be finished for a couple of years.'

The traffic moved a few inches. When it came to a halt again, Jimmy called down, 'I suppose you wouldn't want a lift? I'm going your way.'

She thought walking would be quicker but if she accepted his offer she might get to know him better. 'Thanks!' She pulled herself up and sat sidelong on the wooden seat so she could look at him. Despite the greasy cap and his well-worn working clothes he still looked good.

'You're staring,' he said, without looking at her.

She said glibly, 'I was just seeing if your jaw had gone down.'

He laughed. 'That's ages ago. Bloody Billy! You've no idea what a bloody swine he is.'

'I suppose he's back at sea?'

'Yeah! Won't be seeing him for months.' He glanced at her. 'Anything exciting been happening to you?'

She pulled a face and smoothed down her skirt. 'I suppose you heard about our break-in? I'm to be a witness at the trial soon.'

He blinked long golden eyelashes and looked thoughtful. 'I think Pops mentioned it.'

She had forgotten Mr Brodie had dropped by to pay off some of his debt. 'Of course.'

'I bet he surprised your aunt with that nice big payment.'

Rita chuckled. 'She hit the roof when he said it came with love from a horse.'

Jimmy grinned. 'That was down to Mam. She nagged him into backing it. The horse was out of a dam her father had once owned so she knew it had breeding. We all won money. You've no idea what it feels like to have a couple of pounds in your pocket after being skint for ages.'

The traffic moved and Rita clutched the seat with both hands as Jimmy took a corner too sharply into Parliament Street. It was hard work for the horse because the street veered steeply. She asked after his mother.

His face clouded. 'Better for proving that she can still be of use to the family but I'd rather not talk about her, if you don't mind. She's not too good.'

Rita remembered the haggard-faced woman shaking her fist at her, and wondered what was wrong with her. 'How's Alice?'

'Got a job. Pops insisted, saying he'll keep his eye on Mam, as well as get a woman to come in for a few hours a day.'

'Doesn't that defeat the object of Alice getting a job?'

'Pops thinks she's too much at home. A member of the church choir spoke for her and she's sewing for Weatheralls.'

'Well, I'm pleased for her,' said Rita. 'Jobs aren't easy to come by.'

His face lit up. 'Thanks! I can tell you mean that.' He rested a hand on her knee and squeezed before taking it away.

The intimate gesture caused her heart to race; she had to look away, conscious of a sudden happiness. He must like her! She glanced up towards the unfinished Anglican Cathedral, which appeared to claw at the sky, perched high on St James Mount. She caught a whiff of salt-laden air blowing up from the Mersey, and knew there was nowhere else she wanted to be in the world at that moment.

Jimmy dropped her off outside the shop and asked would she like to go for a walk in Sefton Park with him on Sunday. She said yes. Certain that her aunt would disapprove, she arranged to meet him by St Luke's church at two.

Mr McGinty's trial took place two days later. His wife was not at the trial; she was staying with her sister. The McGinty males were there in force.

During the trial no mention was made of an intruder in black, even by the defence lawyer, so Rita was not called upon to perjure herself. Obviously, no one believed in Alf's mystery attacker, and there was the matter of the stolen lead. He was pronounced guilty, not only of theft but also of assault, and sentenced to ten years' imprisonment. As he was being taken to the cells he cursed Margaret and Rita and shouted that they hadn't heard the last of him.

The following day, Rita was minding the shop while her aunt went to visit Mrs McGinty to see when she would be back at work. When Margaret returned, her face was white and a bruise showed on her cheek. The brim of her new hat had been torn and she was trembling. Rita came out from behind the counter. 'What's happened? You look terrible!'

'I was attacked. There's some brandy in the sideboard cupboard. Get it for me!' She lifted the flap and followed Rita through and sank onto the sofa.

The girl poured an inch of brandy and handed the glass to her. 'Who attacked you?'

'He wore a balaclava helmet so it covered his face. I can only guess.' Margaret's hand shook as she held the glass to her lips.

Rita had never seen her in such a state and knelt on the rug at her feet. 'You think it was one of the McGintys?'

'Could be. He was crafty enough not to open his mouth.'

'So what are you going to do? Report it to the police?'

'When I've stopped shaking.' She tossed off the brandy and held out the glass for more.

Margaret sipped slowly. The bell rang in the shop and someone shouted. 'I'll go,' said Rita.

'No, we'll both go in case it's the McGintys,' said Margaret, with some Dutch courage down her. She seized the poker.

Rita was alarmed. 'We need a bodyguard!'

'What are the police for? I'd have to pay a bodyguard.' Margaret drained the brandy glass, then thumped her chest. 'That went down a fair treat,' she croaked and, swaying slightly, she made her way through the storeroom to the shop, followed by Rita.

Margaret did not have to use the poker because here was the police in force. Well, one bobby, but he was huge. At least six foot six and with a handlebar moustache; a very different man from their usual bobby on the beat. He reassured them that they were in no danger and could put the poker away. 'I've come to tell you that we've had a phone call saying you've been threatened. I want to assure you that there's nothing for you to fear.'

Margaret thanked him profusely, the brandy having gone to her head.

'Who called you?' asked Rita.

'The woman didn't give her name.'

'What about the name of the attacker?'

He shook his head. 'Sorry, miss. But acting on suspicion of a certain family I'll be giving them a warning to keep their noses clean or else they'll be in trouble.'

Rita thanked him and saw him out before turning to Margaret. 'What did Mrs McGinty have to say when you saw her?'

Margaret leant against the counter and yawned. 'She's decided to pack in her job here and stay on at her sister's. She knows where there's another cleaning job going apparently.'

Rita thought it was just as well – until she found out from Jimmy that Mrs McGinty's sister was the woman Mr Brodie was employing to help in the house and that sometimes she helped out, too. It was some coincidence and Rita would rather the McGintys were out of their circle of acquaintances altogether, but there was nothing she could do about it.

That coming Sunday she and Jimmy went and listened to a brass band in Sefton Park. They sat on the grass and he talked about horses, the business and the May Day Horse Show. It was his ambition to have one of the Brodie horses win a rosette.

He enjoyed talking of the future he envisaged for himself and the yard. She was content to gaze into his handsome face and let his words wash over her.

Sunday afternoons fell into a pattern for Rita. Sometimes he would drive her to the Pierhead and they would walk along the landing stage, watching the ships coming and going. Reminded of Billy she asked for news of him but Jimmy only said that it was Alice who kept in touch. One Sunday Rita suggested they window-shop in the city centre, but Jimmy said that it was a waste of time if you couldn't buy anything, so they went for a drive along the dock road as far as the Dingle. He kissed her for the first time; a moment she relived for days after.

The following Sunday Jimmy did not turn up and, worried that something bad might have happened to him, Rita went up to the yard. The place looked deserted. Then a man came out of the cookhouse and stood in the doorway, drinking from a steaming mug. She waved to him and asked after Jimmy's whereabouts.

'They're all up at the hospital.'

'Is it Mrs Brodie?'

'Yeah! They cut her open yesterday and they sent for them today. Nothing down for her if you ask me.'

Rita was shocked, imagining how Jimmy must be feeling. She had not realised his mother was so seriously ill.

When Rita told the news to her aunt, Margaret did not comment immediately but went and made a cup of tea. She sat down in front of the fire and asked Rita what she was doing up at the yard.

'I've been seeing Jimmy.' She could see no point in keeping quiet any longer. After all, he had kissed her, which must mean that he was perhaps serious about her. Before Margaret could say anything about her deceit, Rita added, 'It's going to be hard on him if she dies. He's really fond of her.'

'I'm sure! But death comes to us all and if she's been ill for some time it could be a relief to them,' murmured Margaret. She wondered how William would deal with it, as well as searching her own feelings. 'Alice will find it difficult, too. She's bound to miss her mother, but she'll also have to give up her job and stay at home to look after the house and her father and brother.'

'Perhaps Mrs Brodie won't die,' said Rita.

'If she does or doesn't you're best not seeing Jimmy again. He's a man with a man's needs. You're not even seventeen yet. Don't be like your mother; show some sense. There's plenty of time for courting when you're twenty-one.'

Twenty-one! That birthday was ages off and Rita had no intention of doing what her aunt said. Jimmy would need comforting if his mother died and she wanted to be there to provide it.

Her aunt eyed her speculatively, guessing exactly

168

what she was thinking. She was determined not to let her out of her sight on Sundays in future.

The following day Margaret was alone in the shop when William staggered in. His clothes looked like they had been slept in and his tie was askew. On his chin was several days' growth of beard. 'You'll come to the funeral, Maggie?' he said without preamble, slumping over the counter.

'She's dead, then?' Margaret was determined to remain calm and businesslike.

A laugh escaped him and he rubbed his eyes. 'Aye! Would I be burying her if she weren't?'

'Sorry. It was a daft thing to say but that's all it was: something to say. I never knew your wife but I know how difficult it is seeing someone you've lived with die. I don't suppose there's anything I can do to help, but if there is let me know.'

He looked surprised. 'That's very gracious of you, Maggie. I have to admit that I'd hate to go through the last few weeks again. She was a stubborn woman and hated doctors. She knew about you and what was between us, unfortunately.'

Margaret was taken aback. 'You told her?'

'No! She found an old photograph of the gang taken years ago and wouldn't rest until she knew who everybody was. Perhaps if I hadn't been drinking at the time I wouldn't have reminisced so much and betrayed how I felt about you.' He rubbed his jaw and grimaced. 'It ruined our marriage, which never had much going for it. She smoked opium, you know?'

Margaret was shocked. 'How could I know? Where did she pick up that habit? From you?'

'The hell she did!' William glared at her from bleary eyes, his chin on his hands as they rested on the counter. 'A pipe of ordinary tobacco's enough for me.'

'Sorry! But I thought maybe the pair of you went along to one of those dens in Chinatown.'

'You're not far off the truth. I didn't realise it until Billy told me that he'd seen her there. I chose not to believe him at first. I mean, he hated her. I thought she was ill and got the doctor out. You can have no idea how many doctors I've had look at her. The bloody money I paid out trying to get her sorted out and all the time he was telling the bloody truth.'

'Poor Will,' she said softly, placing a hand on his bowed head.

'My own fault. I should think more before I go marrying people.'

'You mean Bella as well?'

His eyes drooped and he was quiet so long she thought he had fallen asleep. Then he said in a tired voice, 'I didn't see how I had any other choice there.'

'What d'you mean? You weren't engaged to her like I was to Alan.'

'If you'd stayed friends with her instead of dropping her and me like hot chestnuts because I flirted with her once or twice, then you'd know why I had to marry her.' He stared at her intently. 'Am I getting through to you?'

She returned his stare. 'You mean she was having a baby?'

'Hip, hip, hooray! The penny's dropped at last. You were supposed to be good at arithmetic but you hadn't worked that out.'

Margaret felt the blood rush to her face, remembering how she had fought the urges inside her when they were young. Dear Lord, the times she had wanted to melt into him. Once they had almost made love. It had been a May afternoon out in the country near Speke. The air had been rich with the intoxicating scent of hawthorn blossom. They had cycled there, picnicked and lain among the buttercups. How they'd kissed, biting kisses because they were so hungry for each other, but in the end he had pulled back and insisted they cycle home. Now he had the nerve to tell her that he had been unable to resist Bella. Oh, the pain of that thought! Much worse than when he'd married Bella, because she had believed herself in love with Alan. She felt angrier than she had ever been before.

'Get out of my shop! I don't want you here! Haven't you hurt me enough?'

'I never meant to hurt you!'

She came from the other side of the counter. 'That's the trouble. You don't think!' She pushed him, and he staggered back, almost fell over but managed to grab the display cabinet and steady himself.

'Maggie, will you listen to me?'

'I don't want to listen to you anymore. You'd probably tell me a pack of lies just to get round me.' She flung open the door. 'Out! I never want to see you again.' She trembled with the strength of her emotions.

His face screwed up in disbelief. 'Maggie, listen, please? I want to marry you.'

'What – marry *you*? I wouldn't have you if you were the last man on earth.' She shot out an arm and pointed outside. 'Now go!'

'God! You're unforgiving!' He released his hold on the cabinet, pulled back his shoulders, and with his eyes fixed on the doorway he walked carefully towards it, not looking at her as he went out.

She closed the door and bolted it top and bottom before resting her back against it. She took several deep breaths trying to calm down. How dare he ask her to marry him!

The latch rattled and someone tried to push the door open. When it did not give way, a voice called, 'Aunt Margaret, it's me. Mr Brodie's collapsed on the pavement!'

'Then get him up! He's been drinking.'

'I can't get him up. He seems dazed. I think he's banged his head.'

Margaret had an urge to swear, burst into tears, kick the door, but she unlocked it instead.

Rita was kneeling on the pavement, clasping William's hand.

'Here, darlin'! I'll be helping yer up with him,' said a big burly Irishman.

Margaret watched as they got William to his feet. 'He's not coming in here. Take him home.'

'You're hard, Maggie.' His words were slurred.

'What's going on?' said Rita, gazing at her aunt's flushed face.

'Never you mind. Just get him away from here.'

The Irishman looked at Rita. 'I can't be helping yer any further, girl. I've got to get to the docks. Will yer be orlright with him, yerself?'

'It's OK. Thanks,' said Rita. But immediately the Irishman let go of William she had a struggle holding him up. She stared at Margaret. 'Why can't he come in? What's he done?'

'Nothing to do with you,' said her aunt harshly. She went back into the shop and slammed the door.

CHAPTER NINE

Rita helped William to rest against the shop window and peered inside but her aunt had already vanished into the back.

'Never you mind her,' said William, smoothing back a lock of hair that had stuck to the graze on his forehead. 'I'll get off home.'

He pushed himself away from the window and began to walk in the direction of Berry Street, but was swaying so much that Rita ran after him, and without a word, dragged one of his arms about her neck and placed her arm about his waist. 'Thanks,' he muttered.

'You're welcome.'

They reached the bread shop on Berry Street before Rita said to rest before crossing into Leece Street. He slumped against a wall, his eyes shut. Worried about him, she glanced at passers-by, looking for a likely helper. Then she spotted the padre from the Sailors' Home crossing the road near St Luke's. She darted towards him and seized his arm. 'Padre, you've got to help me. I've Billy Brodie's father here and he's had a fall. I need to get him home.'

The padre wasted no time asking questions but went with her to where William rested. He looked at his grazed forehead, smelt his breath, then hoisted him upright.

William opened his eyes and squinted at the padre. 'Jerry! What are you doing here?' he slurred, then his head lolled to one side and his eyes closed.

Rita looked across at the padre. 'You know each other?'

'From way back, lass.' He smiled. 'Now, are you sure you can manage him that side?'

She chuckled. 'With your help it'll be a doddle.'

It was not that easy, especially as William kept falling over his own feet, but they reached the yard and got him to the house.

Alice opened the door and as soon as Rita saw her tear-stained face, she knew what had happened and felt sympathy for the whole family.

Alice stared at the clergyman. 'Padre, what are you doing here? What's wrong with Pops?' She reached out a hand to William.

'He fell outside our shop,' said Rita.

'If you could step aside, Alice, we'll get him inside,' said the padre.

'It's been terrible these last few days. I'm so glad you're here.' Alice led the way along a passage to the back of the house and into a large room with windows either end. It was furnished with a shabby but comfortable-looking sofa and two easy chairs; the remains of a meal were on a dining table over by a window that looked out on a paved area. William was lowered into one of the chairs by a blazing fire.

'I felt cold,' said Alice, as if she felt the need to explain the fire being lit on a warm summer day. 'Did Pops tell you Mother's passed away?' Her eyes were large and sad in her wan face.

'No. I am sorry,' said Rita, going over to her and touching her gently on the shoulder.

Alice's eyes filled with tears. 'Jimmy's taken it really bad. He's gone off and I don't know what to do. Pops vanished too, and the funeral needs arranging.'

'Don't you worry, my dear,' said the padre, a hand on the back of William's chair. 'You go and have a lie down and I'll talk things over with him.'

'Thanks!' Alice sighed. 'I don't know what to do about Billy. Could you get in touch with his ship? Pops might change his mind about having him here now Mother's dead. He'd cheer me up.' She dabbed at her eyes with a handkerchief.

'I'll see what William says,' said the padre.

'Perhaps you could go up with her, my dear,' he added to Rita.

'Yes, please, do come with me,' said Alice, clutching Rita's arm. 'I don't want to be on my own.'

Rita knew she should be getting back to the shop, but how could she leave when the girl obviously wanted her to stay? They went upstairs. Inside the bedroom Alice kicked off her shoes, undid the button of her skirt and sat on the bed. She picked up a framed photograph from the bedside table, gazed at it, then lay down and closed her eyes with it clutched to her.

Rita perched on the edge of the bed, glad to get off her feet. She eased back aching shoulders and glanced round the room. There seemed no lack of money here. She had never seen so many ornaments, frills and so much pink in one small space. The curtains, the bedcover, pillowcases and skirt around the dressing table were all made from the same floral material. A vase on the glass-topped dressing table caught her eye. It looked familiar and she got up to have a closer look.

'Don't go,' cried Alice.

'I'm not going! I'm just looking out of the window to see if there's any sign of Jimmy.' She went over and picked up the vase. It looked very much like the one that Alice had brought into the shop and had been stolen. Could Billy have brought her another one to replace it? No, he couldn't have known about the theft when he came home. He wouldn't have had the time to bring her another. Besides, would she have told him that she had sold it? If this was the same one, then that meant that Alice knew the person who had broken into the shop. There was only one person who Rita could think of who had promised to get it back for her – and that was Jimmy in that conversation she'd overheard here in the yard.

'You like my vase?'

Rita almost jumped out of her skin. She looked at Alice, sitting up against the pillows, staring at her. 'Yes, it's—'

'The exact replica of the one I sold to your aunt. Billy brought me another.'

'So you told him you sold it?'

'No! He-he just brought it to match the other one. He hasn't been in this room so he doesn't know I sold it.'

Rita was starting to feel confused but she did have a vague feeling that Billy had been told about the break-in at the shop and that a Chinese vase brought in by Alice had been stolen. She thought she remembered him mentioning it to her.

'He's very generous, is Billy.' Alice glanced at the photograph and then closed her eyes. 'You can go now if you want. Thanks for helping with Pops. I'll tell Jimmy you were here, and you will come to the funeral, won't you? I'm sure he'd like you to be there.'

'Yes, OK.'

Rita replaced the vase and left the bedroom. Downstairs she found William looking much better. The padre was there and they were drinking tea. 'I'll go now,' she said. 'I'm sorry about your wife, Mr Brodie.'

'Thanks, Rita, you're a good girl. I really appreciate your help.' William smiled warmly.

'You're welcome, as I said.' She laced her hands behind her back and shuffled her feet. 'I'm sorry about my aunt's behaviour.'

'Forget it. I upset her – a misunderstanding, I'm sure. Is Alice OK?'

Rita nodded.

The padre looked at her, a twinkle in his eyes. 'Shall I give Miss Turner your regards? She's mentioned your name several times when I've visited her.'

Rita felt uncomfortable, wondering just what her former teacher had said to him. She said *tarrah* and let herself out of the house, still wondering about the Chinese vase and whether Alice had told her the truth.

As she neared the shop Rita wondered what kind of reception she would get from her aunt. She was relieved to find the door unlocked and Margaret serving a customer. She told Rita to put the kettle on.

Five minutes later Margaret entered the kitchen. 'Well, did you see him home?'

'Yes. The padre from the Sailors' Home helped me with him. It seems they know each other.'

'Not surprising, I suppose. William was a seaman at one time and was bound to have dropped in there at some time or other.' She shrugged. 'Now you're back I don't want you having anything to do with them up at the yard. I'll see to William when he calls here next.'

Rita banged her cup on the table. 'What's he done to make you act like this? His wife's just died. You should be showing some compassion. I felt embarrassed and ashamed when you shut the door on him. I'd come to believe you were a nicer person than that!'

'I won't have you criticising me like this!' Margaret sat down and gazed into the fire. 'You're like your mother; a man only has to smile at you and you'll go chasing after him.'

Rita was indignant. 'That's not true.'

'Isn't it? You keep away from the Brodie family or you'll be out on your ear.'

'Jimmy's not a Brodie. His sister said his mother's death has affected him deeply and I said I'd go to the funeral.'

'He has his sister. Let her fuss over him.'

'She needs help, too.'

Margaret's expression was uncompromising. Her hurt and anger had not abated and, if William had fallen flat on his face in front of her right now, she would have left him lying there. She could not forgive him for what he had done with Bella and she intended making him suffer. She looked at her niece and decided it might be useful to have a spy in William's camp. So she said that she could go to the funeral and be a friend to Alice.

When Rita saw Jimmy at the funeral her heart went out to him in his grief. If she could have suffered for him she would have. It seemed impossible to think that he could have anything to do with the stolen vase. It had to be as Alice had said.

In the weeks that followed there did not seem anything Rita could do to cheer Jimmy up. When she mentioned that to her aunt, Margaret said sharply, 'You can't cheer people up when they've lost someone they love. The Bible has that right, at least. You have to weep with those who weep or at least give them a bit of peace and quiet and time to come to terms with their loss.' She put a hand to her breast. 'I've been through it so I know.'

The girl sighed and went to rearrange the shop window. She determined to be patient with Jimmy, who only spoke to her in monosyllables and did not seem to care if he saw her or not. But she had to believe that one day all would come right. At least it was a lovely day. The autumn sun was glinting on a brass bowl that Rita had polished earlier. She found such tasks soothing and they left her mind free to wander, not only to think about Jimmy and her aunt's antagonism towards William, but also about Sam and his not getting in touch, as well as her mother and the little brother she had never seen. Why couldn't people write?

A knock on the window drew her attention to the man standing outside. She smiled in surprised delight at Billy. 'Had a good trip?' she mouthed.

He vanished to reappear at her side. 'Not bad. Is your aunt around?'

'She's in the back but I'll tell you now that she might be very short with you. She's fallen out with your father. Have you something to sell?'

He patted his pocket and she did a double-take, noticing that instead of his reefer jacket he was wearing a navy pinstriped suit. 'Why, you're all done up to the nines!' She fingered the sleeve. 'You didn't have this made at the Fifty-Shilling Tailors.'

'No, Hong Kong. Like it?' He did a turn.

'Is that Billy's voice I hear?' Margaret came out of the storeroom and for a moment stared at him in silence, stirred by memories. 'What's the suit in aid of? Got yourself a girl?'

He grinned, his teeth white in his tanned face. 'Can't get anything past you, can I?'

Shock quivered down Rita's spine. What kind of girl would he fancy . . . a blue-eyed blonde? According to her mother men preferred blondes. 'Where did you meet her?'

'Gibraltar. She's part of an all-girls band entertaining the passengers on one of those cheap cruises the White Star Line started up. You mightn't have known that their ships were lying in dock a few years back, men laid off, because the rich could no longer afford luxury cruises.'

'How old is she?' Margaret raised her eyebrows. 'If I was a parent I'd think twice about letting my daughter go off like that.'

'She hasn't got a mother and her father's with the army in India. Her ship'll be docking in Liverpool this week.'

'So where'll she be staying?' asked Rita.

Billy grimaced and rattled the change in his pocket. 'That's something I've got to sort out. She's paid buttons so it's got to be cheap. I offered to sub her but she refused.'

'Well, that's something in her favour,' said Margaret. 'I don't suppose you've been up to your father's yard.'

'No, I'm staying at the Sailors' Home – and yes, I know my stepmother's dead. The padre wired me but I couldn't get home any quicker.'

'Jimmy and Alice really miss her. Don't you think you should go up there? Your father's attitude towards you might have changed since your stepmother's death,' said Rita, thinking that he really suited a tan. Lucky girlfriend!

'Ever the optimist, Rita?' She felt the colour rise

in her cheeks. 'But perhaps I should have a bit of your faith.' Billy slipped a hand into his pocket and brought out a package. 'But first things first.'

Margaret reached for her spectacles and the scissors. She snipped the string. 'By the way, your father hasn't paid me any money for three weeks.'

'If that's a hint for me to hand over some of the money from this to pay his debts then you can forget it. I have plans for it.'

'You want to wine and dine your lady-love, do you?' Margaret was distracted momentarily from the carved piece of jade.

'Something like that. She's seen a bit of life and is used to getting out and about.'

'Then I'll be sending in the bailiffs. You can tell him that, if you change your mind about seeing him.'

'I'll mention it to Alice as I'll definitely be seeing her, but it's not going to make her happy.'

Margaret stiffened. 'That's not my problem. Now, this piece of jade, I can offer you . . .' She named a sum. He laughed and she told him that he could go elsewhere if he wasn't happy with the price. He stared at her. 'Rita said you and Dad have fallen out. No need to take it out on me. I'm on your side. Did he take someone else's side against you? That's what he did to me.'

'Something like that,' said Margaret.

'What were his reasons?' said Rita.

They both stared at her and it was as if they

drew together, forming an alliance and, turning their backs on her, began to barter amicably until they settled on a price.

Billy took his money and said that it was nice doing business with them and with a wink at Rita he left.

Two days later a shapely young woman wearing a bum-hugging scarlet coat and a black cloche hat decorated with a small bunch of cherries, entered the shop. She was carrying a musical instrument case. Rita was dealing with a customer so gave her only a cursory glance, but when she placed it on the counter, Rita said, 'D'you mind, love? I need that space.'

'Sor-ree! But my arm's killing me and I don't want to put it on the floor.' She flashed a wide smile and Rita noticed she was wearing lipstick and her eyebrows were pencilled.

'Just shift it over a bit, then? I'll be with you soon.'

'Fine!' The girl moved the musical instrument case a few inches and then from a pocket took a packet of Woodbines and lit up, drawing in a lungful of smoke with a sigh of satisfaction. 'My nerves are shot to pieces. Some of those passengers on the liners are enough to send you up the wall.'

Rita paused, then continued writing out the customer's pawn ticket. As soon as the woman left the shop she turned to the girl. 'You've come off a ship?'

'That's right!' She flashed her wide smile again. 'Girls Quintet. Only we've split up now because two of them have met men and are getting married and the other two have gone home to see their families. I want to stay in Liverpool.'

What were the odds against a girl musician off a liner coming in here a couple of days after Billy had mentioned one? And if this one was Billy's girl, then it was as she thought. Blonde curls peeped out from beneath her hat and she had baby-blue eyes.

'Remember me next time, will you?' said the girl with a twinkle.

Rita did her best to twinkle back. 'Sorry! But would I be wrong in thinking you know Billy Brodie?'

'Nope! He sent me here. I want to pawn this.' She patted the case on the counter. 'I'm a bit short of ready cash.'

'Aren't most that come in here?' said Rita, wanting to like the girl for Billy's sake. Instead she felt rip-roaringly jealous of her clothes, her make-up and the fact that she was going to be wined and dined by Billy while she languished, waiting for Jimmy to notice her again. She unfastened the case and saw that it contained a saxophone and her interest was stirred. 'Do you play jazz?' She had heard snatches of what her aunt called 'jungle music' when passing Crane's music store in town.

'Amongst other things. Why, do you like music?'

'I listen to the wireless. I'll have to call my aunt as I've no idea what this is worth. I take it you'll be going out with Billy tonight?'

'Too right.' The girl's eyes were lively and she stretched languidly. 'I could do with a good dinner and some smoochy dancing.' She flicked ash on the floor.

Rita experienced another dart of envy. She'd never learnt to dance and what wouldn't she give to be able to do so. Everyone was doing it and in all kinds of places. She had seen couples dancing the Black Bottom and the Charleston in the streets during summer, and in the park some girls had being doing the Bunny Hop, as well as the kind of dance exercises encouraged by the Health and Fitness Movement.

Rita found Margaret in the kitchen talking to Mrs Richards, who had taken over from Mrs McGinty. The new char was a widow who was rearing her granddaughter, an orphan. She told her aunt about the latest customer and, curious to see this girl of Billy's, Margaret hurried into the shop. Her eyebrows rose at the sight of her. 'So, you're Billy's girl!'

'That's right!' She treated Margaret to one of her wide smiles. 'He said you'd be fair. It's in good nick.' Her touch on the saxophone was like a caress. 'My mother was musical and encouraged my brother and I to follow in her footsteps, but Sandy prefers acting and has just joined a travelling theatre company.'

'Very interesting,' said Margaret without any change of expression, and named a sum.

The girl's face fell and suddenly she appeared much younger and vulnerable. 'Oh, come on! It's worth more than that!'

'Probably, but if you don't reclaim it I might end up with it on my hands. We don't have much call for saxophones round here.'

'But I have every intention of reclaiming it once my brother arrives in Liverpool. Couldn't you forward me a little more because I'm a friend of Billy's?'

'Ha! You think that's a recommendation? This is a business I'm running.'

'But he said you'd help me.' Her voice quivered.

'I think we should,' said Rita.

'We?' said Margaret, giving her niece a look that should have silenced her.

'Yes! But not necessarily by offering her more money.' She looked at the girl. 'Have you found somewhere to stay yet?'

'No. That's why I need money. You don't finish a cruise with plenty of dough in your pocket, because the shipping line provides you with bed and food but not much money. We might have been a bit of a novelty but . . .' She dropped her cigarette stub on the floor and ground it out with a heel.

'You can stop that for a start,' said Margaret, frowning. 'Pick it up.'

The girl apologised.

Rita turned to Margaret. 'Couldn't we put her up? We've got rooms to spare upstairs.'

'Have you gone out of your mind?' said Margaret, looking fierce. 'We don't even know this girl's name.'

'It's Ellen. Ellen Hannay. And listen . . .' she added with a wave of her hand. 'I can understand you thinking I might be desperate enough to steal but I was brought up to be honest. You could trust me with the crown jewels.'

'Well, you're safe saying that, aren't you?' said Margaret. 'Fat chance of you getting your hands on them. Still . . .' She eyed the girl up and down before glancing at Rita.

She had been hanging on to every word, fingers crossed, having decided it would be fun to have another girl about the place. Maybe she could learn something from her.

'I could pay something,' said Ellen, taking out her cigarette packet and then thinking twice about lighting up with Margaret's eye on her. 'And I'll help about the place.'

'I suppose I could move the chest of drawers and bed out of Donald's room,' muttered Margaret. 'Although my mother would turn in her grave if she could see me.'

Ellen's face lit up. 'Thanks! I really appreciate this. How much will you want?'

'You buy your own food and give me a shilling a

189

week towards lighting and heating. I have a cleaning woman but there's still plenty to do that you could help with.'

'Right!' Rita clapped her hands and smiled. 'We'll get moving the bed. Which room shall I put her in?'

'Business first,' said her aunt, reaching for the pawn tickets. 'And I'm telling you now, I'll not have you using Miss Hannay's presence to skive off work. Now go and make a pot of tea.'

Rita hurried into the scullery. As she poured milk into cups and buttered the scones she had made yesterday, she was thinking of other ways in which she could use Ellen to bring fun into her own life. Over a cup of tea, Rita suggested that Ellen might like to entertain the cinema queues with her saxophone. 'I could accompany you on the squeeze box we've got in stock.'

Ellen giggled. 'You're joking! Picture us among those poor unemployed men with their fiddles, trumpets and baritone voices. Besides, I've just hocked it. No! I'll find some other way to earn money.'

'Perhaps Billy might have some ideas.'

Ellen looked amused. 'He knows nothing about music so I wouldn't ask him.'

'Why didn't he come here with you?'

'Because he booked me into a guest house and I had to be out by ten. He was supposed to be there by then but didn't turn up. I wasn't going to hang around so I left a message telling him where I'd gone and put my suitcase in the left luggage at Lime Street.'

'I wonder what's happened to him? He might have gone up to the yard and been delayed.'

'What yard?' asked Ellen, looking surprised.

'His father's yard. He's in the carting business.'

Ellen shrugged. 'Didn't know he had a father. I presumed when he didn't talk about his parents that they were dead.'

It was Rita's turn to be surprised. 'His mother's dead but his father's very much alive, but they don't get on. He has a stepbrother and stepsister. Surely he told you about them?'

'He told me nothing,' said Ellen cheerfully. She held out her cup for a refill. 'But then I didn't ask. Don't we all fall out with our relatives at some time or other? Any more scones?'

Billy turned up an hour later and seemed on edge, but when Ellen told him that she was going to stay with Rita and Margaret, he seemed pleased. 'That's great! But how did you persuade Miss Sinclair?'

'It was Rita.' Ellen tucked her hand in Billy's arm and smiled at Rita.

'That's real good of you,' said Billy, and he kissed Rita's cheek. 'You're a real pal.'

'What are friends for?' said Rita, trying to sound cheerful, but she felt forlorn seeing the two of them together. A few minutes later they went to collect Ellen's luggage from the station.

Rita was all knotted up inside so found the brass cleaner and set about polishing the brasses with an energy that would have delighted her aunt if she had been there to see it.

The atmosphere in the household changed with the advent of Ellen. She liked a laugh and had plenty of anecdotes about people she had met and the places she had seen. Even Margaret could not conceal her interest and amusement.

Billy became a regular visitor. The first day of Ellen's stay he arrived at nine in the morning, only to be told firmly by that young lady that she was an owl not a lark and to come back later. He took to calling just before lunch and did not return with Ellen until five o'clock. Then he would return at eight to take her out for the rest of the evening.

Rita found his coming and going as unsettling as Ellen's presence. At the end of a long day's work Ellen would come and sit on Rita's bed and talk about the places Billy had taken her to, such as the State Restaurant in Dale Street. She told her the title of every tune the little orchestra had played and would drag her out of bed and onto the landing to teach her the dances she and Billy had performed. Margaret came out of her bedroom to complain, but that did not stop the girls for long. The next night they did the same thing all over again until Rita knew every dance step going. At least it compensated for seeing little of Jimmy. Then Billy's money ran out;

in no time at all he was signing on again and was back at sea.

Rita expected Ellen to be down in the dumps once he had gone, and it was true she was subdued for a couple of days. But on the third day Margaret asked what were her plans.

'Oh Lor'! Have I worn my welcome out already?' said Ellen ruefully. 'I'll leave if you want me to but I've nowhere to go. You can't imagine what it's like not having a proper home and this feels so like home.'

'You can cut the soft soap,' said Margaret, her eyes speculative as they rested on the girl. 'You haven't handed over your shilling this week and you've been eating our food. So you're out on your ear unless you hand over some money and I see food in the larder bought by you. Now, I've some business to attend to elsewhere. When I get back I'll expect you to have done something about both these things. Keep your eye on the shop, Rita.'

After Margaret had gone, Ellen said mournfully, 'I wanted to stay here until Sandy comes to Liverpool with the theatre group. Once they arrive I can move in with him and hopefully get some work with the group.'

'When will that be?'

'A week, or is it two? It's difficult keeping in touch with him moving around, but he wired the ship a month or so ago with his schedule so I'd know where to find him.'

'How about a job in a factory? I heard there's some going at Barker & Dobson, the sweet factory in Anfield. There'll be plenty of girls queuing up for jobs but my aunt could put in a good word for you. She knows a few people of influence.'

Ellen grimaced. 'I've only ever wanted to be a musician or a rich man's wife. I can't see me making Everton mints or chocolates.'

Suddenly Rita felt exasperated. 'You'll have to do something! You heard Aunt Margaret.'

Ellen sighed and then said softly, 'Do you think while your aunt's out I could play my saxophone? Sometimes I come up with some really good ideas when I'm playing.'

Anything to get her doing something! thought Rita.

As luck would have it, half an hour later the padre came into the shop. He and Rita greeted each other like old friends and then he asked to see her aunt, which surprised her. 'She's not in. Anything I can do?'

He smiled. 'No. I need to speak to her.'

'Would you like a cup of tea while you wait? She mightn't be long.'

He thanked her. When she reappeared with the tea and biscuits, he appeared to be listening, his head held to one side. 'Who's the musician?' he asked.

She told him about Ellen and her need for a job.

'Know any other musicians, does she?'

'She used to play in a group but they broke up.'

He looked thoughtful. 'Alice Brodie can play the piano and sing. I've been trying to persuade her for some time to come and entertain the sailors at the club. She needs to get out of that house, according to what Billy said last time he was home. Maybe it would be a good idea if the two young ladies got together.'

'Would you pay them for playing?' said Rita.

He smiled. 'We could work something out.'

'Right!' She took a deep breath. 'I'll go and get Ellen.'

In no time at all Ellen was charming the padre while Rita listened. By the time they had finished talking Ellen had been hired – if she could persuade Alice to join her. Rita wanted to say *What about me?* She could picture herself playing the squeeze box, but didn't have the nerve.

As soon as the padre had gone, Ellen dragged Rita into the back of the shop. 'What do you think?'

'I think it's a great idea!' She found her nerve. 'But if she doesn't want to do it, I can play the squeeze box a bit.'

'Oh!' Ellen appeared startled by the idea. 'Well . . . perhaps! Although the padre seems keen on this stepsister of Billy's playing; it would please him, wouldn't it?' Rita could not deny that. 'You'll come with me to the yard?' said Ellen.

Rita did not need asking twice if there was a chance of seeing Jimmy – and it was near enough to lunch to close the shop.

CHAPTER TEN

As soon as they entered the yard, Rita spotted Jimmy talking to the man she had seen in the yard the day before his mother died. Her heart went out to him and she touched Ellen's sleeve. 'There's Jimmy. What d'you think?'

'I'd need a closer look,' said Ellen, narrowing her eyes. 'Billy told me about him but they'd fallen out over something so we've never met.'

'Shush! He's coming over.' Rita's heartbeat quickened and she moved towards him, only to realise as she got closer that his expression was surly. She wondered what had upset him now. 'How are you? It seems ages since I've seen you.' She could not conceal her concern and took his arm.

'I'm OK!' He removed her hand, leaving a smear of black polish on the back of it. 'Who's she? And what's that she's carrying?'

'Her name's Ellen. She's Billy's girl and a musician. The padre thought that she and Alice could get together and—'

Before she could finish, he went over to Ellen. She held out a hand. 'You must be Jimmy! Billy's told me such a lot about you.'

'I can imagine.' He gazed at her from beneath hooded tawny eyebrows. 'Rita shouldn't have brought you here. Alice has enough to do in the house. You'd best go.' He turned away abruptly and walked towards the stables.

Ellen's expression would have been comical if Rita had been in a mood to see a funny side to Jimmy's behaviour. 'I don't know what's got into him,' said Rita, flushing with hurt, embarrassment and anger.

'Well! I can tell you what I think of him now, Rita. He's rude and you're wasting your time with him. Come on, let's go! We'll see how you play the accordion.'

It was what Rita wanted but she found herself shaking her head. 'No! Let's see what Alice has to say. I think the padre's right in saying she needs to get away from this house.'

The front door was ajar. Rita knocked but when no one came she walked right in, followed by Ellen. Hearing voices, they headed in the direction of the sound. Rita knocked on the door of the room where she and the padre had taken William.

The voices stopped and then the door was wrenched open. Alice stood there. Her normally pale face was pink and there were lines of discontent about her mouth. Her wispy fair hair looked like it had not been brushed that morning. 'What do you want?' she said crossly.

Rita was amazed at the change in her. 'Sorry to disturb you but the padre from the Sailors' Home thought it a good idea if we came to see you.'

'Oh!' Alice looked past her to Ellen. 'I've seen your photograph. You're Billy's girl. Come on in. Ignore anything Pops says. He's been drinking.'

'Perhaps we should come another time,' said Ellen, but Rita seized her sleeve. 'No! He's not going to harm you. Tell Alice why you're here.'

'The padre thought you might be interested in forming a duo with me,' said Ellen.

Alice's mouth trembled. 'Is-is this a joke?'

Ellen said cheerfully. 'Far from it, ducks! Shall we discuss it?'

'OK! You'd best come in. We're standing in a draught.'

After the freshness of the air outside, the room felt stuffy and yet at the same time damp. It appeared less tidy and gloomier than the last time Rita had been here. Maybe that was because the two sash windows were shrouded in nets.

'Who is it?' The words were slurred and came from the figure slumped in a winged armchair near the fireplace.

'Nobody you need bother yourself with, Pops,' said Alice.

'I'll decide that. Put the light on! It's dark in here. I want to see their faces.'

'It's me, Mr Brodie,' said Rita, going over to him. 'How are you?'

The face turned up to hers was haggard and in his hand he held a half-full glass of what looked like whisky. Then slowly he smiled. 'Ah, it's Maggie's niece. The witch has been here today on her broomstick, spitting out fire and brimstone. We had a lively quarrel.' He reached out a hand to Rita. 'But you're not going to spit at me, are you? You helped me that time when I fell outside the shop.'

'No, I'm not going to do anything of the sort,' she said, taking the hand he offered, which was calloused, hot and dry.

'What are you doing here?'

'I'm here with Ellen, a . . . a friend.' She thought it best not to mention Billy. 'The padre thinks Alice might like to entertain the sailors with her.'

William made a noise in his throat, which was a cross between a snort and a laugh. 'I presume you don't mean that how it sounds. Jerry might be a fool in some ways but I really don't think he's in the business of procuring girls for sailors.'

'Oh no!' Rita flushed and laughed remembering the padre rescuing her from the attentions of the fluke who had been a pimp. 'It's to do with music. Ellen plays the saxophone and used to be part of a girls' band.'

'So she's come for Alice.' He drew a deep breath. 'Make her go. It'll be good for her.'

Rita was pleased. 'You don't mind her performing in a roomful of sailors?'

'No worse than a roomful of missionaries.' He took a gulp of whisky and held it in his mouth for a moment before swallowing it. 'I have a brother in holy orders, you know? Maggie thought he was a bloody saint but he was only human like the rest of us. If only she'd accepted that, he wouldn't be where he is and I wouldn't be here. This place is bleeding me dry and soon there'll only be my bones left. I gave Jimmy money to pay your aunt but she says she hasn't had it and is asking me for it over again. I thought I could trust her to be fair and honest with me but she's got it in for me, so whatever I say she's not going to believe me.' He drained his glass and, lifting his arm, he flung it at the fireplace. The sound of the tumbler shattering caused Alice to come swiftly over to them.

'What did you do that for, Pops?' She turned on Rita. 'What have you been saying to him? Isn't it enough that we've had your aunt here today?'

'She's not here about money,' said William, struggling to his feet and placing an arm about Rita's shoulders. 'She's got a heart . . . must have to still be living with Maggie . . . and she must be behaving herself because Maggie has high standards.' He removed his arm from about Rita's shoulders. 'You have my permission to go and entertain the sailors, Alice.' He left them to meander across the room and managed to get through the doorway and close the door behind him.

'He's killing himself,' said Alice, dabbing her eyes with a handkerchief. 'It's losing Mother. Jimmy's always so angry, not only with Billy and Pops but me as well.'

'And me,' said Rita, feeling better because Jimmy's anger wasn't solely directed at her. She smiled. 'But Mr Brodie said you could play and that's good.'

'Yes! It would be if we could practise here but we got rid of the piano ages ago.' Her voice shook and tears filled her eyes. 'What's going to happen to us? I heard your aunt threaten him with the bailiffs.'

Rita remembered her aunt making that threat when Billy had turned up with the piece of jade but apparently she hadn't done anything about it until now. Why? She thought about Mr Brodie just telling her that he had sent money with Jimmy. Who was telling the truth? Was it how he had said and her aunt wasn't being honest and fair with him because she held something against him from their past? She made a decision. 'I'll speak to her. Can Ellen stay with you while I sort something out?'

'But what can you do?' cried Alice, twisting her handkerchief between her fingers. 'As soon as the money comes in, it goes out. We've none to spare and it's money she wants.'

'Then it's money she'll get,' said Rita in a soft voice.

Rita emptied the half-crowns, thrupenny bits, sixpences and shillings in a silver stream onto the table to the accompaniment of the crackling fire.

Margaret looked up from her magazine and stared at the glistening heap. 'What's this for?'

'For Mr Brodie's payments that are due. That should keep the bailiffs away a bit longer.'

Margaret's dark eyes rested on Rita's set face. 'So you've been up to the yard.'

'Yes! The padre thinks Ellen and Alice could form a duo and entertain the sailors. He came here to see you.'

'Me?'

'Yes, but never mind that now. I found Mr Brodie drunk and talking about you not believing he had sent money through Jimmy. He said that you've got it in for him. Alice is in a state because she thinks they're going to be put out on the street.'

Margaret's eyes sparkled. 'If he can drink it shows he's got money. The money he says he sent with that stepson of his! Well, I've seen no money, and I'm sure if you had, then you'd have written it in the ledger. Will's lying! He thinks because it's me that he owes money to I'll keep on giving him more time to pay.'

'He doesn't!'

'Well, there's a limit to my patience . . . and you're only encouraging him in that belief, so put your money away.'

Rita made no move to do what Margaret said, but instead tried to make sense of things. She would swear on the Bible that Mr Brodie had been telling the truth but, if he was, that could mean only one of two things – either her aunt was lying or Jimmy had kept hold of the money. Could her aunt be lying? It would be out of character, but this thing between her and Mr Brodie was making her really narky. The girl scooped up the coins and put them back in the tin, saying firmly, 'I still want to do it.'

'You'd go against me? Against the good advice I'm giving you?' Margaret was really annoyed. 'What about visiting Eve and your half-brother? That's not important to you now?'

'Yes! But it'll keep.' She shoved the tin across the table, a hand on the lid. 'Please, do what I say?'

Margaret made no move to take the money but wrinkled her nose. 'What's that smell?'

'Don't change the subject!'

'Can't you smell it?' Margaret brought her head down and sniffed Rita's hand. 'It's you! What's that on your hand?'

The girl rubbed at the stain. 'Polish. I thought I'd got it off but it's strong stuff.'

'It's a wonder you couldn't smell it, but perhaps you haven't got my nose.'

'I did and tried to wash it off.'

'You need a touch of spirit.'

'OK! I'll see to it!' cried Rita exasperated. 'Now, the money – will you take it, please, Aunt Margaret?'

She scowled. 'You're not doing this for the girl or Will. It's that lad – because it's him who's desperate to hang on to that yard.' She rested her hands on the table. 'Listen to me, Rita. Falling in love at your age will bring you nothing but trouble. I'd advise you to put Jimmy completely out of your mind.'

Rita removed a strand of copper-coloured hair out of her eyes. 'I'm doing it for them all. Take my money and do what I ask again, please?'

'You're still determined to go against what I say?'

Rita's stance was defiant, shoulders back, head held high. 'Yes!'

Margaret drew in her breath and there were two spots of colour high on her cheeks as she reached for the tin. 'I wish you wouldn't but perhaps you'll learn something from this. Fetch me the ledger! I also want to see the credit agreement. It's ages since I've had a look at it and I want to check exactly what I put in it.'

Rita went to do as she said but could not find the agreement. She looked through the file and then riffled through every other file in the drawer but it was not there. Puzzled, she hurried into the kitchen and placed the ledger on the table. 'I can't find the agreement.'

Margaret frowned. 'Have you gone through the whole drawer in case it was filed in the wrong place?'

'Yes! It's not there.' Rita sat across the table from her. 'It's a mystery.' She nibbled a fingernail.

'Don't bite your nails,' said Margaret automatically. 'I can't see it going missing just like that. Someone must have taken it.'

'Who?' As soon as she spoke Rita knew there was only one answer.

'Who's had access to the drawer? Which member of the family has been in the storeroom?'

'None of them,' said Rita.

'Then you must have taken it for them!'

Rita's eyes flashed with annoyance. 'You accused me once before of stealing and it was proved I was innocent. It wasn't me!'

'All right! Don't take offence. I believe you.' Margaret looked down at the ledger. 'We need to think this through carefully before we make a move. You do realise that without the agreement I only have the ledger as proof that Will is in debt to me. How much that could be counted as a legal document in a court of law I'm not sure.'

'You're not thinking of going to court over this?' said Rita, shocked. 'It was bad enough being called as a witness at Mr McGinty's trial.'

'Not at the moment; I was just thinking aloud. I can't make any sense of the different things that have been said and done today.' Margaret opened the ledger and her eyes lighted on Ellen's name. 'Where's Ellen?'

'She's up at the yard.' Rita explained about the padre overhearing her play the saxophone.

'You shouldn't have let her have it,' said Margaret. 'But it's done now.'

'So is it OK for her to borrow it? She needs to practice and make money and once she's done that she can pay you what she owes you.'

'I don't run this place as a charity, you know!'

'Don't I know it,' said Rita, tossing her head back. 'Anyway, her clothes are still here. Perhaps you can keep some of them as a pledge in place of the saxophone.'

'I will! And perhaps you can go up to the yard again and ask can they keep her there. Take her a change of clothes. You can also have a nose round Will's office.'

Rita gasped. 'I'm not going sneaking in there. Mr Brodie trusts me.'

Her remarks irritated Margaret. 'Then it should make it easier for you to gain access.'

'I'm not doing it,' said Rita, folding her arms and looking defiant.

'Then don't,' said Margaret, a quiver in her voice. 'Although it's about time you realised which side your bread's buttered on and were a bit more willing to do things for me. At least go and ask can Ellen stay up there. I want a bit of peace and quiet to count these coins. Although at the moment I can't see any point in taking this sum off the account. I'm expecting him to come in any minute and say he doesn't owe me anything. Although, if he had taken the agreement then he wouldn't have argued with me the way he did this morning.' Margaret wondered if the padre wanting to see her had anything to do with Will. Perhaps it wouldn't be a bad idea to tell him about the missing agreement if he knew the family and see what he thought.

Rita was glad to get away, and went upstairs and packed a couple of changes for Ellen, just in case Mr Brodie agreed to her staying there. She was going to miss her, but perhaps it was best she was out of Margaret's way if she was going to be playing the saxophone.

Alice could scarcely believe it when Rita told her that the family had a stay of execution. She promised to do her best to persuade her stepfather to stop drinking. 'Not that I haven't tried already,' she said earnestly.

'My aunt suggested that perhaps Ellen could stay here. Would that be possible?'

'We've been talking about it,' said Alice, her eyes shining. 'I've mentioned it to Pops and he said she'll be company for me. I could ask to use the piano in the church hall and we could rehearse there.'

With that sorted out, Rita went in search of Jimmy because there were several questions she wanted answers to. However, he had left the yard for the docks and would not return until that evening.

Rita poured a little methylated spirits on a piece of rag, but before using it to clean her hand, she sniffed at the stain again and her brow knitted. Could she be right? If she was, then something had to be done but she knew it was not going to be easy.

That night Rita had her old dream about Mr McGinty, although he was not the only suspicious character creeping about in her mind. She woke the following morning to the mournful sound of ships' foghorns on the river. For a moment she did not move, reluctant to get out of her warm bed, but her aunt was calling and there were things to be done.

The light was on in the kitchen and Rita could just about make out the shape of the galvanised bath hanging from its hook in the yard.

Margaret handed her the toasting fork and a round of bread. 'It's just the kind of weather to fill the graveyards. I'm going down to the Sailors' Home to have a word with the padre. I can't see it being busy here today.'

Rita's head jerked round as she was in the act of stabbing the bread with the toasting fork; the bread fell on the fire. 'Will you be back for lunch? I was going to go up to the yard.'

'Again! Had second thoughts of spying for me?'

'You could say that.' Rita blew black bits from the bread. 'Give my love to the padre,' she said with a mischievous smile.

'Huh! You're turning into a flirt just like your mother.' Margaret put on her coat and hat and hurried out of the kitchen.

Fog hung over the river like an old army blanket and Margaret stood a moment, a scarf covering her mouth and nose, thinking of the men she had cared about sailing away to distant lands, two of them never to return again.

Alan had been so resolute, his eyes alight with zeal. Determined to do what he could for his Lord in China. She had been as excited as he was, stirred by his fervour, wanting to be a partner with him in an adventure. His letters were few and far between because he was travelling about that great land, but when he settled for a while in Shanghai she had written to him asking when she could join him. His reply had never come. Instead, William had told her of his twin's death in an uprising. How devastated she had been, furious with William for not keeping Alan alive and closing the escape route from the humdrum life with her father. Now it was as if history was repeating itself. She had allowed herself to dream of marrying him for a while but his behaviour, echoing the past, had ruined the dream. She turned away from the river and made her way to Canning Place and the Sailors' Home.

Margaret stood on the multicoloured tiled floor in the rhomboidal court looking about her and half-wishing that she had not come. She felt out of place amongst the seamen coming and going about her. Most spared her a glance and quite a few winked at her. She supposed it was flattering in a way, not that any of these men were anything to write home about.

She looked at the clock attached to the wrought iron railing of the first-floor gallery and wondered how much longer the padre would be. Then someone touched her elbow and she started apprehensively, only to realise that the man at her side must be Father Jerome, who not only knew Rita, but William, Billy and Sarah Turner, her niece's former teacher.

'What can I do for you?' he said with a smile.

She gazed at the strong bones of his face and the prominent nose and returned his smile. 'You came to see me – but as it is there is something I want to ask you. Perhaps there is somewhere we can talk privately?'

'Certainly.' He inclined his head. 'A cup of tea in the kitchen? It's much warmer there than in my office.'

'That would be welcome.'

He led the way and soon they were seated at the corner of a well-scrubbed table, drinking tea and partaking of buttered toasted teacakes. She was hesitant at first to tell him what was bothering her.

He could be one of those clergy who looked down on her kind, bracketing her with the tax collectors in the Bible, yet she needed to speak to someone.

At first she stumbled over her words, but his manner was so attentive and sympathetic that soon she was telling him more about her troubles than she had ever told anyone else before. He let her talk without interruption.

When her voice finally tailed off, he said, 'I think you should go and see William and tell him the agreement has been stolen. It's a pity we don't know exactly when. I will say this because I am sure he is innocent. It can't be Billy, despite his having served on the reformatory ship, the *Akbar*, when he was twelve.'

This was news to Margaret. 'Was it for theft?'

The padre hesitated, then resting his elbows on the table, put his hands together as if in prayer and tapped them against his chin. 'No! Youthful high jinks! Destructive, nevertheless, and he had to be punished. There was a lot of anger in him when he was younger. I'm sure you know something of what it was like for him after his mother died.'

Margaret nodded. 'What was his crime?'

'He smashed nearly every window of Dunlop's rubber factory on Brownlow Hill. You know where I mean?'

She nodded. 'There was no doubt of his guilt?'

'No. He admitted it . . . was quite defiant. He's calmed down a lot since, all things considered.'

211

'What d'you mean by that?'

'He was banned from the house after his first trip. He had left the *Akbar*. Something about his being a bad influence on Alice and Jimmy. Most likely Jimmy did try and follow in Billy's footsteps. It's surprising what some lads find admirable. The stepmother was always more likely to believe her son innocent than Billy, whom she accused of theft on more than one occasion. Although a year or so ago she supposedly had a change of heart, but Billy said she was a hypocrite and wouldn't have anything to do with her. He always denied the thefts and I believe him. He is genuinely attached to his stepsister and was to Jimmy, until recently.'

'Why only until recently?'

The padre shrugged. 'That's something he chose to keep to himself.'

'What caused him and Will to fall out?'

'I've no idea. Apparently the rift between him and Billy started long before this last trouble. In fact Sarah Turner . . . you know Sarah, I believe?' Margaret nodded. 'Her mother knew the family, too, and apparently it started even before the first Mrs Brodie died.'

Margaret found all this very interesting. 'I knew Bella. I don't understand why there should be such antagonism between Will and his son. Unless . . .' She was remembering what William had told her about Bella being pregnant when they got married.

Perhaps he had felt trapped and resented the boy for that reason.

'Unless what?' prodded the padre gently.

She shook her head, tracing a pattern on the table with a finger. 'Just a thought. It's strange. Will spoke about having a son. He looked forward to showing him things. I think most men want a son.'

'Ahhh!' The padre smiled. 'Then I'm the exception. If I ever marry I would like a daughter. Girls are much less trouble. More biddable.'

'You think so?' Margaret's voice was dry. 'You have met my niece?'

'More than once.' There was a twinkle in his eyes. 'The first time she would have nothing to do with me.'

Margaret would have liked to know more about that meeting but decided now was not the right time to ask. Instead she said, 'So despite Billy's past you're convinced it wasn't him who stole the document? He was on shore leave at the time of the second break-in.'

The padre leant back in his chair. 'But not the first. I think we both have a fair idea about the person most likely to have taken it. The one who cares about the yard most! I repeat – have a word with William.'

'I will.' She glanced at the kitchen clock. 'I must get back. It's been very informative talking to you.'

'And you,' he said getting to his feet. 'I never

213

realised you knew the Brodie twins so well. I'll see you out.'

As they walked towards the door, he spoke about Sarah Turner. 'She's lonely since her mother died despite having a worthwhile job teaching and doing voluntary work here at the Home. Like you, she lost a fiancé. By the way – I met Alan.'

'You did!' She was amazed that he hadn't mentioned it before. 'Where?'

'Hong Kong. It was where I first became interested in the Seamen's Mission. Alan came in with William. Now, when was it? It only seems like yesterday.'

'It must be over fifteen years ago.'

'That long? Surely not!'

She nodded. He looked thoughtful. 'I remember they were arguing over something. It was incredible how alike they were.'

'Like two sides of a double-headed coin,' she murmured.

'We spoke at some length; both being in the same line of business, you might say.' He took her hand and patted it. 'I really would try and put the past behind you. People are seldom what we think they are. You could do with a woman friend with whom you could share your little worries. Sarah could be the very person.'

Margaret was not so sure about that, having never had a woman friend, so she just smiled and said, 'I believe you've asked Billy's girlfriend and stepsister to play at the Home.'

'Yes. I'm thinking of having an experimental dance. We've never had one before. Perhaps you'd like to come. The more women, the better.'

She thanked him and left the building. The fog still hung over Canning Place, and the sound of the ships' foghorns was just as mournful as before, but she was feeling a little better. Perhaps she would go up to the yard and have a talk with William sometime – but not today. After all, she had called him a liar to his face on more than one occasion, and he might slam the door in her face. She would wait and see what Rita had to say when she returned from the yard.

CHAPTER ELEVEN

Rita hunched her shoulders against the damp chill of the fog, burying her mouth and nose inside the fur collar of her coat. There had been little traffic on the roads and so she was hoping to find Jimmy at home. How to get him alone if the two girls and William were around could be a problem, but what she had to say was for his ears only.

She was in luck. Alice and Ellen had their heads together discussing music, and although they broke off to say hello, to ask how things were and thank her again for what she had done, it was obvious that they didn't really want to be interrupted. She asked after Jimmy's whereabouts.

'He and Pops are over in the stables. Something

about getting the place tidied up,' said Alice, smiling. 'I told Pops what you did for us and he knows Ellen is Billy's girlfriend.'

'What did he say to that?' asked Rita.

'He looked resigned,' said Ellen with a wink.

'But your speaking to your aunt has helped him to pull himself together, I'm sure,' said Alice. 'And he knows it'll be good for me having Ellen here.'

Rita left the house, uncertain whether she could carry out her plan. She could hardly order Mr Brodie out of the stables, but neither could she suggest to Jimmy they go for a walk in the fog. For a moment she considered returning to the shop without seeing him, but then decided that, as she was here, she might as well try and get him alone.

The fog deadened all sound so that it was not until Rita was outside the stables that she became aware of raised voices. The doors were shut so she put her eye to the gap in the middle and, although it was gloomy inside, was able to recognise William's back. She eased one of the doors open an inch.

He was standing beneath a hatch with his head flung back, speaking to someone in the loft. On either side of him were several bales of hay and, even as she watched, another dropped through the hatch and would have hit him if he had not dodged out of the way. 'Will you bloody be careful! Did you hear what I said?' shouted William.

'I'm not deaf!' Rita recognised Jimmy's voice.

'Well, what have you got to say for yourself? What did you do with the money I gave you for Miss Sinclair? She said she never got it. If it weren't for young Rita, the bailiffs would be here this morning and us out. So what the bloody hell do you think you're playing at?'

'I'm not playing at anything.' Jimmy's tone was sullen. 'I needed a harness mending and new boots. I knew you had no cash to spare so it would have been a waste of time asking you. Anyway, there's no need for you to worry about paying her.'

'What d'you mean by that?'

The sound of feet on the stairs which led up to the loft caused Rita to keep perfectly still so as not to draw attention to herself as Jimmy came into sight.

'I've had this by me for a while,' he said, producing a sheet of paper from a pocket in the bib of his overalls.

'What is it?' William glanced at the paper.

'It's all that stands between us and being free of debt,' said Jimmy earnestly. 'I had thought of burning it but I decided you might enjoy doing that. I took it from Miss Sinclair's filing cabinet. We can stop worrying! The business is safe. We could buy another horse or even that lorry you go on about. What other proof has she than this that you owe her money?'

'Bloody hell! What's got into you? Are you crazy? She doesn't need proof!' William's voice shook with anger. 'I know I owe her money! It's a debt of honour. I can't welch on the agreement I made with her. Especially after accusing her of being a cheat and a bloodsucking vampire. No wonder she called me a thief and a liar!'

Jimmy scowled. 'She's a moneylender! Probably has stacks of the stuff hidden away. What are you worried about?'

'It's dishonest! And I care what she thinks of me – that's what!'

'She doesn't think much of you from what Rita said to me. You gamble and drink and the old witch is really against you doing both. So why be so fussy about me doing a bit of thieving to save the yard?'

'My God!' cried William, raising his arm, but the blow stopped short a few inches from Jimmy's face. 'You say *you* stole it? Stealing from me might be one thing but breaking into a house – that's more Billy's style.'

Jimmy bristled. 'You think I haven't got the guts?'

'I don't know if you have or not because you haven't been tested but I just can't see you doing it.'

The younger man shrugged. 'What if I told you Billy took it for . . . for Alice's sake?'

'That sounds more like the truth. Even so, the agreement's going back. I won't welch on a deal.'

Rita heard the heavy tread of his boots coming towards her and sped away into the fog, which soon swallowed her up. She was angry with Jimmy for saying things about her that weren't true. Never had she said anything about his stepfather's gambling and drinking – and to say that Billy had stolen the agreement because he was fond of Alice, she didn't believe it.

As soon as Rita arrived at the shop, she told Margaret what she had overheard. 'You've done well, my little spy,' said her aunt. 'So I can expect a visit from William any time now?' There was a satisfied note in her voice.

Rita walked her fingers along the counter. 'Yes! Shall I make myself scarce so you can argue with him?'

Margaret's expression was severe as she looked over her spectacles. 'Who said anything about arguing? I'm sure Will and I can converse without losing our tempers. I'll invite him into the back while you look after any customers.'

Ten minutes later a grim-faced William entered the shop. He did not waste any time getting to the point. 'I'm sorry, Maggie, but this is yours I believe.' He placed the agreement on the counter.

She feigned surprise. 'What's this?' She picked up the paper and read the first few lines before lifting her head and staring at him. 'I presume this isn't your copy?'

'It's yours.' He dug his hands into his overcoat pockets and did a turnabout the shop before stopping in front of her. 'Billy took it. Jimmy's idea! He thought, without it, you'd have no proof I owed you anything. Thinking of ways to save the yard, you see.'

'No, I don't see.' Her brows knitted. 'What kind of man does he think you are, Will, that he'd believe you'd agree to such a scheme? You'd best come in the back so we can discuss this.' She unlocked the tiny bolt under the flap and lifted it up, trying to hide a smile at his incredulous expression.

'You're inviting me inside?'

'Why not? I can trust you to behave, can't I?'

'Yes, but . . .'

Margaret called Rita, who came hurrying out of the back. She stopped at the sight of William and smiled. 'Hello, Mr Brodie. I was up at your place earlier. You feeling better today? How's Jimmy? I was going to talk to him about polish but changed my mind.'

'Polish?' William looked baffled.

'That's enough, Rita!' Margaret's voice held a warning. 'You mind the shop.'

Rita sighed and, brushing past the two adults, went to do as she was told.

'Polish!' repeated William, following Margaret through the storeroom into the kitchen.

'Sit down, Will.' She waved him to one of the chairs in front of the fire and sat in the other.

He glanced about him. 'This reminds me of old times. It doesn't seem to have altered at all. I remember Jimmy asking me what it was like inside after he found out we knew each other when we were kids.'

That information caused Margaret's ears to prick

up. 'It hasn't altered. This room was repainted the same old cream time after time. After Father died I intended having the paint stripped off and the walls papered but now I'm thinking more along the lines of moving to a new place.' She bit her lip, wondering what had made her tell him that.

He could not conceal his surprise. 'You mean you'd sell the business?'

'I'm not sure. But that's neither here nor there, right now. Let's get back to the subject of polish.'

He screwed up his face. 'What is this about polish? I'd have thought you'd consider the agreement being stolen more important.'

'There's a connection.' To give herself time to collect her thoughts, Margaret picked up the poker and hit a lump of coal, which split and burst into flames. 'A while ago I was broken into and several things were stolen, including a Chinese vase which Alice sold to me.' He went to speak but she held up a hand to hush him. 'Six months ago I was broken into again. This time we caught someone and he had my stolen property in his pocket.'

William leant forward, frowning. 'Are you saying the burglar came back to return what he had stolen?'

'There were two burglars, only one was caught and convicted of the theft – Mr McGinty, whose wife used to be my char. He was also convicted of stealing lead from church roofs.' She paused. 'I don't believe he stole my goods and returned them.'

'You're saying Billy did?'

She shook her head. 'I'm saying Jimmy did.'

William sat back in the chair and his frown deepened. 'What proof have you?'

'A stain and the smell of polish – the fact that Rita saw a similar Chinese vase in Alice's room the day she went with you back to your place.'

William went to speak but she hurried on. 'I believe it was the same vase that was stolen from me. That Jimmy took it. She didn't want to part with it but he persuaded her to so he could buy feed for the horses.'

'But Jimmy's not a thief he—'

'What about the money you gave him for me?'

'OK! I accept he took that but it was for necessary things. He shouldn't have taken it, but—'

'No buts, Will.' Her tone was steely. 'He stole what was mine.'

He sighed. 'OK! But where does the polish come in?'

'Jimmy left a smear on Rita's hand when she went with Ellen to the yard. It was black polish, and although she wiped it off, it left a stain. It also has a distinctive smell. Suddenly she was reminded of the break-ins. I remember her saying to me that all she could see of the mystery burglar was the gleam of his eyes. She realised then he must have blacked his face.'

'But black polish, Maggie? It could have been used by anyone.'

'Jimmy told Rita he used special stuff to polish the black harnesses. She said he was forever talking about the yard and horses when they were out. Apparently it's a special mixture one of the old carters makes up. There was something about the burglar that reminded her of someone but she couldn't remember who until she tried to get the stain off her hand.'

'Then she did,' murmured William, looking upset.

Both were silent for several minutes.

Then he said, 'I'm sorry about all this, Maggie. But he's returned the stolen stuff but for the vase . . . if I pay for that, can we forget the theft took place? The lad's been through a lot – his mother dying, and I couldn't help but keep him short of money.'

She fixed him with a flint-like stare. 'You amaze me, Will. What about Billy when he got into trouble? He'd lost his mother and you were away at sea most of the time; you didn't let him off scot-free. Jimmy needs to be taught a lesson.'

William looked mortified. 'You're right, of course.'

'You can say that again! I did think Billy might have taken the agreement, actually. That he might have done it when Ellen was staying here, but Rita said that he couldn't have. He was never left alone. Besides . . .' Margaret laughed shortly, 'he wasn't out to do you any favours.'

'He'd have done it for Alice.'

'Maybe, but you could say that was what was behind the first break-in. Jimmy's concern for Alice and his mother. I tell you what I'd really like to know . . . why didn't he sell the stuff? It must have been why he stole it in the first place.'

'I wish I knew.' Wearily William rose from the chair. 'I'll ask him.'

'Sit down, Will. Have a cup of tea to warm you before going out in the fog. Just because you're a rotten judge of character, I'm not going to condemn you.'

He looked about to argue but instead sat down. 'None of us are perfect, Maggie. And we all have our reasons for thinking the way we do. I'd appreciate that cup of tea.'

She went into the scullery feeling better for having had her say.

As she handed his tea to him, she said, 'So what punishment are you going to dole out? The padre said Billy was sent to the reformatory ship for "youthful high jinks".'

She so startled him that he spilt tea in the saucer. 'You've spoken to Jerry about this?' His voice was harsh.

'Yes! I was undecided as to whether both Jimmy and Billy were involved. You do realise that Jimmy must have climbed onto the roof for the first break-in? It can't be the first time he's done such a thing. It takes practice to climb like a cat.'

'Now, Billy is to blame there,' said William emphatically. 'He'd get out of their bedroom that way when he was a kid and climb back up the drainpipe. We caught him at it eventually. Jimmy thought Billy was really something. Adventurous! Daring! I don't doubt Jimmy copied him.'

'Jimmy's not a kid now. I know his mother's death has hit him for six and he works for you for buttons, but you always were one for seeing things from the other person's point of view and that swayed your judgement. But you'll rue the day if you don't show Jimmy that crime doesn't pay.'

'You want me to take him to the police? What about that woman's husband?'

'He was punished for a crime he did commit! But no, I don't want you to take him to the police; so you'll have to find your own way of dealing with him, Will.'

He looked drained. 'You don't have to labour the point. I've got the message.' He placed his cup on the hearth and delved into a pocket, drew out several creased banknotes. 'The money I owe you and a bit over for the vase. I blame myself. Jimmy seems to think that because I've gambled and got drunk in my time I'd burn the agreement and not pay you. It seems that it's me who's had to learn a hard lesson.'

She nodded, taking his money, thinking it was not enough to cover the price of the vase, but what did it matter. He wasn't the thief. 'What dreamers the young are, Will.'

'We were the same but at least we enjoyed our youth. What with the war and the Depression, life isn't the same for them. Jimmy should be having fun. All work isn't good for people.'

'I agree, but now isn't the time for him to have fun. Although having Ellen in your house will cheer your place up. She certainly caused a stir here. As long as Jimmy doesn't forget that she's Billy's girl.'

'Just like you used to be my girl. Thanks for everything.' William planted a swift kiss on Margaret's mouth and walked out.

She was too astonished to go after him and see him out. Later she could still feel the impression of that kiss.

Rita asked how things had gone. Margaret told her. 'So what punishment d'you think Mr Brodie'll hand out?' said the girl.

'I don't know but I suppose we'll find out sooner or later.'

The next day the fog lifted and just before noon a horse and cart drew up outside the shop. Rita watched Jimmy climb down, remove his cap, smooth back his hair, polish his toecaps on the back of his trouser legs and march towards the door.

'It's Jimmy,' she hissed to her aunt and hastened to get behind the counter.

When he entered, they were shoulder to shoulder

with their elbows on the counter and eyes fixed on him. He almost retreated but then thrust his handsome head forward, gripped his cap in both hands and advanced.

'I've come to say sorry. I don't know what got into me. I behaved in a way that was rep-rep-reprehensible.' His left eyebrow twitched.

'Were you the guilty party both times?' asked Margaret, wanting things absolutely clear.

'Yes! I didn't come intending to take the rings and things but only Alice's vase, but I was tempted, and then when Rita came nosing about I panicked. I didn't mean to hurt you,' he said stiffly, inclining his head in her direction. 'I'm sorry.'

Rita decided that she had never liked him much but, seeing him humbling himself, she almost felt sorry for him. It was true that she had fallen in love with his looks, but his self-absorption had begun to get on her nerves. She accepted his apology.

'So why did you hang on to the rings and things?' asked Margaret. 'You could have sold them.'

'I did think about it, to be honest.' He looked her straight in the eye. 'But something Billy said years ago about crooked fences and the police checking honest pawnbrokers and jewellery shops made me think again. By the way,' he added hastily, 'you're not to think that Billy was into that kind of thing, but he mixed with some right tearaways, whose fathers were crooks, when he was on the *Akbar*. He used to tell me about them.'

'But what made you risk getting caught by breaking in to return the stolen goods?' she asked.

He sighed heavily and rubbed the back of his neck. 'To be honest, it was Billy who said I had to return them. I didn't know what to do. He heard about the vase being stolen and came to see Alice and saw it in her room like you did, Rita. He got the whole story out of her. We discussed ways of putting the other things back but then I had the bright or stupid idea of stealing the agreement, not that I mentioned that to Billy. I thought it would be handy to have if things got really desperate up at the yard. I wasn't thinking about the dishonesty of it all. Mam was so ill, I was worried sick and not thinking straight. I'm sorry.'

'Well!' said Margaret, gripping the edge of the counter. 'That's some story and I don't doubt you'd rather have kept it to yourself.'

'It makes me look an idiot,' he said ruefully. 'But in one way I'm glad to get it off my chest. Pops said you're to choose my punishment.'

Rita glanced at Margaret. 'That's good of him,' she said sarcastically. 'I'll need to think about it. You can get on with your deliveries now. I'll be in touch.'

He thanked her and left the shop.

Rita said, 'So what are you going to do?'

'Think about it, as I said.'

She was annoyed with William for passing the buck to her but could see his problem. The younger

Billy would have been easier to deal with but, Jimmy being the age and size he was, how did you punish him if you couldn't thrash or lock him up and not involve the police? It did seem that he had seen the error of his ways, and being made to apologise had humbled him. Was that enough punishment? She was unsure. Maybe William felt the same. If Jimmy was to misbehave once more, then she would think again about going to the police.

Next time William came to pay off some of his debt she told him of her decision.

'Thanks,' he said, gripping her hand and shaking it warmly. 'I think the greatest punishment I could have given Jimmy was to order him to leave the yard and I don't really want to do that. He works hard and appears genuinely sorry, and I can't see him going in for burglary again.'

'Not if he's got any sense he won't. I hope my not issuing any punishment at the moment doesn't make him think he can do what he wants, and not worry about hurting others in the process.' She would have said more if at that moment a customer had not entered the shop. William lingered, inspecting the stock, but when several more people turned up he left.

Margaret told Rita her decision concerning Jimmy, and the girl felt dubious about it. She could sympathise with the anxiety he must have felt due to lack of money and his mother's illness, but at the same time she could not forget he had hit her over the head and also put the stolen items in Mr McGinty's pocket. Rita felt uncomfortable thinking about his doing the latter. Yet what could she do? It was out of her hands.

Within days she put the whole episode aside when the travelling theatre, of which Ellen's brother was a member, came to town. Rita was given a complimentary ticket to one of the plays and looked forward to it with excitement.

The play was to be performed at the Royal Court Theatre in Great Charlotte Street, not far from St George's Hall. Rita had not visited the theatre since her mother had been part of a variety act. Once inside, despite feeling initially uncomfortable seeing Jimmy for the first time since he had apologised, she was determined to enjoy herself. Besides, Alice and Ellen were there, too, so it was not as if she had to talk to him.

Rita gazed about her with a rapt expression on her face, admiring the fancy decorations on the walls and ceilings. The plush seats were comfortable and the audience chattering nine to the dozen only served to increase her pleasure. She held her breath as the curtains parted and the play began.

Afterwards Ellen took them backstage to meet her brother, Sandy. As soon as Rita set eyes on him she decided that if she wasn't off the whole idea of being in love she could have fallen for him. He was beautiful, with delicate features and hair as black as coal and wavy as the Oxo bull's forelock. He had strong shoulders and flat hips and moved like a dancer.

'I really enjoyed the play,' she told him. 'You were marvellous and the dialogue was so clever.'

'Thanks! I'm really glad you liked it.' He dazzled her with a smile before turning to Jimmy. 'What about you?'

'Not really my kind of thing!' He wriggled his shoulders as if he had an itch. 'It's not real, is it? People don't talk to each other the way you lot did on the stage. I couldn't understand half of it. By the end it seemed to me you lot had gone through the whole thing without saying what you meant but something completely different.'

'But people often don't say what they mean,' said Rita, annoyed by his rudeness. 'Lots of people are scared of being hurt, so they put on an act.'

'But the main characters were nasty to each other and yet ended up in each other's arms. It was unbelievable and they could have saved each other a lot of trouble by being honest,' said Jimmy.

Rita was about to say that he was a right one to talk about honesty when Sandy spoke again, obviously keen to help Jimmy understand why it had been that way. 'It's necessary in a play to have conflict. A crisis near the end is also essential. It causes the characters to show that honesty you're talking about. The chimney pot that fell and hit Marcus could have killed him. Pauline just had to tell him how she really felt, knowing she couldn't let him go to the grave believing she hated him. See?'

'Yeah! But it still seems unnecessary to me.'

'But there'd be no story without misunderstandings,' said Sandy lamely. He exchanged a look with his sister before moving away to talk to someone else.

Jimmy stretched his arms and smiled. 'That's got rid of him. We can go home now. Come on, Alice! Ellen! I've got to be up early in the morning.' He glanced at Rita. 'You might as well come with us. We're going your way.'

'Yes, do walk with us,' said the girls.

Rita would have liked to stay longer enjoying the atmosphere, but with Ellen leaving she knew she had no choice but to go.

The metal caps on Jimmy's boots made a ringing sound on the pavement as he strode along. Alice and Ellen were talking about the music for the dance that the padre was organising and fell behind. Jimmy told Rita to keep up. That annoyed her because his legs were so much longer and to keep up she had to do a little run every now and then. She wanted to discuss the play but knew that he wouldn't want to. Perhaps she should ask how things were up at the yard. That had always been a good ploy to get him talking – but did she want to listen? No! She'd had enough of hearing him talk about the things that only interested him. She thought of Billy and felt warm inside.

'I bet Ellen wishes Billy was home,' she said.

'So do I,' he said, surprisingly. 'You've no idea how different the atmosphere is with her in the house. She takes up so much of Alice's time. They're always giggling, and even Pops is behaving differently with her around.'

'In what way?'

'I can't explain.'

'Is he still drinking?'

Jimmy shook his head and looked moody. 'He doesn't touch the stuff.'

'Isn't that a good thing?'

'You'd think so, wouldn't you?'

She was amazed. 'You don't?'

'I don't know what to think,' he said gloomily, brushing against her. 'He and Ellen talk about ships and places they've been. Apparently she's been to Hong Kong, just like Pops and the padre.'

Is he jealous? Ellen was the kind of person who was friendly with everybody. 'If they enjoy talking together, then I think that must be good for your stepfather. He hasn't had things easy for a long time, has he?'

'I think you're wrong,' muttered Jimmy, kicking a pebble. 'Pops can be really good company when he puts his mind to it. He could turn her head.'

Rita laughed. 'You're letting your imagination run away with you. She's Billy's girl and he knows it. Anyway, she's much too young for him.'

'Young women have married older men before for what they can get. Imagine if she married Pops? They could have kids and they'd end up getting the yard.'

Rita halted beneath a lamp post. 'You're obsessed with that yard. What has Mr Brodie got but a load of debt at the moment? No girl's going to marry him for that. Ellen likes him because they can talk about the same things, just like she and Alice discuss music. He probably enjoys there being some laughter in the house after months of gloom.'

Jimmy did not look convinced. 'He's had two wives, and there was something between him and your aunt. He's the kind of man that needs a woman, so who's to say that he doesn't have something like that in mind?'

'If you think that, then write to Billy,' said Rita exasperated. 'If there's anything going on between Ellen and your stepfather then he should know. Otherwise, drop the subject. I'm fed up with it.'

His eyes narrowed. 'I can see what's going on. You like him, too. That's why you're getting all worked up about him and Ellen.'

Rita could not believe her ears. 'You're an idiot and you can get lost!' She walked away, wondering how she could ever have fancied herself in love with him.

CHAPTER TWELVE

A week later Ellen called round. 'I've come to get my clothes out of hock and to pay anything else I owe,' she said, resting her elbows on the counter.

'The dance hasn't been and gone already, has it?' said Margaret.

'No!' Ellen chuckled and placed her pawn ticket and several banknotes on the counter. 'You're not going to believe this but Mr Brodie knew this horse and persuaded me to put the money I'd borrowed from Sandy on it. It won!'

Margaret swore.

A startled Rita stared at her. 'I've never heard you swear before.'

'Well, you have now,' said her aunt fiercely. 'That

man! I could strangle him. He said he'd learnt his lesson but he's leading this girl astray.'

'No, he's not! I like a flutter. He also gave me this for you.' Ellen produced an envelope from her pocket.

Margaret had very mixed feelings about taking the envelope, guessing what was inside. Maybe he'd borrowed money elsewhere and there were hundreds of pounds in the envelope. Perhaps it would pay off all he owed her and that would be that, and she would never see him again. Unable to bear the suspense she slit open the envelope. A handful of banknotes fell out and she sighed with relief.

That evening Margaret placed three pounds, ten shillings on Rita's bread plate. 'What's that for?' asked the girl.

'I think it's only fair that your money is returned to you.' Margaret sat down, pulling her chair in with some force. 'Again Will's been saved in the nick of time. If you hadn't given all your savings, though, I'd have had them out . . . sold the place and got my dream house. You're too soft-hearted for your own good! I only have to think of the price you gave for that squeeze box to know that.'

'Sam needed the money. I wonder what's happened to him?' She sighed.

'Never mind him. You buy yourself a new frock for the dance.'

'You don't mind if I go?'

'No! I'm thinking of going myself.'

Rita almost dropped the money. She didn't want her aunt there watching her every move. 'Why? Who asked you? I didn't know you danced.'

Margaret smirked as she buttered a slice of bread. 'There's lots of things about me you don't know. As it happens, the padre invited me along. He thought I might enjoy it.'

Rita could not think what to say. It seemed there was no end to the surprises some days.

The room where the dance was being held was nothing to write home about, but balloons and garlands festooned the walls and a twisting sparkling ball hung from the ceiling. Despite the fact that only soft drinks were being served, there were plenty of sailors present. They outnumbered women and girls by at least eight to one. A lot of the girls were from local churches doing their bit to keep the seamen away from such dens of vice that would fleece them of every penny.

Jimmy stood behind Rita's chair, which annoyed her no end. She had hinted him away but he refused to move, saying he had a good view of the stage from where she was. Ellen and Alice, after a couple of nervous introductory pieces, had begun to relax and were playing 'I Wish I Could Shimmy Like My Sister Kate!' The dance floor was awash with shimmying couples. Rita was desperate to dance, tapping her foot in time to the music, but Jimmy's presence was acting as a deterrent to any sailors who might ask her to dance and he wasn't doing any asking.

Margaret was also waiting, having hopes that the padre would come and ask her to waltz or foxtrot. Her hair was newly washed and set and she was wearing the cream and peach outfit she had bought at Bacon's in Bold Street.

'I hope there's not going to be trouble,' said Jimmy, in Rita's ear.

'Why should there be? There's no alcohol being served.'

'You're a right innocent. I bet some of these sailors have smuggled in spirits and are mixing it with the lemonade. I must say, Rita, you look lovely in that frock.'

'Thanks!' The dress was lemon crêpe de Chine with a scooped neckline and several layers of frills falling from a dropped waist. It fitted her perfectly.

'I'd forgotten how much of you there was.'

'I beg your pardon!' That didn't sound very complimentary and Rita was annoyed. 'Are you saying I'm fat?'

'No! I mean you've got curves. You're growing up just like my sister.' He gazed at the stage and must have seen something he did not like because he squeezed Rita's shoulder and said, 'You'll be OK a minute, won't you? There's an American sailor talking to Alice. I can't allow that.' He disappeared onto the crowded floor.

Thank God for that! Rita was gratified when a few minutes later a royal naval rating came up and asked her to dance. She accepted like a shot and without even a glance in her aunt's direction was soon shimmying with the best of them, grateful to Ellen for those lessons when she had stayed at the pawnshop.

Margaret's mind drifted to another era when she was young and had danced the evening away, either at a church social or in a friend's kitchen, laughing and giggling like the carefree girl she had been then. When an off-white tropical-suited figure stopped in front of her and bowed, he was obviously part of that world.

'May I have the pleasure of this dance?'

She stared at William and without speaking offered him her hand. He drew her onto the dance floor and it made no difference that other couples were dancing a few feet apart. He placed his arm about her waist and they did a sort of very fast foxtrot. It was exhilarating and soon her cheeks were glowing.

When the music stopped they stood there, gazing at each other. 'I'd forgotten what it was like to have fun,' she said breathlessly, her breasts rising and falling.

'Me too!' The expression in his eyes caused the flush in her cheeks to deepen.

'What are you doing here, Will?'

'I'm an old sailor. Jerry asked me along. He thought I might like to make sure that Alice was OK, but Jimmy is doing that.' He sighed.

Very aware of his arm about her waist Margaret glanced towards the stage. 'She seems to be enjoying herself; really knows how to vamp it up, just like you did once.'

'We did have some good times, didn't we?' he said softly.

She nodded, suddenly unable to speak because emotion had her by the throat. Maybe if things hadn't gone so wrong at home . . . if Donald hadn't died . . . if his death hadn't disturbed the balance of her mother's mind . . . if Eve hadn't gone off the rails and left her alone to cope. Then maybe she wouldn't have felt so insecure and minded so much when Will paid attention to other people. Yet it was that caring about folk which had drawn her to him in the first place.

Alice launched into the 'Blue Danube' and William led her into a waltz. Margaret's footsteps followed his without any hesitation; she was aware he was taking care to keep a space between them.

'I took a gamble when I asked you to dance.' His eyes were on her face.

'Please don't talk about gambling.'

'Sorry. I took a risk then. When you said yes, it was as if my ship had come in loaded with goodies.'

She was touched. 'Christmas goodies?'

'Yes.'

They were the best, she thought. His lips brushed her temple and his arm tightened about her waist and they danced cheek to cheek with no need for words. When he escorted her back to her chair and said that he wanted to have a word with Jimmy and Alice, Margaret watched his tall figure shouldering its way through those still crowding the dance floor. For the first time in a long time she felt as if a spark had been lit inside her and experienced a cautious optimism.

'Who was that you were dancing with?' A rosy-cheeked Rita sat next to her.

Margaret clasped her hands in her lap and said demurely, 'That would be telling. Are you enjoying yourself?'

Rita's brown eyes glowed. 'Yes. But I'm not sticking to one fella. I told Reg there are plenty of other sailors sailing the seven seas and he had to take his turn.'

Margaret was about to ask which one was Reg, when Jimmy stopped in front of them with his jaw set rigid. Without even asking her did she want to dance he seized Rita's arm and pulled her onto the dance floor.

'Don't be so rough!' she hissed. 'You're hurting my arm.'

'Sorry!' He frowned down at her. 'But all the things I worried about this evening are coming true.'

'What d'you mean?'

'Pops has turned up. He seems to think it's OK for Alice and Ellen to flirt with all and sundry.' Jimmy steered Rita round the dance floor with only a perfunctory attempt at the dance steps.

'He's showing sense . . . and will you stop holding me like I was a bag of flour? You need to learn how to treat a girl. Ouch! That was my toe.' She realised they were heading for the stage where an American sailor, who she presumed was the same one that had got Jimmy's goat, was leaning on the piano, singing to Alice.

'He's got a nerve,' growled Jimmy. 'Pops should put a stop to it.'

'He's got more sense. It's just a bit of harmless fun and Alice could do with having more of that, just like me.' Her words were no sooner out than they bumped into Father Jerome and Sarah Turner.

'Hello, Rita! Enjoying yourself?' Her former teacher positively bloomed.

'Yes thanks, miss,' she said politely.

Sarah laughed. 'You don't have to call me that anymore. I see your aunt found herself a partner.'

'Your stepfather, Jimmy,' said the padre with a twinkle. 'I'm all in favour of quarrels being made up.'

They danced away.

Rita looked at Jimmy and his expression made her feel uneasy. She was glad when he left her to visit the Gents and immediately accepted an offer to dance from a merchant seaman, who informed her that he had recently returned from Australia. They had an interesting conversation. Then she noticed Margaret talking to the padre and Sarah Turner. The next time Rita saw her aunt she was dancing with a captain of a similar age to herself. Pleased that Margaret seemed to be entering into the spirit of things Rita did her best to avoid Jimmy.

By the end of the evening she was footsore but happy. There was no dancing partner that she particularly wanted to see again, so she was glad to have her aunt as an excuse to turn down those who asked to see her home, including Reg, the naval rating from Portsmouth. She wasn't ready yet to give her heart to a sailor.

She expected Margaret to mention William being at the dance but her aunt was mute on the subject. Even so, it seemed to Rita that the older woman was happy for once because she sang as she got ready for bed.

That mood was soon to change as two weeks went by without seeing anyone from the yard. Margaret's cautious optimism evaporated and she dismissed the emotions she had felt at the dance as so much moonshine. Just for a short while she and William had allowed their past youth to live again, but there was too much in between, and that boat he had talked about had sailed away on the river of time.

She was snappy with Rita and muttered about getting the bailiffs out to the yard if Will, Jimmy or Alice did not show their faces soon. Then the padre called Sunday afternoon and told them that Billy was home and asked for a private word with Margaret. She suggested her niece get some fresh air.

Rita decided to go up to the yard, curious to see what was going on there. She had no idea if Ellen was still staying with Alice or had left Liverpool with Sandy and the travelling theatre.

The first person she saw was Jimmy over by the stables and, realising she could hardly ignore him, went over to him. 'How are things?'

'What are you doing here?' His blue eyes were as cold as ice. 'Your aunt sent you for money, has she?'

'No! But now you've brought it up there's been mention of the bailiffs.' She paused. 'Is Ellen still here?'

'Not Ellen, nor Alice! That bloody dance!' His expression was ugly. He threw a blanket over a horse and led it inside the stable.

Curious, she followed him. 'What's happened? Have they both gone off with the travelling theatre?'

'Alice has only bloody run off to America! Probably gone after that bloody Yank!'

Rita was amazed. 'Honest?'

'You think I'd lie about something so bloody serious?'

'But you and Alice were so close.'

'That's what I thought. But it didn't stop her running off without even a proper goodbye.' His voice cracked. 'She left a letter for Pops, and he's not even related to her. I'm her brother!'

Rita felt genuinely sorry for him. 'What about Ellen? Didn't she know Billy was due home?'

'He's upset about Ellen, of course. But he had the bloody nerve to say that he thought it was a good thing Alice getting away from me. Can you believe that?'

She was silent.

He glared at her and seized her by the shoulders. 'Answer me! What's going on in that pretty little head of yours?'

'Let go of me!' She tried to wrench herself free but his fingers dug into her shoulders.

'He's always been jealous of Alice and me being close. We've never been separated! I can't understand how she could do this to me.'

'That's nothing to do with me, Jimmy. Will you please let me go?'

'No!' His hands slid down her arms and about her waist. He rammed her against him so hard she felt that she could not breathe. She struggled. 'You're hurting me,' she gasped. 'Will you let me go?'

'You've changed your tune. Not so long ago you would have been glad to have me holding you like this.'

'That was before I found out that you were a thief and a liar!' She flung the words at him. 'Now let me go!'

'I don't like being called a thief and a liar.' Before she could realise what he was about his mouth came down over hers, pressing her lips against her teeth in a way that hurt and almost stopped her breath. There was something so cruel about the act that it frightened her. She managed to free her arm and elbowed him in the stomach, but except for a slight intake of breath it seemed to make little impression on him. He carried on kissing her, forcing his tongue into her mouth in such a way that she baulked, thinking she would choke.

He lifted his head. 'What's wrong? This is what you want, isn't it?' His voice was silky soft.

'No, it isn't! Don't you be taking your anger out on me, Jimmy Martin!' Her tongue probed her mouth where she could taste blood.

'Why shouldn't I? You brought Ellen here and if it wasn't for her there would have been no dance and Alice would never have met that Yank.'

'She would have met someone else sooner or later. You can't hang on to people when they want to be free. You want her to be happy, don't you?'

'Of course I do,' he said fiercely. 'But I want her here and happy. It helped having her look up to me.'

'You'll find someone else.'

'I want her, but if I can't have her then I'll have

you. I bet you're no little Miss Innocent.' His look was calculating. 'I saw you dancing with all those sailors and I remember where and when it was that we first met.' He lifted her off her feet.

He startled a scream out of her. 'What are you doing?'

'Doing what I should have done ages ago. All those Sunday afternoons wasted listening to a band playing or walking along the landing stage when we could have been doing this!' He flung her on a heap of straw and dropped on her. She gasped for air and tried to scream but no sound came. He raised his body and she tried to slide from under him but he gripped her with his thighs and forced up her skirts.

Hazy memories of her mother being with men filled her thoughts and she pushed at Jimmy with both hands but could not budge him. 'No, no, no! You can't go there!' She was terrified as he pulled down her drawers. His breath was coming fast, like a locomotive getting up steam. She had dreamt of a wedding first . . . church and a long white dress . . . flowers . . . and there was something else trying to get into her mind . . . being loved and cherished. Where was the love in this? She screamed.

'For God's sake, Rita, what are you making that noise for? This is what you've been dying for,' he muttered. She managed to scream again, to struggle madly to escape as he raised himself again and fumbled with his flies. 'I'll marry you!

We can live here. Your aunt'll cancel the debt and I'll . . . we'll . . . be happy.' He was poking at her as he talked, trying to get inside her.

'Let me go, let me go, let me go!' she shrieked.

'What's going on here?'

Thank God! Rita did not recognise the voice at first. Then she caught sight of Billy. He seized hold of Jimmy by the back of his collar and pulled. Rita discovered a reserve of strength and managed to bring up her knee and ram it into Jimmy's groin. He groaned as he was dragged away from her, along the floor through straw and muck, his braces dangling, trousers about his ankles.

Rita knelt up, aware of a deep shame because Billy had found her in such a position. She watched as he heaved Jimmy upright and with a hand to the small of his back sent him flying to the other side of the stable. She felt sick but forced the vomit down. The mother of all pains was throbbing between her legs. She pulled up her drawers and, dragging her coat close about her, she stumbled outside and headed towards the Judas gate.

'You bloody selfish git! What the hell d'you think you were doing?' Billy picked Jimmy up and rammed him against the side of a stall.

'Let me go! You're tearing me shirt. She wanted it, I'm telling you. She loves me!'

'She was bloody screaming! She's only a kid!'

'You haven't seen her lately,' gasped Jimmy. The metal toecap of his boot found Billy's knee; he grunted with pain and punched Jimmy in the stomach. The horse shifted restlessly in the stall and whinnied. 'You're upsetting the horse,' cried Jimmy.

'You and your bloody horses! You care more for them than people,' said Billy wrathfully, stepping back and rubbing his knee. He looked round for Rita but she was not there. 'You've bloody frightened the life out of her now!'

'I didn't start off meaning to frighten her,' said Jimmy sullenly, pulling up trousers and buttoning his flies. He went to the horse's head.

Disgusted with him, Billy made for the door, only to find William standing there. 'So you're back,' said the older man.

'I believe you've been away, too,' said Billy, 'but I haven't got time right now to ask questions.' He made to brush past William but he stayed him with a hand.

'What's been going on here? I've just seen young Rita running out of the yard as if all the hounds of hell were after her. What have you done to upset her?'

The breath hissed between Billy's teeth. 'It would have to be me, wouldn't it? Always me that's to blame! Well, again you've got it wrong!'

'OK! I deserve that,' said William, pushing his trilby to the back of his head. 'I haven't always treated you fairly.'

Billy was so taken aback by those words that he was rendered speechless. Then Jimmy surprised them both by saying out of the blue, 'I'm going to marry Rita.'

Billy looked at him as if he had run mad. 'She's not going to want to marry you, you bloody fool! You need to learn how to treat women.'

'She might have to,' said Jimmy, swaggering over to them.

Billy raised his fist. William gripped his shoulder and leant on it. 'What the bloody hell have you done, Jimmy?' he said hoarsely. 'Haven't you caused enough trouble? You frightened Ellen away and even your sister's had enough of you. Rita's only a kid, and have you forgotten whose niece she is?'

'That's why I want to marry her.' There was a fatuous smile on Jimmy's handsome face. 'If we're family her aunt won't get the bailiffs in.'

Billy's expression was grim. 'You're a bloody fool! And what's this about frightening Ellen? You told me she was fed up of waiting for me and had gone off with her brother.'

William said brusquely, 'She's not with her brother. I traced him to Rhyl and he told me that she planned to go to America with Alice to try and break into the music scene there.'

'That's a red herring,' said Jimmy, his face white. 'Chasing Yankee sailors – that's what they're about!' He smashed his fist into the wooden wall a few inches from William's head. Then, nursing his hand, he stalked out of the stables.

Billy went to go after him but William held his arm. 'Let him go! Come into the house. I need to talk to you.'

'I think you've got the wrong son,' said Billy, finding it difficult to accept the change in his father's attitude towards him. 'It's your stepson who's always been your favourite.'

'That's what I need to talk to you about.' William looked him straight in the eye. 'You're not my son.'

Rita did not stop running until she reached St Luke's. Her heart was thumping so heavily she felt dizzy and had to sit down. She slipped inside the church grounds and, finding a secluded bench, sank onto it and with trembling fingers fastened her coat.

She knew what people called girls who went with men before marriage. Spoilt goods! She didn't want her life to imitate her mother's. Jimmy had been horrible. She stuffed her fist into her mouth and bit on her knuckles. Tears rolled down her cheeks unchecked. What if Jimmy had given her a baby? Oh God! Aunt Margaret would say she was just like Eve and throw her out and what would happen to her then? And what were Billy's thoughts right now? It had been such a relief and so good to see him. He had behaved like a knight in shining armour rescuing her from a wicked dragon. She was a damsel in distress but could see no happy ending in store for her with him. He loved Ellen and had behaved like the big brother Rita had never had.

She sat there, with thoughts bouncing around in her head, but eventually the damp got to her and she rose and went out onto Berry Street, feeling a little calmer. She might not have a baby and everything could go on as before, although she would have nothing to do with Jimmy. Right now her everyday routine seemed extremely appealing so she hurried home, cold, hungry and desperate for hot sweet tea.

As Rita stood outside the side door she remembered the padre's visit and wondered what he had wanted. If only her aunt had not insisted on her going out she would not have gone to the yard and would be feeling so different right now. She rat-tatted on the door knocker and waited, shivering on the step.

Margaret opened the door and her expression was as austere as that first evening they had come face-to-face almost on the same spot. 'And where have you been all this time, miss?'

'I-I'm sorry.' Rita pushed past her and almost ran up the lobby.

Margaret hurried after her. 'Where are your manners? You don't push me aside like that and you haven't answered my question.'

Rita dived into the scullery where she filled a bowl with hot water and, taking a towel, went to her bedroom.

'I don't believe this,' said Margaret, following her upstairs. She stood in the doorway, arms folded, watching her take off her coat. 'What is it? Why this sudden need to wash?'

'Please, Aunt Margaret, could you give me some privacy?' pleaded Rita.

Margaret took a deep breath. 'All right! But I want to know where you've been. Something's wrong.'

Too right something was wrong, thought Rita, closing the door and proceeding to strip and wash herself several times underneath before dressing in warmer clothes. She felt so cold.

Downstairs she found the table set for tea. 'So what's wrong?' asked Margaret, removing the cosy from the teapot.

Rita watched her aunt pour tea. She seized a cup and raised it to her lips. Her teeth chattered against the rim.

'You *are* in a state,' said Margaret, frowning. 'Am I such an ogress that you can't tell me what's wrong?'

'A-Alice has r-run away with an-an American s-s-sailor. Ellen's gone too.'

She could not have surprised Margaret more than if she had said the moon really was made of cream cheese. 'Good God! How has Will taken that? And how's Jimmy feeling? Now that *is* a shock; it must be the reason why we haven't seen anything of them. Has Will gone after her?'

254

'I-I didn't see Mr Brodie but-but Jimmy's very upset.' Her cheeks burned as she relived those moments in the stable. Dear God! She hated violence.

'I'm surprised it's upset you so much.'

'Well, it has.' Rita drank the tea and felt better for it.

'Did you see anything of Billy?'

'Not to talk to.' Rita did not want to think about him. It hurt. What must he think of her?

Margaret topped up her niece's cup. 'I can't understand why Ellen left if she knew Billy was due back in Liverpool.'

Rita wished her aunt would shut up about Billy.

'Eat something,' ordered Margaret, placing a slice of coffee and walnut cake on her plate. 'You still look pale. I wonder how Alice will get to America. I can't see her having a passport, and what about money?'

'Perhaps the American sailor smuggled her aboard his ship. I read in the *Echo* about some kids stowing away.' Rita looked at the cake with distaste. Her appetite had completely deserted her.

'Will would know about such things,' murmured Margaret, recalling waving him off at Birkenhead docks on the other side of the Mersey. 'And perhaps the padre could help by getting in touch with his opposite number in America. The trouble is that it's such a big country.'

Rita remembered the padre had been here. 'What

did he want? Anything you can tell me or is it private?'

'He's got himself engaged to your former teacher. Isn't that good news?' Margaret's smile was forced. She had felt so jealous when he had broken the news. She envied Sarah finding love and a husband at her age. She thought of those moments on the dance floor with William and longed to forgive and forget, to be able to love unconditionally.

'It's great!' Rita was delighted.

'She'd like you to be a bridesmaid.'

'Me!' Rita was flabbergasted.

'She's got no family and has a soft spot for you,' said Margaret with a wry smile.

'We did get to know each other better when she gave me those elocution lessons.' Rita felt really flattered.

Margaret sighed. 'Let's put that aside. About Alice – she wouldn't be the first person to want to leave her old life behind and build a new one in another country.'

Rita thought her aunt probably had something there but did not want to discuss Alice. She switched on the wireless and the distinctive dance music of Ambrose and his orchestra flooded out. She took one look at her aunt's face and switched it off.

That night Rita had nightmares and was relieved when morning came. She hoped that by keeping busy she could forget what had happened in the stables; but she was still sore underneath and that served as a constant reminder.

Billy came into the shop just after eleven during a lull in the stream of customers hocking their Sunday best. She felt so embarrassed she wanted to bolt into the storeroom and shut the door. Instead she had to stand her ground because Margaret was elsewhere. She avoided looking him straight in the eye. 'What can I do for you?'

He placed a package on the counter. Relieved that he was here on business, she reached for the scissors and snipped the string. Wrapped inside the brown paper was a gold and red lacquered bird. Her sore spirit was enchanted. 'It's beautiful,' she said in a low voice. 'You have a real knack for finding the right things.'

'It's a phoenix. The Chinese believe they bring good luck. The myth is that they rise out of the ashes when something's been destroyed. I want you to have it, Rita, to help you remember you can put the past behind you and start over again.'

She stilled, aware of the quickened beat of her heart. Tears filled her eyes so that she saw him through a blur. 'I didn't mean to lead him on.'

'I don't believe you did. Here, don't cry!' Billy took a handkerchief from his breast pocket and wiped her eyes. 'It was Jimmy's fault. He seems to have flipped his lid. P-Pops says he's been acting strange for a while. He was jealous of the friendship between the girls; then he made a play for Ellen, got a bit rough. That's probably the reason for them both disappearing, without a word to him. It was the last straw. So don't be thinking you're in any way to blame for what happened back at the stable.' He stroked the back of her hand with a work-roughened thumb.

She was so relieved; a rush of warmth enveloped her. 'You're so kind.'

'Why shouldn't I be? You're a nice girl.'

She wanted him to think her more than nice. 'So are things all right up at the yard now?'

'P-Pops is trying to sort things out with Jimmy. Then he'll have another go at finding the girls. They mightn't have left the country yet.'

'You won't be helping him?'

His expression changed. 'I've someone else to find first.'

Before she could ask who was more important than the two girls the door opened and in walked Jimmy.

CHAPTER THIRTEEN

Jimmy stopped short at the sight of Billy but then advanced towards them, walking jerkily. Rita felt she couldn't breathe. 'What are you doing here?' asked Billy. 'Have you come to apologise?'

Jimmy snorted, holding his head to one side as he gazed at their joined hands. 'I've come to ask Rita to marry me. I don't care what you and Pops say. So don't you go muscling in on my territory.'

'You're crazy!'

'Crazy, am I?' Jimmy did a hop, skip and a jump and bopped Billy on the jaw. Caught off guard he went reeling back against the counter and if Rita had not held onto him he would have slid to the floor.

259

Anger replaced her fear of Jimmy. 'Have you lost your head, you idiot?'

'No! I've come to my senses.' He blew on his knuckles. 'He's got hard bones, has our Billy.'

'Get out,' ordered Rita.

Margaret appeared in the doorway of the storeroom. 'What's going on here?'

'I've come to ask permission for Rita to marry me,' said Jimmy.

'I wouldn't marry you if you were the last fella on earth,' said Rita, and making sure that Billy was not about to collapse on the floor she came from behind the counter and slapped Jimmy across the face. He swore, seized her wrists and lifted her off her feet.

With an angry gasp Margaret reached for the cane. 'Have you been drinking?'

'I'm not drunk!' Jimmy was indignant. He released Rita abruptly so that she stumbled and fell against the display cabinet. 'I want to make an honest woman out of her.'

Margaret stared at him and then at the recovering Billy. He swore. Rita wanted to leave the shop and never come back. Jimmy grinned maniacally. Margaret looked at her niece. 'What have you done?' she whispered.

'It's not what she's done. It's what he's bloody done!' said Billy.

'You keep out of this,' snapped Margaret, bringing

the cane down with a mighty whack on the counter. 'You can both leave.'

Neither man made a move. Her face set in grim lines, Margaret swished the cane left and right, stinging them on their hands, necks and faces. Rita made a grab for the cane. Margaret wrenched it out of her grasp, and lifting it high, brought it down on Jimmy's head.

He swore and stumbled out of the shop.

Billy faced the angry woman. 'I'll go peaceably but don't take it out on Rita. It wasn't her fault.'

Margaret held the cane aloft. 'I'll not be taking orders from a Brodie! Get out!'

He hesitated. 'Go, Billy!' urged Rita. 'I'll be fine. I hope you find who you're looking for!' He went to say something but Margaret advanced on him. 'Go!' repeated the girl.

Sucking his knuckles he left the shop.

Margaret flung the cane the other side of the counter and stared at her niece. 'Right, miss! You can tell me exactly what happened yesterday when you went up to that yard.'

Rita baulked at the very idea. 'No!'

'Don't use that tone with me, my girl! It's a long time since I took the cane to you but you're still not too old for me to do it again.' Margaret felt such a sense of failure. She had tried to do her best with her niece, but just like Eve she had gone off the rails.

'If you think I'd let you have a go at me then

you've another think coming. I don't have to stay here and put up with being threatened. I'm going.' She snatched up the phoenix and fled upstairs.

Margaret, who was feeling the strain of having been on an emotional roller coaster for weeks, lost her temper and rushed after her. 'You're just like your mother! You want to have your cake and eat it . . . Will was the same! He got her pregnant, you know! The heartache I've suffered. Well, I'm not going to be left this time to pick up the pieces.'

'You don't have to because I'll sort myself out,' shouted Rita, slamming her bedroom door and placing a chair beneath the handle. She kissed the phoenix before placing it on the chest of drawers. Billy might love Ellen but he liked her, cared enough to give her such a lovely present when he could have sold it.

Margaret tried to open the door but to no avail. She opened her mouth to tell her niece to take the chair away, only the shop buzzer sounded. She hesitated but a shout decided her. She told Rita that she would deal with her later and hurried downstairs.

Those words decided Rita. She took some underwear, a couple of jumpers and a skirt from the chest of drawers and wardrobe. Then she counted her savings. She didn't have much because she had bought the dress for the dance. Still, the money should get her part of the way to Cardiff; she would walk the rest.

She crept downstairs and placed her change of clothing in a shopping bag before donning her best winter coat and hat. She drew on her gloves and left.

Buoyed up by a sense of adventure and relieved to be escaping something she really didn't want to face up to, Rita walked briskly in the direction of Berry Street. She hurried down Renshaw Street and past the Adelphi Hotel, to enter Lime Street station by its rear entrance. Then she faced her first setback. The train which would have enabled her to make the connections to reach Cardiff that day had departed and there would not be another until tomorrow. The price of a ticket also came as something of a shock.

At the look on her face, the teller suggested she took a train to Warrington, which was due in a quarter of an hour, change for Chester, then catch the Shrewsbury train. 'Nice place, Shrewsbury. Worth a look and you're more than halfway. You've time to go on to Ludlow, if you like, which is another nice place – has a castle, and Broad Street is reputed to be one of the handsomest thoroughfares in Britain with real old buildings.'

Rita cut him short just in case he was about to extol the attractions of every place on the way to Cardiff. 'I'll take a ticket to Ludlow.'

She went and looked at a map of the railway system of the British Isles and saw that she had a good way to go after Ludlow, but she was wearing stout shoes so should be OK. She did have another problem, though; due to leaving in a hurry she did not have her mother's address. She knew that the boarding house was situated in Tiger Bay and that was all. But she had a tongue in her head and could ask around when she arrived there.

After Rita changed at Chester, she allowed herself to think about what had happened in the shop. Surely after her reaction to Jimmy's advances yesterday he should have known how unwelcome his proposal was. Thinking afresh of those times they had spent together, it was obvious he had no idea the kind of person she was at all. Thank God Billy had turned up when he did. She thought of the beautiful red and gold phoenix he had given her and wished she had brought it with her. She had never received a gift like it in her life and would have liked to be able to show it to her mother. It was something else for her to be grateful to Billy for and her heart ached. If only he wasn't in love with Ellen; if only he didn't just see her as a kid needing rescuing from a big bad wolf.

She sighed and hoped that her aunt would not sell the phoenix. Perhaps she should drop her a postcard and explain that it belonged to her and that one day she'd be back for it. What Margaret had said still smarted. Rita was not like her mother and she had never had her cake and eaten it. Eve might have, and Mr Brodie, but not her.

Having reached the point of mental and emotional

exhaustion, Rita yawned and her eyelids drooped. She fell asleep, not waking until the train arrived at Shrewsbury.

As she stood on the platform waiting for the train to Ludlow she remembered it was here that Sam's aunt lived. Why had he never written? If only he had she could have visited him. They'd been mates and it would have been good to see him again. Perhaps he was dead! She did not like that idea; there had to be another reason why he hadn't been in touch.

The train came in and Rita climbed aboard. By the time she arrived in Ludlow it was almost dark. The air was cold and crisp and she was glad of her warm clothing. Which way to the town centre? She gazed up and down the unfamiliar road. She felt so alone. Her stomach rumbled, reminding her that she had not eaten since breakfast. 'Food first,' she muttered.

Remembering what the ticket seller had said about Broad Street she asked directions from a passer-by. It was quite a walk from the station but at last she arrived there. The street sloped steeply, and she set off in search of a fish and chip shop. For a moment she forgot her troubles in the pleasure of seeing a different town. The Angel Inn had a bow window with leaded panes on the first floor, jutting out above the pavement. She imagined gentlemen in doublets and hose, drinking ale and eyeing the ladies in silken gowns.

At last she found what she was looking for and, after a short wait, emerged with a vinegar-soaked newspaper package and a bottle of ginger beer. Fish and chips had never tasted so good. She ambled along the street, listening to the different accents of the passers-by. Desperate men were on the move, tramping the roads of Britain looking for work. As she passed a side street there came the sound of raised voices and she stopped.

'You snivelling little faggot! Give me it or I'll let you have a taste of my knuckles.'

'Let me go! How can I reach it if yer keep a hold on me like that?'

Sam! It couldn't be, thought Rita. But the second voice sounded so like his that she decided to listen a bit more.

'I don't trust you. You'd be off like a rocket if I let go of you. Let me have that rucksack and see what else you've got in there. Share and share alike! That's what I said when I allowed you to come with me.'

'I didn't wanna go with yer. I'd rather be on me own. I got this loaf meself. I don't need you.' The accent was unmistakably Liverpudlian, but was she right about its owner?

Rita turned into the narrow street, hugging the wall on her left. A few yards ahead she could see a bearded burly bloke with his arm about the throat of a youth. She caught the gleam of a knife and got such a shock that she ran towards them. She swung her shopping bag and caught the man a blow on the side of his head. 'Pick on someone your own size, yer big bully!'

'Get off!' He rubbed his head and stared at her before abruptly thrusting his victim against her and grabbing the package of chips out of her grasp. He stalked off.

'Well, he had a nerve,' said Rita, holding the youth away from her so she could get a better look at him. He was really scrawny but there was no mistaking that thin face. 'It really is you!' she said gleefully.

Sam was more cautious. 'Do I know you?'

'Of course you know me. Let's go into the main street where it's lighter.' She linked her arm through his left one.

He looked at her askance, clutching his rucksack tightly. 'Yer do remind me of a girl I knew but yer couldn't be her.'

'It could. It's me!' she said happily.

His eyes widened and his jaw dropped. 'Bloody hell! Is it really you, Reet?'

'Really! From now on, Sam, I'm going to believe in miracles.'

'What are yer doing here?'

'Going to Cardiff to visit my mam and baby brother. I didn't have enough money to take me all the way so I'm shank's ponying the rest of the way.'

He held up a hand. 'Stop right there! What happened to yer rich aunt?'

'It's a long story.' She hugged his arm. 'Are you hungry, Sam?'

'I'm always hungry.'

'Fancy some chips?'

He grinned. 'Yer on. And this story, long or short, I'd like to hear it.'

'You first. Why didn't you write?'

'I was too ashamed. I wasn't wanted, was I? Me aunt's fella said he didn't need another mouth to feed so he turfed me out. I've been on the road ever since, finding work where I could and begging when I couldn't. Did some of me pavement drawings. I didn't write because I felt I'd failed you. Besides where would you post your letters to me? *The nearest hedge to his majesty's highway, Shrops?*'

Her heart was wrung with pity. 'Oh, Sam, fancy being on the road in all weathers. How have you survived?'

'Plenty of us out there. I've had to learn a trick or two or I'd have gone under.' He grinned, revealing two chipped front teeth. 'It pays sometimes to be small and weedy. Plenty of farmers' wives want to feed me up. I chop wood or feed the hens, help mend a fence . . . in return I gets a nice bacon butty or even a chop sometimes . . . as well as a cup of char. If yer'd like me company I could go your way. I'd prefer putting some miles between me and Blackie back there.' He indicated the alley with a jerk of his head. 'He used to be a posh nob until he lost all his money. So if you don't mind?'

'Mind! You're manna from heaven, Sam.' They had arrived outside the fish and chip shop so went inside.

Several hours later Rita had changed her mind about Sam being a blessing. He was a slave driver, setting a cracking pace. She was footsore, the muscles in her legs and hips aching. She could have curled up in the hedgerow and slept for a week but he seemed set on walking forever. Eventually she dug in her heels and told him that she could go no further.

He looked about him at the rolling hills, hoary with frost where sheep huddled together. 'No good stopping here – too open, too cold. We'd freeze to death. There's a derelict place a couple of miles on.'

A couple of miles! She groaned. 'I've got blisters.'

He turned a smiling face on her. 'You'll survive.'

'I didn't realise you had a cruel streak, Sam.'

'I can promise yer a hot drink when we get there.' He patted his knapsack. 'Always carry the makings of a fire.'

She stumbled on, wincing at every step.

'Now what happened to ol' McGinty?' asked Sam.

Telling her story helped Rita to forget her sore feet for a while. At last they reached a house with no roof but at least some of the ground floor rooms were intact. She huddled in a corner, watching Sam produce a candle, matches, and kindling. Soon he had a fire going and was boiling water in a tin.

Tea sweetened with condensed milk and tasting of smoke warmed her up nicely and sent her off to sleep. She woke to find herself covered with an old army blanket. It was daylight and Sam had the water for their morning tea on the boil. Needing the lavatory, she got to her feet with difficulty and stumbled outside.

When she returned he produced a poke of newspaper. 'It's grease. If you rub it on yer feet it'll stop them getting worse. I've some lint and sticking plaster, as well.'

She wrinkled her nose. 'It stinks.'

'Mutton fat, but it'll do the trick. I'll put it on if yer don't want to touch it, Miss Fusspot.'

She accepted his offer and found having her feet rubbed amazingly soothing. They drank tea, but there was no food. She was hungry but saw no point in complaining.

They set off and it was hard going, but the countryside was pretty with gently rolling hills. It was so peaceful that Rita was able to set her worries aside. She suggested they buy bread at the next town. Sam said that she could save her money; he knew a farmer's wife near Hereford, but she would have to stay out of sight because she looked too well fed.

That afternoon they dined on bread and cheese and windfalls.

By evening Rita was exhausted and wishing herself back in Liverpool. That night they slept in a barn. The next morning they breakfasted on scrambled eggs. She did not ask where they came from but demanded they take things easier that day. He told her that they would make for Abergavenny but do it in two days instead of one. 'With a bit of luck we could be in Cardiff by the weekend.'

Rita pulled her hat down further. The wind was sharp and was nipping her ears, and she put her best foot forward.

Sam entertained her with anecdotes of his adventures on the road. 'I was almost shot by a farmer! He accused me of stealing one of his chickens. He was a liar. The nearest I got to them was pinching eggs.'

She laughed. 'You're a terrible fella, Sam.'

He grinned. 'I like to see yer laugh. Yer know I'd never hurt yer, Reet?'

'Of course I do,' she said softly.

'I'd like to punch that Jimmy on the nose for trying it on with yer.' Sam glowered. 'He always fancied himself. His stepbrother sounds a nice bloke, though.'

'He is,' said Rita, and fell silent.

Sam took the hint and told her about the writer he had met, who had told him that he was a vanishing way of life. 'He wanted to put me in a book. He thought me a real tramp and was willing to pay me, so I took his money and made a few stories up for him.'

Rita was amused. Sam had obviously gained confidence since he had left home and taken to the highways and byways of England.

Sometimes they walked along with other men, who spoke of their concern for their wives and children back home. Some were so poorly dressed that she could have cried for them. Despite having lived with her aunt for more than two years she had not forgotten what it was like to be deprived of so much that made life worth living. She remembered what her mother had said about the government having promised a land fit for heroes after the war. It was a long time coming.

She told Sam about the travelling theatre and the play she had seen. He was fascinated and asked after every twist and turn of the plot. She thought of how Jimmy hadn't been interested at all.

They had reached the Brecon Beacons and that night it was very cold; the only place they could shelter was in the lee of a wall. Rita insisted they shared the blanket and they huddled together. Sleep did not come to either of them but she did not fear Sam would get amorous. She trusted him. It was comforting, though, to be held in his arms and to rest her head on his shoulder.

It rained the next day and the going was arduous. Neither talked. At last they reached Abergavenny. Exhausted, cold and wet she told Sam enough was enough. They found the bus station and discovered there was a bus that would take them to Pontypool where they could get another bus to Cardiff. She pawned her spare clothing and, with the money she still had left, it was enough to buy two bus tickets for the following day.

She used most of the money she had left to buy a meal of eggs and chips and they spent the night in a shelter in the park. Rita lay on a bench curled up against Sam's back. She pictured her mother welcoming her with open arms. She refused to think what she would do if that did not happen. She thought of Billy, pretending it was him she was nestling up against. If only he could love her. She would marry him and they'd live happily ever after.

She sighed, wondering whether her aunt was worrying about her and if Margaret had thought of getting in touch with Eve. How was her aunt managing without her? Rita felt an unexpected longing to be back in the shop, talking to the customers, sleeping in her comfortable bed, eating good food and chatting about the day's happening with her aunt. She had been good to her in so many ways but shouldn't have said those hurtful things about her being like her mother and wanting to have her cake and eat it. *Eve and Will!* Her aunt had said something about his getting *her* pregnant!

Rita wriggled, her thoughts uncomfortable. Sam murmured in his sleep. She put her arm around him to prevent him falling off the bench. She must have misheard her aunt. Surely Mr Brodie and her mother couldn't have had an affair? Yet it would explain why Eve had run away and never got in touch with her sister again. What if Billy was the result of an affair between them . . . he would be her half-brother! And that meant that even if there was the remotest chance of Ellen and Billy falling out, she still wouldn't be able to marry him. She moaned, hating her mother at that moment, and asking herself what the hell she was doing making such an effort, suffering in the process, just to see her. She must be as crazy as Jimmy!

CHAPTER FOURTEEN

Tiger Bay was an area east of the River Taff and as Rita stood with Sam on the quayside she could hear familiar sounds: the cry of the gulls, the hoot of a tug, and voices coming to her on the breeze from the docks and river. The only difference was that the accents were mainly Welsh, not Scouse.

'So where will we start?' said Sam, tucking his thumbs into his belt and turning away from the river to gaze across the road to the streets that ran off it.

Rita's eyes followed his. 'Why not over there?'

He nodded. 'Is yer mam married to this negro?'

'Yes! But I've forgotten what her married name is.'

He chuckled. 'Yer completely crackers coming

this far without knowing that. We're gonna have our work cut out finding her. It could take days.'

'Let's look on the bright side, Sam; we could find her today.' Her voice was light despite the heaviness in her chest. She had come this far to get the truth from her mother and wasn't about to give up on finding her just yet.

They began their search, going up and down streets, knocking on doors of likely-looking places, or going inside in some cases where it was obvious the building was a guest house due to a sign in the window. They met with no luck. Several times they were told to beat it as soon as they opened their mouths and on more than one occasion they couldn't understand what the person was saying because they spoke Welsh or heavily accented English.

Then they had a bit of luck. A woman suggested they make enquiries at the corner shops or the post office. Rita had begun to feel desperate and was grateful for the suggestion. Sam said they should have a break first. 'I don't know about you but I'm hungry. Have you any money left?' They were standing outside a sweet shop.

Rita did not need to look to know that she had exactly tuppence. 'How about some pear drops? They'll last and stave off the hunger pangs.'

'They'll give us energy as well,' said Sam.

They went inside the shop and a small, smiling woman served them. On the way out Rita thought to ask about her mother. After all, Eve had a child, and sweet shops were popular places for mothers with children.

The woman told them that lots of white women with half-caste children came into her shop. 'I can't give you names, lovey. But why don't you try the preacher's house? Lots of them go to chapel.'

Not my mother, thought Rita, but decided there was no harm in trying. They asked directions and, sucking a pear drop apiece, followed the woman's instructions to the letter. Soon they were being shown into a room filled with shabby old-fashioned furniture. A white-haired man came into the room a few minutes later and they explained to him why they were there.

'Well, well,' he said in a deep musical voice. 'I've only met your mother a few times if it's the right woman I'm thinking about. She plays the accordion and is from Liverpool.'

Rita nodded, excited. Eve must be doing well if she had managed to buy another squeeze box and was setting foot in church.

'High days and holidays, that's the only time we see her, but when Caleb's home from sea he worships here. He comes with his sister and they bring his son Joshua with them.'

Rita was surprised to hear that her mother's husband was sailing again. 'I thought he'd given up the sea.'

The preacher smiled. 'All sailors give up the sea at sometime or other but for many the call remains too strong to resist.'

'Yer have an address?' asked Sam.

The man shook his head. 'I know where the house is and the name of the street but I can't tell you the number. It does have a Rooms to Let notice in the window and . . .' He looked thoughtful, then his eyes brightened and he snapped his fingers, 'a wooden antelope in the fanlight.'

Rita thanked him and they set off on what would hopefully prove to be the final leg of their journey. The days were short at this time of year and soon it would be dark. As it was they didn't have to find the house to find Eve. As they walked up the street checking fanlights for antelopes, she heard her mother's voice.

Rita looked about her and there was Eve on the other side of the street arguing with another woman. Her mother's deep husky voice was unmistakable and so was her blonde hair; she had a dusky-skinned toddler with corkscrew curls clinging to her hand.

Rita was so relieved to have found her that she forgot about Sam, running across the road, calling, 'Mam! Mam!'

Sam hung back, suddenly feeling in the way.

Eve turned and her expression was one of shocked disbelief. Instantly she put several yards between her and the other woman. 'What are you doing here?'

she demanded crossly. Rita stopped in her tracks and angry tears filled her eyes. 'Don't look like that,' groaned Eve. 'You didn't come when I asked you so why should I welcome you with open arms now?'

'I didn't come because Aunt Margaret burnt your letter before I could see it,' she said fiercely. 'Anyway, you have a nerve saying that to me after dumping me the way you did.'

'I didn't dump you. I left you for a reason. Why are you here? Is she dead?'

'Of course not!' Rita was shocked at the very idea of Margaret being dead. 'We had an argument, so I left.'

'What! Are you bloody stupid, Reet?' Eve's blue eyes widened and her pencilled eyebrows shot up. 'Why d'you think I sent you to her?'

'Two reasons,' snapped Rita. 'One, because you bloody wanted to get rid of me and two—'

'Don't swear!'

'And two . . . you're daft enough to think there might be money in it for both of us.'

Eve smirked. 'What's so daft about that? Our Maggie's unlikely to marry after all this time. Her money should come to us. I was Father's daughter as much as she was.' Eve gave a sharp nod of her platinum-blonde head and began to walk with that peculiar little wiggle she had of the hips, dragging her son behind her.

Rita glanced down at him and his expression was

one of resignation. She winked at him and he smiled shyly and attempted to bury his head in the skirts of his mother's coat.

Eve stopped abruptly, causing Joshua's head to bump her leg. 'What did you argue about?'

Rita flushed. She had considered unburdening herself on her mother but had no intention of doing so now.

'Answer me!' Eve tapped the toe of her patent leather high heels on the pavement. 'Well?'

'Do we have to talk like this in the street?' said Rita, trying to control her temper. 'I've walked most of the way, sleeping rough. I'm hungry and would love a cup of tea.' Suddenly she remembered Sam and glanced behind her but there was no sign of him.

'Walked! You've no money?' said Eve.

Rita faced her mother. 'No! I was angry and just ran way.'

'You . . . are . . . a . . . fool,' said Eve, stressing each word with a stab in the air of a scarlet-tipped finger. 'You'd better go back immediately and make it up.'

'Didn't you hear a word I said, Mother? I . . . haven't . . . any . . . money,' said Rita slowly and distinctly. 'You will have to give me some if you want me to go back to Liverpool.'

Eve sighed exasperatedly. 'Do you think I'm made of money?'

'You can't be doing too badly by the look of you.

That coat hasn't had much wear.' Rita dropped her gaze. 'And the shoes are really smart.'

'Aren't they just?' said Eve, smiling. 'Well, you can come in but you're not stopping. I thought Caleb had run out on me when I wrote that letter asking you to come but he'd just gone back to sea without telling me. Couldn't stand being on shore for long. His ship's due in tomorrow.'

Rita was hurt and baffled by her mother's summary dismissal of her. 'Why can't I stay and meet him?'

'Ask no questions and you get told no lies,' said Eve, mounting a flight of steps. 'All I'll say is that you've improved since living with our Maggie, which is what I hoped, but I don't want any competition.'

'Competition! Me?' Rita found it hard to believe her mother had said that.

Eve took a key from her pocket and opened the door. She led her daughter through to a kitchen on the ground floor and lit a gas lamp protruding from a wall. 'You can stay the night but no longer – and you'll have to sleep in Josh's room.'

'He sleeps on his own?'

Eve raised her eyebrows as she put on the kettle. 'I can't have him in my room. Every movement he makes disturbs me.'

Rita realised what her mother was up to and was unable to conceal her disgust. 'You mean you're entertaining men while your husband's away.'

Eve pointed a finger at her. 'You keep your thoughts to yourself. That's why I can't have you here when Caleb comes home. You have too much to say for yourself. Now, tell me what the argument with our Maggie was about.'

'What's the point?' said Rita, her eyes smouldering. She sat sideways on a kitchen chair and rested her arm along the back. 'You're not really interested in me. If I were in trouble you wouldn't help me. She's done more for me than you ever did.'

Eve looked unmoved by that comment. 'Then why run away? If you've come all this way you must be desperate to get something off your chest. What set Maggie off? She used to have so much self-control when we were kids, it was unnerving.' Taking a loaf from the bread crock she picked up a knife and cut several slices. Joshua reached up to take one and received a rap across the knuckles with the handle of the knife for his trouble. 'Wait until you're given.' His bottom lip quivered.

Rita rose from her chair. 'D'you have to do that?'

'Don't interfere, Reet. You don't know what it's like until you have one.' Rita blushed. 'God, it's not that, is it?' cried Eve, dropping the bread knife. 'You haven't gone messing about with fellas and got yourself caught?'

The colour ebbed from Rita's face. 'I don't know.'

'What d'you mean you don't know?' snapped Eve. 'You either have or you haven't!'

Rita told her what had happened in the stables. Her mother listened without interruption. Then she asked her a few questions before saying, 'I don't know what you're worrying about. I'd say he didn't do enough to get you pregnant, but you can never tell.' She poured boiling water into the teapot. 'Who did you say the fella was?'

'Jimmy! I don't know his second name but his stepfather is William Brodie, who's up to his eyes in debt to Aunt Margaret. She's been threatening to have the bailiffs in for ages but there's something between them that stops her.'

Eve's expression froze. 'Well, who'd have believed they'd meet up again and our Maggie would be in a position to have her revenge on him. They were mad about each other once but then Alan came between them.'

'You mean his brother?'

'So she's talked about them, has she? She couldn't make up her mind which one she wanted and in the end she made a damn daft choice and let Will slip through her fingers.'

'Aunt Margaret seems to think you were very close to him.' Rita watched her mother's eyes carefully.

Eve's pencilled brows drew together. 'What's that sister of mine been saying?'

Rita took a deep breath. 'That he got you pregnant.'

Eve threw back her head and laughed. 'She always was jealous as hell of me! But that's plain daft! I'm not the sort he goes for.' She handed a cup of tea to Rita. 'Your father Harold was a very nice man. He was besotted with me. A steward on one of the liners, he died at sea of blood poisoning. My life and yours would have been very different if he hadn't.'

This information was a relief to Rita but she was also puzzled. 'Then who was she talking about?'

'Probably Bella, his wife. Although . . .' Eve frowned.

'Although what?' asked Rita.

Her mother shook her head. 'I'm not sure. Anyway, if that's what our Maggie thought, then no wonder things went wrong between them.'

'You knew Billy's mother?'

'Of course.' A cynical smile twisted Eve's painted lips. 'Now she always looked like butter wouldn't melt in her mouth but you know what they say – appearances can be deceptive.'

So Bella was a sexpot, thought Rita. 'Anything else you can tell me about when you were all young?'

'Not really. I'm not one for living in the past.' She paused to butter bread and gave half a round to Joshua. He sat on a low three-legged stool, chewing on the bread and staring at Rita from big brown eyes 'He's the apple of Caleb's eye, you know?' said Eve.

'I'm not surprised. He's a sweetie.' Rita smiled at her half-brother.

'I can tell you something our Maggie doesn't know,' said Eve, waving the knife about. 'I'd put it out of my mind until now. She was waiting to hear from Alan about joining him in China and Father didn't want her to go. I was paying one of my rare sneaky visits trying to cadge money from him, and a letter arrived by the afternoon post. The envelope had foreign stamps and the address was in Alan's handwriting. I commented about it to Father and he told me not to mention it to our Maggie and he'd give me some money.'

'So you kept your mouth shut,' said Rita slowly, unable to take her eyes from Eve's face. 'How could you?'

Eve shrugged. 'I needed the money. Besides, I didn't want her to go. I knew I was right when the news came that Alan had gone missing during some riots and was presumed dead. If she'd gone out there she could have been killed alongside him. I saved her life.'

'You would see it like that,' said Rita, shaking her head. 'I don't think she's ever forgotten him either. She's led a really unhappy life.'

'She hasn't done so bad. She's got the shop and all Father's money.' Eve pushed a plate of bread and butter across the table towards Rita and smiled. 'William asked her to marry him after Bella's death and she turned him down because she blamed him for his brother's death. Just because he was out there at the time! Crazy, if you ask me. Anyway, you can tell our Maggie that she's wrong about me and William – and I've got your birth certificate to prove it. Besides he did long trips and wasn't around. It can be very frustrating being married to a sailor, I can tell you that much.' She leant across the table. 'Now, tell me all about you and our Maggie and how you got on before this row that sent you flying down here?'

Rita told her about working in the shop, about the McGintys and her aunt's dream house. The information about the latter caused Eve to appear very thoughtful indeed.

It was not until Rita was lying on a mattress in the tiny box room where Joshua slept that she thought of Sam again. Thoroughly ashamed of herself for forgetting him, she crept downstairs and eased back the bolts on the front door. She gazed up and down the street but could not see him. Wondering where he was and feeling terribly guilty, she went slowly back upstairs.

The following morning Rita stood outside the lodging house, peering about for a sign of Sam, wondering where he had slept last night and feeling sad that she might never see him again. She was resigned to having to leave the boarding house that day, but at least all her efforts to see her mother had not been wasted. She had met her half-brother and Eve had reassured her about the identity of her father. She had also given advice on how to get rid of an unwanted baby, which Rita prayed she would not have to use. She had also been told how to turn men on and off like electric light bulbs, and not to be put off by her experience with Jimmy. 'Men can be beasts but there are good ones out there. Sex can be fun with the right lover. Otherwise, sweetie, I wouldn't have been so good at it and made money,' said Eve, more frank with her daughter than she had ever been. As it was, Rita did not want to think about sex at that moment.

Eve came and stood beside her. 'Well, it's been nice seeing you but you're better off with our Maggie.'

Rita turned to her. 'In that case, Mam, as I told you, I've got no money so you're going to have to sub me. I can't walk all the way back to Liverpool. I need enough for a train ticket and something to eat.' She held out her hand.

Eve sighed and opened her purse. 'I was waiting for you to ask me for money.' She offered a ten-shilling note.

Rita arched her eyebrows and took the money, but said, 'Thanks, but it's not enough. Home's over a hundred miles away.'

Once more Eve delved into her purse, shoving coins around. She brought out half a crown. Rita shook her head. Eve muttered under her breath and, lifting the side of her skirt, fiddled with her stocking top and brought out a banknote. 'That's my last offer!' She snatched the ten-shilling note out of her daughter's hand. 'Don't say I never give you anything.'

Rita gazed at the white banknote in amazement. 'Five whole pounds!' Her voice was jubilant. 'Thanks, Mam!'

Eve held up an admonishing finger. 'There'll be no more. I've been saving that for a rainy day. Write to me at Christmas and let me know how you go on.'

'Rightio!' Rita kissed her mother's cheek, and then looked down at her half-brother and ruffled his hair, feeling a deep sadness. She wondered what Margaret would have made of her nephew. At least one thing could be said for her aunt, and that was she seemed to have no prejudice against people of other races. 'Nice meeting you, Josh.'

She brushed the top of his head with her lips and then, with tears in her eyes, jumped the steps and marched along the street, head held high. She looked back once and saw her mother standing on the pavement with Joshua in her arms. Rita waved and then, with purpose in her stride, she headed for the railway station.

'And where are you off to? Forgotten about me, have yer?'

Rita stared at the skinny figure leaning against the lamp post on the corner of the street. Her face lit up. 'Sam, I'm really glad to see you. I'm sorry! I did forget you for a short while and by the time I remembered, you'd disappeared.'

'Felt in the way, didn't I! But I wasn't going to go off without saying *tarrah*.'

'Where did you sleep?'

'In a doorway.' He moved towards her. 'How did yer get on with your mam?'

Rita grimaced. 'She thinks I'm mad to have left my aunt the way I did. I'm not needed here so I'm going back. Besides, I've been asked to be a bridesmaid at a wedding so I have to get home. Mam did give me the money for my train ticket so I should be back in Liverpool this evening, with a bit of luck.'

His face fell. 'I'm going to miss yer. Yer me best mate!'

'Why don't you come back with me, then? I've got enough money to get us there. It's going to be tough on the road with winter coming on.'

Sam looked thoughtful. 'What about me dad? If he was to find out I was in the neighbourhood he'd have me life.'

'You've got to stop being frightened of him, Sam.' She slipped a hand through his arm. 'What you need is a Charles Atlas bodybuilding course so people won't bully you. My aunt's been saying for ages that we could do with a man about the place.'

He looked gratified but sighed and said, 'She'll take one look at me and say . . .' He put on a falsetto voice, 'You a man! You're nothing but a shirt button, milad!'

Rita's eyes twinkled. 'You've got a real talent there. But don't you think it's worth a try? I'm not even sure if Aunt Margaret'll take me back, and in that case we'll both be looking for work and a place to stay. I'd really like your company, Sam.'

'Would yer?' he said wistfully.

'Haven't I just said?'

'OK!' He jerked his head sharply. 'Let's go and buy them tickets.'

Margaret gazed at the broken window, angry and fearful. Part of her had been waiting for this to happen for some time. Whether the McGintys were responsible she didn't know, but at least it helped her to make up her mind about a house she had seen in Abercromby Square, similar to her original dream house. It had four storeys and a marvellous spiral cast-iron staircase going up from the ground floor to the roof.

She would make an offer and hope for the best. Estate agents were having trouble getting people to take over the lease on properties because there wasn't the money around these days. There would be rent to pay but that could be raised by letting out some of the rooms. Although that might be risky because moonlight flits were common occurrences. She would have to vet her tenants carefully. Without them she would rattle around the house like a dried pea in an empty tin now Rita had gone.

It had been a bad moment discovering her niece missing. In fact she had been near to tears, knowing she should not have lost her temper. Rita had worked so hard to improve herself and had become a real asset in the shop, as well as good company in the house. For several days she had waited, hoping her niece would return, worrying about her safety, knowing she had little money. When Rita hadn't turned up she had written to Eve but had yet to receive a reply. If her niece did not return, Margaret knew she would not get the same pleasure out of redecorating and furnishing the house. But still she was determined to move.

She turned away from the broken window, left the glazier to get on with his job and set off to visit the estate agent in North John Street, thinking she needed to bring more pressure to bear on her clients to pay what they owed her. Perhaps she should visit William, not having heard a thing from those up at the yard since the rumpus in the shop with Billy and Jimmy.

Margaret found William in the stables talking to a middle-aged man; both were wreathed in pipe smoke and had their backs to her. She waited a moment for them to finish their conversation before making her presence known. 'Good afternoon, Will! You'll set yourself on fire one of these days.'

He turned slowly and looked at her. 'And will you come and dance round my funeral pyre, Maggie?'

The other man excused himself.

'Maybe! I was sorry to hear about Alice.'

'Nice of you to say so.' William pointed his pipe at her. 'You understand her going off the way she did is the reason why you haven't seen me? I've some money for you.'

'That's what I like to hear.'

'And you're going to get it regularly from now on. I'm doing what I should have done when my uncle died and am putting a man in charge of this place.'

That shook her. 'So you're taking my advice! Goodness, Will, what next? Giving up gambling and smoking?'

'I'm going back to sea.'

He couldn't have surprised her more than if he'd said he was going to hang upside down from the mammoth crane down at the docks. 'After years on shore? Will you be able to get a ship? These are difficult times for seamen.' She hated the thought of him going away.

'I've still got contacts. We got a card from Alice a few days ago and yesterday Jimmy vanished. She's in America. I can only think he's gone in search of her. I'd much rather he'd leave her alone. I thought I'd go over there myself . . . work my passage. Don't want him upsetting her.'

'So are the girls together? Couldn't Billy have gone?'

William tapped his pipe against the wall, knocking out ash. 'He has his own fish to fry.' She thought he appeared ill at ease. 'How's young Rita?' he added.

Margaret felt suddenly weary and rested her back against the stable wall. 'She's gone off, too. What are we going to do with these young people, Will?'

He looked anxious. 'I'm really sorry to hear that, Maggie. Did she give you a reason?'

'If you mean Jimmy, then yes, he probably has a lot to do with it.' Her tone was brusque.

'I can only apologise for his behaviour.'

She sighed. 'I didn't exactly act in a way that made her believe she could depend on me to help her. I was reminded of Eve and that made me say things that I shouldn't have. I just hope she's with her mother and is all right.'

'Me, too,' said William, making a move outside. 'Nothing changes, does it, Maggie? Today's youngsters make just as many mistakes as we did when it comes to dealing with their feelings.'

She could not deny it. 'So how did Alice get to America?'

He smiled ruefully. 'Ellen did some fast talking and got them on a liner crossing the Atlantic as a musical double act.'

'Clever Ellen!'

'She was supposed to stay in America with Alice but met up with a couple of old friends and decided to stay on the liners.'

'I see. So is Alice with that American sailor she met?'

'She's staying with his sister in Chicago. He's gone back to sea.'

'So when will you be leaving?'

'Within the next few days. I'll come and say goodbye.' He smiled faintly. 'Now let's go into the office and I'll give you that money.'

That night Margaret had a nightmare. William hadn't changed at all but turned up at the shop drunk and smashed the new window. She had remonstrated with him by calling him a fool. 'Drinking, gambling, unable to face the truth of what you are! You've destroyed what could have been a good business and'll end up in hell!'

'Then I'll see you there, Maggie,' he'd whispered. 'You're a bloody hypocrite, unforgiving and miserly, and to top it all you've frightened that poor girl away. She could have put bricks in her pockets and thrown herself in the Mersey.'

Margaret had been unable to speak and William had vanished. Then she was running down to the river and there was Rita in the water, her hand stretched towards her. Margaret had tried to grasp it but the tide took her away.

When Margaret woke she prayed for the first time in a long time, prayed that Rita would come home. It did matter if she was pregnant but the main thing was that she was safe.

CHAPTER FIFTEEN

'There's some money in here,' said Sam, gazing in the pawnshop window.

'Of course there is, but getting your money to work for you is the way to make more and you need to have nous to do that, Sam.' Rita's brow knitted in thought, as her fingers dug into fresh putty. 'Come on, let's go and face Aunt Margaret . . . and I warn you now not to touch anything. You know what she's like.'

'Has eyes in the back of her head.' He pushed the door and held it open for Rita.

Margaret had just been reading over the clauses in the lease, and thinking she would have to consult a solicitor before signing anything, when the shop door opened. She glanced up and saw Rita standing in the doorway. Relief showed in the woman's face and then she saw Sam and her expression changed.

Rita forced Sam towards the counter. 'Hello, Aunt Margaret! Who broke the window? You been having trouble while I've been away?'

'You could say that.' Margaret pointed a finger at Sam. 'Don't I know him?'

'I'll go,' said Sam, his expression that of a mouse encountering a female tabby, and would have hightailed out of there if Rita had not kept a firm hold on him.

'Of course you know Sam,' she said. 'He's kind, generous, resourceful and has been a real help to me. I wouldn't have got to Mam's if it hadn't been for him.'

Sam blushed and mumbled something incomprehensible.

'So what's he doing here?' asked Margaret.

Rita smiled. 'I thought he might be useful to you. Contrary to his looks he's quite strong.'

Margaret sniffed and came from behind the counter and sniffed again. 'He smells.'

Sam moaned. 'I'm goin'!' And he tried to escape again but Rita hung on to him with both hands. 'You'd smell, too, if you'd lived on the road. You can't carry a bath on your back, you know! And the streams and rivers are freezing at this time of year. He left Liverpool because his sister died and his father was a bully.'

'Then what's he doing coming back? You don't expect me to take him in?'

Rita smiled sweetly. 'You've got plenty of room and if windows are getting smashed then it'll be good to have him around.'

Margaret could scarcely believe her ears. 'How do I know that he's trustworthy?'

'Because I'll vouch for him! I've trusted him with my life. If you're not prepared to give us both jobs then we'll look elsewhere.' Rita's brown eyes sparkled defiantly.

At that Margaret laughed. 'Oh, the nerve of the young! I wish I had half your courage.' She sobered. 'So you got to see Eve. How did you find her?'

'Looking good but she wasn't having me staying there.' Rita shrugged, resigned as her half-brother to her mother's ways.

'So that's why you're back?' said Margaret dryly.

'Nope! I had every intention of coming back,' said Rita, crossing her fingers, knowing she'd thought no further than seeing her mother when she made the journey to Cardiff. 'I thought you'd be lonely without me.' Her eyes twinkled.

'Uhh! So you thought I'd miss you!' Margaret thought that it was good to see that twinkle.

Rita said boldly, 'I bet you have.'

'I thought you might have gone to your mother's so I wrote to her.'

'Your letter hadn't arrived before I left, but then

letters have a habit of going missing – and people do get things mixed up. You were wrong about Mr Brodie and Mam – if it was her you meant. My dad's name was Harold and he died at sea.'

Margaret was completely baffled. 'I don't remember saying anything about Eve and Will – and what's your father got to do with it?'

Rita knew her mother had been right. 'Forget it,' she said cheerfully. 'I misunderstood you. But I'm not mistaken about the letter.'

Margaret was getting even more confused as to why Rita should go on about a letter. 'You mean the letter I wrote to your mother?'

'No! The one your father got rid of because he didn't want you going off to China.' Rita yawned. 'Can Sam and I stay or not? Because if we can't I'd like to get something from my room before we leave. It's a red and gold phoenix that Billy gave me. I hope you haven't sold it.'

'No, I haven't sold it,' said Margaret, resting against the counter, trying to get things sorted out in her head. Had she misheard Rita? 'Can you repeat that about my father getting rid of a letter to stop me going to China?'

Rita shifted uncomfortably. 'Perhaps I shouldn't have mentioned it just like that.'

'Well, you have! So you'd better tell me everything our Eve said about it.'

'There's not much to tell. Only that it was from

Mr Brodie's brother and your father destroyed it. She had no idea what was in it.'

Margaret paled. 'When was this?'

Rita shrugged. 'It must have been after she left home because she came back here to try and wheedle money out of him.'

'And she kept quiet all this time,' whispered Margaret.

The shop door opened and a customer entered. Rita recognised the woman and said to her aunt, 'Let me deal with her. I've really missed the shop.'

Margaret turned on her heel and went into the back premises.

Sam looked at Rita. 'Just stick around,' she said in a low voice, going behind the counter. She faced the customer with a smile. 'Right, Mrs Swift, what can I do for you?'

From a tatty shopping bag the woman drew a chipped jug. 'Can yer give me a tanner for this, girl? Me kids haven't had anythin' to eat today, and I wanna get some neck ends to make soup.'

The jug wasn't worth sixpence, tuppence more like, and Rita told her so, but she felt sorry for the woman so gave her fourpence and wrote out a pawn ticket, knowing it was highly unlikely the jug would ever be redeemed.

No sooner had that customer left than another entered. 'Glad to see yer back,' said the woman, leaning on the counter. 'I see Miss Sinclair's had the window fixed. That must have cost her a few bob.'

'What happened? I haven't had a chance to find out yet.'

'Someone threw a brick through it, didn't they? Real big hole it made.'

'Was anything stolen?'

The woman tightened her headscarf and laughed. 'What d'you think? Nobody goes and does that for the fun of it.'

Rita served her as quickly as she could to get rid of her and was soon ushering Sam into the back.

There was no sign of Margaret. 'Where is she?' said Rita, looking about her. She went into the scullery but her aunt was not there. She put the kettle on and made tea. She took the teapot into the kitchen and found Sam standing in front of the fire, his hands held out to the blaze. She told him to pour the tea and went upstairs. There was no response from Margaret's bedroom, which was locked. Slowly Rita returned to the kitchen. She and Sam were hungry so she made toast, wondering where her aunt could be.

Margaret almost flew up Leece Street. She had to see William. Why she should be so certain that he knew what had been in the letter that her father had destroyed she could not explain. Perhaps it had something to do with him and Alan being twins. Despite their differences, they'd been alike in many ways. She reached the yard. A couple of men were talking by the stables. One of them was the man she had seen with William two days ago. She called over, asking if Mr Brodie was about.

'He's not here, Miss Sinclair. He collapsed shortly after you left. Peritonitis! They've operated but it's touch and go. He'd said he'd been feeling a bit off but none of us expected this.'

For a moment Margaret could not speak and then she found her voice. 'Where is he?' she croaked.

'The Royal Infirmary.' The man hesitated before adding, 'We're not sure what to do about things here with him gone – buying feed and the like. His credit's not good, as you know only too well. What d'you advise?'

Margaret managed to pull herself together. 'What's your name?'

'Dixon. Albert Dixon!'

'Then, Mr Dixon, you will do what should be done. You tell the tradesmen to send their bills to me.'

He looked relieved and touched his cap. 'Right you are, Miss Sinclair.'

Although she was feeling dreadful, Margaret made her way to the Royal Infirmary in Pembroke Place. She could have taken a tram but she was in a dreamlike state and just set one foot in front of the other. She prayed earnestly as she had prayed for Rita's return. At last she reached the soot-begrimed red-bricked Victorian building and went inside.

She asked at reception for the whereabouts of William Brodie and, although it was not visiting hours, her manner was such that she received the information she required and was not prevented from proceeding to the ward where he had been taken.

Margaret hated hospitals. Their distinctive smell of disinfectant and floor polish was mixed up with a natural fear of death. Too often people didn't come out, except feet first. The corridors seemed endless and voices were muted. It was as if people were scared to speak aloud of the thing they dreaded in case it came to pass. She came to the ward and pushed open the door.

The ward sister looked up at the pale-faced, upright figure. 'You can't come in here. Visiting hours are . . .' Her voice trailed off as Margaret ignored her and walked past her desk.

She hurried along the long line of metal-framed narrow beds with their coughing, moaning or unconscious patients. She almost walked past William. It was he who called her name and brought her up short. The lack of strength in his voice frightened her. She looked down at him and knew she was going to have a fight on her hands if she was to keep him alive.

Rita placed a steaming bowl of soup in front of Sam, who said, 'This looks good. But d'yer think it's all right us eating her food without permission?' He cocked an eyebrow.

She laughed. 'Come off it, Sam! Think of all those eggs you stole from farms. Besides, she's my aunt so it's not stealing. Just eat, then you're coming out with me.'

He grinned. 'OK! Perhaps I'm being overzealous in wanting to win her over to believe I'm the perfect lodger. But will she let us in again if she gets back before us?'

Rita winked. 'I know where the spare key's kept.'

It was eight o'clock in the evening and there was still no sign of Margaret. Rita had decided to waste no more time hanging around but to visit the yard. It was the only place she could think of where her aunt might be. Jimmy was the last person Rita wanted to bump into but she knew that, sooner or later, she would have to face him – and anyway, she would not be alone.

Tears rolled down Margaret's cheeks as she held tightly onto William's hand. Over his head hung a notice saying NIL BY MOUTH. He had dozed off and soon she would have to go. The ward sister had told her to leave but she had refused and the nurse had gone away. From the staff's behaviour she sensed they didn't hold out much hope for him, but she was not going to give up yet. She would get him out of this place. He needed special nursing and here there were too many other patients; if he caught an infection from any of them it could finish him off.

She rose from the chair and wiped her tears away. Time to do something! Squaring her shoulders, she marched down the ward to where the sister was sitting at a desk, watching her. She guessed that the woman hated visitors disturbing her routine.

'I want to see whichever doctor is looking after Mr Brodie,' said Margaret imperiously. 'I can pay and if you don't pussyfoot around I'll give this hospital a generous donation. I want him out of here and taken to this nursing home.' She picked up the fountain pen from the sister's desk and wrote an address in perfect copperplate. 'And I want it done as soon as possible.'

Rita stood gazing at the shop window, wondering who was responsible for smashing it. They had just returned from Brodie's yard where she had received triple shocks. She could only guess her aunt had gone to the hospital. Poor Mr Brodie, not expected to live. She would be upset. Then there was the news that Jimmy had gone to America! He would never have done so if he'd known Mr Brodie was so ill. After all, he had always wanted the yard. Still, she was glad he was out of the way but sad that Billy had gone off too.

'Are we going to stay out here all night?' asked Sam, hunching his shoulders against the cold. 'Your aunt might be in by now.'

'Let's hope so.' Rita opened the door to the private entrance. Feeling her way along the darkened lobby she called her aunt, but there was no response.

It was gone eleven before everything was arranged to Margaret's satisfaction, and now she was on her way home. She felt worn out and was still worried sick about William but she had done her best and had to be content with that.

She entered the house and almost immediately heard Rita's infectious chuckle and then a responding male laughter. Only then did she remember that her niece had come home with a young tramp. Margaret pushed open the door and saw Rita perched on the edge of a chair, smiling down at Sam. He was kneeling on the rug but as soon as he saw Margaret he rose to his feet and stood with his hands clasped in front of his chest, wearing an expression that reminded her of a dog expecting to be thrown out.

She thought fretfully that it wasn't fair of Rita expecting her to take him in. What was she supposed to do with him? If she told him to go Rita said that she'd leave as well. Oh, what it was to be young and have the courage of your convictions! Rita reminded her of herself as a girl, prepared to go to the other side of the world. Adventure had beckoned and she could be with the man she believed worthy of her love; they would be working in harness for God.

How could her father have destroyed the letter most likely summoning her to be with Alan?

Gazing down at the two young people, she was filled with anger, envy and despair. They had their lives before them and most likely would find love and companionship and have children, whereas she had more years behind her than in front of her. Her past could have been so different. Yet she should be thankful to Rita for shocking her out of her shell. Otherwise she would never have met up with William again. But maybe it was too late and she would lose him.

Panic gripped her and a sharp pain darted through her left breast. Sweat broke out on her forehead and her mouth went dry. She was going to die! Stretching out a hand to Rita, she gasped, 'Please, help me!' Then she slid down the wall into a heap on the floor.

Rita flew over to her and fumbled for a pulse, scared out of her wits. It was a relief to feel the beat, beat, beat. A minute later Margaret stirred. Her eyelids fluttered open but her eyes looked blank. That was enough for Rita to say to Sam, 'I'm going for the doctor. You stay with her.'

'Will I get her onto the sofa?' He looked nervous. 'I mean, will she let me touch her?'

'Just stay with her.' Rita delayed no longer and ran out of the house.

The doctor who lived above his surgery was not pleased at being roused from his bed but when the maid told him who needed him and what had happened he did not delay. He put his overcoat over his pyjamas and grabbed his black bag.

By the time they reached the house, Margaret was lying on the sofa with her eyes closed. Her face was pale and clammy. Rita thought she looked dreadful. The doctor took out his stethoscope and told Rita to make some hot sweet tea. 'You've had a shock,' he said.

Rita dragged Sam into the scullery. 'Will she go to hospital? Can we stay here if she does? I'd almost forgotten what it was like to be so warm and have a full belly,' he said.

'I don't want her to go into hospital,' said Rita fiercely. 'This is my fault. I shouldn't have told her about the letter – and on top of that Mr Brodie could die. Perhaps he's already dead! She used to get real mad at him and threaten to take his business but she's known him for years and used to be in love with him.'

When the doctor called Rita she was pleased to see that, although Margaret looked exhausted still, her colour was much better.

'She's had several upsets lately from what she's told me,' said the doctor, writing out a prescription. 'I'm pretty certain that her heart's fine and it's her nerves that are letting her down. I've given her an injection and she's to take the tablets I've prescribed. See that she rests and don't let her get worked up over things.'

'Your bill, Doctor,' whispered Margaret, her eyelids fluttering.

He wrote with a flourish and placed it on the mantelpiece. 'Payment will do tomorrow.'

'No. I'll not be in debt. I'll pay now.' She made to get up but the doctor stayed her with a hand. 'Do as you're told, Miss Sinclair,' he said sternly. 'I'll not charge you interest. Send this young lady with the money tomorrow, and if you need me again, don't hesitate to get in touch.'

Rita offered him a cup of tea. He thanked her with a smile but said that he was for his bed. She saw him out and then returned to the kitchen. She would have liked to ask her aunt how Mr Brodie was but knew this was not the time and offered instead to help her upstairs.

Margaret thanked her but said she would stay where she was for a while longer and could Rita put a hot-water bottle in her bed. She took a key from about her neck and handed it to her. She trusts me, marvelled Rita, and filled the hot-water bottle and took it up to her aunt's room.

She gazed about her, remembering that first night she had spent there after Margaret had chopped off most of her hair. How they had resented each other – but now they had come to depend on each other. Rita gripped her bottom lip between her teeth to stop it trembling and then hurried downstairs to help her aunt to bed.

* * *

When Margaret woke it was daylight but she still felt as weak as one of those women who'd had the blood sucked out of them by that vampire creature played by Bela Lugosi. She tried to sit up, found it a struggle and was aware of a rising panic. There was so much to do. William to visit . . . the house in Abercromby Square to cancel. She felt a momentary overwhelming disappointment. She had come so close to getting her dream house, but thank God she had not signed the lease and had money to draw on to pay William's medical bills and to keep his business going.

Rita appeared with a tray. 'You OK?' she said cheerfully.

Her solicitude made Margaret want to weep but old habits die hard. 'I'm not dead yet,' she said gruffly. 'Has that scruffy little tramp you brought home run off with my money yet?'

'With you here? He wouldn't dare! He's making the fire and I've told him to light one up here, too.'

Margaret was shocked. She had never had a fire in her bedroom in her life. 'Think of the expense of all that extra wood and coal! I'm getting up!' But when she tried to stand she realised how weak she was and sat down quickly.

Rita said anxiously, 'Are you OK? Need help?'

Margaret put her head in her hands and wept.

'Oh, don't cry!' said Rita, sitting on the bed and putting an arm round her. 'You're going to be fine.

Get into bed and have your cup of tea and I'll go and get the tablets the doctor prescribed.'

Margaret wiped her eyes with the back of her hand. 'I need the lavatory.'

'Use the po!'

'I'd rather go downstairs, and besides, I want to wash my hands and face . . . and thinking of washing, has that young man had a bath yet?'

Rita smiled. 'I thought I'd give him the money to go to Cornwallis Street and have a bath there. It'll be less messing. I've still got a few bob from the money Mam gave me, so I'll pay.'

'Eve gave you money?'

Rita chuckled. 'How did you think I got home? I was skint.' She got up from the bed. 'D'you want me to help you downstairs?'

'Later. I'll do what you say and drink my tea first.' She looked up at her niece and there was warmth in her dark eyes. 'Thank you, Rita.'

'For what?'

'Coming home.' Her voice was husky.

'Get away with you!' said Rita, but she was touched and left the bedroom before she started crying, too.

In the past Margaret had scorned those women who took to their beds with nerves but now she understood how they felt. She was exhausted and the least effort or worry could bring on a panic

310

attack. Even so, she could not stop herself worrying about William and his business. Ten days had gone by since she had seen him, and despite Rita having made several telephone calls on her behalf at the nearest post office, and having reassured her that he was in a stable condition at the nursing home, she fretted.

So the following Sunday morning when Margaret was sitting in a chair in front of her fire she told Rita to visit him. 'Get some fruit from that shop that's open all hours and take it to him. Surely he'll be able to eat something by now. We could do with getting in touch with the padre. He might know where Billy is and send him a wire.' She sighed. 'Oh, why did Alice have to go to America just when Will needs her! And as for Jimmy . . .'

'I'm sure they'll write,' said Rita, not wanting to be reminded of Jimmy. She'd had a period so that was good. 'Is there anything you want? Chocolate?'

Margaret looked more cheerful. 'Chocolate. And make sure you close the side door properly behind you, and that the shop doors are locked. I haven't really said much about the window being smashed, but I can tell you I've never been frightened being here on my own before but I am now. That's the trouble with having company. You get used to it.'

'What was stolen?'

'Just a few trinkets. The good stuff I keep locked

up elsewhere, as you know. I'm worried in case they come up here the next time.'

Rita did not need to ask who *they* were. The McGinty lads! But it wasn't doing her aunt any good talking about break-ins. 'There's not going to be a next time because you're not alone. Sam's downstairs, remember?'

'That really makes me feel better,' said Margaret, giving her one of her looks, and reaching beneath her cushion she produced a heavy doorstop. 'I'm not taking any chances. I was one of the best bowlers in our rounders team when I was young. Now off you go. I'll decide if I can trust my life to that young man or not.'

Rita smiled, wondering what Sam would make of her aunt's defensive action and decided she had best warn him in case he took her up a cup of tea.

She found him spreading butter liberally on a doorstep round of bread. 'This is the life,' he said, grinning at her. 'We can pretty well do what we like with your aunt ill in bed.'

'You can rid yourself of that attitude,' said Rita, poking him in the chest. 'You're not here for a free ride. If you want to stay once she's up and about again you've got to pull your weight and show her that you're not only a worker but that you can be trusted with her last farthing.'

'OK! There's nothing you want me to do today is there? It *is* Sunday, the day of rest.' He picked up the *Wizard* comic from the arm of the chair.

'You know what they say, Sam. There's no rest for the wicked – even on Sunday. You could dust all that stuff on the top shelves in the shop. It hasn't been done for God only knows how long. There's a ladder. Don't go falling off it.' She chuckled at his expression. 'Only joking! But be warned if you take her a cup of tea; don't make any sudden threatening moves because you'll end up with a smashed skull. She's got a doorstop under her cushion.'

It was the first time she had left him alone in the house with her aunt and she hoped that if they spent just a little time in each other's company to start with, they would slowly get used to each other.

Rita felt apprehensive as a nurse showed her to William's room overlooking the green expanse of Sefton Park, but when she saw him she felt much better. He did look careworn and his skin was pallid but the blue eyes, so like Billy's, had plenty of life in them. He asked after Margaret.

'She's getting on OK. The doctor said she'd had too many shocks lately.' Rita offered him a pear from the fruit she had brought and took one herself.

'You disappearing, for example!' There was an amused expression on his face as he watched her eat.

Rita flushed. 'I had my reasons. Besides, Aunt Margaret guessed I'd gone to see Mam.'

'How is Eve?'

'Mam never changes.' Rita removed a pip from her teeth and placed it in a handkerchief. 'She told me a few things I wanted to know but I wasn't needed there so I came back. I've got a younger half-brother.' She couldn't disguise the pride in her voice. 'His name's Joshua and he's got the curliest hair. I wish I had curls like his.'

'You should eat more crusts. Although your hair is pretty as it is.'

She smiled. 'Mam tried to get me to eat crusts by saying that I'd get curls and I believed her. I wanted blonde curls like hers. I've even thought of bleaching my hair, but I think Aunt Margaret would hit the roof. I was amazed when she took notice of me, got her hair cut and had a perm as well. It made her look younger and she's a nicer person.'

'A woman needs to look her best to feel her best, and that affects her whole outlook.'

Rita thought what a wise man he was and how well he knew women, but then he'd had two wives so must know something about what makes women tick.

There was a silence and his eyelids dropped. 'Are you tired? Would you like me to go?' She leant towards him. 'I know I've only just come but Aunt Margaret said I mustn't tire you, just see how you are.'

William forced his eyes open. 'No, stay a little longer. Tell me about these other things that have upset Maggie.'

'The shop window was smashed. It was probably

314

the McGintys bent on revenge. Their father didn't steal from us that time, as you know.'

'It was Jimmy and he got off scot-free. When did the window get smashed?'

'While I was away.' The expression on his face caused her to add, 'You don't think Jimmy did it before he left? She went for him with her cane, you know?'

William smiled faintly. 'Billy told me. She's some woman is Maggie. You're thinking Jimmy might have done it for spite. It's possible.' He sighed. 'You think you know someone, then find out you don't at all.'

'How well do you think you know Billy?'

'Better than I used to. There's lots of things I never gave him the chance to tell me and matters I just couldn't talk to him about for a long time. I'm glad we got round to doing so before it was too late.'

She felt as if a cube of ice had been dropped down her back. 'What d'you mean, "too late"?'

William grimaced. 'We never know when the final trumpet's going to sound for any of us, luv.'

'But Billy's OK and you're going to get better, aren't you?' Her tone was anxious.

'I treated him badly through no fault of his own.' William closed his eyes. 'As for me – the doctor says I've got to look after myself if I want to make old bones.'

'You must do as he says then,' said Rita firmly,

remembering her mother saying that the man who admitted to being wrong was a rarity.

'I'm not very good at looking after myself,' said William with a sigh.

Another thing Eve had said was that men were useless at doing that very thing. Rita smiled. 'Then we'll have to find someone to look after you when you come out, so you'll stay out of mischief.'

'I like that "we".' His voice was drowsy. 'Anything else you can tell me?'

She told him about Sam and how he'd helped her reach Cardiff. Also about Margaret's letter from his brother being destroyed.

William frowned. 'So Alan wrote to Maggie. I wish I'd known, and whether he told her the truth.'

'The truth?'

He said, 'Thanks for coming. Give my love to Maggie.'

Her curiosity unsatisfied, Rita left.

CHAPTER SIXTEEN

Margaret was eager for news when Rita arrived home. 'So how is he?'

'Pale but smiling. He asked after you.' Rita knelt on the rug in front of the fire, holding her hands out to the blaze, and thought how much more lived-in the bedroom looked with the shadows of the flames flickering round the walls and an open magazine and crochet on a small table.

'Did he say anything about going back to sea?' asked Margaret anxiously.

'No!' Rita was surprised. 'The doctor said he's to take things easy. I should imagine the work would be too strenuous on a ship.'

Relieved, Margaret asked what else they had talked about.

Rita hesitated, unsure whether to mention the letter.

'Out with it!' said Margaret, the glow of the fire illuminating the fine lines about her eyes and mouth. 'I'll only worry, and that's not good for me.'

'I mentioned the letter from his brother and he said something about him telling you the truth.'

'The truth?' Margaret frowned.

'I shouldn't have told you,' said Rita glumly. 'You'll only worry more now.'

Margaret did not deny that but decided she would try not to think about until she could ask William what he meant. 'Anything else?'

'He said he wasn't very good at looking after himself and I said . . .' She hesitated.

Margaret smiled faintly, 'Go on!'

'That we'd help him.'

'And what did he say to that?'

'He liked the idea and sent you his love.'

'Did he now?' Margaret blushed. 'He must be getting better. We'll have to see what we can do to make his life brighter and more comfortable when he comes out of the nursing home.'

But within days she decided something should be done before then and sent Rita to the yard to see how things were. 'And ask for the account books,' Margaret called after her.

Rita found Mr Dixon in the cookhouse frying

eggs. 'We're not doing badly,' he said in answer to her question. 'I could do with an extra man and there's a machine I'd like to buy. It cuts hay into chop which would save time and labour. I know where one's going second-hand if your aunt doesn't mind forking out.'

'I'll mention it.' Rita asked for the account books.

'You'll find them in the office.' He reached into his pocket and handed a bunch of keys to her. 'You could tell your aunt, too, a couple more slates blew off the roof in the storm last week and water's getting in.'

Rita thanked him and swapped the warmth of the cookhouse for the damp chill of the house. She picked up the accounts book from the office and then walked through to the sitting room. She remembered Alice and Ellen discussing music in here and wondered how long it would be before they received a reply to the letter Margaret had written to Alice about William's illness. There were still ashes in the grate and she was reminded of Billy giving her the phoenix and what he had said about starting a new life. The padre had sent a wire to his ship but they had not heard anything from him. Her heart ached, thinking of him.

She cleaned out the grate. Then went over to a window where the heavy curtains and dingy nets shut out the wintry sunshine. Standing on a chair, she took down nets and curtains from both windows before going upstairs. There were pools of water where the rain had come through on the landing and in Alice's room. She mopped them up and placed buckets beneath the leaking ceilings.

Then she went into William's room, took down the curtains and stripped the bed. Looking at the walls she decided the room needed brightening up. She would speak to her aunt about buying paint and wallpaper for this room and the sitting room downstairs.

When Rita broached the subject of repairs to the roof and redecoration to the two rooms, Margaret said, 'You think I'm made of money?' Her tone was mild, so the girl pushed the issue.

'You could use the profits from the yard.'

Margaret looked up from the accounts and laughed. 'Any money coming in is going out again. Still, we have to speculate to accumulate. Tell Mr Dixon to buy his cutter and if he knows an honest roofer to get those slates fixed.'

'The decorating?'

'I'm sure Sam could splash a bit of paint about.'

Rita smiled, thinking that was a good idea.

'Maybe he could also help them up at the yard one day a week. I'm sure we could spare him.' Margaret's tone was dry.

Rita found Sam in the bedroom across the landing. She had been as astonished as he was when Margaret had given him Donald's old room. 'Time it was used. He'd have never wanted it to be a shrine,' she had said.

Sam had replied that it was real man's room and treated everything in it with respect. When Rita entered he was sitting on the bed with the ship in a bottle in his hands. 'Have you seen this?' he said.

'Of course I've seen it, dafty!'

'What I mean is, *really* seen it. It's a work of art.'

'Yes, it's very nice. But put it down! There's a couple of jobs for you up at the yard.'

He returned the ship in the bottle to its place and gave her his full attention. She told him what her aunt had said and immediately Sam perked up. 'I'd enjoy doing both. I feel like a spare part round here sometimes.'

So the following Wednesday afternoon when the shop was closed Rita and Sam went to the yard. She showed him William's bedroom first. He stood in the middle of the room, eyes narrowed, gazing round, before nodding. 'He was a sailor like your Uncle Donald, you said?'

'Yes.'

'Then I know exactly what I'd like to do with this room.'

'Good,' she said, relieved. 'I can leave you to see to buying what's needed, then?'

He agreed.

They went to see Mr Dixon and she told him what her aunt had said. The yard manager eyed Sam up and down and his lips twitched. 'I'm sure we can find something for you to do, lad, and it'll put a bit of muscle on you.'

Rita returned to the pawnshop and told her aunt

that everything had been set in motion. Margaret asked if there had been any letters from Alice or Billy. The girl shook her head, gazing out over the street. 'You keeping your eye on things?'

Margaret's crochet lay still in her lap. 'Yes. There's the constable. He's been more attentive since the brick came through the window. He said he's given the McGintys a warning, although they deny responsibility.'

'Perhaps they're telling the truth. Mr Brodie and I did wonder if it was an act of revenge on Jimmy's part for you hitting him with the cane.'

'Good God! I never thought of that,' said Margaret. 'I'm glad there's the Atlantic Ocean between us if that's so.'

'We've got Sam now to protect us,' said Rita seriously.

Margaret laughed. 'He wouldn't scare a cat.'

'I reckon he'll surprise us one day,' said Rita. 'In the meantime we could buy one of those wire mesh guards to put over the window.'

'People won't be able to see what's on display,' said Margaret, shaking her head. 'And it'll cost money. No, I think it was Jimmy, as you've said, and there's no need for us to worry about any more bricks coming through the window.'

A fortnight later Rita went to the yard to hang the clean curtains and make up William's bed, he was due home in a couple of days. Sam had been busy and now she had the chance to see what kind of job he had made of the painting.

Her eyes widened in wonder as she surveyed first the sitting room. 'But it's marvellous! I knew you were good at drawing but I didn't realise you were so talented, Sam.' He had not just distempered the walls in a delicate shade of peach but painted curls and whorls and leaves and flowers.

He looked gratified. 'I enjoyed doing it. It relaxes me. I hope Mr Brodie likes it, and what I've done to his bedroom.'

Rita grabbed his hand and literally ran him upstairs. She gasped as she stood in the middle of William's room, because here Sam had given full rein to his creative muse. On the wall facing the bed he had painted a ship in full sail against a pale-blue background.

'What d'you think?' He sounded anxious.

She said delightedly, 'I'm sure he'll think it's great!'

Sam whooped and putting his arms around Rita he swung her round. 'I really love you, Reet.'

'I love you, too. Now put me down.'

Immediately he did as told but kept an arm round her shoulders, hugging her against him as he gazed at his creation. 'I've never been happier than I am right now.'

'Well, you've cause to be pleased with yourself. You're really clever.' She kissed his cheek and he surprised her by kissing her right back on the lips.

Then he released her, a faint blush on his cheeks.

'Are we going to hang the curtains?'

While they busied themselves, Rita spoke about doing something to build him up despite the strength she had felt in those arms that had lifted her. 'You're not the seven-stone weakling you used to be but you need more muscle if Aunt Margaret's going to take you seriously as a protector.'

'Yer mean I really should do some bodybuilding?' He took a couple of monkey nuts from his pocket, shelled one and offered her the contents before cracking another shell for himself.

She munched the peanuts. 'You could learn ju-jitsu.' He looked blank. 'Oriental self-defence.' She feigned a blow, holding her hand flat. 'I've seen posters in Chinatown. You can have lessons.'

'They'll cost money.'

'Then we'll have to ask Aunt Margaret for some. You are working here as well as at the pawnshop so you deserve some pay as well as your keep.'

Sam smiled. 'That'd be good. I've enjoyed the painting and I like going to the docks with the men. We could do with a lorry up here, though. More deliveries would get done.' He brought out more peanuts, taken from the heaps stacked up at the oil-refining and soap factory down by the docks. He had been told to help himself.

Rita said she would mention the lorry to her aunt. Margaret almost blew a gasket, saying neither

William nor she could afford one. Margaret had been thinking seriously about the future and knew she must talk to him. Her emotions were still in a tangle where he was concerned but she'd had an idea that she could not get rid of and, nervous as she was about broaching the subject, she felt she must.

When she knew William was home and had given him a chance to settle in, Margaret went up to the yard. She had heard about Sam's paintings and considered it a reasonable topic to break the ice.

He opened the door to her and all the careful words she had prepared were forgotten. She was shocked by his appearance and wanted to put her arms round him, hug him tightly and then take him home with her. He needed building up if he was to cope with all the ills that plagued folk in the winter and killed many.

'Come in, Maggie. It's good to see you. Are you feeling better now?' His voice was deeper than she remembered and seemed to resonate round the yard.

'Yes! But you've lost weight.'

'And you've put it on. It suits you.' He grinned, taking her arm and helping her over the threshold. 'Have you come to see Sam's painting?'

'I've come to see *you*.' She was very conscious of that hand on her arm. 'But yes, I'd like to see what the lad's made of it. Rita seems to think he's done a marvellous job.'

'She's right.' William led Margaret into the sitting room.

The last time she had been there she had thought it a cold hole, but now she drew in a breath and smiled. 'It's . . . it's . . .'

'Different,' said William, smiling.

'But so clean and cheerful and warm-looking.'

'He's a talented young man and Dixon speaks well of him. Says he's willing to have a go at anything. Come over to the fire!' William's hand slid down her arm and took her gloved fingers. He led her over to one of the fireside chairs. 'Tea?'

'Thanks.'

Now she was here Margaret knew it was going to be difficult to say what she wanted. It was so much easier for men, she thought crossly, removing her coat and hat. She sat down and gazed into the fire, wondering how William felt living on his own. She remembered Billy saying this had never been a happy house. Was it possible to get rid of the ghosts that haunted it and make a fresh start?'

'I'd like to see what you think of Sam's work in my bedroom.' William placed the tea tray on a gate-legged table in front of the fire.

'Will I pour?' she asked.

He thanked her and sat down, and only now did she notice that there were more silver threads in his black curls. We're both getting old, she thought sadly. 'Rita told me that with just a few lines he's created a ship.'

'I imagine myself sailing away in her every night.' His eyes gleamed.

She handed him his tea. 'Are you sorry you can't go to sea?'

'I'm a realist. Drink up, then I'll take you to see my dream ship. First, I want to thank you for all you've done for me. When I'm solvent again I'll repay you every penny you spent getting me on my feet.'

'There's no need for that. I did it for old times' sake . . . for the good times.' Her voice was low. 'For a long time I wouldn't think about them, but during the last few weeks I've had time to think and remember.'

'I'm glad of that, Maggie. The bad and ugly should be buried and forgotten, leaving alive only the good.'

'It's not been easy,' she whispered.

He took the cup from her and placed it on the table. Then he drew her to her feet and into his arms. She looked up and saw an expression in his eyes that caused her pulse to leap with nervous excitement. She would have moved away but his arms tightened, and he drew her closer. His breath was warm on her cheek . . . her nose . . . her mouth.

His lips moved over hers in a way that she could not resist and, when that kiss ended, he kissed her again, before his lips moved to caress her chin, throat and the hollow beneath her collar-bone. His hands slid up from her waist and paused just beneath her breasts.

'Marry me, Will?' she said in a throaty whisper.

He froze and for a moment Margaret was

frightened of she knew not what. Then he held her against him and kissed her hair before resting his cheek against hers. 'I can't!'

'Can't?' Forcing her head up, she looked into his eyes and was shocked by what she saw. 'What's made you change your mind since the time you asked me? My terribly unsympathetic, judgemental, unforgiving behaviour? Or did you meet a pretty young nurse in the home?' Margaret was so hurt she could not control her tongue.

A derisive smile curled his mouth. 'Trust you to think up another woman! It's neither that nor your behaviour. There are other reasons.'

'Such as?'

'Your money could prevent me from jumping at your offer.'

She stared at him in astonishment. 'Not for one minute! You'd have to be mad not to accept the chance of having your debt wiped out and me putting the rest of my money behind you.'

'I have my pride, Maggie! Give me six months to pay off my debt and then ask me again.'

'Six months! You want me to wait another six months?'

'I want to make sure I get things right the next time I marry. What d'you say?' His eyes held hers.

Her head was in a whirl. 'I think you're daft.' She reached for her coat and he helped her on with it, holding her against him.

'I have to do it, Maggie.' He kissed her ear.

She closed her eyes and leant against him. 'What if you don't succeed?'

'That depends on Billy.'

He had surprised her again. 'You think he won't approve? We get on well.'

'It's not his approval I'm after.'

She felt frustrated. 'Don't start your old tricks by teasing me.'

He kissed the tip of her nose. 'I'm not. When you marry me I want you to have no doubts that I'm the right man for you.'

She was baffled. 'There's no other man in my life!'

William made no response to that but asked if she wanted to see Sam's artwork upstairs before she left.

'Another time,' she said, in no mood to see inside his bedroom with no chance of sleeping in his bed just yet.

He looked disappointed but she would not be persuaded so he saw her out. Her parting shot was that he shouldn't forget to keep up his payments. She was still hurt he had turned down her proposal. She wanted him now, not in six months, but knew there was no shifting him once he had made up his mind.

It was four months later and the padre was marrying Sarah Turner. Rita posed in a dress of primrose organdie and she clutched a huge confection of daffodils, narcissi, hyacinths and trailing fern. She stood next to the matron of honour, smiling at the camera, aware that Margaret – whom she could see out of the corner of her eye – was far from happy. As the photographer signalled to the padre, Sarah and her bridesmaids relaxed. Rita excused herself and made her way across the church grounds.

'What's the matter? You look like you've lost half a crown and found a farthing. Don't you like weddings?' She slipped her hand through her aunt's arm.

'Of course, I like weddings.' The green-eyed monster had Margaret in its grip, wishing she were the bride. 'I'm just wondering how Sam's coping in the shop,' she lied.

'The customers aren't going to try anything on with him; he's twice the bloke he used to be. He knows to tell those he can't deal with to come back when you're there.'

Margaret was only half-listening because she had noticed a late arrival. So Will had dragged himself away from work to make an appearance after all. She gazed at him hungrily, thinking how good he looked in a charcoal lounge suit. Like Sam, he had put on muscle in the last few months. Strange that after years of keeping her emotions battened down she could not stop dreaming of going to bed with him. They were never alone and some of that was due to him working hard which was paying off. His income had risen far in excess of his outgoings – despite his having increased the men's wages. She had advised him that now was not the time to give his employees more money, but he had told her that he knew what he was doing.

'Come on, Aunt Margaret!' Rita tugged her arm.

The photographer's assistant was calling the wedding party for a group photograph. Margaret managed to manipulate herself into a position next to William. She asked was there any news of Billy or Alice.

He lowered his head and his mouth brushed her ear. 'Alice says that she's seen Jimmy and that he didn't hang around but has gone out west.'

'Let's hope he stays there. What about Billy?'

'Not a dicky bird! I'm worried.'

She reached for his hand and squeezed it. 'Have you any idea where he is?'

'China!'

She looked at him in astonishment. 'I thought he was looking for Ellen on the liners.'

'No. Smile at the camera, Maggie. I haven't told you how lovely you look. The new hairstyle suits you and that peaches and cream outfit does wonders for your skin.'

She flushed with pleasure but said no more because the photographer was telling them to hold that pose and say *cheese*.

At the wedding breakfast the padre came over to William and Margaret. He had received news from his opposite number in Hong Kong, who said Billy had left for the mainland. There had been no news of him since.

'What's he doing in China?' burst out Margaret, who hadn't had the chance to ask William that question due to their talking to other guests. 'He's taking a risk with all the fighting between Chiang Kai-shek and the Communists. You should have stopped him going, especially with the Japanese on the move as well. Remember Alan getting caught in an uprising and being killed?'

'Neither of us could prevent Alan doing what he'd set his mind to,' said William, drawing her away from the padre as another couple came up to speak to him.

She could feel the tension in William. 'You knew he was going to the mainland and that's why you've been worried. What's he up to?' A crazy idea struck her. 'He's not . . . he couldn't be after more artefacts?'

William blinked and pushed back a hank of hair. 'Could be that you've hit the nail on the head, Maggie. He did mention artefacts last time I spoke to him but I hadn't reckoned on his being away so long. Perhaps he's hit a snag and I need to do something.'

'Such as what?'

'If he's not home within the month, go and find him.' William took two glasses from a trestle table and handed her one.

She paled. 'Have you forgotten what the doctor

said? You're already putting yourself under enough strain the way you're working up at the yard.' She twisted the glass between her fingers. 'It's dangerous. You could be killed.'

'It's my fault Billy's gone there. I've got to do what I can to find him.'

'You mean you gave him money to buy artefacts for you? You saw that as a way of paying off your debt?' She was incredulous.

He smiled. 'I didn't think the idea that bad. If I go, will you keep an eye on Dixon? Keep the yard going, and if there's any letters from Alice, answer them for me without worrying her.'

Margaret drained her glass and put it on the table. 'You've no need to concern yourself about that.' Her tone was sharp. 'It goes without saying that I'll see to things. You will be careful?'

'Stop worrying, Maggie. I'm heaps stronger than I was and the British treaty ports out there are protected by our armed forces. You'll see. Everything'll be OK.'

She wanted to believe him so she returned his smile, but deep down she had a sense of foreboding. If only Billy would come home everything would be all right.

But a month passed and still there was no word from him. It was as if he had vanished from the face of the earth.

CHAPTER SEVENTEEN

'I wish I was going with you,' said Margaret, a dull ache in her chest as she watched William stir a huge pan of beans, oats and treacle for the horses; Dixon was having a day off. 'I dreamt of visiting faraway places before a house replaced that dream.'

William had a berth on a merchant navy vessel and would be working his passage to Hong Kong. Later that day he would take the ferry to Birkenhead docks and his ship would leave on the morning tide.

He flashed that smile which still had such power to charm. 'I promise when I get back if you still want to go travelling we'll go.'

'I'll keep you to that,' she said, getting up from

her perch on the empty treacle barrel. 'You will come back, won't you?'

He put down the ladle and took her into his arms, smoothing back her hair with an unsteady hand. 'Of course.'

'Promise?' There were tears in her eyes.

'Cross my heart.' He kissed her and she snuggled into him.

'I wish we could have got married before you go.'

'Me too. But we'll have the rest of our lives.'

Despite his reassurances, what if all there was is now? She wanted him, needed to ease the ache inside her. Surely he wanted her in the same way? She would regret it for the rest of her life if she let him go without showing how much she loved him.

'Can you leave this mix?' she said abruptly. 'I never did get to see Sam's work of art upstairs. I want you to show it me now. I want to lie on your bed and look at it and dream what you dream. I want our ship to come in now full of goodies.'

William was silent but the expression on his face caused a lump to rise in her throat and she knew he understood what she was trying to say. 'Come on, then!' He seized her hand and ran with her to the house.

Once inside his bedroom, neither of them spared a glance for Sam's sailing ship. They undressed hastily and snuggled down beneath the bedcovers and gazed into each other's eyes.

'I'm not going to talk about being in love with you since we first met,' said William. 'You should know that by now. And I know you care about me despite all the arguments we've had and the times we've fell out.'

She was almost too scared to admit how much she cared for him. Her silence did not seem to bother him. He kissed her gently, then exerted more pressure as she responded and clung to him with all her strength. There was no holding back now. She returned his kisses with a passion that even surprised her. He kicked down the bedcovers and began to kiss her naked body, trailing his lips in a downward path. She gasped with pleasure, never having thought being caressed in such a way could be so delightful at her age. His hands were on her hips and then he was inside her. It was a new experience in a relationship that went back to their youth and she wasn't going to waste a moment in letting the pain of his entry detract from the act she had wanted to share with him all those years ago. She was definitely not going to worry about what might be the outcome. He clasped her buttocks firmly with both hands and moved slowly inside her, tantalizingly slow, the movement soothing, sensual and she could feel excitement building up. Suddenly she felt a wonderful explosion inside her and clung to him, moaning that she loved him. All the frustrations of the past were forgotten. They had come full circle and she felt that she was where she belonged.

Afterwards they lay drowsily gazing at Sam's work of art. 'I wonder what he was thinking of when he painted it?' murmured Margaret, idly twisting a curl on William's chest round her little finger.

'Of my reaction. He's someone who needs someone else to tell him he's good. Doesn't have confidence in himself.'

'Don't we all feel like that at times?' She hugged William and wished they could make love all over again. Now she knew what real intimacy was like and wanted it to be permanent. 'Oh, why do you have to go?' she whimpered, and nibbled his ear.

'Ouch! Why did you do that?' There was laughter in his voice.

'Because I'm hurting here.' She held his hand against her breast.

The laughter faded in his eyes. 'Me too. So don't make it any harder for me to go than it is already.' He kissed her long and hard and then pushed her away from him and got out of bed.

They dressed and went downstairs. He accompanied her to the gate and they stood a moment in the shade out of the sun. Sparrows pecked at the crumbs in the road and she watched them, remembering what was written in the Bible about God knowing even when a sparrow fell. She looked at William and said, 'If you don't come back I'll never forgive you.'

He held her hand and said tenderly, 'Trust me! I'll be back before you know it. Thanks for everything.' He kissed her.

She did not say goodbye but walked away, knowing that the months to come were going to be difficult without him.

A couple of weeks later Margaret received a postcard from Gibraltar. She had written to William, hoping a mail boat would reach there before he left. He had written that the Bay of Biscay had been rough but they were making good time.

The next postcard arrived the day Margaret woke feeling sick and threw up. On the front was a photograph of the pyramids; on the back he had written that they'd passed through the Suez Canal and it was hot. He was well and she was constantly in his thoughts. He thanked her for her letter and asked if Billy was home. She pinned the postcard on the wall above the fireplace and wished she could write, Yes! Come home. I'm ill and I want you. But, of course, she didn't do anything of the sort.

Margaret continued to be sick every morning in the weeks that followed and her emotions were all over the place. One minute she was filled with fear and shame and the next she felt joyful and exhilarated. Should she write and tell William those too brief moments they had spent making love had resulted in a child? She felt certain he would return

338

immediately, but what of his need to find Billy? Besides, she could miscarry and it would be a wasted journey on his part. For now she had to go it alone and hope he would find Billy and that they would be home before the baby arrived.

The thought of giving birth filled her with trepidation. She squirmed with embarrassment, imagining the chin-wagging in the neighbourhood. She would never live it down. The gossips would have a field day. As for telling Rita and Sam, she couldn't face up to it yet. Maybe she should go on a long holiday until the baby was born, she thought in panic. Yet not once did she consider getting rid of the baby. If anything was to happen to William it was all that she would have left of him. She would pray that when he reached Hong Kong, by some miracle Billy would be waiting for him. William was behaving like a proper father to his son, so how could she come between them? As it was, there was news of another baby. Alice was pregnant.

Months passed before Margaret received the next missal from William. Postmarked Bombay it described the sights he had seen and informed her their next ports of call would be Ceylon and Singapore before finally docking in Hong Kong. He had received the letter about Alice's pregnancy and written to her. He hoped Margaret was well and the yard still doing OK. Lots of love, Will.

With a sinking heart Margaret placed a hand

over her swelling belly, knowing there was little likelihood of him getting home in time for the birth.

She glanced at her niece and knew she could no longer delay telling her about the baby.

Rita had borrowed a globe from Sarah for them to trace William's journey to the other side of the world. 'I knew it was a long way but I never realised just how many thousands of miles Billy travelled when he breezed in here as if he'd only just been round the block. He must have had to cope with all sorts of scary things – storms at sea, unrest at ports when the ship had to take on water, fuel and provisions. The ports might be part of the Empire but the British aren't always welcome.'

'I don't want to know about such things!' cried Margaret, twitching nervously. She took a deep breath. 'I'm having a baby and I need you to help me to cope with what lies ahead!'

Rita's hand stilled on the globe and the muscles of her face froze in an expression of pure astonishment. For a moment she could not speak, then she said, 'Surprise, surprise! There's no use me asking whether you're sure. You wouldn't be telling me otherwise. Is it Mr Brodie's?'

'Who else's could it be? I'm not one for jumping into every Tom, Dick or Harry's bed.' Her voice broke and she buried her face in her hands and added in a muffled voice, 'After all the things I said to you that time over Jimmy.'

'That was natural! You felt responsible for me.' Feeling awkward but strangely protective, Rita put an arm round her aunt's shoulders. 'When's it due? What are you going to do?'

'Round about Christmas, and I plan to move.' Margaret glanced up at her. 'Thanks for taking it so calmly.'

Rita choked on a laugh. 'I don't feel calm inside. But I'll tell you something: I'm glad it's you and not me.'

Margaret's eyes filled with tears.

'Don't,' pleaded Rita, hugging her. 'Everything's going to be all right.'

Margaret lifted her head and gave her one of her looks. Rita grinned. 'That's more like you. So where are we going to move to and when?'

Margaret had no answer to that until a while later when she received two letters on the same day. One was from William, who after speaking to a padre who had seen Billy, was off to Peking. He made no mention of the Japanese and anti-foreign feelings running high in China that she had read about in a newspaper. The other was from Alice, who had given birth to a daughter. She asked about Billy, saying she had not heard from him for months.

Margaret's expression was strained as she looked at Rita and Sam across the breakfast table. 'I don't know what to tell her about him. I want to give her some hope but it's over a year since we've seen him.'

'You mustn't give up hope,' said Sam, buttering a slice of toast. 'Don't forget things are topsy-turvy in China. Mr Dixon told me there's warlords ruling over different parts of it, and they haven't trains and buses like we have. It's rickshaws, long marches and horses. Even the Japanese have control of only a chunk of China where they've built a railway – and half the roads and bridges have been blown up in the fighting. Still, yer've got to hang on and have some faith in Mr Brodie and Billy.'

'Sam's right!' Rita placed her hand over her aunt's. 'All what he's saying is horrible but it could explain why we haven't heard from them. They could be cut off somewhere, unable to get to a port.'

Margaret placed the letters back in their envelopes. 'You're right! But I've been through this waiting game before. What's making it so difficult is trying to believe Billy's gone there after artefacts. It doesn't hold water! There's something Will hasn't told me and when he gets back I'm going to have it out with him. In the meantime we've got to move. People will be putting two and two together once I get larger.'

Sam and Rita exchanged glances. She had already told him about her aunt's condition and he had been silent for at least an hour, before asking would it make any difference to them. After being reassured it wouldn't, he had accepted it, although Rita had noticed him looking at Margaret with an anxious expression on his face. Perhaps he feared, like her, that her aunt might die in childbirth. 'So where are we going?' asked Rita.

Margaret pleated the tablecloth between her fingers. 'I'll let you know as soon as I work some figures out.'

Her dream house was back on the market, the leaseholder having gone bankrupt. She determined to make an offer, having discovered the lease would cost her only half of what it would have done three years ago. It was a risk because her income from the shop had also dropped. The Depression had deepened. The queues outside the Employment Exchange in Renshaw Street were growing week by week, and those frequenting the pawnshops could no longer afford to get their possessions out of hock. It was a sad state of affairs for her customers. Fortunately the income from the yard was steady. She had spent out on a lorry going for a song and Sam had learnt to drive. He was ruthlessly competitive when it came to grabbing any business there was; the yard was building up a reputation for getting deliveries done at top speed. Thinking of her baby's future, if anything should happen to her she had also invested money into an automobile firm in the Midlands, as well as a film company. Just as during the Great War people had needed to escape the misery all around them, so they did now and the new talkies were extremely popular.

She took a chance and made an offer for the house. It was accepted and she breathed easier. Exhausted by the strain of everything, she told Rita and Sam what she had done, and thrilled her niece by giving her certain orders and sending her off to the house with Sam while she put her feet up.

'Wow! It's some size,' he said, his head thrown back as he gazed at the central staircase winding its spiral way up through each floor of the house to the top in decorative wrought iron splendour. Sunshine flooded through a central dome. 'She must have more money than I thought to afford this.'

'She got it cheap and said if things get any tougher she'll be renting out rooms. It's beautiful, isn't it?' said Rita, trying to imagine throwing a party in this hall on a summer evening. She had never had a party in her life. She scolded herself. What was she doing thinking of parties when there was still no news of Billy and Mr Brodie? She worried as much as Margaret but kept it to herself. She slipped her hand through Sam's arm. 'Come on! Let's go and pick our bedrooms.'

'I thought Miss Sinclair wanted me to carry on living over the shop.'

Rita grimaced. 'I'd forgotten. I must admit I don't like that idea. I'm going to miss you. These days you're either up at the yard or out delivering so that I hardly see you much as it is.' She paused as they came to the first floor and her brown eyes widened as she gazed about the huge landing. 'We're going to need more than Mrs Richards to keep this place clean and do the cooking. Unless Aunt Margaret does let out rooms.'

Sam followed Rita into a front bedroom. She gazed out of the window at the bare branches of the trees, thinking it was heavenly having the garden in the centre of the square to look out on. If her mother could see her now she'd be green with envy. Margaret had said Abercromby Square had been named after a professor at Liverpool University, who had designed a youth hostel in North Wales for the YHA. Hundreds of young Liverpudlians had taken to rambling or cycling in the countryside to escape the city.

Sam sidled up to her. 'We could get married and then take turns at staying in each place.'

Rita's heart flipped over. She stared at his pleasant face, thinking how the scruffy runt she had befriended had turned into the man at her side. They had discussed marriage several times but she had always said no. She loved Sam and knew he loved her but they were not in love. Yet he was such a kind person she knew she would be safe with him. Besides, she would like to have children and if she could not have Billy's, then Sam's would do. He would make a good father.

'I'll let you have an answer later today,' she murmured, then changed the subject. 'I believe years ago this room would have been a family sitting room and that's why it's so large. Perhaps Aunt Margaret would like to keep it as one.'

'I prefer small rooms myself. They're cosier!'

She did not argue with him but opened the catalogue obtained from Wades Furnishings. Margaret had ticked the items she was interested in and Rita tried to imagine the furniture in place.

She picked a bedroom for herself on the second floor overlooking the rear walled garden and pencilled notes against the illustrations in the catalogue. It seemed to take ages to go over the house. Sam got fed up halfway and sat on the stairs, reading an Edgar Wallace thriller.

When she had finished Rita squeezed up beside him. 'Perhaps I will marry you, Sam.'

She had to say it twice before he heard her and dragged himself out of the book. His face creased into a smile. 'Honest? I'd feel better married.'

'Good!' She kissed him lightly on the lips.

He hugged her. 'I'll buy you a ring. There's one in the shop I've had my eye on for some time.'

'Let's go and tell my aunt.'

Margaret was not the least surprised when they told her. 'I've never heard the pair of you utter a cross word to the other. So when's the wedding to be?'

'June,' said Sam firmly. 'I'm going to be busy until then. The horse show's coming up in May and that means more work for all of us.'

Rita agreed June was a lovely month to get married. Sam bought a garnet and pearl ring that Margaret let him have for a special price and on Saturday they splashed out and had supper at the Silver Grill in Dale Street. On Sunday they went to matins and booked the church.

They moved into Abercromby Square the week before Christmas. Margaret took to wearing a wedding ring. She was getting more and more frightened as the birth drew near. She changed her doctor. There were three women doctors who shared a house in the square. When she went into labour on Boxing Day, Rita was hammering on their front door at the first twinge.

Dr Foley examined Margaret and smiling said she would be back after lunch. As it was, the baby did not arrive until evening. A tight-lipped Margaret had stopped trying to be brave and was giving vent to her feelings by cursing everyone she knew by name – including William. The doctor rolled up her sleeves, told her to behave herself and to give some nice little pushes.

Within the hour Margaret's son made his appearance. She fell in love with him immediately. His hair was dark and curly and his eyes blue just like his father's. She named him Jonathan William and he weighed in at seven pounds six ounces. As she put him to her breast, a fierce pride filled her. She thought of William and tears filled her eyes and she prayed one day he would see their son.

CHAPTER EIGHTEEN

Rita's high heels click-clacked on the cobbles as she hurried across Oxford Street, quickening her pace as she approached Abercromby Square to avoid a man mooching in the gutter. He had the gait of the seafarer, taking a few short paces one way and then the same number back. She felt guilty watching him bend down and pick up a fag end. He took a tin from his pocket and placed the cigarette butt inside. She opened her handbag, took a sixpence from her purse and tried to slip the coin into his pocket without him noticing.

'What are yer doing, girl?' He grabbed her hand.

'It's just sixpence!' She did not want a fuss.

He took the coin from her and his rheumy eyes held a tear. 'God bless yer!'

'And you, too!'

She made her escape, angry and sad. There were so many like him on the streets of Liverpool these days; they made her remember the poverty of her childhood. She would hate to go back to that again. As she approached the square she thought of her mother and wondered what she was up to. There had been no word from her for a while, although a letter had winged its way to Eve telling her about her engagement and the wedding planned in June, not that she expected her mother to attend. She wondered what Eve would make of the new house. Rita could easily picture the family of a rich merchant passing in and out of the lovely doorway topped by a decorative fanlight. He would be dreaming of the money he would make on cargoes of tobacco and cotton from New Orleans and rum and sugar from Jamaica. She could imagine his wife and daughters, long silk skirts brushing the floor.

She smiled thinking how times had changed. The square housed professional people or contained departments of Liverpool University these days. She thought of the brass plate that Sam had screwed into the wall next to their front door. It bore the words MARGARET SINCLAIR, *Financial Advisor and Broker*.

Shortly before they had moved, several advertisements had been placed in the local newspapers. At first there had been only a couple of inquiries and Margaret had talked of renting out several rooms, but so far nothing had been done about it. Business was picking up but they were still some way off from making a living. If it were not for the income from the yard and Margaret's investments they would be in trouble. Money was tight but none of them were complaining because they were so much better off than lots of other people. Most of their clients were wives of professional men, and they had several medical students on their books. All were carefully vetted to make sure they could keep up with their payments or had some kind of collateral.

Birds twittered in the trees and outside the house stood a horse and cart. Sparrows pecking at the droppings from the horse's nosebag flew up at her approach.

A man stepped out from beneath the overhang above the door. 'I'm looking for Miss Sinclair. I believe she lives here but I can't get an answer.' He had a transatlantic accent but his features were barely distinguishable because the wide brim of his felt hat cast a shadow over his face.

'Can I have your name, please?' said Rita.

'Jimmy Martin.'

She froze. The memory of his attempted rape came vividly to mind despite all her attempts to forget it. Anger welled up inside her. What the hell was he doing back here? Obviously he had not recognised her, but then, they had both changed. They were a couple of years older and she was better dressed and her hair styled differently, and she now carried herself with confidence.

'Well?' he demanded. 'Cat got your tongue?'

She controlled her temper. 'I'd heard you were living in America, Mr Martin.'

'I was! But obviously I'm here now.'

'What have you come for?' She fumbled in her handbag for her door key.

'I don't think that's any of your business. I'm here to speak to the organ grinder not the monkey.'

Rita wanted to hit him. 'I think you'll find it *is* my business.' Her tone was icy. She stepped over the threshold and noticed an envelope on the floor. She picked it up and slipped it in her pocket before beckoning Jimmy inside. He was taller than she remembered, but there was none of that restless energy that had attracted her in the early days of their acquaintance.

'What d'you mean by that?' He removed his hat to reveal hair the colour of sun-bleached cotton. He was shabbily dressed, so whatever he had been doing in America he had not been able to avoid the effects of the Depression.

'Last time we met you were hell-bent on making an honest woman of me after attempted rape.'

'Rita? Bloody hell! It was hardly that! A misunderstanding!' His blue eyes took her in from head to toe.

'Keep your eyes to yourself! It was no misunderstanding! You tried it on and don't think you've got away with it. Let's be hearing why you're here. My fiancé'll be here in a minute and he's got muscles like Charles Atlas. One wrong move and you'll be spitting out teeth.'

She saw the flash of anger in his eyes and watched him struggle to keep his temper. He managed a smile. 'Don't be like that, Rita! My mistake! Put it down to your being such a looker I couldn't resist you.'

'You can cut the cackle and keep your soft soap. I'm nobody's fool these days.' Her voice was hard. 'What the hell do you want? Out with it!'

'I want the deeds to the yard. With my stepfather and stepbrother dead it belongs to me.'

His assumption infuriated her. 'Been talking to your sister, have you? Well, you've been misinformed. We haven't heard they're dead so we're not giving up hope. She shouldn't have either!' Rita walked away from him and into the office.

He followed her. 'You're just being bloody awkward. They must be dead if nothing's been heard from them. Your aunt just wants to keep her filthy hands on what's mine.'

'Mr Brodie's debt, you mean? Yeah, well, that's outstanding. When are you going to pay it off?' She went behind a large oak desk to put a barrier between them. She moved the ivory dragon pen and inkstand that her aunt had taken in exchange for a debt from a Chinese man in Pitt Street and rested her hands on the desk.

His eyes smouldered. 'It must have been paid off by now. The yard looks like it's doing well.'

'Well as can be expected in a depression. But I hate to disappoint you; even if the debt has been paid off there's another claimant to the property.' How she enjoyed saying that and seeing the shock in his face.

'You don't mean a bloody long lost Brodie cousin? I don't believe it.'

She had no intention of telling him about Jonathan, who held her heart and her aunt's between his chubby little hands. 'Someone like that. Of course, you can take it to court but it would cost money and even if you won I think you'd have to wait seven years before the court would declare Mr Brodie and Billy as dead.'

'You're bloody loving this, aren't yer?' He slammed his fist on the desk. 'I've had it tough. You in your posh suit and high heels have no idea what I've been through! I've walked and walked from Texas to get here.'

'Walked on water, did you?'

His eyes darted her a venomous look. 'I want that Dixon up at the yard out and I'm putting myself in charge.'

'Get lost! You haven't got a cat in a dogs' home chance of that happening.'

Jimmy lunged across the desk, caught her off guard and seized her by the throat. 'I'd enjoy choking the life out of you right now,' he said through gritted teeth.

She believed him and clawed at his hands and drew blood. He swore and his fingers tightened on her windpipe. Then came the sound of voices in the hall and he dropped her like a hot coal; he looked about him and spotted the filing cabinet. 'I'm not going without those deeds.'

'Don't be bloody stupid!' gasped Rita, feeling her throat. 'Sam! Aunt Margaret!' She made for the door but it opened before she touched it.

Sam entered, took one look at her face and then at Jimmy, who was struggling to force open a locked drawer in the filing cabinet, and shot across the room. Jimmy aimed a blow at him but Sam seized him by a wrist and elbow and performed a series of quick movements. The next moment Jimmy was on the floor with Sam's knee in the small of his back.

'Who is it?' Margaret had entered the room in his wake.

'Jimmy! And he's come for what he claims is his inheritance. I told him to get lost and he tried to strangle me. Thanks to Sam he now realises his mistake. How did you manage that trick, Sam?' said Rita.

He grinned. 'Ju-jitsu! What d'yer want me to do with him?'

'I'd like him battered, fried in boiling oil and then thrown to the dogs,' she said.

'I'll take him to the chippy,' said Sam.

'Wait!' said Margaret, eyeing Jimmy up and down. 'You believe Will's dead?'

'Yeah! I bet you do, too, but yer want what's

mine,' gasped Jimmy, struggling to get up, furious at being so humiliated by Sam.

Margaret was rigid with pain and anger. 'You own nothing, so don't you come round here again throwing your weight around. It's time you learnt manners. Your stepfather cared about you more than you deserved. Take him out, Sam!'

Sam hoisted Jimmy to his feet. 'But I've got nowhere to go!' he yelled. 'You can't do this to me! Pops wouldn't have done it!'

'Your Pops was an old softie! Now get out.' Margaret's gaze shifted to Sam. 'You'd better take the cart back. Heads will roll when I find out who let him take that.'

'I'll get you for this!' said Jimmy, fixing Rita with a furious glare.

'You and whose army?' she said softly, picking up his hat and ramming it on his head.

Sam frogmarched Jimmy out of the room, calling over his shoulder, 'I might be late. I'm teaching a new bloke how to drive.'

Rita looked at her aunt and saw the worry in her eyes and knew what she was thinking. 'He's wrong! They're not dead.'

'Is he?' whispered Margaret.

'Of course he is! Jimmy's a selfish G-I-T.'

'Will treated him like a son.'

'That was his big mistake. He encouraged him to have expectations.'

'I need to think,' said Margaret. 'I suspect he's not going to go away.'

Rita thought she was probably right and a chill ran down her spine. The swine, she thought, as if we didn't have enough to worry about. She hugged her aunt. 'Don't think on an empty stomach. Let's have lunch. You're feeding Jonathan, remember.'

They both left the room, Rita considering how love made you vulnerable. She went downstairs to the basement kitchen to see what Mrs Richards had left them. A widow, she shared the attic with her daughter, Babs, and looked after Jonathan. Today she was visiting her sister and had taken the baby with her.

There was a casserole in the oven and Rita put on the kettle before returning upstairs. She found Margaret at her desk, perusing Will Brodie's file. 'So what are you going to do about Jimmy? He attacked me. We should have called the scuffer. A few months in jail would give Jimmy a fright.'

Her aunt removed her spectacles and rubbed her eyes. 'There's a thought, but he's family.'

'Not yet he isn't! And he's not got our blood, thank God! Or any Brodie blood either.' She perched her bottom on the edge of the desk. 'If he comes near us again you should threaten him with the police.'

Margaret shook her head. 'I can't do that. But I'd like to know where he is so I can keep my eye on him.'

Rita frowned. 'You mean hire someone like Sexton Blake to tail him?'

Margaret gave her one of her looks. 'A job at the yard, where Mr Dixon and Sam can keep their eye on him.'

Rita slid off the desk. 'You're crazy! That's a reward! The last bloody thing he deserves!'

Margaret's eyes glinted. 'Don't you bloody swear at me! I'm running the place, not you! I know what I'm doing!'

Hot words sprung to Rita's lips but she bit them back. Time would prove her aunt wrong – she just knew it. In the meantime she would carry a pepper drum around with her. Jimmy was not going to get the chance to take her by surprise again.

Sam was to surprise them the next morning when he came storming round to the house at what felt like the crack of dawn. 'There's been a smash and grab raid at the shop.'

'Jimmy?' said Rita, biting back a yawn.

'I wondered, but I've got no proof,' said Sam.

'You can't believe Jimmy would be so stupid?' said Margaret, tightening the belt of her dressing gown.

'He's the obvious suspect. He did threaten us,' said Rita.

'So did Mr McGinty,' said Sam in a hollow voice.

They stared at him. 'Why d'you bring him into it?' asked Rita.

He hesitated. 'He's escaped from prison.'

'You're joking!' Rita clutched her aunt's hand.

'When?' said Margaret.

'I forget!' Sam looked uncomfortable. 'I've had other things on my mind. I saw a poster outside the bridewell. There's a price on his head.'

'You had no right to forget!' snapped Margaret. 'You know the kind of maniac he is.'

'He'd be a fool to come here,' said Sam, flushing. 'It's the first place the police would look for him. I shouldn't have mentioned it. I didn't tell you before because I didn't want to worry you.'

'Thanks, Sam,' said Rita. 'I'd be thinking "I'm glad Sam didn't want to worry me" as he cuts me throat!'

Sam muttered. 'D'yer have to go on? I've told you now, so there's something else for you to worry about.'

'I'd rather worry and be on me guard,' said Rita.

Margaret nodded. 'You can wait while I get dressed, Sam. I want to see the damage for myself. I just hope there won't be any more surprises.'

She might as well have saved her breath, thought Rita a few days later. As happens in life, a string of events were to happen that were to completely take them by surprise.

'Salt, pepper, mustard, vinegar!' chanted Babs, turning the skipping rope.

'Excuse me, duck, but is this the house where Miss Sinclair and her niece Rita have moved to?'

Babs turned a flushed face to the woman. 'Yeah! Who are you?'

'An old friend!' The woman waved a cigarette holder. 'Who are you?'

'Babs! Me mam works here. Who shall I say is calling?' said the girl, carefully pronouncing every word, remembering her orders for when people called.

'Just say Ellen's come to call.'

'Ellen!' repeated Babs, slinging the skipping rope round one of the railings that fenced off the entrance to the basement and opening the gate. She ran down the steps into the kitchen where her mother was cooking supper. 'Visitor for Miss Rita called Ellen.'

'Run up and tell her.'

Babs ran up the stone steps which led to the rear of the hall and shouted, 'Miss Rita! Visitor!'

A door opened upstairs. 'Who is it?'

'An Ellen!' Babs jiggled about on the tiles at the foot of the staircase. 'She's dressed like someone out of a pantomime and's smoking out of a long stick.'

'My God!' Rita hurried downstairs, feeling a mixture of emotions. She remembered with gratitude the good times she had shared with Ellen but she could not forget Billy had been in love with her. 'Where is she?'

'Outside.'

Rita opened the front door, wondering what had brought Ellen to Liverpool. Perhaps she had come for news of Billy and, finding none of the family up at the yard, had been directed here. She stared at the woman with her back to her. Smoke formed a cloud about her head and, even from this angle, there was something glamorous about that figure. On her head was a glistening skull-shaped hat. She appeared to be wearing a long cloak in a variety of colours. The heels of her shoes were at least three inches high. Already she was attracting the attention of several of the students clustered round the garden gates in the centre of the square. Rita felt an old familiar stab of envy. No wonder Billy had fallen for Ellen. She was like a tropical bird among sparrows. 'Ellen!'

She turned and her eyes widened. Then she laughed and ran up the steps holding out a hand. 'You've grown up! It's great to see you.'

'Same here!' Rita meant it. Interesting things always happened when Ellen was around. 'Where've you been for the last two years? It was as if you'd been whizzed away in a flying saucer.'

'That'd be different! I've been here, there and everywhere – by ship, mostly – but not once have I bumped into Billy. It's him who's the real missing person.'

'You should have caught a slow boat to China.'

Ellen sighed. 'No thanks. He must be crazy. I visited Alice in the States. She thinks he's dead. It's a sad loss if he is but I'm not going to believe it. He's as tough as old boot leather, so I told her she shouldn't give up on him yet.'

Rita was grateful for those words. She would rather Billy was alive and married to Ellen than his corpse was rotting in some Chinese city. 'You must have supper with us. You look well.'

Ellen pulled a face. 'It's all window dressing, duck. Clothes home-made. I've told you before, us lady musicians are hard done by.' She paused to draw on the long cigarette holder. 'But I have friends and I still love to travel.'

'You know Jimmy's back in Liverpool?'

'That idiot! Alice is worried about him so I said I'd look him up, but he wasn't at the yard.'

Rita said, 'No! He's an idiot, as you said. Come on in.'

Ellen stepped into the hall and stopped. 'Holy Mary, mother of God! This would make a bloody brilliant set for a play. I can just see Gertie gliding down those stairs.'

Rita was impressed. 'You mean you've met Gertrude Lawrence?'

'There's only one Gertie. She and Noel – Coward – came and watched the cabaret of which I was a small part on their way to New York.'

'What a life you lead! I envy you!'

'Don't tie yourself up in knots. It's not all sequins and glamour, but grotty cabins beneath the waterline and being groped by rich old men.' She rolled her eyes and laughed. 'You couldn't give me a bed for the night, could you?'

'I can let you share mine if Aunt Margaret gives the wink.' Rita noticed Babs watching them, obviously taken with their guest. 'Go and tell your mam there's an extra one for supper. Right now we'd like tea and some of her delicious scones.'

Rita took Ellen upstairs who lauded praise on the sitting room with its embossed ceiling. 'Perfect for Oscar Wilde's *An Ideal Husband*. Have you seen it?'

'Too busy.'

'You should make the effort. Sandy's travelling theatre is due in Liverpool soon.'

'You crafty thing! That's why you're here. One night will turn into a week, and so on.'

Ellen smiled and waved her cigarette holder. 'I always knew you were sharper than you appeared.'

'I enjoyed seeing Sandy act. How d'you keep yourself informed of his whereabouts, though, when you're never in one place for long?'

'Friends of friends in the business.' Ellen curled up in a corner of the sofa. 'You're a lucky duck. Much nicer here than those rooms over the pawnshop.'

'Sam lives there.'

'Sam?' Ellen tapped her teeth with the cigarette holder. 'I heard that name up at the yard – something to do with a lorry.'

'We're engaged. He's a lovely bloke,' she said, trying to sound casual.

'I'm glad you realised Jimmy wasn't.'

They stared at each other and an unspoken message passed between them. 'Poor Alice,' said

Ellen. 'She really does love him, warts and all. I'm glad my brother's not like him.'

No more was said on the subject of Jimmy as Mrs Richards appeared with tea and scones. Sam and Margaret came in and joined them. The latter agreed for Ellen to stay but stated terms right away.

'I'll have to do the impossible and find myself a job,' said Ellen.

It was not until they went to bed, Ellen saying she would fetch her things from the left luggage in the morning, that she told Rita more about Sandy and the travelling theatre. 'He's planning on going out East because Dad's leaving India and the pair of them never got on and so are best with an ocean between them.'

'You mean Britain isn't big enough for both of them?'

'Dad would seek him out wherever Sandy was. He thinks acting is for sissies, not real men, and he'll get at him.'

'Poor Sandy. Where East is the company going?'

'Ask me again when he gets here.' Ellen yawned and snuggled beneath the covers. 'A real bed to sleep in at last. Wake me up in a week.'

Rita smiled and turned on her side. That night she dreamt of being on a stage which was decked out just like Chinatown; sitting in a rickshaw were Billy and Ellen and she wanted to tear them apart. Then Jimmy appeared carrying a brick, which he was going to hit her with and she was running, running.

CHAPTER NINETEEN

Jimmy stood on the step, turning his hat round and round between his tanned fingers, looking the worse for wear.

'You back again?' Rita's voice was unfriendly.

A muscle in his jaw tightened and through clenched teeth he said, 'I've come to say sorry.'

'Oh aye! What do you want me to say? That I forgive you?' She rested her shoulder against the door jamb.

Anger flashed in his eyes. 'It's your aunt I want to speak to, not you.'

'Well, she mightn't want to speak to you. Besides, she's busy right now.' That was not true but why should she make things easy for him? 'Come back in a couple of hours and maybe she'll see you then.'

There were footsteps in the hall behind her and Margaret said, 'Rita, I think that's up to me to decide.'

Rita glanced at her aunt as she came alongside her and said, 'I was only trying to protect you. I know how tired you are.' There were dark circles under Margaret's eyes because she was still waking in the night to feed the baby.

Margaret thanked her but said she was capable of making her own decision. She fixed her gaze on Jimmy. 'What is it you want? The same as before? Because, if so, you're wasting your time.'

'I'm come to say sorry for being so rude yesterday, but I've been under a lot of strain myself lately. I mean, the news about Pops and Billy really knocked me sideways.'

'You managed to pick yourself up quick enough to get yourself over here and lay claim to the yard,' said Rita.

He glared at her. 'I was worried about the place.'

'You mean you wanted to get your hands on it! You don't care about Billy or Mr Brodie.'

'You can think what you like! I don't care,' said Jimmy.

'Enough, the pair of you!' snapped Margaret. 'I will not let you take charge of the yard, Jimmy. I've sunk a lot of money into it and I've no intention of you getting the benefit.'

'But Pops wanted me to have it!'

'That's before you left for America. Things have changed, but if you're stuck with nowhere to stay and no job, then you can work up there and sleep in the house. You'll have to knuckle under and keep your nose clean. You'll take orders from Mr Dixon and do as you're told or you're out on your ear.'

She waited, half-expecting him to refuse.

Jimmy gazed at the ground to hide his fury. 'I don't seem to have any choice.'

'Is that a yes?' said Margaret in a cool voice.

He nodded.

'Right! I'll write a note for you to give to Mr Dixon. Wait here.'

Margaret left him standing on the step and went inside, but Rita stayed. 'A thank you wouldn't have come amiss. You're a selfish sod.'

'And you're a crafty bitch. You and that Sam! I didn't realise straight away that he's the lad who worked at Fitzgerald's. The pair of you done well for yourselves, haven't you? Worming your way into your aunt's and Pops' good books.'

'The pair of us have worked damn hard to get where we are and, besides, it's none of your business.' Her eyes were stormy. 'You'd be better apologising to me for almost strangling me. I hope Mr Dixon really rubs your nose in it and works you off your feet. The horse show's coming up so that should keep you out of mischief. I believe it starts here in this square. Aunt Margaret will be keeping her eye on you – so just watch the way you behave or you'll be brushing the streets.'

At that moment Margaret appeared and handed an envelope to him. 'I've told Mr Dixon you can use the house but the rent'll be part of your wages.'

For a second it looked like Jimmy was going to argue, but Margaret did not give him a chance. He looked at Rita and swore under his breath. She gave a honeyed smile and closed the door in his face. There were far more important people to worry about.

A month passed and still there was no news of Billy or William. Ellen was under the impression that Jonathan was Mrs Richards' baby and nobody had told her any different. Margaret was prepared to put up with her because she had managed to find work at the *Blue Angel* club in Seel Street. Ellen had written to Alice but she had little to do with Jimmy. The police were no nearer to finding the person responsible for the smash and grab.

Outside the office window, the horse show was in full swing but Margaret was refusing to show any positive interest, complaining about the dust stirred up by the horses' hooves and the noise of the crowds. Rita gazed out at horses decorated with ribbons and flowers; leather shone as did every bit of metal, including the brass bells which hung from bridles and saddles; coats gleamed and manes and tails plaited with raffia and ribbons stirred in the breeze.

'I know what you're thinking,' said Margaret.

Rita looked at her aunt and smiled. 'Mind reader, are you?'

Margaret forced a smile, twiddling her pen between her fingers. 'I mightn't be in the mood but the show is the reason why we closed the shop today, so you go and find Sam. Mingle with the crowds, have an ice cream, have fun.'

Rita did not need telling twice. She kissed her aunt's cheek and hurried outside, knowing it was no good moping. Them both being miserable wouldn't do anyone any good.

Harnesses jingled, horses snorted and gaily decorated carts, including the coalman's and the Co-op's, were being admired. People laughed and chattered. Despite the economy being in a mess and unemployment worse than ever, with protest marches being organised, folk seemed determined to enjoy themselves today. Rita bought a yellow balloon because she had never had one as a child, and also an ice cream from a STOP ME AND BUY ONE vendor, pausing to chat to several people she knew. She was looking for Sam but there was no sign of him. Then she caught sight of Jimmy sitting astride a huge dappled grey horse, which exhibited a rosette. They made a handsome duo and were having their photograph taken.

Typical of him to get into the limelight, thought Rita, irritated. Even so she felt compelled to pat the horse's neck after the photographer had moved away, and ask Jimmy how he had managed to twist Mr Dixon's arm to allow him to take the glory.

He smirked. 'I know how to get into people's good books.'

'You mean you're two-faced.'

His expression altered. 'What is it you bloody want? If you can't say anything nice to me, get lost.'

'I intend to. I'm just looking for Sam.'

'You're wasting your time, then. He's up at the yard tinkering with the lorry.'

'Right! Enjoy the glory while you can. It won't last.'

He swore at her, pulled on the reins forcing the horse to turn, and if Rita had not darted out of the way the beast would have trodden on her foot. It was on the tip of her tongue to tell him about Jonathan but she managed to restrain herself and walk away, looking forward to the day when all would be revealed and the smile would be wiped off Jimmy's face.

She found Sam with his head beneath the bonnet of the lorry. As she drew nearer he looked up and, grinning, gesticulated to someone sitting in the cab.

'Sam!' she called, waving a hand.

His head turned in her direction and she thought he looked positively guilty, but then he smiled and the impression faded. 'Hello, Reet! What are you doing here?'

'I was looking for you at the show but Jimmy told me you were up here. How's it going with the lorry?' Rita was aware she was getting the once-over from a red-haired youth sitting in the cab.

'Getting there. This is Archie, by the way. The bloke I told you I was teaching to drive.'

'Nice to meet you.' She held out a hand.

Archie grinned and shook it. 'Sam's told me lots about yer. All good, I might add.'

'Glad to hear it.'

Silence.

Archie glanced at Sam and Rita expected her fiancé to crack one of his jokes, but the silence stretched and she began to get the impression they wanted her out of the way. Men's talk! she thought. 'I can see you're busy so I won't hang around,' she said with assumed brightness.

'That's right, luv,' said Sam, looking relieved and pecked her cheek.

She returned the gesture before strolling out of the yard, feeling slightly hurt. It was not like Sam to make her feel unwelcome. His love was something she had taken for granted for a long time. When she felt blue he was always there trying to cheer her up. What if he suddenly wasn't there? How would she manage if Billy really was dead? A chill seemed to freeze her bones and she shivered. But what was she thinking of? Just because Sam wanted to get on with fixing a lorry there was no need for her to get all worked up, but maybe she had neglected him since Ellen's arrival.

For the rest of the week Rita made a fuss of Sam when he came in from the yard for a bath and supper before going to sleep at the shop. She talked about the wedding and her dress being almost finished at the local dressmaker's. That was until Margaret said Sam was looking haunted and added she was getting tired of the subject herself. Rita felt the blood rush to her face, having given no thought to her aunt's still unmarried state. 'Sorry. I didn't mean to upset you.'

Margaret waved the apology away. 'Take no notice of me. I suppose I just don't want to lose you to Sam.'

Rita was touched. 'I'll still be around.'

'I know, but it won't be the same.'

At that moment the doorbell rang and Rita went to answer it. She flung open the door and caught her breath in amazement. 'Mam! What the hell are you doing here?'

'Well, that's a nice welcome, I don't think!' sniffed Eve. 'Aren't you going to invite me in?'

'I don't know if I should!' She frowned, having very mixed feelings about having her mother around. 'You weren't that keen on having me stay at yours last time I saw you. Besides, this is Aunt Margaret's house and you haven't answered my question. What are you doing here?'

'She's my sister, for God's sake! And we've come for the wedding. Thought we'd come early and have a nice little holiday.'

'Remembered you've got a daughter? You should have written. I wasn't expecting you. You didn't want me when your husband was due home. Where is he, by the way?'

Eve glowered. 'I've left him, but I've brought Josh.' She glanced down the steps.

Rita saw Josh, his arms wrapped round a basement railing as if he needed something to hang on to. Now, him she *was* pleased to see because, after all, he was the only half-brother she had. 'Hi, Josh!' She smiled down at him and held out a hand but he hung back.

Eve told her son to stop skulking down there and come and say hello to his sister. Slowly he stumped up the steps and clutched Eve's skirt. 'Don't do that!' She slapped his hand away.

Rita's lips tightened but she knew it would be a waste of time rebuking her mother. She made up her mind to be extra nice to Josh. As she stared at them, she asked herself how her mother could afford to dress up to the nines. She was wearing a cream and brown checked two-piece and a hat with an enormous feather in it. On her feet were crocodile court shoes and she was carrying a handbag and suitcase. She had to still be on the game. Maybe found herself a rich bloke. Perhaps the husband had discovered what she'd been up to and that's why she was here. She wondered what Margaret would say when she saw her sister again and how she would feel about having a nephew beneath her roof.

'Well, are you inviting me in?' said Eve, an edge to her voice. 'Or are you going to keep me on the step all day?'

'I suppose you'd best come in but I don't know how Aunt Margaret'll feel about you stopping.' She stepped aside and waved her mother in.

Eve entered the house followed by Josh, and she stopped abruptly by the wrought iron staircase, gazing up at the domed glass roof. 'Bloody hell!' she breathed, placing the suitcase on the floor. 'This is some place. Our Maggie really knows how to make the money. Is she in?'

'This is where she works. I'd better warn her you're here.' Rita walked towards the office.

'Don't bother announcing me,' said Eve, skirting round her daughter and pushing open the door. She stepped inside and shut Rita out.

Margaret did not lift her head from the ledger on her desk but said, 'Who was that at the door?'

'Look up and you'll find out. Long time no see, Maggie.'

Margaret glanced up and the muscles of her face froze and several moments passed before she said, 'Rita wrote telling you we'd moved. I wish she hadn't.'

'I love you, too,' said Eve with a mirthless smile. 'But she not only told me that you'd moved but that she was getting married, so I decided it was my duty as a mother to come and give the bloke the once-over.'

'So you've remembered you're her mother? Fancy that! Well, I can assure you that Sam's a good bloke, so you can go back where you came from.'

'What a way to welcome your prodigal sister home!'

'This isn't your home.' Margaret's heart began to thud. The last thing she wanted was her sister finding out she'd had a baby out of wedlock. How Eve would enjoy her fall from grace. No longer able to sit still, Margaret stood up and came round the desk and, leaning against it, she folded her arms. She was wearing a navy-blue suit with white piping round the collar and cuffs and sensible court shoes and knew she looked smart – but glamorous? Eve had glamour, and what the film people called *It*.

'I don't believe you're here just because you decided to cast an eye over Sam. What are you really here for? Out with it!'

Eve raised pencilled eyebrows. 'You're so untrusting. You and Reet are the only family I have – you two and Josh.'

'Where's your husband?'

Eve shrugged her shoulders. 'You tell me?'

'Left you, has he, because he got fed up of your carryings-on?'

Eve's eyes narrowed, became almost catlike. 'You can think what you like. But you wouldn't have this place if it wasn't for Father's money. I reckon I'm entitled to half of it.'

Margaret felt a rush of relief. She could get rid of her sister if it was only money she was after. 'So the truth's coming out now. Well, I'll give it you straight. I've worked hard for what I've got, but because I'm such a nice-natured person I'll give you a handout as long as you take yourself out of here and don't come back.'

'How much?'

'A hundred pounds.'

'Two hundred.'

'Don't push your luck. I've done your job for you where Rita's concerned for the past few years. A hundred and thirty and that's my last offer. These are hard times, even for me.'

Eve hesitated.

'Take it or leave it,' said Margaret, straightening up from the desk. 'Legally I don't have to give you anything.'

The muscles of Eve's face relaxed. 'I'll take it. I've got friends I can stay with. I wouldn't mind a bite to eat first, though . . . and if I could leave Josh here while I look them up I'd take it as a big favour.'

Margaret was surprised. 'You brought him with you?'

Eve's eyelids flickered. 'You surely didn't expect me to leave him behind?'

Margaret made no answer but instead ushered her sister out of the office. Rita was sitting on the stairs with Josh. She was telling him the story of David and Goliath with actions and they were both obviously enjoying themselves. Margaret had to admit he was an attractive little boy but being of mixed race she felt certain he was bound to meet with problems trying to be part of two worlds and felt sorry for him. 'Rita, take Josh down to the kitchen and tell Mrs Richards to give him something to eat, and if she could put something on a tray for your mother and bring it into the office I'd appreciate that.'

Rita looked at her mother, who smiled. 'We've hardly eaten since we left Cardiff so we're starving. I've got to slip out afterwards and see a friend about a place to stay, but you'll keep your eye on Josh for me, won't you?'

'Of course.' Rita had to admit to feeling relief that her mother was not staying at the house. Knowing her the way she did, she guessed Eve would expect her and Mrs Richards to wait on her hand and foot; and it was often much easier to do what Eve asked than argue because she could get right moody. She went downstairs with Josh, giving Mrs Richards a shock when she walked in with him and explained he was her half-brother.

Upstairs, Margaret had gone to her safe and taken out the money to give to Eve. She had also slipped off the wedding ring, not wanting any questions about that from her sister. 'Don't expect anymore,' she said, handing over the wad of notes.

'You're like Father. It was like getting blood from a stone getting money out of him.' Eve opened her handbag, placed the banknotes inside and sat down.

'You don't half push your luck.'

Eve smiled sweetly. 'So, tell me about you and Will.'

Margaret almost jumped out of her skin. 'What did Rita tell you?'

'Why, what is there to tell?' asked Eve, eyes as sharp as a ferret's.

Margaret determined not to let anything slip about her son. She could not imagine Rita having told her mother about him. 'He's missing. He went to find Billy who went off to China and nothing's been heard of either of them for ages.'

Eve rolled her eyes. 'Where's Will's brains? China, for God's sake! Did he forget what happened to Alan?'

'Of course he didn't,' snapped Margaret.

'What's been done to find them?'

'The padre who belongs to the Seamen's Mission has been doing his best by contacting people out there, but I haven't heard from him for a while. I don't like bothering him as his wife's having a baby and that's not easy at her age. I know.' She bit her lip, hoping Eve wouldn't pick her up on those last two words.

Eve looked surprised and amused. 'So Father Jerome took the plunge at his age. It shows you. It's never too late.'

'You know him?'

'We've met. I'd get in touch again if I were you. It's his job to be pestered about problems to do with seamen. And that's what Will was at one time, wasn't he?'

Margaret nodded, and decided to follow up her sister's suggestion as soon as she got rid of her, which was even quicker than she had hoped.

Half an hour later Margaret set out for the Sailors' Home, thinking to find the padre there, only to be told that his wife had just given birth to a baby girl so he was at home. So he got what he wanted, thought Margaret, remembering a previous conversation with him. She was cheered by the news.

To her relief she was made welcome at the house and it was obvious they thought she was there to see the baby. She admired the new arrival and it was plain to see that the padre, whose hair was pure silver these days, would be a doting parent. Afterwards, over a cup of tea, she brought William and Billy into the conversation.

The padre said, 'I was going to ask if you'd heard any more news but I see somehow the letter I posted through your door has gone missing.'

'Letter! What letter?'

'I heard from Billy. It was weeks ago.'

Margaret's heart felt as if it was performing a somersault inside her chest. 'What did he say? Did he mention Will at all?'

'Yes! He's been very ill. Almost died, apparently.'

Margaret felt faint. 'But he's all right now?'

'Let's hope so. The message was sent via the Chinese Inland Mission. William was in a hospital in Hong Kong and Billy was staying there until his father was fit to come home.'

Tears rolled down Margaret's cheeks. It seemed miraculous that after all this time they were both alive. Yet she must not get too excited. Hong Kong was thousands of miles away and they had the long sea journey to complete before she could relax. Even so, it was good news she had to tell Rita, and fresh tears sprung to her eyes.

The padre held one of her hands between both of his and said a prayer for William and Billy and a safe journey home, and then saw her out.

As soon as she arrived home Rita noticed the tearstains on her face and felt sick to the stomach. 'What's wrong? Have you heard something about Mr Brodie and Billy? They're not dead?' she whispered.

'No!' Margaret's happiness burst through and

she flung her arms about Rita and danced her round the room. 'They're alive!'

'Alive!' Rita could scarcely believe it but her aunt's actions reassured her. Billy was alive and he would be coming home; she would see his face again. She began to laugh and cry at the same time, not knowing whether she was on her head or her heels.

CHAPTER TWENTY

Margaret heard her name being called and dragged herself out of a wonderful dream to gaze bleary-eyed at her niece. She looked angry and was cradling a grizzling Jonathan and holding a weeping Josh by the hand.

'You'll never guess what Mam's gone and done.' Rita did not wait for an answer. 'She's left Josh the way she left me. I could scream! Last night I was so happy. How could she do this to him and us?'

Margaret eased herself up against the pillows and groaned. 'I should have known she was up to something. Why should she suddenly want to give the man you're going to marry the once-over? She's never worried about you before. She deliberately

381

came here to dump her son and get money out of me. What a fool I was!'

'She's left a letter.' Rita sat on the bed and Margaret took the baby from her. Josh immediately sat on Rita's knee. 'What were you thinking of, giving her money?'

'I didn't want her staying on here.' Margaret felt like tearing her hair out. 'I didn't want her finding out about Jonathan. You know the kind of thing she'd say and I didn't want to hear it from her.'

Rita could understand her aunt's feelings. 'So what do we do? I feel like strangling her right now but it'll be a waste of time trying to find her. She says in the letter she's going to America. There's a bloke there who says he'll set her up in an apartment and she's got to seize the chance of a whole new life.'

'The crafty madam! If I had her in front of me I'd strip her naked and throw her out on the street. America! No wonder she needed money. Where's she sailing from?'

'Southampton. She was catching an early train. That's to make sure she was out of Liverpool before we found the note.'

'What else did it say?'

'That she's written a letter to Caleb so he knows where to find Josh.'

'Does that mean he'll want the boy so he'll be coming here?'

'Yeah! I can't understand, though, why Mam didn't leave him with Caleb's sister.'

Josh lifted his head from Rita's breast and muttered, 'Auntie Hortense hated Mam and she didn't like me 'cos I was Mam's son. She told me so.' The boy's shoulders drooped. 'Now you don't want me either.'

Immediately Rita felt torn by guilt, remembering how she had felt when Eve had deserted her – and she had been so much older. 'It's not that I don't want you. But this isn't my house and I'll be getting married shortly, and what's my husband going to say? We'll just have to hope your dad gets the letter and comes up with some ideas of what to do with you when he's at sea.'

Josh's bottom lip trembled. 'You're not going to strip me naked and throw me out on the street, are you?'

Rita could not prevent a smile. 'Of course not! But if our mam turns up here again—'

'We'll tar and feather her,' said Margaret, unbuttoning her nightdress and telling Rita to take Josh out of the room and give him some breakfast . . . and she wouldn't mind a strong cup of tea and toast.

Rita took her brother down to the kitchen where Mrs Richards already had a fire going and the kettle on. She gave her brother a bowl of grape-nuts with plenty of milk and sugar and asked him about his father, remembering her mother telling her how fond Caleb was of his son. She seethed with anger, knowing it was going to take her some time to get over her mother's latest escapade. She just hoped that Josh's father would come for him. Otherwise the boy was going to feel worse than she had when deserted by their mother.

Rita took a last look in the hall mirror and knew she had hit the right note in choosing the green frock with white spots and matching bolero jacket. For the last couple of days she had dressed with care, thinking this might be the day when Billy and William arrived home. The padre's letter had been found in the pocket of the suit she had worn the day Jimmy had turned up on their doorstep – and which she had not worn since. Three days ago a postcard had arrived postmarked Gibraltar, announcing the Brodie men should be home within the week.

She smoothed back a strand of hair, which had come loose from her tortoiseshell slide, and winked at her reflection. She picked up her handbag and called a *tarrah* to all within hearing distance. Josh came running and asked was she going to the shop and could he come. He was inclined not to let her leave the house without knowing where she was going and often wanted to go with her. She was fond of him but had to be strict. Keeping an eye on him and trying to work at the same time wasn't easy, so it was shared out between herself, Mrs Richards and Babs. The girl's mother knew better than to complain about her daughter mixing with the boy. Margaret also did her share of keeping an eye on him.

Rita kissed her half-brother's dusky cheek. 'Not today. Who knows – today could be the day when your dad turns up, and what if you're not here waiting for him?'

Josh's face brightened. 'He'll probably come by ship.'

She had already taken him down to the Pierhead so he could see the ships coming and going. 'Probably.' She kissed him again and left.

Rita was only a few doors away from the shop when she noticed Sam arguing with a middle-aged man. Presuming he was a customer with a complaint she increased her stride, but as she approached the man shambled away.

'Who was that?'

'Me bloody father! Pardon my language but he makes me mad.' Sam lifted the wire mesh guard he had just removed and carried it inside the shop.

'He's taken his time finding out you're here. What's he want?'

'Money! There's nothing else he'd want from me.' Sam's expression was grim. 'I told him to get lost and if he pestered me again he'd be sorry he started.'

'Good for you!' She squeezed his arm. 'Everything

else OK?' Her gaze swept the shop's interior and she thought the stuff on those top shelves could do with dusting.

'Fine. I'll just put this up the lobby and be off up the yard. There's a float in the till and the kettle hasn't long boiled.'

'Thanks, luv.' She kissed his cheek and wished he could make her feel tingly all over, like just thinking of Billy did. 'You take care driving that lorry.'

'I'm not doing the driving today. Archie is.' Sam's face lit up. 'He's almost as good as me now.'

'That's great.' Rita saw him out.

She made a cup of tea and brought it into the shop, served a customer and then fastened an apron about her waist and tied a scarf over her hair. She climbed the ladder and began to dust, singing, *'If you were the only boy in the world and I was the only girl.'*

'Nothing else would matter in this world today!'

She dropped not only her duster but lost her footing on the ladder.

Billy seized her by the ankle and steadied her with his other hand.

She gazed down at him and was so overcome by emotion that she could not speak for a moment and when she did her voice was raw. 'About time too! For ages we thought you were dead. I could hit you for putting us through all that pain and worry.'

'Feel free!' He grinned. 'Are you coming down so you can give me a proper welcome home?'

She held out both hands and he gripped them and swung her down, bringing her against him. She allowed herself to gaze at him only briefly, noting lines about his eyes and mouth that had not been there before, and that his skin had been burnt by the weather and he was thinner, much thinner. Her heart longed for him. She wanted to look after him, be all things to him, but knew she had to pretend her feelings were only sisterly. 'Welcome home! It's so good to see you.'

'Give us a kiss, then!' Before she could prevent him he caught her up in his arms and kissed her hard. She found it difficult to resist returning the kiss but kept her lips pressed together. She wanted to cling to him and not let him go but knew she had to be sensible. She was getting short of breath and forced herself to pull away.

'Gosh!' She laughed. 'Do you kiss all girls like that? My fiancé would have your life.' She avoided his eyes as she put up a hand and dragged the scarf from her hair and removed her apron. 'I must look a mess.'

'No. You're a sight for sore eyes.' The tone of his voice was like a caress and she trembled inwardly. 'And I know about Sam. Jimmy wasted no time in telling me. I won't soil your ears with what he called the pair of you.'

'I can imagine,' said Rita, lifting her gaze to meet his. 'I suppose he also told you Ellen's staying with us?'

Billy jingled the change in his pockets and said dryly, 'That too.'

'You'll be wanting to see her.'

'Sure. We had some fun times together.' He paused. 'Are you happy, Rita? You deserve to be happy with this Sam after all you suffered before I went away. Is he a good bloke? Not that I can imagine you tying yourself up to someone who wasn't, but you did make a mistake over Jimmy.'

Rita grimaced. 'You don't have to remind me. Sam's not a bit like him. We've known each other for ages and you're bound to meet him at the yard, so you'll be able to judge for yourself.' She felt if she could keep talking about Sam she would be able to keep the lid on her feelings for Billy.

'Does your aunt like him?'

'Of course!' Rita laughed. 'Do you think she'd have let me get engaged to someone she didn't approve of and trusted to live here and help run the business?'

'I suppose not.' He forced a smile and reached out a hand, took one of hers and squeezed it. 'I want you to tell me everything you've been doing while I've been away. I've really missed you.' He toyed with her fingers.

Rita withdrew her hand gently. 'I've missed you too and I'd rather hear about what you've been up to in China than talk about my life.'

'Give us a cup of tea then, and I'll tell you some of it.'

She thought there could be no harm in the pair of them sharing a cup of tea and talking in the back. She had told him about Sam so they both knew exactly where they were. 'OK!' She led the way, saying to him over her shoulder. 'I could have killed Jimmy when he turned up believing you and your dad were dead and looking to take over the yard.'

Billy smiled grimly. 'I can imagine. You should have seen his face when we arrived home.'

'All smiles, I bet?'

'He's not deceiving anyone. What he did to you hasn't been forgotten; neither has the theft and the lies he told.'

Rita was glad of that. She told Billy to sit and made tea. Having poured, she sat opposite him and hoped the shop bell would not buzz. It seemed incredible that he was really here in front of her. She felt dreamlike. 'Tell me everything.'

He drank his tea before leaning back in the chair, a shadow in his eyes. 'It would take too long to tell it all, and some I'd rather not talk about.'

'Tell me just the important bits.'

He told her about the fighting between not only the Communists and Imperial troops but how the presence of the Japanese soldiers had meant making huge detours to avoid getting caught up in their wars and probably thrown into prison. 'The trouble is, you think before you go out there that you've got a good idea how vast China is, but you can't imagine how great the distances are until you've walked them like we did across valleys and mountains. I broke my leg crossing a river when I was swept away by currents.'

'You broke your leg! That must have been terrible. How did you get it fixed?' She leant forward and touched his knee but withdrew her hand quickly.

'It wasn't easy. Pretty grim, in fact, and dozens of times I thought I wasn't going to make it. I was lucky in the guide I chose. He knew his business and had been taught more than just English at a mission station and that's where he took me to rest up. Fortunate, really.'

'Why? And what were you doing there, Billy? I can't believe you went to all that trouble just for some ol' artefacts.'

Billy laughed. 'Da – told me that's what he'd let you think.'

'Isn't it true?'

He shook his head and said in a low voice, 'I went in search of my father.'

Rita thought, he's suffered a bang on the head as well as breaking his leg. He's confused. 'It was your father who went in search of you,' she said gently.

'No.' He gripped the arms of the chair. 'William isn't my father. My real father is his twin brother.'

She was stunned and for a moment could not think what to say, then, 'I don't understand. You are talking about Alan who's supposed to be dead?'

'Love, betrayal, deception!' Billy took a deep breath. 'Yes. But he's not dead and I reckon right now Da – my uncle – is telling your aunt all about it. You know what it makes me, Rita?'

She slipped from her chair and knelt in front of him and took both his hands in hers. 'Who's to know? You can be sure I won't blab about it and neither will my aunt. Did you find Alan?'

Billy shook his head. 'All that hardship, suffering and money spent was a waste of time. He left China years ago and came back to Britain, and William is determined your aunt's got to know everything before they can even think of getting married.'

It was on the tip of Rita's tongue to tell him about Jonathan but again she managed to keep quiet and instead told Billy to tell her the rest as she tried to imagine what this news would do to her aunt.

'Will, stop pacing the floor!' Margaret's heart felt as if it was somewhere in her stomach. This reunion was going all wrong. Perhaps he had stopped loving her?

When he had knocked on the door she had run to answer it. Despite the initial shock of seeing how ill he had been – his clothes hung on him, his skin was like parchment and the whites of his eyes yellowish – she had flung herself in his arms. For a moment he had held her tightly, his cheek resting against hers. She had wanted to burrow into him and blurt out about the baby, but then he had freed himself and said they had to talk.

'Of course we have to talk,' she had said.

And he had talked but she would have preferred to hear what he had to say while being held by him. In his arms it would have been easier to tell him about Jonathan but while he kept his distance and told his story from a chair three feet away she felt all churned up inside. And what a story he had told. So many adventures avoiding troops and wading across rivers. It had been sheer good luck or an answer to prayer that he had found Billy laid up in a mission station with a broken leg. Even when Billy was on his feet again their progress had been slow. Then more delay when Will had caught hepatitis and nearly died. He had yet to give her an answer to why he and Billy had ended up at a mission station in the middle of nowhere.

'You haven't got a drink, have you?' asked William.

He looked drawn, and although she was not sure whether he should be having alcohol, she decided maybe a medicinal brandy might relax them both. So she got up and splashed brandy and soda into two crystal glasses and handed one to him.

He raised his glass. 'To truth and hope!'

What a strange toast, she thought, but repeated his words and sipped her brandy. The muscles of her stomach clenched as she waited to hear what he had to say next.

'Alan's alive.'

She choked on the brandy. Surely he could not have said what she thought he said? She had to have misheard him.

'Are you OK? I shouldn't have blurted it out like that. Will I get you some water?'

'Shut up, Will!' she gasped.

He sat down and his eyes were anxious.

She got her breath back and asked him to repeat what he said. She felt otherworldly. She was glad now she had done as he said in his postcard and not made a fuss about their homecoming and thrown a party. Besides, she wasn't good at parties, she thought distractedly.

'Alan's alive.'

So she had heard him aright and her heart went off at a gallop. Her mind refused to believe it. 'You're lying. You good as told me he was dead years ago. I grieved for him.'

'He's alive. Do you think I'd really be telling you now he was if he wasn't? He messed up my life in the past and by God I'm letting him do it again. The trouble is I can't stop myself.'

She knew it was true then. 'Why didn't he get in touch with me and tell me he was alive?' She was bewildered.

'Because he wanted to lose himself. He had done things he was ashamed of.' William tossed off his drink.

'What do you mean?'

'He got Bella pregnant.'

Those words were more of a shock than the news Alan was alive. Margaret could not sit still and stood up. 'That's not funny.'

'It wasn't at the time either.' Will's smile was grim as he got to his feet too. 'Alan had gone off to China and I'd just got back from sea. Bella came to see me in a terrible state and told me she was two months gone with his child.'

Margaret drained her glass. 'You should have told me.'

'I wasn't your favourite person at the time. Would you have believed me? You thought Alan the saint and me the sinner.'

'I was only a girl and I was mixed up. You know how it was with me. I don't want to go over all that again.' The drink seemed to be affecting her legs and she sat down heavily. 'All those years I spent being angry and hurt and lonely.' She raised her voice. 'You should have trusted me and put me to the test.'

'I wanted to but you'd already shown that you didn't trust me.'

'I could have gone to Bella and asked her for the truth.'

His laugh was harsh. 'You think she would have told you! Alan was in China and she wanted a quick marriage. She said that if I didn't marry her she

394

would write to the Missionary Society and tell them what he had done.'

'So you allowed yourself to be blackmailed.'

'I saved his reputation,' said Will brusquely. 'He was my parents' blue-eyed boy and the disgrace would have devastated them. Once Bella died, of course, things were different. I saw Alan in China and told him Billy was his son.'

'What did he say?'

'He went to pieces. I asked him to write to you and tell you the truth. He knew that I loved you and I wanted to marry you. He said he would do as I asked, break off the engagement and give his life completely to God.'

'But I never got the letter.'

'I was furious about that.'

'And so you convinced me he was dead. Why couldn't you have told me the truth then?' Margaret felt so hurt.

'You made no sign that convinced me the news would have been welcome without some kind of proof.'

'But you have no proof now. I only have your word.' All kinds of thoughts were popping into her mind. 'You married Maud! Why did you do that? Why didn't you go and look for Alan and bring him back so we could sort it out?'

William was silent and then said in a heavy voice, 'I always told myself I had no choice but to find a mother for Billy when you turned me down, but I suppose the truth is that I was scared that you might still prefer Alan to me if you saw him again. I'm still scared.'

She could not believe he could be so unsure of her love. For God's sake, she had gone to bed with him! And, remembering how she had to cope alone with her pregnancy, she wanted to punish him. 'Where is Alan?'

'Not in China. If the pair of us had taken the trouble to get in touch with the different missionary societies we would have found that out. Apparently he's been working at a mission for seamen in Scotland for years. He got the idea after talking to Jerry in Hong Kong that time.'

Scotland! And he hadn't bothered to come and see her in all that time or written another letter. She felt so angry she couldn't think straight. She wanted to punish Alan as well. 'I must see him,' said Margaret.

'I thought you'd say that,' said William, twisting the stem of the glass between his fingers. 'Billy's already made up his mind to go up there.'

'So you told Billy the truth and not me?'

'I thought he needed an explanation to why I'd treated him the way I did. It was wrong of me but he's forgiven me.' William's expression warmed. 'We really got to know each other while in China. He could have left me and come back home but he wouldn't do that. I can say now that I truly love him like a son.'

'Yet you're letting him go off and see Alan. Aren't you afraid he'll prefer his real father to you?' Her voice was tart.

William winced, knowing why she said it but he made no effort to answer the question. Instead he said, 'Billy will be leaving for Scotland tomorrow. Do you want Alan to come here and visit you?'

'Yes! I need to see him.'

William nodded. He left the room looking weary and afterwards she felt ashamed of not stopping him and giving him reassurance. But at that moment she was stiff with shock, anger and hurt.

CHAPTER TWENTY-ONE

'So what did he say when you told him about Jonathan?' said Rita as she sat down at the dinner table. They were free to talk openly about the matter because Ellen had left for *The Blue Angel*.

'I didn't tell him.' Margaret's voice was short and she did not meet her niece's eyes.

Silence.

'Is that because he lied to you about his twin brother?'

Margaret stopped toying with her food and threw down her fork. 'So Billy told you!'

'He came into the shop and it came out when he was telling me about China. They had a terrible time, didn't they?'

'Daft, the pair of them,' muttered Margaret, picking up her fork again and digging it into a potato. 'It would have been better if they'd stayed at home and Will had kept his mouth shut.'

Rita was silent, thinking she would probably have never got engaged to Sam if Billy hadn't been told about his father; but then he and William's relationship might have disintegrated all together and that wouldn't have been good for either of them. 'Don't you think Mr Brodie acted kind of noble in saving his brother's reputation? You have to forgive him.'

'It's me who'll decide that, miss!' said Margaret, her eyebrows snapping together in a manner Rita had not seen for ages. 'You look after your own business and I'll look after mine. This homecoming hasn't turned out the least how I expected and I don't want to talk on this subject anymore at the moment.'

So nothing more was said between them but they both still carried on thinking about the Brodie men with that familiar ache inside them and wondered what the next few days would bring.

The next morning Rita was in the shop when Billy dropped by. 'I'm off to Stranraer on the west coast of Scotland so I thought I'd come and say *tarrah*.'

She was touched but knew she had to keep her feelings firmly under control. 'Does your father know you're coming?'

'Father Jerome phoned a message through but he didn't speak to him because he was out. Someone was passing the information on without giving too much away. Hopefully I'll only be away a few days.' Billy's hand strayed to hers on the counter and covered it. 'I don't know what to say to him. It's hard to imagine how I'm going to feel seeing a man who's the spitting image of the father I've believed was mine all these years.'

'Take each moment as it comes. I'm sure you'll think of something. One thing, you'll know I'm thinking and praying for you. It's such a hard thing to have to face up to.'

He smiled and toyed with her fingers. 'You're a good kid. I'm glad we met that time in Chinatown. If we hadn't I don't know what would have happened to the Brodies.' He raised her hand to his lips.

A quiver ran through her and she attempted to make light of things. 'Get away with you! You're not thinking what you're saying. If you hadn't met me then you wouldn't have met my aunt and she and your father would never have got together and you'd have never had to go to China and broke your leg and—'

'And on and on. You'd have never run away and met Sam again. He was telling me how you met him in Ludlow.'

'I think these things are meant,' she said. Her heart was imitating a drum beat because he still had hold of her hand; she had an overwhelming urge to press herself against him.

'It was certainly a good thing for Sam. He—' Billy never got to finish what he was going to say because the door opened and Sam staggered in. His face was ashen and a bloodied bandage was tied about his head.

'What have you done to yourself?' Dragging her hand free of Billy's she rushed from behind the counter. 'What's happened?'

'Archie crashed the lorry. He's dead!' Sam choked on the words.

'How the hell did that happen?' said Billy, following Rita over.

Sam moved his shoulders as if he had the weight of the world on them and tried to hold back his tears but a sob broke from him. Rita put her arm around him. 'Don't, Sam! You'll have me crying.'

'Jimmy said I've got to get the lorry repaired. I told him to sod off and he said I'd get the sack for speaking to him like that. I said I didn't care about the bloody lorry. I know that can be fixed but I can't fix Ar-Archie.' He tried to choke back another sob.

'Come on now, mate, pull yourself together,' said Billy, patting Sam's shoulder. 'What you need is a strong drink!'

'I'd like a cup of tea,' said Sam.

'Let's go into the back,' said Rita.

Between them she and Billy got Sam into the

kitchen and she made hot strong tea. Sam stammered out how Archie had swerved to avoid a little boy who ran into the road and crashed into a lamp post.

'It was horrible what happened to him. Horrible!'

Rita had tears in her eyes as she remembered the red-haired youth she had seen the day of the horse show. 'You don't have to tell us anymore.' Her voice was husky. 'You rest while I see Billy out. He's got to go to Scotland today.'

'I can see myself out,' said Billy, his expression intent as it rested on Sam's face. 'You take care of yourself, mate.' He touched Rita's cheek with a finger. 'You, too. Don't go wearing yourself out. If he's got any whisky pour him a dram.' Then he was gone.

Rita would have given a lot to go with him but she pulled herself together. She guessed there would be no whisky in the place because Sam was no drinker. So she took money out of the till and went and bought a small bottle. She poured a half a tumbler and told Sam to get that down him.

He did not argue.

When it was time for her to close the shop and go home he clung to her hand. 'I don't want to be left alone, Reet. Couldn't you stay the night? You can trust me.'

Of course she could trust him. It was the extent of his grief that surprised her and the need to mention it to Margaret that gave her reason not to stay with him. Then she remembered Ellen. Maybe she could stay, too. Margaret and Ellen had had words that morning over the time she was coming in after working at the club so she would probably agree to the idea. 'I'll have to speak to Aunt Margaret. You'll be OK for half an hour or so, won't you?'

He nodded. 'Don't be long, though. Me mind keeps playing over what happened.' He wiped his eyes with the back of his hand and then reached for the whisky bottle.

Margaret appeared to give scant attention to what Rita told her but was quick to agree to Ellen's staying at the pawnshop. Ellen was happy with the idea too. 'It mightn't be as posh as here,' she said, 'but it's nearer to the club and I won't have your aunt snapping at me. What's happened to make her so bad-tempered?'

Rita was not going to tell her but suggested she got a move on as Sam would be waiting for them.

Sam lay comatose on the sofa and the empty whisky bottle was on the rug. As there was only one bed in the house Rita suggested she and Ellen share it. Sam could carry on sleeping on the sofa.

'I understand how he feels, losing a mate,' said Ellen, gazing down at him. 'And in such a way. Tragic!' She sat down and, opening her handbag, began to apply fresh nail polish and changed the subject. 'So how do you find Billy? He's changed, hasn't he? He's much more serious. I was surprised and glad we never got as far as an engagement. Still, I'm in no rush to marry anyone.' She smiled at Rita, not realising the effect her words had on her. 'Switch the wireless on, ducky, and let's liven the place up.'

Rita did not argue; it was easier to give in to Ellen and she doubted anything would rouse Sam at that moment. How she wished Ellen could have said those words years ago. Rita tried to lose herself in her library book but couldn't – despite it being the latest Agatha Christie. Her mind kept wandering to that moment Billy had helped her down from the ladder and kissed her. If only she could have kissed him back. She thought about him meeting his father for the first time and wondered what the outcome would be. She sighed and lifted her gaze from the open page in front of her and looked at Sam and knew she must stop thinking of Billy. Sam needed her.

The following morning Ellen was still asleep in Sam's bed when Rita got up. She had left him still out to the world on the sofa last night. She found him pale and clammy but on his feet and drinking water. 'You look like death,' she said without thinking.

He almost keeled over but steadied himself by putting a hand against a wall. 'I'll have to arrange Archie's funeral.' His voice trembled.

'Surely his family will see to that.'

'He was an orphan. I became his family. He

trusted me to look after him; that's why I've got to see to things.' Sam's voice had strengthened and he pulled back his shoulders and put on his jacket and left.

Rita was in the shop locking the till when he returned much later. If anything he looked more drawn than he had earlier and her heart was filled with pity for him. 'Do you want us to stay tonight too, Sam?'

'Thanks, I'd appreciate your company.' He put both arms round her and rested his head on her shoulder. 'What would I do without you? Me and you, we've looked out for each other for a few years now, haven't we?'

She nodded, near to tears.

Ellen was a comfort to both of them, helping Rita in the shop in the afternoon and, when Sam came in, trying to take his mind off things by playing music and talking to him about her brother and the proposed tour to the other side of the world.

The day of the funeral, Rita did not open up after lunch but went with Sam to church. Ellen said she would have gone too but had to rehearse several new numbers at the club. Very few people were at the service. The minister praised Archie for his bravery in saving the little boy's life. She thought Sam was going to faint and propped his swaying body up with her own. Afterwards he seemed in a dream and she had to keep telling him what to do.

The interment was a nightmare because she kept thinking he might topple into the open grave. He had made no arrangements for a funeral meal for which she was glad because when they arrived back at the shop Billy was waiting outside.

Her face lit up. 'How did things go?'

'He's coming tomorrow because he had a meeting today. Can't say we hit it off. I embarrass him. I'm a reminder of something he'd rather forget. I can admire the work he's doing but . . .' Billy shrugged and glanced at Sam. 'How are you, mate?'

Sam gulped. 'Archie was a hero, you know!' Then he went ahead of them and up the stairs.

'He's probably gone to get changed,' said Rita. 'He's taking Archie's death really hard.'

'When's the wedding?' said Billy, his gaze following Sam up the stairs.

The question coming so unexpectedly took her aback. She did not want to think about it but June was bursting out all over; flowers, trees, birds on the wing, and students with collecting boxes were everywhere because it was Rag Week. 'The end of the month.'

Billy started and he seemed to lose colour. 'So soon! Do you think he's going to be up to it?'

'You mean because of the way he is over Archie's death?' She had not thought of postponing the wedding but maybe they should. 'I'll talk to him. Maybe you can get him to see it might be best to wait until he's got over this upset. While I make tea perhaps you can tell me how you greeted your father when you met him.'

He grimaced. 'Certainly not "Hi, Dad!"' He followed her into the kitchen. 'It was unreal him looking so like Dad—Blast! One of these days I'll stop thinking of William as my dad.'

'Why do you need to? He's been more of one than Alan. Call Alan your father and William your dad.' She smiled.

'That's a good idea.' Billy's eyes were warm as they met hers. 'We're a pair, aren't we? Your aunt has taken the place of your mother and my uncle that of my father. It makes you think, doesn't it?'

'You can say that again and you haven't even heard the latest on Mam.'

'Tell me,' he said with a slight smile.

There was a thud overhead. 'Gosh! I've forgotten about Sam. I wonder what that noise was?'

'You'd better go and take his tea up. I guess this isn't the right time for us to talk. I'll go.'

'No wait!' She touched his arm and said impulsively, 'Stay a little longer.'

Their eyes met and held and she felt breathless. Hastily she poured a cup out for Sam and hurried upstairs. She pushed open his bedroom door and stopped abruptly. Her heart raced as she took in the fallen chair and Sam hanging by a cord from the light fitting. He was twitching and gasping, his face turning purple. She darted forward, set the chair beneath him, and placed an arm around him to take his weight while trying to loosen the noose but it was too difficult. She yelled for Billy and carried on yelling until he came.

'Bloody hell!' He took a jack-knife from his pocket and managed to balance on the edge of the chair. Rita's arms were aching but she felt unable to let go of Sam until Billy sawed through the cord.

Between them they managed to get Sam down and lay him on the bed. 'Is he still breathing?' she gasped.

Billy did not answer but at that moment Sam drew in a rasping breath and reached up a hand to his throat. 'You fool! You bloody fool! What did you go and do that for?' cried Rita.

Sam's eyelids fluttered open but he made no answer.

'Leave him alone,' said Billy, an intense expression on his face. 'He can't give you an answer. Go downstairs. I'll look after him. If you have any brandy we could all do with a tot.'

Rita knew there was no brandy but, relieved that Billy was taking over and still shaken by what had happened, she determined to raid the till again and buy a bottle. Margaret would surely understand why she had to spend the money when told what had happened. Or would she? Rita shuddered as she relived that moment when she had seen Sam hanging. If she had left him hanging there a little longer, then—She buried the thought.

She bought brandy and took bottle and glasses upstairs where she found Sam still lying on his bed and Billy by the window removing the cordless blind.

'Sorry!' croaked Sam, looking up at Rita from damp eyes. 'That bang on the head muddled me.'

Billy turned. 'He felt guilty because it wasn't him who got killed. I told him men who survived the war often felt the same way. Isn't that right, Sam?'

He nodded. 'I'm really sorry for frightening you, Reet.'

'I should think so too!' She forced a smile as she poured brandy into three glasses. 'Promise me you'll never try anything like that again. In fact I'm not going to take the chance of you doing it. You're coming back with me to Abercromby Square.'

Billy and Sam exchanged looks. 'Do you think that's a good idea, Billy?' Sam pushed himself up onto his elbows.

'It's your decision, mate. I've got to go along there and have a word with Miss Sinclair so I could walk with the pair of you.' Billy took a glass from Rita. 'Cheers!' he said, lifting his glass. 'Here's to no more frights. It's not doing my heart any good.'

Rita could only agree wholeheartedly.

Margaret was sitting behind her desk, supposedly reading a report Rita had written about a prospective client but not taking in a word because her thoughts were all over the place. One minute she was rehearsing what she would say to Alan and thinking of what Billy had told her about him, and the next she was picturing herself telling William about Jonathan. She wished she hadn't said she wanted to see Alan now. What was the point? The past was the past and it would be best to let it go. She knew which twin she loved and wanted to marry. She glanced at her watch. He would be here soon.

A child's voice sounded in the hall and there was a crash. 'Damn and blast!' she muttered, and left the room to discover Josh had knocked a vase over. 'Go outside and play! I wish your blinking father would hurry up and get here.'

Josh picked up the ball and looked at her from big brown eyes. 'He'll come on a boat.'

'Probably,' she said with a sigh.

'Per-raps he'll come today!'

Margaret hoped not. She had enough to cope with. She opened the door to let him out and returned to her desk. It was half-day closing and Rita would be home soon with Sam. Surprisingly Ellen had asked could she continue to stay on at the shop as it was nearer to the club. That suited Margaret. The hours the girl kept disturbed the household and she wondered why she had agreed for Ellen to stay here at all. The house was turning into a boarding house! Her mind flitted to thoughts of Sam and what her niece had told her about him and her brows puckered. No! She was not going to think about that today. She wandered over to the window and saw Josh crossing the road to the garden in the middle of the square. If one of the residents saw him with that ball going in there they'd chase him. She thought of Eve and felt a simmering anger. The selfish bitch! Living it up with some man on her money! Thinking about men – her gaze rested a moment on a middle-aged man reading a newspaper, before travelling on to several students in costume with their collecting tins.

Suddenly she caught sight of another man. This one was wearing a black homburg and a clerical suit. Even from this distance she could see the facial likeness to William, but his twin was portly and obviously in the best of health. He was checking door numbers and was getting closer. He stopped at the bottom of her steps and appeared to be able to read the brass plate on the wall from there. She wondered what he was thinking. Maybe he thought her soul needed saving because moneylenders did not get a good press in the Bible, she thought dryly. It was a relief to her that she had not lost her sense of humour.

Deciding not to wait until he knocked, Margaret smoothed down the skirt of her best peach suit and went to open the door.

For a moment neither of them spoke. She was

aware of her anger when she compared his physical well-being with his twin; it was obvious William had suffered in life far more than his brother.

'Hello, Margaret! May I come in?' Hearing his voice after all these years, she was conscious of Billy saying how much plumier than William's it was. Yet there was a similarity in its depth and the hesitant smile could have been William's. Alan being nervous made her feel much better.

'I can hardly say what I want to on the doorstep for the neighbours to hear.' She held the door wider.

He sighed as he removed his hat and stepped over the threshold. 'I don't blame you for being angry with me. If I'd known you hadn't got my letter I'd have done something about it.'

'Such as writing another? Didn't you give any thought to Bella getting in to trouble? You allowed your brother to shoulder your responsibility even after you knew Billy existed. Didn't you want to see your son? Never mind about me. He's the one who got really hurt in all this. It's a funny kind of Christianity that ignores the needs of a child.'

He reddened. 'He was safe with Will. I thought you and he were married.'

'You could have sent money to help with his upkeep, even so.'

'I was ashamed. I wanted to put the past behind me and do the work I believed God had called me to, but maybe I had even that wrong.'

He frowned. 'My work in Scotland is so much more rewarding.'

'How glad I am to hear that.' She clapped her hands together. 'Now you've told me how fulfilling your life is I don't think I need to detain you any longer. I know all I need to know now. You do know your brother is worth two of you? He might occasionally be weak but he has got a heart and you could take a few lessons from him.'

Alan made to speak but she shook her head. 'If it's an apology, I don't want to hear it.' She held wide the door. 'Thank you for coming. I presume you've seen Will? How did you find him?'

'Much in the same mood as you,' he said with a grim smile, replacing his homburg. 'Whatever you might say, Margaret, I am sorry. I did truly love you but I think Will is the man for you.' Before she could respond he left.

Margaret closed the door and suddenly felt on top of the world. She might not have wanted to listen to his apology but his sincerity had affected her and she realised she could forgive him. But now she wanted to see Will. There was so much she needed to say to him. She would go up to the yard. She scribbled a note for Rita and placed it on the hall table before leaving the house.

The yard gates were open but the yard appeared to be deserted. She went over to the house and discovered the door was on the snick. She called

Will's name and walked in.

She found him in the kitchen, walked straight up to him and put her arms round him. Immediately he returned her hug and they stayed like that for what felt like ages without speaking. Then she said, 'I've really missed you. It's been agony without you.'

'You love me, then?'

'Don't be daft!'

'Say it.'

'Haven't I proved it by telling your brother to get lost and that you're worth two of him.'

'Only two?' She could hear the smile in his voice.

'Two dozen.'

'Do you love me madly, passionately—'

'How old are we?'

'So you believe that kind of love is only for the young?'

She gazed up into his face. 'No. And I have your son to prove it.'

It was obvious she could not have surprised him more; in that respect she had to admit he was like his brother. Had the thought occurred to him at all that she could have got pregnant from one moment of passion? His eyes were moist. 'Why didn't you write and tell me?'

'You were too far away. Already had a son, or so I believed. You were set on finding him and I didn't want to prevent that. I just didn't think it was going to take so long for you to find him and that you'd get sick. I had to cope – so I did.'

'My God! You're a strong woman! Are you sure you don't hate me for not being there to make an honest woman of you?'

'Not hate,' she said, stroking his face. 'But you'd better do it soon. Jonathan is growing and I want you there to enjoy him, like I do.' He kissed her and they went on kissing, unaware of what was happening outside.

CHAPTER TWENTY-TWO

Rita read the note on the hall table and smiled. 'You can eat Aunt Margaret's lunch,' she said to Billy, who had turned up at the shop half an hour ago, wanting to talk to Sam about getting back to work at the yard. The lorry had been fixed. 'You're not going to believe this but Jimmy's vamoosed and taken the cash box with him. Mr Dixon's told me because he doesn't like breaking the news to Dad himself. He's ashamed of having been taken in and of giving him access to things he shouldn't have.' Sam had not looked too happy but said he would go after lunch. That had pleased Rita.

She went downstairs to tell Cook, expecting to find Josh with her, but Mrs Richards said she had not seen him for ages. 'Perhaps your aunt's taken him out with her.'

'She would have mentioned it in her note,' said Rita.

She went outside via the basement steps and across the square to the garden but could see no sign of Josh. Worried, she went inside and told Sam and Billy about her half-brother being missing.

'He'll turn up,' said Billy.

'He's never gone off like this before,' said Rita, gnawing her lip.

Billy squeezed her shoulder. 'OK! If he hasn't turned up by the time we've eaten lunch, then I'll go and look for him. I bet he'll come in, though. Kids always know when it's time for food. Isn't that right, Sam?'

Sam agreed absently.

That was of some comfort to Rita but Josh had still not turned up by the time they had finished their meal. Really worried now, she said, 'I'm going to have to search for him.'

'Does he know his way around the city at all?' said Billy.

'I've taken him to the Pierhead a couple of times. He's convinced his dad will come sailing up in a big ship for him.'

'There you are, then!' said Billy, his gaze meeting hers. 'Sam and I'll go down there and see if we can spot him.'

She felt a flood of relief. 'Thanks! I'll have a look round here.'

She split up from the two men outside and searched the length of the garden which ended in front of St Catherine's church, checked a few more streets and then made her way down towards the river.

Billy was thinking about Rita and how he would much rather be back at the house, sitting in that lovely room, watching the sunlight play over her gleaming hair and the bones of her peach of a face, instead of with Sam. But he had wanted to take advantage of Sam thinking him some kind of saint for not showing disgust or calling him a nancy boy or a pervert when he had sobbed his heart out in the bedroom and told Billy why he should have let him die. Having met several of his kind at sea, Billy had just listened, remembering another bloke saying no one who had the choice would choose to be the way he was because it was no bloody joke.

'Do you think we'll find him?' said Sam.

'I hope so.' Billy paused on the corner of Paradise Street in sight of the Sailors' Home.

'I love Rita, yer know. She's got a heart of gold. That's why she deserves someone better than me.' Sam's expression was sad. 'I won't be able to stick it out at the yard or go through with the wedding.' He fixed Billy with a stare. 'I know you care for her, so could you keep your eye on her for me?'

'Sure I will!' Billy was glad he wouldn't have to bring pressure to bear on Sam. 'But you're going to have to tell her,' he said firmly. 'You can't just go off. You know how it affected her when her mother did that.'

Sam nodded. 'I'm going to have to pick the right moment.'

'It would be an idea,' said Billy, smiling, as he headed down the side of the Sailors' Home. 'You'll have to choose your words carefully. Not that I believe the truth would occur to her in a thousand years.' He slapped Sam on the back, thinking he was going to have to curb his impatience and pick his right moment, too. 'Now let's get on with finding Josh.'

Boats and ships of all different sizes were massed in the river. The sight never failed to stir Rita's senses. She was breathless with running and had taken several shortcuts to get here fast. Now she slowed down, thinking, what lad used to the Cardiff docks wouldn't wander off down here to mingle among the crowd and listen to the call of a ship's hooter and the cry of the gulls and breathe in that intoxicating smell of the sea? No wonder so many Liverpool lads and some lasses succumbed to its lure despite the danger and low wages. She thought of Billy and wished he didn't have to go back to sea but knew it was for the best if she was to stick by Sam.

Suddenly she spotted Josh talking to one of the men tying up a ferryboat and pounced on him. He struggled. 'I want to find me dad!'

'Well, you're in the wrong place for the ships from Cardiff.' She put an arm round him and steered him in the direction of Canning Dock, remembering her search for her mother and her meeting Billy for the first time.

As if her thoughts had conjured him up, she heard her name being called and there he was with Sam. Billy gave her such a smile, her heart turned over and she devoured him with her eyes. He looked so good to her despite the fact that he wore grubby trousers, his corduroy jacket had seen better days and his shirt was collarless. He wore his seaman's cap pushed to the back of his head and a lock of dark hair curled on his forehead. She felt goose pimply all over and gave into impulse and kissed Sam so she could kiss Billy, too. Her excuse being that she was so glad to see them both. Billy laughed and then swung Josh up on his shoulders. Sam offered Rita his arm and they asked at the dock gate about ships from Cardiff and were told there was one due in three days' time. Then they headed for Abercromby Square. Several times Sam started to say something but when she looked at him his voice trailed off. She asked him what it was but he said that he would tell her another time and that he had to get up to the yard.

Finding Margaret still not at home and Josh having dozed off, Rita decided she would walk up to the yard with the two men. She told them to hang on while she put Josh to bed, certain she would find her aunt at the yard.

As they turned into the street where the yard was situated, Sam sniffed. 'I can smell something burning!'

The next moment a man came tearing down the street whom Billy recognised and he seized his arm. 'Where's the fire, mate?'

'Your dad's place,' gasped the man. 'But the gates are locked and he isn't answering. 'I'm off to ring the fire brigade. If something isn't done quickly the whole place could go up and there's some horses going mad in there.'

The three of them began to run but Rita could not keep up with the men and let them go ahead. Smoke and sparks filled the air and a few passers-by were gathering outside. Billy climbed the gate. Within minutes he had both open. She and Sam were with him in seconds, followed by those who had lingered outside. All stopped abruptly at the sight of the flames because not only was part of the stable block on fire, but so was the house.

Billy paled and so did Rita, but he told Sam to direct people to the horse trough and pump and to get buckets while he checked the house. Rita would have followed him but he told her to stay back and to help someone get the horses out. There were two who were lame.

Rita grabbed a likely looking youth and told him to come with her. The horses were frantic, attempting to drag themselves loose of the iron rings on the wall to which they were tied by handling reins. She went for the smaller grey and with unsteady fingers began to unfasten the rein, careful to avoid the horse's rump that threatened to squash her against the wall of the stall.

She was unprepared for the strength of the animal when, with the rein looped about her hand, she freed it. She was pulled off her feet as it bolted, spun round by one arm and dragged through a mess of straw and dung into the cobbled yard. She screamed and carried on screaming. Her arm felt as if it was being pulled from its socket. People scattered as the horse headed for the open gateway.

Billy came tearing out of the smoke followed by Margaret and William. 'Let go!' he yelled.

Afterwards Rita could not remember how she managed to drag her hand free but she did. As the other horse thundered towards her she curled herself into a ball with a moan, protecting her head with her arms. It swerved and followed the grey through the gateway.

Billy and Margaret, Sam and Will gathered about her. 'Are you OK, luv?' rasped Billy, his anxious face sweaty and streaked with dirt.

'I don't think I'll ever move again,' she groaned.

He smiled and slid his arms beneath her and lifted her up. 'Take her home, Billy,' said Sam. 'I'll help here.'

'It should be you taking her,' said Margaret to Sam, caressing Rita's cheek with the back of her hand.

'No! Let Billy,' said Sam hastily, and he turned away and hurried over to the line of people emptying the water trough. William looked at Billy, who shrugged, then William turned and followed Sam. Margaret stared at Billy and then Rita and wondered. But she made no comment, and went after William.

Aware of the clang of the fire engine, Rita determined to make the most of being held in Billy's arms. Although halfway along Hardman Street she remembered that he had broken his leg and had only recently returned from his adventures in China, so she suggested he put her down. He told her she was no weight at all and continued past the Philharmonic Hall and the eye hospital, gymnasium and eventually into Abercromby Square.

Outside the house they found Josh and Mrs Richards holding the baby, surrounded by an excited chattering group of students. Billy placed Rita on her feet while keeping his arm round her. 'What's going on?'

Mrs Richards, her eyes as round as gobstoppers,

said, 'You two look as if you've been having trouble just like us. Someone tried to set fire to the place.'

'There's a fire up at the yard,' said Billy, frowning at the blistered and blackened paint on the front door. The smell of paraffin hung in the air.

Mrs Richards' eyes widened and she shook her head. 'There must be an arsonist about. He not only tried to burn the door down but put a lighted newspaper through the letter box and singed the coconut mat. If it wasn't for these students, the whole place could have gone up and us with it. Why should anyone do this?'

Rita and Billy were as puzzled as she was, but remembering her manners, Rita thanked the students and told them to call round later with their collection boxes. They drifted away. She suggested to Mrs Richards that a gallon of tea wouldn't come amiss and they all went inside.

'I'm desperate for a bath,' said Rita, sniffing her clothes and pulling a face.

'I don't exactly smell of attar of roses myself.' Billy took hold of her hands where the skin had been scraped off and the grazes bled sluggishly and kissed her fingers. 'You were very brave.'

The tenderness of that gesture touched her deeply. 'I'm going to run a bath,' she said unsteadily. 'I suppose you'll be going back up to the yard? Who do you think caused the fires?'

'I think now the fire brigade's there they'll manage

424

without me . . . as for who started them? Maybe it was Jimmy.'

She had started up the stairs but stopped. 'I wouldn't put it past him.'

'Me neither. But I hope I'm wrong.' He caught up with her on the stairs. 'I think Dad can cope with his stealing money, although he's deeply disappointed in him, but to try and destroy the stables and set fire to this beautiful house . . . that's really nasty.'

'He is nasty. So how do we find out if it was Jimmy?' She entered the bathroom.

Billy followed her and, as she struggled to turn the knob on the water geyser above the bath, he removed her hand and did it for her. 'I think it's going to be a job for the police. But let's forget about him for now.' As the water gushed into the bath, he took her hand and said, 'You do know I love you, Rita? I know we haven't spent loads of time together but I'm sure of my feelings. You're kind, you're brave – as I said before – you've got a head on your shoulders and you're beautiful. Any man would be proud to have you as their wife.'

Her cheeks burned and her heart beat a tattoo. 'You're forgetting Sam,' she whispered but her eyes shone like stars.

'No, I'm not. You might find he's been having second thoughts about marrying you.' Billy took Rita's face between his hands and kissed her long

425

and deep, enough to make her toes curl. Then he left her alone.

Rita was trembling and her hands shook as she turned on the cold tap, automatically reaching for the jar of bath salts and flinging a handful of pink crystals into the water, thinking hard and wondering if Billy and Sam had talked about her while looking for Josh. She could easily imagine Sam thinking he had let her down because of his suicide attempt but she had to be certain that wasn't his only reason for telling Billy he no longer wanted to marry her. She felt dizzy, and whether it was due to shock or happiness or both, it didn't matter. So many things happening at once were enough to put anyone in a tizzy. She could still feel the pressure of Billy's lips on hers and she hugged herself. If only she could be sure Sam could cope without her, then she could be happy. If he couldn't . . . she knew only too well what it felt like to be rejected.

Rita turned off the taps and swished the water round with her hand, poured in a little more cold while she undressed and then climbed in.

Pure bliss! She and Sam were going to have to have a heart to heart to get to the bottom of his suicide attempt; only then would she allow herself to dream of being married to Billy.

She left her filthy clothes in the bath water and, wrapped in a towel, she went into her bedroom. She presumed Billy was downstairs talking to Mrs

Richards about the arson attacks. It seemed too much of a coincidence to believe they could be anything else. She took clothes from the wardrobe and placed them on the bed, slipped into her dressing gown and sat on the stool in front of the dressing table, beginning to rub her hair dry. Her mind drifted to thoughts of Billy and marriage.

She began to brush her hair. A face loomed in the mirror, bearded and one-eyed and for a moment she froze with shock and terror. Then she whirled round, clutching the hairbrush and opened her mouth to scream but Mr McGinty silenced her with a hand over her mouth and jerked her to her feet.

'You thought you'd bleeding got away with it, didn't yer?' he sneered, his foul-smelling breath making her recoil. She caught him a blow on the side of his neck with the hairbrush. He swore and slipped his hand down the front of her dressing gown and dug his fingernails into her breast. It hurt! She wanted to scream and tried to bite the hand over her mouth as she struggled. He began to drag her towards the bed and she hit out again with the hairbrush.

'Will you stop that!' He squeezed her breast that hard she felt faint with the pain. 'If it wasn't for you and yer bitch of an aunt I wouldn't have been locked up and had to work me bleeding guts off smashing bleeding stones.' He wrenched the hairbrush out of her hand and threw it.

She heard it hit the door and despaired. If only she could get his hand from her mouth for a moment she could scream and bring Billy running. The edge of the bed dug behind her knees and she was forced down. He laughed and removed his hand from her mouth and pulled apart her dressing gown. She screamed. He slapped her across the face and fumbled with his flies. Her head was ringing and now his body was on top of hers. This was some terrible nightmare. He was going to rape her and this time Billy would not arrive in time to rescue her. Oh God!

The rap of knuckles on the door caused the man to freeze and Mrs Richards' voice told her that the tea tray was in the sitting room and that Mr Billy Brodie was borrowing some of Mr Sam's clothes. Rita tried to yell for help but Mr McGinty's hand silenced her. Then she heard the sound of footsteps retreating.

Mr McGinty laughed weakly and wiped his sweating brow. 'That was a close thing.' Then the laughter died in his eye and all she could see was evil. 'Now's the time to pay your dues, girl.'

From somewhere deep inside her Rita dredged up the strength to claw at that dark eye. He went berserk, arms flailing. She tried to cover her face as he hit her over and over again, yelling at her, telling her how he had done for his missus.

The door burst open and Billy appeared, carrying

a poker. Behind him came Margaret holding a high-heeled shoe.

Mr McGinty dragged Rita to her feet, an arm about her throat. 'One step nearer and I'll choke the life out of her. I've got nothing to lose.'

Neither Billy nor Margaret spoke but the expression in their eyes was uncompromising as they continued to advance. Rita felt the pain in her body as a distant thing as she struggled and managed to get her hands between Mr McGinty's arm and her throat. She could feel him trembling and his breathing was noisy in her ear. Then unexpectedly he cracked and flung her at them and turned towards the open window. Billy went after him, but he was already outside on the ledge and as Billy made a grab for him, he jumped.

Rita lay on the sofa in her dressing gown, having refused to be treated like a child and ordered to bed. Witch hazel and iodine had been dabbed on most of her body and she had a black eye. She had downed a large brandy and had a good cry.

Mr McGinty's body had been taken away and the police had been and gone. At the moment Ellen held the floor because there had also been an attempt to set fire to the shop. 'It was lucky I was still in bed and heard the letter box go. I thought it was the late post so went to have a butchers. That's when I found the mat on fire and the door smouldering.'

Sam's expression was grim. 'I ought to have known me father wouldn't let me get away with telling him to get lost. I never thought he'd do anything as stupid as hiding Mr McGinty and joining forces with him to get revenge.'

'I think he must have been the man I saw outside the house reading the newspaper,' said Margaret. 'I wondered what he was doing hanging about.'

'I remember you telling me they were drinking mates, Sam,' said Rita, her vision blurred in her black eye as she stared at him. 'I must admit that I still find it difficult to take in that both Mr and Mrs McGinty are dead.'

'She didn't deserve what happened to her but it's all over now and your father's going to spend a good few years behind bars, Sam,' said Billy.

Sam nodded. 'At least something good came out of all the mess. What's going to happen about the yard?' He turned to William, who was standing behind Margaret's chair with Jonathan in his arms.

Before he could answer she said, 'No need for you to worry, Sam. I had the place insured. We can rebuild.'

'We'll be getting married in a few days by special license,' said William, smiling despite his obvious weariness. 'We don't want a big fuss. We don't want to take the gloss off your wedding.'

Sam glanced at Rita and then Billy but did not speak.

William, Billy and Sam left an hour later to help Mr Dixon and the men to carry on bringing some semblance of order to the yard.

Rita was drooping and this time her aunt insisted she went to bed. She told herself she had to think what to do about Sam but the happenings of the day caught up with her and she fell into an exhausted sleep.

CHAPTER TWENTY-THREE

Margaret walked into the pawnshop and found Ellen talking with one of the handsomest young men she had ever seen. He was definitely not a customer – too exotically dressed. His trilby was set at a rakish angle and instead of a tie he wore a yellow and red spotted scarf tucked inside the neck of his shirt. His suit was a deep blue and in his buttonhole he wore a red rosebud. She hazarded a guess to his identity. 'Is this your brother?'

Ellen smiled and straightened up from the counter. 'You've got it in one. Sandy, meet Rita's aunt, Miss Sinclair.'

Sandy bowed before shaking her hand. 'Thank you for being so kind to Ellen.'

Margaret felt a little discomforted and said, 'Well, she's pulled her weight this time. But you must come and see Rita. She's spoken about you and the company and needs cheering up. I presume Ellen's told you what's been happening?'

He looked grave. 'Terrible! But it would make a good story. Man imprisoned on the word of a beautiful girl seeks vengeance.'

Margaret was amused. 'Don't say that to Rita. At the moment she can't stand looking in the mirror. She has a black eye, swollen jaw and is so stiff she can hardly walk. There's my wedding in two days and her own in a couple of weeks and I can see it's getting to her.'

'Poor kid,' said Sandy, looking concerned. 'Tell her I'll be around later with Ellen.'

Margaret thanked him, had a look at the books and the fire damage and left, having decided it was time to get rid of the shop. What with the yard and her other business, which she had told Will she had no intention of giving up, and a husband, baby and house to run she already had far too much on her plate. Sam was going to be busy up at the yard and probably he and Rita would start a family right away, and running the shop and having babies might prove too much for her niece. Then there was Josh. His father had yet to turn up.

She grimaced. But she was happy so was in a

mood to want the whole world to be happy, too, even Alan. He had gone back to Scotland after saying to his twin and Billy that it was regrettable, but after all this time it would be foolish to believe they could start forging strong bonds. They had their lives and he had his but maybe they could still keep in touch. Billy had said that he hadn't really expected any different and shrugged, saying all the people he really cared about were here in Liverpool, and he had continued with the task William had given him.

Her face had softened, thinking of Billy, remembering him bursting through the back door like a pantomime demon, sooty-faced and panting as she and Will canoodled, to tell them the house was on fire. She thought of Jimmy and her expression darkened. William had said to write the stolen money and his stepson off and no longer would he take responsibility for his actions.

Families were a right mixture. Margaret thought of her sister and niece. They couldn't be more different. She'd still like to tar and feather her sister at times but her niece . . . Again Margaret's face softened, but she wasn't going to get all sentimental. She loved the girl and wished she would regain her good spirits soon.

Rita had been having a lovely dream, standing in front of St Catherine's altar in her wedding dress and saying 'I do' to Billy, who was standing at her side. It was the knocker being violently wielded which woke her up. She eased herself upright and retrieved her book from the floor and placed it on the arm of the sofa. She remembered that Mrs Richards had gone shopping and taken the baby and Josh with her so as she could rest. Slowly she made her way downstairs.

She blinked in the sunlight and put a hand over her black eye but was able to see clearly with the other one the large good-looking black man on the doorstep. He removed his seaman's cap. 'You have ma boy?'

Her face lighted up. 'You must be Caleb. I'm Rita.' She held out her hand.

He looked relieved and took her small pale one in his large calloused hand. 'Joshua is OK?'

'He's fine, just not here at the moment.'

His face fell. 'Eve wrote—'

'Mam's not here. If you were hoping to see—'

'No, no! I just want ma boy.'

'That's a relief,' said Rita. 'He's only gone to the shops and should be back soon.'

The words were no sooner out of her mouth than Josh's joyous voice cried, 'There's me dad!'

The next moment the boy had flung himself at his father and the bear hug the man gave the lad convinced Rita that Caleb's feelings for his son were of the right sort and she invited him in.

Rita placed a steaming cup and a plate of sandwiches in front of Caleb and asked what his plans were for Josh.

'You've no need to worry about ma Joshua. I've got a woman to look after him.' His expression was earnest.

'In Cardiff?'

'Here in Liverpool. I know her from way back but her husband was alive then and I allowed ma self to be sweet-talked into taking Eve to Cardiff with me. Now ma Agnes is a widow woman so I'll be staying at her place. She has no kids of her own and is happy to look after ma boy while I'm away.'

Rita decided not to ask whether he'd be divorcing her mother. It was plain to see that Eve and Caleb weren't bothered about it, so why should she worry?

'Agnes isn't a looker like your mam but she's kind and if you want to come and see Josh any time you'll find a welcome.'

Rita thanked him and said she'd like that. Then she went to pack Josh's clothes.

Shortly after, father and son left but not before Josh gave Rita a big hug and Caleb asked who'd hit her and said to send them to him. She explained what had happened and his eyes were like organ stops. Then she waved them off, convinced Josh was in safe hands and pleased she would be able to see him when she wanted. If only she could sort her own life so easily; she had hardly seen Sam since the day of the fires and it had been the same with Billy. She was starting to feel desperate.

Margaret arrived back at the house after shopping and visiting the padre and Sarah to find that Ellen and Sandy had arrived and were seated at the dining table with Sam, Billy and Rita, eating fish and chips. At least the brother and sister were – the other three were only picking at theirs. She said hello and then went upstairs to unpack her shopping and have a bath.

Rita was in some discomfort but did not want to miss any of the conversation that was about parents. Sam's expression was tense and she wondered when they could talk about them and the wedding.

He must have noticed her gaze on him because suddenly he said, 'I've got a helluva headache.'

'I'll get you some aspirin.'

'You stay there,' said Billy, placing a hand on her shoulder. 'Tell me where they are and I'll get them.'

She did so and watched him leave the room.

Sandy said to Sam, 'None of us can be responsible for our parents. Yours sounds a brute. Mine was the same. Always wanting to toughen me up – cold baths and ten-mile runs with bricks stuffed in a haversack.'

'That's terrible,' said Sam, his eyes wide as he absently reached for a chip. 'Where is he now?'

'He's on his way back from India. I'm glad to say his return's come at the right time. I don't know if you know, we're planning on going out there with the company?'

'I've told him all about it,' said Ellen, lighting a cigarette.

'Good!' Sandy smiled at Sam and continued what he was going to say. 'Dad would only pull me down – denigrate what I'm doing and I'd rather not have to put up with that.'

Sam nodded and taking a deep breath, said, 'I wouldn't mind getting away for a while. I lost a mate recently, you see.' Rita stared at him and so did Ellen. Sam reddened, aware of the effect his words must be having on Rita in particular. 'I could paint scenery for you, Sandy – you ask Mr Brodie if I'm any good.'

'He is,' said Rita, making up her mind to seize this opportunity to straighten out matters between her and Sam. 'He can drive a lorry, too. Didn't you mention having some trouble with your driver? Something about him not being too keen on going abroad?'

'That's right,' said Sandy, his startled eyes going quickly from her to Sam. 'But I thought you two were—'

'I won't need much in the way of wages,' said Sam, reaching out for Rita's hand and squeezing it. 'Just a place to doss down and some grub until I get the hang of things.'

438

'Sam!' said Rita. 'There's something I must tell you.'

'Me too. I can't go through with the wedding, Reet.' He stared at her unflinching.

Sandy glanced at his sister, who said, 'Let's slip outside and leave them to sort this out.'

As soon as they were alone Rita said, 'So Billy was right, Sam!'

'I'm not your Mr Right, luv. You'll be better off with him.' He squeezed her hand.

'It's to do with Archie, isn't it? He was the first real mate you'd ever had.'

'You were that, Reet.' His voice was husky. 'I don't really want to talk about it. But, honestly, the closer the wedding came the more I realised I didn't have the right feelings for you. Billy really loves you. I could see it in the way he looks at you and I've seen that look of longing when you look at him, too.' She went to speak but he placed his fingers gently on her lips. 'Don't deny your true feelings. I'll be OK. I've been getting itchy feet lately, and even if Sandy turns me down I'll be leaving Liverpool.'

'Oh Sam!' Rita's eyes were moist. 'I'm going to miss you.'

'Aye! I'll miss you too. But never say die, Reet!' He kissed her and then blundered out of the room.

Rita stared through a haze of tears at the engagement ring on her left hand. Slowly she removed it. Sam could sell it. He would need the money it would bring.

Ten minutes passed before Billy entered the room. He looked at her face and without a word took her into her arms and held her close. 'He's going to go with Sandy and Ellen. He'll be OK with them. They'll see he doesn't get too low and do something stupid.'

'I know. He gets on with Ellen. Perhaps, one day . . .' She lifted her head and looked up at him.

Billy said nothing but hugged her.

At that moment Margaret entered the room and stopped in her tracks. 'What's going on here?'

They turned to face her. Rita searched for the right words but in the end just said, 'Sam and I have broken off our engagement. He's got itchy feet and we've discovered that being fond of each other isn't a good enough reason in our case to get married.'

Margaret was silent a moment. 'I see. I suppose that's why the pair of you have been miserable lately. Isn't it a good job you've got Billy around to cheer you up?'

'Isn't it!' said Billy with a sudden gleam in his eyes. 'But you've still got your wedding to look forward to. So you're not going to be too disappointed over Rita's and Sam's being cancelled, are you?'

Margaret smiled. 'I think I'll cope. Who knows? There might be another one on the cards before too long.'

* * *

Two days later Rita helped her aunt into a cream organdie frock with matching coat for her wedding. On her gleaming hair Margaret wore a close-fitting hat made of cream chiffon petals. Billy was best man and Rita was bridesmaid. The bruising about her eye had turned yellow but she had toned it down with face powder. Jerry and Sarah, Sam, Ellen, Sandy, Mrs Richards, Babs and baby Jonathan attended the ceremony. Afterwards they returned to the house where William would live with Margaret. A wedding breakfast had been prepared by Mrs Richards and it was sumptuous and an enjoyable time was had by all. Especially as it was obvious to Margaret and Rita that Sam was getting on fine with Sandy.

There was to be no honeymoon until the work at the yard was completed because Margaret and William wanted to keep an eye on things. Hopefully the work would be finished by August so the newly-weds could have a delayed honeymoon, a twelve-days cruise to the Mediterranean at the bargain price of a pound a day. These had been started by the White Star Line to provide work for laid-off crews, as well as to bring in some much needed revenue to the shipping company. As she sat at her desk, Margaret dreamt about getting away with Will, having put the pawnshop up for sale.

She was not the only one who dreamt of getting away. After saying goodbye to Sam, Rita knew she and Billy would not wait long before tying the knot. They desperately wanted each other and it was not easy controlling their physical feelings. He was camping up at the yard in two rooms and working his socks off helping run the place. When William suggested that he give up the sea and go into partnership with him he agreed: Margaret had returned the deeds of the yard to her husband on their wedding day. Rita was delighted and so they decided to break the news to Margaret and William that they wanted to get married.

'We saw it coming, didn't we?' said William, beaming.

'We couldn't be happier,' said Margaret, hugging them both. 'You can have the second floor of the house for your own.'

Rita looked at Billy to see if that was OK with him. He nodded, knowing how much she loved the house in Abercromby Square.

It was decided that Mr Dixon and his family would move into the one at the yard when the repairs were finished.

The wedding day was set for August.

Rita was glad she had that short time to get used to not having Sam around. She shed her tears in private. She might not have loved him as a lover but they had been close and she missed him.

In Billy's company she blossomed. He took her dancing, to the theatre and cinema and they crossed the Mersey on the ferry and had all the fun of the fair in New Brighton. They loved, they laughed and they told each other things about their childhood they had never mentioned to anyone else.

Almost unbelievably, considering how far the postcards had to come, two arrived on their wedding day. One was from Sam saying he was in Calcutta and it was hot, hot, hot! He was fine and she was not to worry about him but to be happy with Billy. She put the card next to the phoenix that Billy had given her and then, tight-lipped, gazed at the picture of the Statue of Liberty on the other postcard. As she read how Eve's new fella had dumped her and that she was living in a two-bit place in Brooklyn and was it possible for her to arrange to have some money sent to her, Rita started laughing. Her mam would never change. She would be selfish to the end, but at least she no longer had the power to hurt her.

There was a tap on the door and Margaret said, 'Can I come in?'

'Of course! Read this.' She handed the postcard to her aunt.

Margaret read it and said in a satisfied voice, 'Everything comes to *she* who waits. We'll let her stew. See if we get any more postcards. Today we've got more important things to think about.'

She helped Rita into her long white satin gown and placed the chaplet of white roses holding a trailing lace veil into place. 'You look lovely,' she said unsteadily, wiping a tear away.

Rita smiled. 'You look pretty good yourself. Very different from the first time I saw you.'

'You too!' Margaret hugged her and then together they went downstairs where William was waiting to give Rita away.

The organ swelled and the first notes of the 'Wedding March' filled St Catherine's. The men at the yard had been given the day off and all those who'd frequented the pawnshop were there to see Rita marry her Billy.

She gazed at the back of his head where his black hair curled in the nape of his neck and her heart seemed to swell with love.

He turned as she came alongside him and there was such a look in his eyes that she could feel the heat of his desire. He reached out a hand and she placed hers in it. The ages-old words of the service began.

The vicar had got to the bit where he was announcing Rita and Billy as man and wife when there was the sound of a scuffle at the back of the church and a voice yelled, 'It's not right! I should have been the partner! The yard should have been mine!'

A murmur rippled through the congregation and all heads turned to stare at the wild-eyed figure struggling with the verger. 'As for that slut you're marrying she—'

'You never give up, do you, Jimmy?' Billy's voice was thick with fury. He turned to Rita. 'Don't go away, luv.'